continued . . .

Bound and Determined
(by Shayla Black writing as Shelley Bradley)

"This story explores one of my favorite fantasies . . . a desperate heroine takes a handsome alpha male hostage. Much sexy fun is had by all. Especially when the yummy captive turns the tables!"

—*New York Times* bestselling author Angela Knight

"Steamier than a Florida night, with characters who will keep you laughing and have you panting for more!"

—*New York Times* bestselling author Susan Johnson

"A searing, frolicking adventure of suspense, love, and passion!"

—*New York Times* bestselling author Lora Leigh

"Will have you grabbing for the nearest fan (or man)!"

—Jenna Petersen, author of *Lessons from a Courtesan*

"A flawless story that grips readers from page one and doesn't let up."

—*The Road to Romance*

Decadent

"Wickedly seductive from start to finish."

—National bestselling author Jaci Burton

"A lusty page-turner from the get-go, *Decadent* lives up to its title, grabbing readers from the very first chapter and not letting go until the very end with a shuddering climax worthy of any keeper shelf."

—*TwoLips Reviews*

Wicked Ties

"A wicked, sensual thrill from first page to last. I loved it!"

—*New York Times* bestselling author Lora Leigh

"Not a book to be missed . . . Just be sure that you have something cold to drink while reading it, and hopefully someone there afterward to ease away the ache."

—*A Romance Review*

"Absolutely took my breath away . . . *Wicked Ties* wound itself around me and refused to let go. Full of passion and erotic love scenes."

—*Romance Junkies*

Strip Search

SHAYLA BLACK

writing as

SHELLEY BRADLEY

HEAT
NEW YORK

THE BERKLEY PUBLISHING GROUP
Published by the Penguin Group
Penguin Group (USA) Inc.
375 Hudson Street, New York, New York 10014, USA
Penguin Group (Canada), 90 Eglinton Avenue East, Suite 700, Toronto, Ontario M4P 2Y3, Canada
(a division of Pearson Penguin Canada Inc.)
Penguin Books Ltd., 80 Strand, London WC2R 0RL, England
Penguin Group Ireland, 25 St. Stephen's Green, Dublin 2, Ireland (a division of Penguin Books Ltd.)
Penguin Group (Australia), 250 Camberwell Road, Camberwell, Victoria 3124, Australia
(a division of Pearson Australia Group Pty. Ltd.)
Penguin Books India Pvt. Ltd., 11 Community Centre, Panchsheel Park, New Delhi—110 017, India
Penguin Group (NZ), 67 Apollo Drive, Rosedale, North Shore 0632, New Zealand
(a division of Pearson New Zealand Ltd.)
Penguin Books (South Africa) (Pty.) Ltd., 24 Sturdee Avenue, Rosebank, Johannesburg 2196,
South Africa

Penguin Books Ltd., Registered Offices: 80 Strand, London WC2R 0RL, England

This is a work of fiction. Names, characters, places, and incidents either are the product of the author's imagination or are used fictitiously, and any resemblance to actual persons, living or dead, business establishments, events, or locales is entirely coincidental. The publisher does not have any control over and does not assume any responsibility for author or third-party websites or their content.

STRIP SEARCH

PRINTING HISTORY
Berkley Sensation mass-market edition / July 2006
Heat trade paperback edition / July 2009

Heat trade paperback ISBN: 978-0-425-22925-5

PRINTED IN THE UNITED STATES OF AMERICA

10 9 8 7 6 5

This book is dedicated to the memory of
a great fan and friend,
Elizabeth Benway.
You never failed to make me smile,
and touched me with your kindness
far more than you ever knew.
I miss you!

Acknowledgments

With special thanks to Jenna Petersen and Lora Leigh. Both of you contribute to my mental health (in a good way!) by assuring me I'm not writing drek and providing needed laughs when I'm ready to go postal. You share your talent, your time, and your tears with me. I'm so grateful!

Chapter One

"How do you feel about spending every night surrounded by adoring women eager to worship your body?"

Mark Sullivan stared at his brother-in-law across the desk in the posh Manhattan office as if he'd lost his mind. "Is this a trick question?"

With a rueful smile, Rafe said, "I got a call from my pal Norton over at the FBI yesterday. He needs a little freelance work done."

"Really? Is that regulation?"

"It's a favor. I owe Norton for keeping my ass out of a sling while I was . . . bending the law to prevent you from doing ten to twenty in beautiful Leavenworth."

"Then I owe him, too. Big time. But why don't you want this? He asked for you, right?"

Rafe hesitated. "This is a little beyond my realm. You know my business is primarily electronic security. This case really needs a CPA, my man, and that's you."

"Okay. What's up?"

"Norton wants to send in a civilian, someone who has fewer

rules to follow, someone fresh. The FBI has an agent in this location already on a separate case but . . . they suspect something is up, that maybe the agent has gone rogue. They haven't heard from this person in nearly three months."

"Got a name?"

"Nope." Rafe shook his head. "Norton wouldn't spill it, just in case the agent is even deeper undercover or has temporarily stopped communicating because things are hot. In either event, watch for signs and steer clear."

"Sure." Mark grinned. "When do we get to the part with the adoring women?"

"Ha! I knew that would get your attention." The smile slid off Rafe's face. "We'll come back to that. Have a seat."

Frowning, Mark stared at his sister's husband and lowered himself into a black leather club chair. The jagged Manhattan skyline jutted up into a gray sky, but the sight did nothing to distract him now. Why the secrecy? Why the formality?

"Okay, I'm sitting. What's this about?"

"Here's the deal: The Feds are chasing a Mafia connection. Money laundering. If they can figure out where the money is coming from and where it's going, they hope it will net them a big fish."

"Makes sense." Mark shrugged. "So why are you looking at me like I'm a big game hunter and you're about to tell me guns have been outlawed?"

"The tip came from your ex-wife, Mark. She finally gave up some information about her connection. With her trial starting soon, she's looking for a plea bargain."

Apparently she valued her plea bargain more than her neck. While he was glad she was finally cooperating, it didn't surprise Mark that Tiffany failed to grasp the fact her freedom would be worth nothing if she was dead. Appreciation for lasting things had never been her strong suit. She'd certainly valued quick, easy money more than their marriage.

"So what did Tiffany say?" Mark finally asked.

"She didn't have the guy's name, just a description and the name of the place he worked at the time of their connection. She claims her contact told her he would gain control of the money pipeline this summer."

"Okay." Mark realized Rafe held a manila envelope in his hand and wore a reluctant expression. "What's in the envelope?"

"Nothing, really," Rafe said, looking away and tossing the brownish rectangular envelope on his desk. "Just some papers and . . . nothing."

"Bullshit." Mark stood and crossed the space in three long strides. "When I came to work with you, we agreed up front to complete honesty. Don't go back on your word now, man."

Rafe rolled his eyes. "Now I know why your sister can sniff out even the tiniest white lie. You trained her too well, damn it. I can't even surprise her for Christmas, while she managed to blow me away with the announcement that she was pregnant."

"Stop trying to sidetrack me. What's in the envelope?" Mark said through gritted teeth, feeling his temperature rise.

Whatever it was, Rafe wanted to hide it bad. Since coming to work with his brother-in-law, they'd been nothing but even, equal. After a rocky introduction, they'd settled into a great working and familial relationship.

So this shit just pissed him off.

Rafe sighed and reached for the envelope. "Don't look at this. It's really unnecessary. What you need to know is, the guy we're after is Caucasian, stands just at six feet, is somewhere between twenty-eight and thirty-five, has dark brown hair and brown eyes, no distinguishing tattoos or birthmarks."

"Gee, that narrows the suspects down to ten percent of the male population. Hell, that could almost describe you. Let me see what's in the envelope."

Without further comment, Rafe sighed and handed Mark the packet.

First, he withdrew a piece of paper with a candid headshot taken out on the street during a cloudy day, along with small bio. "Blade Bocelli? This is the guy we're after?"

"With the description Tiffany provided, I called a PI who owed me a favor. He narrowed the list of suspects down significantly. This is the most viable one. Bocelli is a mid-level thug, but he has a direct line to the upper echelons of the Gamalini Family, we think, through Pietro DiStefano. Bocelli's brother was Mafia, but he went to prison a few years ago for murdering a federal judge. Anyway, it appears Blade Bocelli is the dude the Feds want to nail."

"Great." Nodding, Mark reached inside again and withdrew an eight-by-ten glossy photo.

The breath left his body in a single rush. *Tiffany.*

Mark stared at the picture of his ex-wife, taken during their marriage, as evidenced by the fact she was wearing the wedding ring he'd put on her finger one rainy November afternoon. She had her skirt hiked up to her hips, her black high heels spread wide and a dark-headed man standing between them, his pants loose about his hips. Black leather stretched across the man's wide back and shoulders as he held Tiffany in place with a white-knuckled grip. In the heat of the moment, her red hair had fallen askew and her mouth opened wide.

"Son of a bitch," he muttered.

"You didn't need to see that, Mark. Seriously. I tried—"

"It's not as if I didn't know she cheated." But it didn't keep the sight of it from curling rage through his stomach. "Some computer tech head, the janitor at the bank, now this guy. That's the least of her crimes, really."

Tiffany didn't have the power to hurt him now, nearly a year after their divorce. Shock, at times. Annoy, every time.

She'd only married him to frame him for embezzlement so that she could launder money for the Mafia and take her cut. A year ago, when he'd first learned the truth, it had devastated him. The knowledge he'd meant nothing to her beyond the means to a profit had flattened his heart. He'd loved her—or thought he had.

Today, she was just a stinging reminder of his failure to see her for what she was, his piss-poor ability to recognize what true love wasn't, and his really, really bad taste in women.

"I'm sorry," Rafe muttered. "Look, if this case is too personal . . ."

Too personal? Being humiliated and duped was personal. Catching the jerk who helped orchestrate his downfall—that sounded like a good time.

"No, I want it. If this Blade Bocelli is the scumbag who helped Tiffany on her way to prison"—*while plowing his way between my ex-wife's thighs*—"and he's laundering money, he deserves to do hard time."

Rafe slapped him on the shoulder. "You're a better man than me. If I saw a picture like that of my wife with another man, I'd dismember him slowly and painfully."

"My *ex*-wife, thank you very much. Besides, you don't have anything to worry about. My sister would never do that to you. She loved you, even when you were too stupid to know you reciprocated."

"Point taken." Rafe smiled. "So, want to hear your cover? This is the part where the adoring women come in."

Mark tossed the offending picture of Tiffany and her Mafia thug lover onto Rafe's desk. "Finally, a subject of great interest. Lay it on me."

"You're going to Las Vegas. Blade Bocelli appears to still be living and working at the same Vegas nightclub he started at last year, shortly after it opened."

"What do we know about the club?"

"It's called Girls' Night Out. It's actually a male strip joint. Hence the adoring women."

Mark hesitated. "I'm going in as the accountant, right?"

Rafe's cat-ate-the-canary smile warned him that something was deeply wrong. "The club is actively seeking dancers. I hope you don't have two left feet."

Mark stood. "Wipe that freakin' smirk off your face. I'm *not* going in there as a male stripper and taking off my clothes so bored housewives can shove dollar bills down my G-string."

"It's our only in."

Cursing a blue streak, Mark paced to the other side of the room and gazed absently over the midtown view. "I'm a hell of a lot better prepared to demonstrate karate than shake my booty. I've never done anything like that."

"We have two weeks to prep. I've got a line on someone who's 'retired' from the biz and can teach you what you need to know."

"But an exotic dancer? C'mon . . . be serious."

"That's the gig. You want to catch this guy or not?"

Mark stewed in silence, contemplating all the ways he'd make an idiot out of himself onstage wearing nothing but a scrap of cloth with a piece of string up his ass.

"Oh, and before you answer, let me introduce you to one of the major perks of the case," Rafe said, cutting into his brooding.

Rafe reached into the packet again, this time to extract yet another photo. Only this one was of a woman in brief denim shorts and a red tank top, holding a pen and a few pieces of paper. Her head was turned toward one shoulder, facing whoever had been holding the camera, her expression looking slightly off-guard. Dark hair framed her face, drifted halfway down her back. Slanted blue eyes looked a bit wide and startled, while full lips parted in question.

Mark grabbed the photo and stared harder. She had a face beautiful enough to qualify as a starlet's and a body tempting enough to belong to the Devil's daughter. Immediately, his imagination turned unruly. He pictured himself parting her lips—with his tongue, with his cock. Her cleavage peeked out above her tank top, and his pants grew a tad too tight as he thought about peeling it off, holding her pert breasts in his hands, and kissing her nipples. Brown? Pink? Coral? Didn't matter. He wanted her.

"I thought she might get your attention."

"Who is she?" Mark demanded.

"The club's owner, famous New York party girl Nicola DiStefano, Pietro DiStefano's niece and . . . your new boss."

A smile crept across his face. "Seriously?"

"Before you start thinking about what a cushy assignment this is, there's one catch: The Feds think it's likely Nicki is in the dark about her club being used by Bocelli to launder money, probably for her uncle, a big-time Mafia man. But they don't know for certain that she's unaware, so she can't know her place is being investigated."

"No problem. I'll maintain my cover."

"Which reminds me, you'll be going in as Mark Gabriel. I'm having a phony driver's license and Social Security card made for you as we speak. But it's a bit more complicated than that. You've got to get into her club's books and study them. Find out what's going on, see if there are any patterns, try to glean who might be behind it all. To do that, you'll have to earn her trust."

"Earn her trust. How?"

Rafe sent him a sly grin. "Be creative."

Mark had ideas, juicy, salivating, lustful ones . . . though not deeply ethical. Being a guy, Rafe's mind obviously ran in the same direction.

"C'mon. What are you suggesting I do, fuck it out of her?"

"Whatever works."

He rolled his eyes. "So while I'm working for her, I get her to trust me. Fine. I'll find a way to get it done."

"It's still not that easy. The job isn't just yours. You still have to . . . ah, audition."

* * *

BRING in the next victim," Nicki DiStefano called with a long-suffering sigh.

Within moments, her younger half sister Lucia appeared, thick auburn hair restrained in an elegant French twist and white librarian sweater perched on her shoulders. Nicki laughed as she stared down at herself. The black bra she hadn't realized she was wearing was visible through her yellow tank top, and her diamond navel ring winked in the club's dimmed lights.

"So how was the first audition?" Lucia asked.

Nicki pushed aside all thoughts of the ways she and her half sister were different and realized this was one thing they would agree on wholeheartedly.

She made a face at Lucia. "Blech! He'd been watching too many old Michael Jackson videos, I think."

"Really?"

Lucia laughed, managing to sound so refined and mature, despite being a mere twenty-three, more than three years Nicki's junior. Then again, earning a Ph.D. the same year she could legally drink, rather than learning intimately the inside of every nearby evening hot spot, did make Lucia more mature. Nicki had never finished college . . . but she'd sure known every nightclub worth knowing in New York. She grimaced at the realization and shoved the thought away.

"All the crotch grabbing . . ." Nicki said with a shudder. "I think he liked the self-touching for an audience way too much. Put a whole new meaning to the song 'Beat It.'"

With a hand over her mouth, Lucia stifled another laugh. "Well, maybe your second candidate will be an improvement. He's certainly *very* easy on the eyes."

With that cryptic comment, Lucia disappeared. She might be a refined history professor, but that twinkle in her eye was pure mischief. Maybe her sister was being facetious.

"Bring him on," Nicki called.

A moment later, the stage door creaked, then slammed shut. Dang it, she really needed to buy some WD-40 for that . . .

Oh. My. God.

Through the stage door and past the black curtain, her second audition entered the room. Nicki lost her breath—and the ability not to gape like an utter idiot.

Who was this Adonis dressed in a crisp white collared shirt and black leather pants? A glance at her list told Nicki that his name was Mark Gabriel. Such an innocuous few syllables to term the embodiment of every sexual fantasy she ever remembered having.

The room felt warm suddenly as he stepped onto the stage, under the dimmed lights, a worn leather backpack slung over one shoulder. Lord, he was huge—very tall, broad, bursting with muscle. Blond hair an amazing golden color hung past his collar. His eyes—green? Maybe darker?—pierced her as he nodded.

"Miss DiStefano."

Wow, his deep, powerful voice alone was orgasm-inducing. Would he be offended if she told him she wanted to take Polaroids so she could fantasize about him the next time she spent a lonely morning with her battery-operated boyfriend? And could she get an MP3 of him saying her name, just for effect?

"C-call me Nicki."

Was she actually stuttering? He hadn't danced a step, and she was acting like a groupie. Most likely, he got that a lot.

"Nicki," he returned smoothly.

Was it her imagination, or were her panties actually turning damp?

"And you're Mark?" she managed to say in a somewhat even tone.

"Yes."

Not a big talker, apparently. That was just as well. All she really wanted to do was look at him . . . fantasize about touching.

Wait! It's an audition, not a grope fest, logic screeched. Wishing that logic would keep its nose out of her thoughts, she returned her full attention to Mr. Yummy-Enough-to-Drool-on.

"Ever done this sort of work before? I didn't get a resume from you."

"No."

No explanation. No offer to get her a resume. Interesting . . .

"Where are you from?"

"Florida."

Which explained the gorgeous golden skin. "That's a long way from Vegas."

"Looking for a change of scenery."

Nicki hesitated. Something in Mark's face, a certain tenseness maybe, seemed to say it was far more complicated than having grown tired of looking at palm trees and beaches. But it really wasn't any of her business. The man was here for a job. If she hired him and he did it well, then the rest, his past, whatever—it didn't matter.

"Can you dance?"

He shrugged one massive shoulder, even as his lips—oh, how did she miss that scrumptious mouth earlier?—curled up in a smile. "I get by."

Lord, he gave her the tingles. Why was she interrogating him? He could stand perfectly still and make them both a small fortune. A fortune she desperately needed, if she ever wanted financial independence and freedom from the tight press of her uncle Pietro's thumb.

Still, it wasn't in her nature to take anything at face value, especially men, even if her hormones were doing the mambo.

"Can you flirt?" she asked. "This job requires it."

As if she had challenged his very manhood, Mark set down his backpack, eased off the stage, and strode toward her table. He didn't swagger—it would have been too cheesy on him. He . . . prowled, as if hunting someone. Her, by the look on his face.

And what a face it was. Square jaw, square chin, covered with a fine five o'clock shadow.

As he edged closer, Nicki realized his eyes were neither green nor brown. They were somewhere in between, like moss growing over rich earth. They were gorgeous, and she wondered if he was aware of her awestruck stare. Lord, bury her in a hole now if he was.

Mark sat on the edge of her table, leaned forward, and sent her an amused smile.

Dimples. Real, live dimples creasing each side of his face. On any other man, they might have looked girlish. On him, oh no. He looked all man. She'd died and found heaven.

"I can flirt, if I have to. I'd rather just talk to you. About you."

It had to be a line, and she'd be stupid to be affected by it. Ignoring her speeding heartbeat, Nicki cocked her head and regarded him with what she hoped was a cool gaze. "That's laying it on a tad thick."

He leaned in. "It's being honest. I searched for you on Google before this meeting. You run with quite a crowd. What was it like hanging out with Paris Hilton at parties?"

"Relatively dateless. And once she got into home movies . . . well, then I really couldn't compete," she said flippantly.

"So all the men you met in the past were stupid?"

"Excuse me?"

"To be more interested in a careless bimbo than you, they've got to be stupid. To run a business takes some guts, brains, and substance."

A burst of pleasure flushed her body at his words. For years she'd wondered why men failed to see the qualities of a woman beyond her waistline, ass, or breasts. Maybe this guy did. And maybe he was blowing sunshine up her skirt. She couldn't deny, however, that he was good.

"You have the most interesting eyes," he murmured. "They're so blue and exotic next to your beautiful olive skin."

"My dad was both a typical Italian and a typical man. I got his skin. Everything else, I got from my mother. She was half Norwegian, half Chinese."

"No kidding?" His smile widened. "That's a unique combination."

"My father liked possessing unique mistresses. She was a beautiful woman."

"So is her daughter."

Boy, he looked at her. Right at her. With those vivid hazel eyes, he stared, taking her in. She didn't want to be affected by his praise or his gaze on her. It was stupid, unprofessional.

You don't always get what you want, a pesky voice in her head reminded her.

"You going to dance for me, or you going to sit here and gab all day?"

"Whatever you want, boss." He winked and turned away.

From his backpack, Mark extracted a CD and placed it in the portable player located stage left. Moments later, a rich, sexy techno rhythm filled the air. To the beat of the music, he strutted to the front edge of the stage, his expression mysterious, arrogant, as his gaze locked on to hers. For a man who stood about five inches over six feet, he moved with a slick grace, a smooth prowl. Generally, if a man was a good dancer, he was also good in—

Get your mind out of the gutter, girl. He's here to audition, not light your fire!

Nicki knew she should be more jaded. She saw this kind of stuff all the time. Every night, in fact. But something about Mark made being impervious utterly impossible. She had no idea why he affected her more than any other hottie working here. But when a bump of his hips had her catching her breath, she couldn't deny that he did.

A large hand raking through the pale sheen of his hair as he prowled closer had her heartbeat racing. The pure sex attitude and intent stare had her lamenting every last moment of her two years of celibacy.

But when he grabbed the edges of his shirt and ripped them wide, exposing a chest bulging with muscle and abs rippling with definition, Nicki pretty much lost her mind.

The white shirt hung loose on his wide shoulders, stark against his golden skin. Every muscle in his sleek torso bunched as he took a deep breath. His incredible pectorals tightened as he raised his hands from his sides.

They stopped at the waistband of his pants.

His gaze honed in on her again, rich with promise and knowledge. This man knew a thing or two about sin. His thumb glided down his fly, directly down the length of a bulge a blind woman couldn't miss.

Nicki sucked in a breath and held it.

A reproachful half smile taunted her just before he yanked on his shirt, stripping it clean away from his body, exposing miles more muscle heaped on his beefy shoulders. A Celtic knot tattoo encircled one of the hard swells of his very healthy biceps. Even his thick forearms, lined with wide veins, attested to his strength and vitality. Holy cow, he looked like he could bench-press her Crossfire convertible.

He grabbed his shirt in his large fist and, with it, stroked his way down his chest, throwing his head back to expose the long, strong column of his throat.

Lying to herself was useless. She'd love to be the one to put ecstasy on his face. And thinking that about a prospective employee was about as smart as cranking her air-conditioning on and flinging her doors wide to the Vegas summer.

Mark fastened his hot gaze on her once more. He tossed his shirt away with a snap of his wrist and strutted closer, so close she could see a rivulet of sweat sliding down his corded neck. There was no doubt this time; her panties were definitely damp.

Wearing nothing but a naughty smile from the waist up, the Adonis look-alike gyrated his hips in a deep, lazy movement, demonstrating a sure rhythm to the music. The perfect rhythm, in fact, for—

Stop there, she told herself. For God's sake, she was a grown woman who'd had her fair share of gorgeous men. What was her problem?

Besides not having had a flesh-and-blood man in so long her sexual skills had moved from rusty to corroded beyond salvage?

The notion that sex was like riding a bike seemed too easy, especially when confronted with a man who could probably win the bedroom Tour de France, blindfolded. Not that she'd ever know personally.

Suddenly, he turned away. Nicki's eyes widened at the sight of his naked back and leather-clad ass. Views of his front and back were equally drool-inducing. No doubt, he got a woman both coming and going . . . and coming again.

Bad, bad girl.

She drew in a deep breath. Now would be a good time to get her head on straight, rather than mooning over an auditioning man like a thirteen-year-old with her latest *Teen Beat* magazine. Mark Gabriel was here to serve a purpose, potentially to make her money.

Business, her club's future, financial independence—those were her priorities. Period.

But then he grabbed his leather pants at both sides and pulled. Suddenly, he wore a small black G-string that showed his taut, sculpted ass. And well . . . the future seemed really far away.

Aware that her mouth gaped open, Nicki closed it. Again, he swung his hips. The muscles in his legs and backside moved in fluid harmony. Every shift in his position showed off his rippling back to perfection.

Where had this guy come from, Hunks R Us?

Finally, he turned and faced her, arms swinging at his sides, as he and his taut belly undulated closer. Now she had to peer up at him, and the new angle had her wishing she had invested in a video camera. It also gave her a really up close and personal view of the fact he wasn't small anywhere.

Resisting the urge to wipe her sweaty palms down her jeans, she sat on her hands instead, to restrain herself from the powerful temptation to touch. Her panties had gone beyond damp.

Mark smiled, as if he could read her mind.

He dropped to one knee in front of her on the raised stage, and they were nearly eye-level. His gaze seemed to say that he would love nothing more than to master her body, grant her every midnight fantasy. Everything below her waist wholeheartedly accepted.

The music throbbed around them, hot and insistent. He reached out. Toward her. Closer, closer, those long fingers and that broad palm came. He held a lock of hair that framed her face between his thumb and forefinger and slowly drew it through his grasp. Then he feathered his thumb along her jaw as he stared deep into her eyes, as if she was the most fascinating creature in the world.

Her heart all but stopped. Her skin tingled. Everything between her legs ached. She'd run out of adjectives to describe how amazing Mark Gabriel was—a first for her.

With a wink and a dimpled smile, he stood, swung his hips once more, and struck a bodybuilder's pose that delineated every muscle of his mind-blowing body as the music stopped.

Nicki didn't know whether to clap madly or run to the stage to attack him, ripping off her clothes as she went. Or send him away before she indulged in the latter.

Instead, she sat stunned, mute.

Mark uncurled from his pose. Casting her a quick glance as if to gauge her reaction, he casually gathered his clothes and music, then hopped off the stage. He stood right in front of her, glistening and gorgeous and—oh God—she could smell him now . . . pine forest, a hint of sweat, and a whole lotta man.

She exhaled and pasted on a smile. "Well done."

The smile toying at the corners of his mouth displayed his amusement. "Thank you."

He shifted right, directly into her line of vision, so that she was suddenly staring at his rigid six pack and ample . . . attributes. Hot tamales, he was temptation on two legs. It would be so easy to indulge her craving for a little afternoon delight and put an end to the lengthy celibacy that suddenly constricted like a spiked collar. His golden skin sliding over thick muscle just brought on fantasies of the power he could bring to bed, the—

"Nicki?"

Great, he'd caught her staring. Well, duh! She'd been as subtle as a dog panting after a whole pile of juicy bones. She glanced again at his . . . package and figured any analogy that contained the word "bone" was just a bad idea right now.

Clearing her throat, she stood and met his gaze. "Sorry. Zoned off for a minute. Remembering some things I left unfinished in my office."

And if you buy that, I've got a bridge to sell you . . .

"I know you're busy. Sorry if I kept you too long." He shrugged into his shirt.

"It's fine. Um, since all I have is a name, I'm going to need some contact information. I've got a few more auditions over the next few days, but I'll call once I've made a decision."

He gave her the number to his cell phone as he donned his pants. Thinking it was a shame to cover up such awe-inspiring scenery, she scribbled his number greedily. Gee, if she called him during a weak moment and lured him into great phone sex, would he know it was her?

"I've got caller ID. I don't always answer the phone, but for you I will."

Nicki bit her lip to hold in a gasp. Had he read her mind?

No, he wants a job, you idiot. Focus!

"Address?" she asked.

He hesitated. "I just got into town yesterday, so I don't really have one. Once I find a job, I'll be looking for a place. For now, I'm staying at a motel."

"No sweat. I'll just . . . call."

"I'll look forward to it." He extended his hand in her direction.

Oh, goody, she was going to get to touch him. Even if he only offered her a handshake instead of an invitation to do the wild thing. Her belly knotting, she folded her much smaller hand in his. Lightning singed its way from her hand, up her arm, straight to her chest the instant he touched her. From the moment she'd set eyes on him, she'd known he had potent written all over him in big red letters. His handshake more than confirmed it. The knot in her stomach tightened . . . just like her nipples.

Lord, what would happen if the man kissed her, spontaneous combustion?

"Thanks for coming out." She hoped her smile looked nice and impersonal, as if she were talking to her uncle or old Mr. Piedmont who bagged at the grocery store a few blocks away.

"My pleasure. And hopefully yours, too." He winked.

Oh, yeah. If the gods were kind, he had no idea just how much.

Chapter Two

FOUR o'clock already? Nicki sighed as she climbed the stairs to her second floor office. Dancers would start arriving in another hour. The club opened at seven. She'd wasted the afternoon on five auditions, each less inspiring than the last.

Because you were hung up on bachelor number two, Mark Gabriel?

Shoving aside the irritating voice in her head, Nicki opened the door to her office. And stopped.

Mr. Tall, Dark, and Unsettling was sitting in her chair.

Blade Bocelli. Six feet of Italian machismo, with an intimidation factor of about a thousand. Blade had made it his personal crusade to watch every move she made, snoop through her files, and act like he owned the joint.

"What are you doing in my office?"

He turned toward her in his own good time, his cheekbones wicked slashes down his chiseled face. His dark stare hovered somewhere between flat and challenging. "Your accounting."

"What?" Nicki snapped. "I better not have heard you right."

"Your ears aren't broken."

"Damn it, no one said you could—"

"Your uncle said I could. In fact, I think his exact words were 'Update her fucking books, because she's not.'"

"He only owns thirty percent of this club. The rest came from the inheritance my father left me and the willpower I used to stop buying Jimmy Choo shoes. I worked my ass off doing PR for clubs in New York and saved every penny I could. I'm here every day, every night. I've dedicated my life to Girls' Night Out. It's *mine!*"

"I represent your uncle's interests, and he thinks otherwise," he said, then dismissed her by turning back to the late Marcy Hamilton's computer.

No way was she going to let some big testosterone-oozing lug tell her how to run her place. Unfortunately, talking to Uncle Pietro about Blade's overbearing presence did absolutely no good. Why was it that all old-school Italian men assumed that anyone with a vagina was automatically missing a brain?

Feeling her blood pressure soar, Nicki reached for the phone anchored to the waistband of her shorts. "This is crap, and I'm going to put a stop to it."

"Pietro is in Sicily. He ain't gonna answer you."

Damn it. Reluctantly, she let go of the death grip on her phone. "When is he due back?"

"Don't matter. Someone killed Marcy two months ago. You haven't done jack since," his voice rumbled. "Face it, you need help. Pietro is just making sure you get it."

"It's my business; I'll deal with it."

"When?" Blade's gaze, sharp as his name, cut her with demand. "Receipts need to be tallied, expenses logged. You were running on a shoestring and a prayer when you opened. The club may be crowded more often than not, but these books still need watching."

He was right. As much as Nicki hated it, she'd been avoiding the math portion of the business ever since her accountant, Marcy, had been gunned down in the parking lot one night after her shift.

Putting off her bookkeeping wasn't an Einsteinian move. It had to be done.

"And I'm telling you to stay the hell out of my books. I'll hire someone to take care of it."

"Do you have that much extra cash? Once I finish, I can tell you for sure."

"You won't finish a damn thing," she insisted through gritted teeth. "I said I'll do it."

His terse laugh grated across her nerves. "You can't balance your checkbook."

"I could if I really tried," she blurted.

Instantly, she wished she could take it back. Her comeback sounded as mature as a six-year-old. *My sandbox is better than yours.*

He shot her a skeptical stare. "The fact you don't try only proves you're no accountant."

"Neither are you!"

"I manage."

With a lightning bolt dangling from one pierced ear, a gun holstered inside his leather jacket, and shoulders as wide as a bus, he looked like he managed to do a lot of things, none of them very legal.

"Look, who else you got to do this?" he challenged.

Nicki paused, thinking. Zack Martin, her lead dancer and stage manager, had his hands full. Besides, she wanted him focused on making money, not crunching numbers—assuming he even knew how. None of her employees had any accounting in their backgrounds that she knew of. Some hadn't even finished high school. Still, she wasn't helpless.

"Lucia. She can do it for me."

He hesitated, but his poker face gave nothing away. "Yeah, I guess your books are more important than that research paper she's writing. It's just her full, tenured professorship on the line."

She resisted the urge to wince. Lucia had come to her for the summer, begging for a change of scenery and the chance to write for a very important publication with a minimum amount of interruption. Nicki knew her books were so off balance, it would probably take even a whiz like her sister several weeks to sort it all out.

And that left her with no one. Except Blade.

"Listen to me." She wagged a finger at him. "This is temporary. The minute I have the money, I'm going to find someone else to keep these books." *Someone I trust.*

He shrugged as if he couldn't give a shit. "I'm just doing what the boss asked me. You hire someone else who makes him happy and you can afford it, I'm done."

The day couldn't come soon enough for her.

"Anyone call while I was taking auditions?"

"I'll keep your books. I'm not a fucking receptionist."

The man made her grit her teeth. "Do you have to be an asshole all the time?"

Blade shot her a tight, dangerous smile. "Just doing my job."

* * *

IF someone had asked him before tonight what his definition of a good time *wasn't*, Mark could have come up with a fairly healthy list: root canals, being in jail, speaking publicly. But after tonight, he knew that watching oiled-up pretty boys take off their clothes ranked up there, too.

Tossing back the last of his third beer in as many hours, Mark scanned the club again. Hordes of women of all ages, whose behavior ranged from horrified to on the prowl, filled the club's dim, mirrored interior. A few of the male dancers strutted their stuff around the perimeter of the two stages, flirting, smiling. One guy grinned as a woman old enough to be his mother shoved a ten in his G-string. In response, the dancer bent her over his arm and gave her a kiss Mark was fairly sure included tongue. That part of the job was paradise, though, when compared with dancing onstage, actually stripping under the harsh lights, to pounding music, urged on by catcalling strangers.

He really hoped he didn't have to do this job for long. Provided he even got the job. Learning to rip off Velcro-seamed clothes and prance around in a G-string had been humiliating enough in the privacy of a dance studio with just his instructor as a witness. In a club full of bachelorettes, birthday babes, and party girls, taking it off and gyrating for the crowd was bound to be sheer torture.

Yet doing it for Nicki, watching her stare and flush, seeing her ogle him like a chocoholic about to fall off the wagon, had been a sublime pleasure.

Why had something he'd dreaded for weeks been so much fun to do for his sexy audience of one? His enjoyment consisted of more than knowing he'd succeeded in learning the skill necessary to complete this assignment, more than realizing a beautiful woman desired him. Mark couldn't put his finger on it. He only knew it had something to do with Nicki.

"Where is she?" he muttered to himself.

No one noticed. Oh, his presence had raised a few brows among the bachelorette party occupying the table nearest his, but they shrugged him off. Probably assumed he was gay.

Not a comforting thought.

"Want another beer?" a waiter paused near his table to ask.

"No, thanks. Is Nicki DiStefano around?"

Instantly, the waiter's face closed up. "Nicki doesn't talk to strange men."

"I'm not strange."

The waiter's look pointed out that he was the lone man watching a show of mostly naked men. "Whatever you say, dude."

Mark held in an impatient sigh. "I mean that I'm not a stranger. I auditioned for her yesterday, to replace one of the dancers. She suggested I come by and check out the act," he lied. "I had a few questions."

"Oh. Nicki doesn't circulate the floor until most of the acts have finished. She usually watches from her office."

The waiter tossed his head up, motioning to a location above the bar. Mark glanced that way, saw a panel of smoky glass amid a row of solid black chrome. His gaze traced the slim outline of a woman's silhouette.

Nicki. Just the thought of her, the suggestion of her curves through the obscured glass, had his cock rising.

Mark handed the waiter a twenty. "How do I get up there?"

Empty tray in hand, he hesitated, looking undecided as he pushed his long, dark hair from his face. "I don't know, man. I could get fired."

Without pause, Mark slid another twenty across the table. "How? I've never seen you before."

Cutting his eyes toward Nicki's box, then the stage, and apparently relieved by what he saw, the waiter snapped up the second twenty-dollar bill. "See the door behind the bar? It leads upstairs. Leon will take a break soon. Jeff, the other bartender, will be too busy trying to get laid to notice you."

At a glance, Mark had no trouble discerning who was who. Leon mixed drinks with grim efficiency near the door that led up to Nicki's office. Jeff leaned in and smiled at a pretty brunette as he served a glass of wine farther down the bar.

"Thanks," Mark said.

He was talking to air. The waiter had long since gone.

Impatience riding him, Mark stood and eased toward the center of the room. A handful of minutes later, Leon tapped Jeff on the shoulder and stepped out from behind the bar.

Once assured of the fact Jeff was shaking a blonde's martini and trying to charm her out of her panties, Mark ducked behind the bar and quickly eased the mirrored door open. He shut it with a quiet click. No one followed.

First hurdle down. Now for the bigger one: gaining Nicki's trust. Today, he had to keep his thoughts on disarming her enough to persuade her to hire him, not wondering what she smelled like when she was aroused. Not visualizing what she'd look like when he held her against a wall and impaled her on his cock. Not imagining her voice as she cried out his name while she came.

Soon, though, all bets were off. Somehow, someway, he'd make sure he had the opportunity to satisfy his curiosity—and more.

He crept up the stairs, marveling at how quiet it was above the chaos, then paused at the top of the landing. Here, the music was just a dull throb in the otherwise silent room.

Mark stared down the terra-cotta tiled hall at the lone closed door. She was down there, in a darkened room, probably all alone. Just the way he wanted her. He crept down the hall, heart pounding, heat rising off of him like an inferno.

Nicki made him hot. Denying it was as pointless as trying to stop a semi with a butterfly net. Her reaction to him during his audition made it clear she reciprocated. Hopefully, that would help him. If not, he'd find another way to earn her trust so he could persuade her to help him catch Blade Bocelli. He wouldn't give up until he had fucked up the gangster's life, much the way Bocelli had nearly ruined his. If using Nicki's desire turned out to be the most expedient means to achieve his goal, it was ugly . . . but so be it. He'd just turn on the charm, persuade her to hire him, then be helpful, polite, sexy, caring, a bad boy . . . whatever she needed in order to feel comfortable with him in her life, in her books—and in her bed.

As Mark pushed the door open to her office and saw her standing in a shimmering black halter dress, most of her slender back bare, and dangling a pair of killer stilettos from her fingers, he acknowledged that the likelihood of him keeping his hands off Nicki was about the same as Snoop Dogg recording a gospel CD.

"Knock, knock," he murmured, drinking in the sight of her in black silk.

She whirled to face him, and the view sucker-punched him in the gut. Her halter top dipped low, displaying the soft valley between her breasts and a hint of the lush swells on either side. The fly of his jeans couldn't expand fast enough to comfortably encase his pike-hard cock. The woman was like a livewire to his libido. Would she object too loudly if he told her that he wanted to lift her sinfully short skirt, lay her across her cluttered desk and ride her until she screamed?

Damn it, he needed to focus on business here.

"Mark Gabriel?" she frowned, trying to peer through the dark. "How did you get in here?"

Clearly, the short-term answer to his X-rated question was that she would mind. Sighing, he wrenched his thoughts away from her body and the things he'd like to do to it. Time to refocus on the job.

"I came to see the show, take in the vibe of the club, and saw your silhouette through the glass."

"This is a private area of the club, for employees only."

"I hope to be one of those soon." He smiled without apology. "None of your waitstaff would ask you to come down to see me, so I hoped you wouldn't mind me coming up. Do you have a few minutes? I'd like to talk to you."

Her eyes narrowed in her suspicious expression. "About what?"

"Look, I'm not trying to creep you out. I just . . . wanted to ask you to give me a fair shake. I can do this job."

Nicki tilted her head, sleek dark hair caressing her bare shoulders. "You seemed very capable. I'm just not done evaluating all the auditions."

"I understand."

Mark studied Nicki. She moistened her lush lips with the tip of her tongue in seeming invitation, but crossed her arms over her chest. She tossed her hair, so he got a peek at the velvet curve of her neck, but she lowered her gaze. Even in the near darkness of the room, he saw her interest. But he couldn't miss her hesitation, too. What was she looking for, just an employee? A friend? A lover?

He really hoped to hell she wasn't looking for a big brother.

Mark studied her face, fastened his gaze deep in her blue eyes, trying to discern the fastest way to her trust. She looked a bit tired and lonely, and more than a bit wary. While he didn't know her well, he'd start with the premise that she wanted someone in her life and see where it took him.

He sighed and paced closer . . . until she tensed. Then he stopped. He had to tread carefully here. Smooth, but not too smooth.

"It must be hard to keep this place running mostly on your own." He thrust his hands into the pocket of his jeans and ducked his head. "I can't imagine how many hours you work, so I didn't expect that you'd have your mind made up yet."

"I keep busy, yes. Mostly because I do a lot of things around the club myself so it stays true to my vision."

"You must have done a lot of things right. It looks pretty crowded for a Tuesday night."

"Vegas never sleeps." She smiled tightly.

"Do you take care of the business side all day, then patrol the place at night?"

"Usually. Why?" Her wariness returned.

Mark intentionally relaxed his stance more. "Just admiring the fact you work hard. I'd be lying if I said I didn't wonder when you might make a decision, but I'm sure picking a replacement dancer is probably the least of your worries."

"No, it's very important. I try to pick only the best-looking men for the show."

She hesitated and stared as if pondering him. Mark let the silence stretch between them. Whatever was going on in that pretty head of hers was more likely to come out if he didn't fill the awkward pause. It would eventually wear on her, and she'd say something.

"And actually, you're one of the reasons my job is so hard this time," she offered.

"Me? If I don't have what you want for the show—"

"On the outside, you do. But it's not just looks. I try to pick interesting men, too. Conversation goes on here, you know. It's one thing to know how to flirt. But some women want to connect, relate. You can't spend a lot of time with any one woman, but part of the experience for her is in knowing that you really got her, even if just for a moment."

"You're not sure I can connect?"

"Oh, you had the charm part down. It was practiced and polished until it gleamed like my grandmother's silver tea service on Easter Sunday. But some women see through that." She paced closer, stepping to his side and glancing his way. "Some women find that insulting. Sure, they want you to undress them with your eyes, but they want you to talk to them, as well."

Mark returned her stare, getting her hesitation. "I insulted you."

Her eyes narrowed, and he could see the intelligence gleaming in her gaze. Thoughts seemed to bounce off her; energy sparked. Besides being a good businesswoman, he'd bet she was rarely anyone's fool. Kinky home movies aside, probably another reason a lot of the losers she'd known in the past had picked Paris over her. Some guys just couldn't handle a woman with brains. After Tiffany's airhead act, Nicki's sharp mind turned him on.

Except this wasn't about him. It was about earning her trust. He really needed to keep his mind on the conversation . . . and out of her panties.

"You didn't insult me, but I knew your charm was an act. I didn't try to get you to connect with me, true. But you sidestepped every one of my questions a bit too well."

Mark rubbed his chin and smiled. "I hoped you hadn't noticed."

Nicki snorted. "In this business, I've dealt with every charmer, loser, playboy, mama's boy—you name it. Believe me, I've learned to notice when my questions are being avoided."

"Sorry I didn't answer you. It's . . . complicated."

"Try me," she challenged.

Now what? Making up a background was too risky. Best to stay close to the truth.

"I'm here because I need a new start. I had to get away from my old life. Las Vegas is the most different place I could think of, compared to the Florida gulf coast. Exotic dancing is the farthest occupation from working in a bank that I could dream up."

Hopefully, that would satisfy Nicki's curiosity—at least about his past. Now if she was interested in knowing exactly how he'd like to kiss her, rake his tongue through her wet slit, and make her beg . . .

"A bank?" Surprise lit her features. "I visit my bank a lot, and I've never seen anyone like you work there."

"I was a branch manager, the expert in deposits and withdrawals." He winked.

Nicki rolled her eyes. "So you worked at a bank. What happened?"

"I quit, drifted to Manhattan. My sister and her husband live there." He shrugged. "But it didn't fit me. The place feels too dirty and rude. My thin Florida blood can't take the winters. Rent that amounts annually to a Third World country's GNP made me choke every time I wrote a check to my landlord. I loathed the subway, thought the Rockettes were overrated. And I got so damn tired of hearing about the Yankees."

He was one of the few who didn't love New York, but had never shared that with a soul. Mark frowned, wondering why he'd told her.

"As a native New Yorker, I have to say, I think that's harsh."

"Yeah? If you love it so much, why aren't you still there?"

"My uncle. I had to get away before he started trying to dress me every morning and cut my food into little bites. The man thinks he needs to control every part of my life, like he does his five-year-old grandson. At least two thousand miles away, it's a little harder for him."

"You miss New York?"

Nicki grimaced. "Not as much as I should. But this isn't about me, and you're trying to change the subject. No more crap. If I hire you, what makes you think you'll like Vegas any better than the Big Apple? It's loud and chaotic here, too."

"Yeah, but there's excitement, too. I like the hot desert wind. You can feel Lady Luck hovering in the air. Frankly, I could use a little of her magic."

Nicki hesitated. "Why? What was so bad about your life in Florida?"

"You don't want all the gory details."

After placing her shoes on the table beside her, Nicki turned back to him and anchored a hand on her hip. "I've asked twice, so obviously I do."

He sighed, mentally editing all the shit that had happened in his life in the last few years. "One of my . . . coworkers at the bank, who was embezzling money, framed me. Finally, my sister and brother-in-law helped prove the claims false, while I formed an intimate acquaintance with the county jail."

"That sucks. But if everyone eventually realized that you were innocent, why not stay?"

"It just wasn't the same, working with people who had believed me guilty once."

"Smart people don't leave good jobs because of a little wounded pride. There are holes in your story, Mark Gabriel." Her savvy gaze raked him. "I don't have time for this. If you came to say something, say it. Otherwise, I have a business downstairs that needs attention."

Direct. No sugarcoating her words. Mark admired her ability to cut to the chase even as he held in a curse.

He sighed. "Don't say I didn't warn you . . ."

Not knowing what else to say, he started with a watered-down version of the truth. "At nineteen, I petitioned the court for custody of my younger sister. Our parents were both dead. Not long after, I found out I had stage two melanoma. I had surgery, chemo, all kinds of medication. I lost my job, had no health insurance, and had to rely on my sixteen-year-old sister for virtually everything."

"*You* had cancer?"

"I got the skin grafting on the back of my neck to prove it. My sister tells me I look like a refugee from an eighties metal band, but I keep my hair long to cover the scars."

Nicki smiled. "You look more than healthy now."

Her smile contained enough suggestion to turn up the temperature of his blood. He'd ten times rather pursue that than this conversation, which was getting out of hand.

"I'm definitely healthy and cancer free. I use sunscreen when I'm outdoors, get checked regularly, exercise religiously, flirt with pretty girls."

Was it his imagination, or had she relaxed a little?

"Yeah, you got the flirting part down. So the bastards you worked for fired you?"

He nodded. "But once I got well, I found another job. That's when the embezzlement thing came up. Around that same time, my sister got married and moved away. I . . . got out of a relationship. I realized I had nothing to tie me to Florida but bad memories. I left."

Mark clenched his jaw and looked away. As explanations went, that was too much. *Way* too much. He needed to shut up. Nothing like opening his mouth and vomiting out the lowlights of his life. God, why not just tell her that he'd gone completely bald during chemo? Or that Tiffany, his ex-wife, had married him solely to ensure he went to prison for her embezzlement? Maybe he should give her the blow-by-blow of the cavity search he'd endured when entering jail. Seriously, if he was going to spill his guts, why not go for the gold? What the hell had happened to his suave idea of charming her?

Embarrassment stung like a sharp slap to the face.

Out of the corner of his eye, Mark saw Nicki sidle closer. She bit her bottom lip and looked at him, not with pity in her eyes, but understanding.

"Actually, I left New York for a lot of the same reasons you don't like it. I miss the pizza. I loved watching fireworks over Lady Liberty on the Fourth of July. But the rest . . . I could do without. My uncle was a nightmare. He still is. But I know about having a reputation you didn't exactly earn and wanting to leave it all behind."

Amazing. The starch in her posture was gone, arms dropped from their guard-duty across her chest to dangle at her sides. Something he'd said reached her, rather than made her think he was a head case throwing a pity party.

"Really?"

Nicki shrugged, wearing a rueful smile. "I ran with a fast crowd, but could never keep up. I didn't want to. My mom had lived that life. It didn't interest me much."

Something vulnerable shone in her eyes, and Mark had the urge to hold her. "Her life bothered you."

"It's not as if I was some kid at home completely alone night after night. I had a great nanny. Our doorman was the grandfatherly type. I saw my mom every afternoon and spent weekends with my dad, stepmother, and half sister. And you're changing the subject again!" She sent him a sharp stare that seemed to see right through him. "I'll bet you do that a lot."

Mark couldn't keep the smile from creeping across his face. "Busted. It's a common complaint of my sister's."

Laughing, Nicki faced him, her face lit up with amusement. Next to him, she was a tiny thing, small boned and not particularly tall. But her personality vibrated, filled a room. Energy pinged around her, even as her obvious intelligence grounded her. She had a lot of warmth without being syrupy. Really unlike Tiffany, who'd been a Precious Moments kind of woman.

"Do you like Precious Moments dolls?" he blurted.

She hesitated, staring at him as if he'd lost his mind. Given all he'd said about his past, followed by this inane question, he'd have to agree.

"Not really. Why?"

Mark shrugged, feigning nonchalance. "Just curious. Some women do."

"I've heard that. They're too sweet for me. I'm known as Commando Bitch around here."

As he laughed at her remark, the oddest relief slid through him. Not that a woman refusing to fall for the marketing spiels of PMC Doll Company exempted her from selfishness or greed. But maybe it was a good sign.

Then again, it really didn't matter. The goal here was getting inside her books. Getting inside her body was a secondary goal—no matter how urgent it felt.

Ultimately, her character was irrelevant. It wasn't like they were going to have a relationship. After all, he had really, really bad taste in women. Given the fact he liked her, he'd bet Nicki had some horrible flaw, like being an ax murderer, that he just didn't see yet. And he wouldn't until it was too late.

"Do I look like the type who collects Precious Moments to you?" she asked, a frown settling right between her brows.

She looked insulted that he believed she did.

"Not really. If you collect anything, my guess is shoes." He picked up one of the strappy, sexy black sandals off the table. "Bet you got a pair of these in just about every color."

"No, just the black there . . . along with red, lime, and white."

Mark couldn't resist laughing at that female bit of rationale as he set her sandal back on the table—and eased closer. "Bet I can guess how many pairs of shoes you have, give or take five."

Challenge lit her eyes. "Bet you can't."

"You're on. What do I win if I'm right?"

"The privilege of knowing you're right." She tried to put him in his place with a dismissive gaze.

He wasn't about to let her.

"Let's make this interesting. I want a kiss."

Nicki tensed. "I don't think that's a good idea."

"Backing out?" he taunted.

He was betting a lot here, gambling that Nicki wasn't the kind of woman to retreat from a challenge. If he was wrong . . . well, she'd likely throw him out on his ass, tell him to screw himself, and hire someone else to work in her club. He held his breath, waiting.

"I'm not backing out," she insisted. "I'm being reasonable."

"How is one tiny peck being unreasonable?"

Her eyes narrowed. "I get the feeling you're a give-an-inch-take-a-mile sort of guy."

Oh, she had him pegged. "I swear, one kiss. I won't put a single finger out of line." *At least not right away.* "Besides, you could always win. What do you want if you do?"

"For you to get the hell out of my office and stop shamelessly flirting."

"You might get your way. All you've got to do is agree to play the game."

Nicki rolled her eyes. "Men and their little contests. Fine. I'm in."

"Excellent."

"Why do I feel like I'm going to regret this?"

"Are you a pessimist?"

"I'm a realist, thank you."

"All right, Ms. Realist, write down the number of pairs of shoes you own. Then I'll guess, and we'll compare. Sound fair?"

Pausing, Nicki seemed to be examining his words, looking for the flaw in the plan. Finding none, she finally nodded. Mark watched her cross the room to her desk, hips swaying beneath the sexy-as-sin short skirt that had his mouth watering. With a quick flourish, she wrote on a scrap of paper, folded it in half, and handed it to him.

"This is the truth?"

"Why would I lie about something this insignificant?"

"Point taken."

"What's your guess, Mr. Gabriel?"

Mark closed her scrap of paper in his hand and glanced at her sandals again. They had to be a bitch to walk in for long, which explained why she was holding them rather than wearing them when he entered the room. And she had them in four colors. He'd bet she had lots of these strappy-style shoes for parading around the club and painting the town red. Naturally, she'd have a pair of sneakers, maybe two. She'd have sexy, close-toed shoes for contrast. And she'd have them in multiple colors. He'd bet she had boots, as well. She'd probably been a bridesmaid a time or two along the way and had special shoes for each of those dresses.

"Did you count slippers?" he asked.

"No. They don't count."

Technically they did, since she wore them on her feet, but he wasn't going to argue.

"Hmmm. All right. My guess is fifty-three."

Instantly, her jaw dropped. Shock rippled across her face. And Mark knew he'd come close enough to win. He unfurled his fist and opened up the paper in his hand. Fifty-two. He'd been damned close.

"How the hell did you know that?"

He shrugged. "An educated guess. My sister is into shoes, too. Although she likes to look at them more than wear them."

Nicki took a deep breath, and her posture turned starchy. Oh, a sore loser—or one out of practice. Mark sensed she didn't lose often. He'd bet she had one hell of a temper about it when she did.

"This has to be the silliest bet I've ever made, but whatever. You won."

"Yep, I did."

Mark said nothing else, did nothing. Silence stretched, thick and ripe and so full of awareness, he had to resist the urge to smile. About now, she was probably bracing herself, wondering what it would be like when he kissed her, if he'd try to take advantage of her, go beyond his one promised peck. She was preparing a defense, steeling herself against feeling anything. But she was also likely confused by his lack of action.

"Well, you won. Claim your prize. Let's get it over with."

He grinned. "Here and now isn't the place. I'm patient. I'll wait for the right time."

"What? The invitation doesn't get any more engraved than this. Look, you said yourself it's a peck. No big deal."

"Yeah, but I want it to be a big deal." He winked and headed for the door, brushing his body with hers. Feeling her pebbled nipples against his shirt just about killed his good intentions, but he managed to pull it together, block out the feel of his raging erection and murmur, "I'll collect later."

Chapter Three

"Zack is complaining that Sean isn't . . . um, equipped to be both Conan and a cowboy."

Frowning, Nicki glanced up from the order forms swimming in her vision. Normally, she'd welcome the distraction Lucia provided from the endless columns of food items and numbers. She'd already finished this week's alcohol order, thank goodness. Her reward? Getting to buy exciting paper goods like toilet paper next. Gee, what a treat.

The only subject that could put a damper on her enthusiasm to ignore these dull but necessary tasks? A new dancer for the club.

"Really? Guests have always been enthusiastic about Sean's equipment."

Lucia flushed. "I'll take your word for it. I didn't look. Just passing a message. Zack is in a bad mood."

"Hmm. It must not have worked out between him and Pedro. He's always in a bad mood when he's between relationships."

Nicki sighed. One more thing to deal with. First, thanks to her overbearing uncle, she had Blade, the asshole accountant she hadn't hired. Then her virginal sister had arrived to spend the summer underfoot . . . in a place full of eye candy dancers, several of whom would be all too happy to give Lucia their version of a sex education. Running a fledgling business minus one buff attention getter, with a temperamental lead dancer and financial records in chaos was no walk on the beach—and they were problems she couldn't avoid much longer.

Lucia pushed her glasses up on her nose. "I know nothing about Zack's love life. I only know he's screaming at Sean."

"Which makes it hard for you to concentrate on your research, I'm sure." Nicki sighed and stood and stretched. "Sean just can't seem to remember to completely change out of one costume before traipsing back out onstage. Three times in two weeks. Conan peeling off his armored breastplate to reveal a Western vest kills the fantasy."

"So when are you going to end Zack's misery and call your Mr. Yummy to hire him?"

"My Mr. Yummy? Who are you talking about?"

As if she didn't know.

Mark Gabriel had swooped through her mind a time—or ten—after she auditioned him four days ago. But when he'd stolen into her office the following night, told her about himself, then won a kiss he hadn't claimed, she hadn't been able to get him out of her mind. What would his mouth feel like on hers? Would he be demanding? Tender? Exceptional, she'd bet.

In her business, this kind of curiosity wasn't a good thing. Lusting after one of her dancers—stupid. Taking the energy away from Girls' Night Out while its outcome was still uncertain and she owed her uncle a huge chunk of change . . . that would make her a candidate for the Darwin awards.

"You know exactly who I mean." Lucia slanted her a skeptical stare. "He's gorgeous. You said he could move. He wants to work, you need a dancer. What's the issue?"

Other than her personal hang-ups and her fear that she'd molest him in . . . oh, the first ten minutes he worked for her? None at all. Nicki sighed. Maybe she needed to invest in a new sex toy. This morning, her B.O.B. just hadn't gotten the job done. Fantasies about Mark and down-and-dirty sex against the wall had worked wonders, unfortunately.

On the other hand, he'd likely make her a fortune. She needed every dime of it. Once she'd paid off Uncle Pietro, then she could give her glorified babysitter, Blade Bocelli, the old heave-ho.

"It's complicated," Nicki hedged. The truth was too embarrassing. "For starters, based on some things he told me, I don't think he'd stay long."

Lucia frowned and tilted her head so her auburn curls slid down one shoulder. "Last time I checked, you weren't offering retirement benefits. Even if he stays a couple of months, isn't that better than nothing?"

Damn it, yes. And she'd hired several of her current dancers knowing they hadn't intended to stay long. That some had, in fact, remained for a while was merely good fortune on her part, not an expectation.

She was running out of excuses . . . beyond not being able to control herself around one beautiful, testosterone-packed man. Time to dig through her mental bag of tricks for a little self-control. Who knew, maybe her attraction was a momentary blip, a hallucination produced by her utterly neglected sex drive.

Nicki leaned over her desk and fished around for her stack of applicants' paperwork. All she had on Mark was a name, a Social Security number, his date of birth, and his cell phone number. Well, and the grainy picture of him she'd had her security company pull from their footage of the parking lot on Monday afternoon. Even that rough still of him from a distance screamed that he was major hunk material.

What was a girl to do?

"Nicki?" Lucia prompted.

She sighed. "Where is the damned phone?"

Half-hoping he'd skipped town or decided to apply for a job at any of the local banks, Nicki called Mark. Clammy palms weren't the usual for her. Nor this odd tightening in her belly. *Quit it already,* she told herself. *You're extending a job offer, not inviting the guy over for an evening of screaming sex and sweat-damp sheets.*

The pep talk failed utterly when, on the second ring, Mark answered.

"Hello?"

Dark and deep, his voice vibrated its way up her spine, resonating inside her body—all from that one little word.

"Mr. Gabriel, this is Nicki DiStefano from Girls' Night Out."

He paused . . . just for a moment. Nicki found herself holding her breath for his response.

"Hi."

Again, one word was like a blow to her gut. Full of invitation and a hint of suggestion. And this was a business conversation. How potent would his tones be when he was aroused, his voice raw, redolent of sex? A telltale flush of warmth crept through her at the thought.

Get your mind between your ears and out of your thong!

"I was hoping you'd call," he offered.

Nicki tried not to think about all the way she could interpret that statement.

"Good. Um, can you come down to the club for a few minutes? I'd like to see you." Realizing how that could be construed, she hastily added. "A-about the job, of course."

The amused surprise on Lucia's face suggested she'd been less than successful in her effort to be strictly businesslike.

Shocker.

"I'd love that. I can be there in an hour."

"Perfect. I'll see you then."

"I'm looking forward to it."

His voice was like warm honey, sliding down her skin, seeping inside her. Addictive, powerful—like she suspected the rest of him could be. She really, really hoped hiring him wouldn't be a huge mistake.

Before she could say something utterly inappropriate and

embarrass herself, Nicki slammed the phone down. She sighed as the sudden tension drained from her.

Behind her, Lucia burst into laughter. "You've got it bad for this guy."

"Bite me."

"I think it's Mark Gabriel you'd rather have biting you."

Nicki rolled her eyes. "How do you know these things?"

"I watch movies. I read. A lot." She shrugged. "Someday, some man will realize I'm a woman, besides being a professor with a scary IQ. When I find him, I'll be ready."

"Honey, you will find someone." Nicki hugged her sister, feeling more than a bit guilty for being so wrapped up in business and Mark Gabriel that she never stopped long enough to think that Lucia might be lonely and want a little romance in her life. "I know you will. And I'll help you if I can. Just make sure it's the right guy. Not anyone who works around here. Broken hearts are no fun."

"I imagine not." Lucia shot her a mischievous glance. "If Mr. Yummy is on his way over, you might want to put on something else."

Nicki stared down her denim Capri pants and red, oversized Mickey Mouse T-shirt. The perfect thing to wear for taking inventory and doing paperwork. Not so perfect for this occasion.

"Good point. I should look more professional."

"I was going to suggest sexy."

"I'm giving the man a job!"

"Maybe, but you'd like to give him more."

The smile Lucia flashed at Nicki was anything but virginal. "Okay, who's been giving you these books you're reading?"

"I'm a smart girl who knows her way around the library."

Then she walked out the door, leaving Nicki all alone with her impure thoughts.

Trudging her way up to her apartment on the third floor, she reconsidered. Did she really want to hire Mark Gabriel? Wave temptation under her nose every night? It wasn't too late to back out . . .

Besides, the attraction might be totally unreciprocated. Not only could he flirt, but he could also seem so genuine, like the woman he looked at was the only woman who truly mattered. Nicki snorted. No doubt, that got him laid a lot.

Even if the attraction wasn't one-sided, Nicki didn't see a lot of options. She needed money, and Mark would definitely make it for her.

Nicki arrived on the club's top floor, which had been divided into four apartments by the building's original owners. She hadn't seen any reason to change that. In fact, living above the club was incredibly convenient.

On her way to her own unit, she passed the other three. Thanks to her uncle's insistence, Pain-in-her-ass Bocelli lived in the first unit on the left. Lucia was crashing this summer in the apartment down the hall from him. Nicki enjoyed having the place farthest back, since it was the biggest and offered the most privacy.

The unit on the right, just before hers, sat empty. Too bad she couldn't rent the silly thing out, not even to another employee. Not for lack of trying. But who wanted to live above a male strip club, other than people who worked there? All of the guys at the club either had wives or partners or live-ins or, like Zack, took care of his ailing grandfather. Despite multiple ads in local papers, the apartment remained vacant. Which sucked. The extra money might have freed up some of her cash to hire an accountant.

Nicki let herself into her place, sailed past the bits of clutter in her old world European living room and headed straight for her bedroom. The sight awaiting her in the full-length mirror nearly made her scream. What had happened to the well-ordered French braid she'd yanked her hair into this morning? And the outfit . . . She looked like a kindergarten teacher on the edge.

Not a sight that would inspire authority and project professionalism.

After a quick ten minutes with her cosmetics bag and another five with a hairbrush, Nicki stepped into her closet. Professional. Yes, that's what she needed.

Biting her lip, she looked through her wardrobe. Being a night-club owner meant she didn't have much that passed for the Brooks Brothers look. Too bad she and Lucia weren't the same size, or she'd borrow one of those cute tailored shirts . . . But Nicki and her healthy B cups had no hope of filling out a shirt her sister's D cups normally occupied.

She sifted through her clothes with a critical eye. *Too short. Too low cut. Too last season. Ugh!*

Nicki sighed. She had to stop agonizing about what to wear. Mark Gabriel was just a guy she planned to offer a job, not Brad Pitt. Not the Pope.

Finally, she pulled out a khaki skirt that reached mid-thigh, a simple black silk shirt, along with some medium-heeled black sandals from her fifty-two pairs of shoes and donned them. Then immediately resisted the urge to change.

A spangled bracelet and a flirty anklet later, Nicki was out the door.

By the time she made it downstairs, Mark was waiting for her in the darkened foyer of the club.

Naturally, he looked completely edible in a body-hugging blue T-shirt, jeans faded in some really intriguing places, and casual loafers. Knowing what he looked like under most of those clothes wasn't helping her pulse rate.

"Glad you could make it," she greeted.

Mark extended his hand. Damn it, the electrical outburst she'd experienced the last time they'd engaged in this ritual was dangerous, not smart to repeat before she'd had a chance to find something about the man she loathed and fortify herself with it. But she didn't want to appear rude, either.

Steeling herself, Nicki slipped her hand in his. Oh, hell yes—just like before. A jolt, the tingles, fire spreading up her arm. If a mere handshake thrilled her this much, what would he feel like deep inside her, pounding hard with long, sure strokes?

Do not *go there,* she told herself. Deep breath. She could do this.

A quick shake later, she hastily released his hand.

"I'm glad to be here," he murmured.

Those killer hazel eyes of his latched on to her. They shimmered with heat and mischief—and blatant interest.

For the sake of her business, her future, and her sanity, she pretended not to notice.

"Let's sit at one of the tables and talk."

He followed her inside the club, down the shallow bank of stairs. Nicki made sure she chose a well-lit table dead in the middle. No cozy corners that would give either one of them more ideas.

As she sat, he folded his long, hard body in the chair directly across from hers. She'd imagined that having a cocktail table between them would give her some level of comfort. It didn't. Mark was closer than ever, his woodsy, musky male scent teasing her.

She cleared her throat. "If you still want the work, I'm offering you the job. You'll be on four nights a week. Zack, the lead dancer and stage manager, will help you with your schedule. You'll be here by six. You're usually out by two-thirty. Rehearsal is every Monday, the day we're closed, from two to four. Naturally, you keep tips. Trips to the V.I.P. room with a guest for a private dance earns you thirty dollars each time. If you elect to serve drinks when you're not onstage, you'll get a cut from the bar, besides your hourly wage. Any questions so far?"

"It seems straightforward. Anything else I can figure out as I go."

"So you accept?"

"Sure. I'll do my best to make you feel good about the choice."

Nicki didn't even ask what he meant by that. Her imagination didn't need the stimulation. "This is the part of the spiel where I warn you to keep some of your money back to pay taxes. If you don't, I won't have to cut off your balls. The IRS will do it for you."

A faint smile curled his mouth as he flashed those landmark dimples. "I certainly wouldn't want to incite you to anything that extreme. Besides, I already spent time in jail and know how unpleasant it is, so I'm the last person you have to worry about breaking the law."

Nicki nodded, conceding the point. "Zack and the other guys will fill you in on specifics. Be here an hour early for rehearsals next Monday so Zack can work with you one-on-one. You'll have a routine or two of your own to work out. Group numbers with all the dancers are at the beginning and end of the evening. You'll need to learn those before we turn you loose on stage. Zack will know when you're ready."

Mark nodded. "Zack sounds like he knows what he's doing."

"He's been with me since I opened the doors."

"So he has a lot of experience."

"Dancing, yes. He's only been my stage manager for a few months. But he understands my vision, and I've learned to trust him to make it happen."

"Then I'll be sure to stay on his good side."

"Not too good." Nicki paused as a terrible thought occurred to her. Had she completely misjudged him? "Well, unless . . . I'm not against employees dating each other, so if you're same-sex oriented—"

"No." He didn't even let her finish the sentence. "Definitely not."

Why did that come as a relief? It shouldn't. It didn't. Hell, he could be into barnyard animals for all it should concern her. Mark Gabriel's sex life was absolutely none of her business.

Her libido protested vociferously.

"Um, I think we're about done here. I'll need a glossy head shot and a full body pose of you in the next week or so. If you don't have one, I'll refer you to a photographer."

Mark leaned in, those warm greenish eyes drilling her, making her next breath difficult to take. Nicki tried to ease back in her chair, but short of standing she had nowhere to go. And putting space between them would only tell him how much he affected her.

"I'm not much for cameras. Maybe you could take the pictures."

Oh, sure. Her, a camera and a mostly naked Mark Gabriel. There was a recipe for her immediate downfall.

"I'm terrible with cameras. If you're uncomfortable with a photographer, Zack can probably take the stills."

The grin lifting the corners of his firm, wide mouth seemed to confess that he'd been outsmarted. "I'll figure it out and get you the pictures soon."

"Great. Any other questions? If not, I've got to start getting ready for tonight's show. Fridays are always busy."

Mark leaned forward a bit more, propping that intriguing square chin on one large fist. "Actually, I was hoping you could help me. I've spent a few days looking for a place to live, and I'm not having much luck. Any recommendations, preferably without drug dealers and king-sized roaches as neighbors? I want to live as close to the club as possible." He shrugged. "I didn't bring my car."

Immediately, Nicki thought of her vacant apartment upstairs . . . the one right next door to hers.

No, bad idea. The worst idea she'd had in years. Decades, even.

"Did something occur to you?" he prompted.

Drat, the look on her face had probably given her away. "Um . . ."

What the heck could she say? Well, she could keep the apartment vacant. But . . . she needed Mark here, ready to dance, not distracted by his living arrangements. She could charge him rent, which would help her bottom line. They wouldn't have to see each other after hours. He'd never be late for work or a rehearsal. She could keep an eye on him so that whatever he did that might need watching was . . . well, watched.

"Help me out here," he cajoled. "I could really use it."

That smooth, honey-rich voice, followed by dimples, was like a one-two punch to her resistance.

She sighed. When had Commando Bitch become such a freaking pushover?

"There's a vacant apartment on the third floor. You can rent it for six hundred a month, if you want. It's one bedroom, one bathroom. Kitchen, living room, and a small washer and dryer. Refrigerator is included."

"Really? That's great! Furniture?"

"A sofa, a kitchen table, and a queen-sized bed. That's about it. I'm sacrificing this for you." *Huh, and pigs will fly!*

"You're great, you know?"

His smile had her feeling faint. How could he do that to her so easily? Other men in her life had been interesting or hot or fun. None had been magnetic or tied her up into more knots than Lucia when she did yoga. He just got to her.

"Can you show me?"

All the ways in which he affected her? Not a chance. "Excuse me?"

A hint of mischief sparkled in his eyes. "The apartment. I'd like to see it."

She nodded and stood. The sooner she dealt with him, the sooner she could excuse herself from his compelling presence. The sooner she could get on with her business and stop being a hormone-happy airhead.

Nicki led him through the club, to the private stairs behind the bar. As she climbed three flights, she not only heard Mark behind her, she felt him. His body heat, his warm breath on the back of her neck, his tempting scent wrapping around her.

Finally, they reached the top of the club. Nicki drew in a deep breath, glad for Mark-free air.

"Wait here just a second," she said, then hustled down the hall to her apartment.

She grabbed the vacant unit's key from the junk drawer in her little kitchen, then joined Mark, who was looking around the narrow landing.

"Is that the apartment?" he asked, nodding toward her door.

"No, this is." She pointed to the door on her right and shoved the key in the lock.

"What do these other doors lead to?"

Nicki hesitated, then realized he was going to figure it out, sooner rather than later. "These are all apartments. The door I just came through leads to mine."

His smile brightened until it could have lit up all of Las Vegas. "I like the neighborhood already."

Rolling her eyes, Nicki did her best to look unmoved by his show of interest. "No normal person I know wants to live close to their boss."

Not waiting for his reply, she opened the door. A blast of hot, stale air whooshed from the unit, into the hall. She stepped back to avoid the draft—and collided with Mr. Yummy's fabulous, hard chest. His hands fell to her waist to steady her. His killer scent surged all around her. She abruptly discovered that the cliché about a woman's knees turning weak was actually true.

"If everyone's boss had your qualities, they would," he whispered in her ear.

Pulse seesawing, Nicki stepped away and cast what she hoped was a warning glance over her shoulder. Restraining herself from jumping on Mark was hard enough. If he was going to encourage her . . . hell, it was as dangerous to her agenda as someone waving a seven-layer chocolate cake in front of her on diet days.

"What?" he asked innocently. "You're smart, driven. You seem fair and easy to deal with. That always makes for good neighbors."

He was good—and quick. She'd give him that. It was on the tip of her tongue to demand he claim that kiss he'd won and get it over with, stop holding it over her head and killing her with innuendo and those lust-tinged glances. But she wasn't about to give him the upper hand, even if she had to bite her tongue.

"Thanks," she said dismissively and walked into the apartment. "Kitchen on your left. Nook and living room directly in front. The bedroom is down the hall, first door on your right. Bathroom is on your left. Washer and dryer are at the end of the hall in the closet. I'll let you look around."

With a shrug of those heavenly wide shoulders, Mark glanced around. Less than a minute later, he said, "I'll take it."

That was quick! "Really?"

"It's perfect. Close to work, low maintenance, already equipped with the basics. And," He flashed her those dimples again, "I have a great neighbor."

* * *

BY Monday afternoon, if the devil had opened up a big hole in the floor of Girls' Night Out and offered eternal damnation to escape his current, humiliating predicament, Mark would have been sorely tempted to agree.

"A what?" he asked Zack Martin, the lead dancer/stage manager.

"A Viking."

Zack handed him a studded metal helmet with protruding horns. Mark frowned. What was the intimation here, that he was *horny*? Wearing phallic symbols on his head in public definitely went above and beyond the call of duty.

Next, Zack handed him a black tunic-like garment with an open *V* to his navel, a pair of thin black pants he'd bet were so tight the club's patrons would be able to guess his religion, and black thigh-high boots. A black cape completed the look.

"Seriously?" he asked Zack. "This looks more like a vampire with bad taste in hats."

"I'm the vampire around here. This is Viking."

"Technically, it's not," a woman called from the shadows.

Mark peered past the glaring lights overhead to see a curvaceous redhead walking his way. She was short with a pretty round face and chocolate eyes, which sparkled with mischief. As she stepped closer, out of the harsh glare of the lights, her image materialized.

She held out her hand. "Lucia DiStefano. We met briefly the day of your audition."

Yes, they had. She'd let him in the door with a smile. He'd been too damned nervous to smile back.

Zack dimmed the harsh lights overhead, and finally Mark got a good glimpse of the woman.

"Hi. Mark Gabriel." He shook her hand.

"I'm Nicki's sister," she added.

From the raising of her brows, Mark knew his surprise rippled across his face.

Lucia and her sister looked nothing alike. Nicki was all sleek and dark with uptilted blue eyes, narrow shoulders, spitfire, and challenge, along with a sculpted mouth he was dying to taste. Lucia was more lush curves, warm auburn hair, insightful eyes the color of decadent milk chocolate, and an inviting pink mouth. No doubt she was making some man who loved breasts seriously happy, since she had plenty and then some. But sisters? Lucia was . . . Rita Hayworth to Nicki's Angelina Jolie—totally different animals.

"Half sisters," Lucia clarified. "Her mother was an exotic Euro-Asian model. Mine was an Italian housewife." A self-deprecating smile played at the corners of her lips. "And your costume is more Teutonic. A Viking tunic would have a rounded neck, a gathered sleeve, and end somewhere around the knee. And black pants that thin definitely weren't in their wardrobe."

"Only a history professor would know." Zack rolled his eyes. "We're creating a fantasy here." He dismissed her and turned to Mark. "This is how Nicki sees you onstage. I agree."

At six feet tall with cropped black hair and equally dark eyes, Zack wasn't anyone's idea of a Viking. So he would never know the humiliation of the horned helmet. For Mark, it was more than that. The thought of tearing off tight black everything in front of strangers while he was supposed to look like a Viking conqueror with lust on his mind was making him queasy.

Gritting his teeth, he asked, "What do you want me to do now?"

"In your spare time, practice with the costume. Mirrors help. Look for sexy ways to take it off."

He'd already done plenty of stripping in front of a mirror to prepare for this gig, thanks for asking. No way he planned to do more.

"I meant right now," Mark clarified.

"Oh, set it aside. We need to get you started on learning the routines."

Right, the routines . . .

This assignment had seemed simple in theory. Anything to nail the bastard who had helped destroy his life. Anything to assist the money-laundering scum who'd all but escorted his ex-wife to prison find his own way behind bars. It was still important. Vital. He just hadn't expected it to be so damn embarrassing.

Stripping for Nicki had been fun—a rush, even. Watching her gaze latch on to him, interest brewing in her eyes. Seeing her cheeks flush, imagining that maybe . . . just maybe, she was as affected by him as he was by her.

Somehow, he knew that stripping for a crowd wasn't going to be like that. But he could either tuck his tail between his legs and give up or stick it out and nail this asshole.

No contest.

"Where do I start?" he grumbled.

The door behind the bar slammed, and Mark looked up to see a man with short dark hair and wide shoulders emerge. He wore tailored black slacks, a white oxford under a black leather jacket, and Italian loafers that had probably cost as much as Mark's rent payment.

Blade Bocelli. The picture Mark had seen of the gangster hadn't included his whole face, but given the guy's cocky attitude, he had no doubt this was the man he'd come to bring down.

Bocelli sailed through the club, hawkish gaze seeming to take in everything, even as he gave off a definite don't-fuck-with-me air. Mark gritted this teeth, restraining the urge to jump off the stage, take the prick down, and beat him senseless. Too bad that wouldn't accomplish anything—except make him feel a whole lot better.

Suddenly, the thug stopped. He glanced from Mark to Lucia. His eyes narrowed.

"Your uncle Pietro don't want you around those pretty boys, Lucia. Don't you have a research paper to write?"

Lucia's back turned rigid. "Don't you have anything else to worry about?"

"Right this minute? No." His ruthless glare riveted to Lucia, and he sauntered closer, until he stood at the base of the stage.

Bocelli and Zack were about the same height and build . . . but the similarities ended there. Zack's slightly pissy air of authority drowned in Bocelli's heavy presence.

"Too bad," she shot back. "I'm introducing myself to Mark. Uncle Pietro can't object to that. And in case it's escaped everyone's notice, I am a grown woman."

Bocelli raked a quick dark-eyed gaze over Lucia. "You are. But I'm here to look out for the club. If the Viking over here isn't learning his routines," Bocelli said with a sneer, "then he's not doing something that's gonna earn this place some money. You're distracting him on company time."

"I'm being friendly."

"Call it what you want, but Pietro don't want you around him and his type." He gave Mark a dismissive glare then proceeded through the club and out the front door.

As the door shut behind him, the tension left Lucia's shoulders. She turned back to face Mark, her expression sheepish. "Sorry. Blade is harmless, really, but . . . difficult. He likes to growl a lot."

Harmless? The good professor might know a thing or two about history. She knew squat about men.

"Growling makes him feel big and bad," Zack agreed.

Well, Mark couldn't wait to teach Bocelli otherwise. And he'd make damned sure the time came soon.

* * *

THE only way to put an end to the insanity, Mark feared, was to hunt Nicki down and talk sense into her. He had an inkling that, in this case, Nicki's version of seeing reason was him nodding as she told him how things were going to be.

That wasn't going to happen.

Besides convincing her the Viking gig was a bad idea, he had to find some way to gain her trust, fast. The fact it had taken Nicki more than a year to trust Zack Martin to do a job he juggled almost effortlessly did not bode well. Mark didn't have a year to give to this endeavor. Even a month was stretching it. While that left his options limited, he had no objection to the one he had: pursuing the sizzling chemistry between them. It was a sure way to break down barriers and build intimacy—all while getting him very close to a woman he was dying to sample, one square inch of skin at a time.

He knew exactly where to start.

Climbing the stairs to the third floor after rehearsal, Mark entered his own temporary apartment. It wasn't his room at the Bellagio, complete with minibar and maid service, but it would do.

A quick shower and a shave later, he dressed in jeans and a tight T-shirt. Nicki had stared when he wore something similar, and Mark was all in favor of giving himself every advantage.

After a quick knock on Nicki's door, he waited. A long minute later, she answered, wearing black yoga pants and a bright pink tank top. What she wasn't wearing was a bra.

Hell, yeah! And it wasn't even Christmas.

"Mark?" she stared at him, her eyes straying down to his chest . . . lower. "Is something wrong?"

He held in a grin as she checked him out. "I was hoping I could talk to you for a few minutes about the show."

"Tomorrow. This is my one day off a week, and I'm beat."

A second look told him she wasn't lying. She looked pale and heavy-eyed. His cock jerked when he thought of lying down next to her sleep-warm body, breathing in her scent, and imagining all the creative ways he could rouse her once she'd rested.

"Actually, I'm tired, too. And hungry. Are you?"

Nicki barely ripped her eyes away from his torso before answering. "No."

"You must be. It's almost seven. Let me take you someplace so you'll have a nice full belly when I try to talk to you out of making me wear that costume."

She laughed. "Well, that's honest."

"C'mon. It'll be more fun than eating alone," he cajoled.

"Maybe I want to be alone."

"No, you don't. You were hoping I'd come over here and make you laugh and offer to feed you."

"You're dreaming."

Mark smiled. "Probably, but a guy's got to have goals."

Another of her lilting laughs bubbled to the surface, and Mark relished the sound. Something about Nicki kicked him in the gut every time he looked at her. Her smile gave him the old one-two punch.

"See. I'm good for your morale."

She groaned. "You don't know when to quit, do you? I don't want to go out."

"Then you can invite me in. We'll share a pizza and talk."

Nicki hesitated for a long moment, biting that lush bottom lip. Ah, she was vacillating. Just a little longer in silence and . . .

"All right. But only because we both need to eat. I don't want anyone getting the idea that this is any sort of date."

Interesting. He'd pursue that in a minute—once he was safely inside. "I doubt they will."

Finally, Nicki stepped back and let him in. Mark shut the door behind him.

Goal one, complete. They were alone.

Nicki's decor was a lot like her, rich and warm with smooth lines. A little exotic. Unique.

After a quick discussion about topping preferences, in which they both admitted loving pineapple on their pizza, Nicki ordered from a local place.

"Twenty-five minutes," she announced, hanging up the phone.

"Good. It's quick, but gives me plenty of time to understand why you don't want anyone to think we're dating."

"I thought you wanted to discuss your costume."

"We'll get back to that. Tell me why it's important no one think we're dating."

Sighing, she sat down in the room's lone chair, rather than next to him on the wide sofa. "It's just not a good idea."

"When you were questioning my heterosexuality and telling me I could pursue any interest I might have in Zack," he snorted, "you said you didn't have a problem with employees dating."

"I still don't."

"Then why would it be different if, someday, we did want to have a date?"

"Because I sign your paycheck, not share your dressing room."

"We're still working in the same place, under the same roof. I don't really see the difference."

He stared, bracing his chin in his hand, and tried to keep his mind on the conversation . . . and off the reality that only a thin layer of cotton separated his gaze from her breasts. Those same breasts with nipples now pointed at him, beckoning him mercilessly.

Mark gritted his teeth. Did she have any inkling that he was about three seconds from pinning her to that cozy chair under the weight of his body and using his tongue to acquaint himself with every inch of her?

Wearing a strained smile, Nicki rose and turned away with a shaky sigh. He grinned. Had it been his hot stare that had put her on edge or the steel-pike erection in his jeans? He made no attempt to hide either. She'd been quick and discreet . . . but she'd looked.

With a grin, he rose and followed with silent steps.

"It's an irrelevant question, anyway," she said, then glanced over her shoulder.

Her eyes widened when she saw him closing in on her.

"Irrelevant how?" he challenged, voice purposely soft.

"I—I don't date, really. Too busy."

"Maybe you just didn't have the proper motivation."

"And you would be the proper motivation?" She managed to inject a hint of disdain in her voice.

"It's possible. You never know until you try."

"Are you asking me out?"

"If I was?" He sauntered another step closer.

A deep breath had her breasts rising, her nipples rasping against the cotton and tightening. Damn, the woman was about to kill him.

Nicki backed away, shaking her head. "The answer is no."

"Because . . . ?"

"I told you, I just don't have time. I'm a serious businesswoman with a club to run, and I think some of the other dancers would think . . . I was playing favorites or something. They'd think it isn't a good idea."

"But what do *you* think?" He edged closer. "If it weren't for the other dancers and all."

"It would still be no," she said, voice turning breathy. "I don't need distractions."

"How do you know I'd be a distraction?"

Her gimme-a-break stare nearly had him laughing out loud. "You're a walking, talking distraction. The fact we're having this conversation when I should be laying down the law about your costume tells me the answer needs to be no."

"Hmm," he murmured and came closer still. "Good thing I didn't ask."

Retreating another step, Nicki did her best to put space between them. If he gave her a second to think about how much ground she was giving, how revealing her actions were, Mark had no doubt she'd stop now and ream him out. He'd bet his last dime that Nicki's idea of a good defense was usually a good offense.

Instead of stopping to think about it, though, she eased back again—until her back hit the wall.

Mark smiled.

"Then I guess I'll just have to settle for pizza . . . and that kiss you owe me."

Chapter Four

"K<small>ISS?</small>"

Nicki's heart beat against her chest hard enough to do a battering ram justice. Mark stared, his hazel eyes sizzling her with intent. His look said it all—sex. Fast, hot, demanding, explosive—just the way she liked it. Now.

Air. She needed more air. Despite quick, short breaths, she felt dizzy. And flushed all over. Damn, he smelled good, like spice and vitality. He oozed musk and mystery. Nicki feared she had all the resistance to his scent that an addict had to crack.

Mark slid a large hand across her cheek, curled it around her nape. Tingles burst across her skin wherever he touched. His hot, insistent fingers tilted her face up to his. Breathless in a way she never had been, Nicki waited. Her sensitive nipples scraped her cotton tank with every breath. He leaned in, not close enough to touch . . . but the heat of his body penetrated her, scorching her like a Vegas afternoon in August. Suddenly, her stomach had more knots than a sailboat in a raging storm.

Mark edged closer still and anchored his other hand to the wall beside her head. A dangerous ache coiled between her legs. She felt every minute of her two years of celibacy.

"Yeah," he breathed as he nuzzled her ear. "A kiss."

Nicki shivered.

Lust and self-preservation arm-wrestled in her mind. To her passionate side, the concept of saving herself for anything, like a less dangerous man, held all the appeal of scrubbing off shower scum with her toothbrush. But her head told her that resisting him now would save her problems in the future. First, she needed all her time and mental energy to run this place. Second, she didn't need romantic . . . complications. Mark didn't seem like a forever kind of man. While Nicki wasn't ready for a picket fence quite yet, succumbing to a charmer who would give her the ride of her life then pack his bags seemed downright stupid. Generally, she had more intelligence than a horror movie victim, and hiding in a closet had never been her style.

"I don't think—"

"You think too much," he whispered, moving his hand off the wall and easing it around her hip. "Your eyes tell me your mind is always moving. Now it's time to just feel."

He knew her. Somehow, someway, he'd seen the constant mental energy, the relentless planning and worrying and hoping going on in her head. She fantasized about just letting go. The fact he understood her both thrilled and terrified her. What else would he be able to guess about her? Her deepest fantasies?

Mark leaned a fraction closer. Her hormones catapulted like an Olympic high jumper.

Nicki swallowed. "The problem is—"

"You think you're going to control this—and me. You're not, baby."

"But—"

"Are you the kind of woman to welsh on a bet?"

Damn it, she hated having her honor questioned. She defended it with everything she had when necessary. But when it warred with her preservation instinct, that just sucked.

"No," she admitted. "But I don't want—"

"Yes, you do," he whispered. "It just scares the hell out of you. But I'm going to kiss it and make it all better."

He wore a smile of lazy challenge as the searing hand on her neck situated her perfectly under his mouth. His lips hovered above hers, and he hesitated like a man contemplating a feast. The green heat in his hazel eyes burned her. Nicki's pulse picked up speed. Near him, dizzy seemed like such a permanent state she might as well make it her middle name.

Robbed of the will to resist, she closer her eyes.

He pulled her flush against his hard torso. Nicki had a mere instant to marvel at the sensation of his wide, muscle-slabbed chest against her breasts before his lips covered hers.

Actually, covered was too weak. Mark seduced her lips apart with a soft swipe, a teasing hot-breathed brush. He gave so little, took even less. Taunted her. He left her wanting, aching.

Damn him.

More. She needed more now. Melting like a cheap candle, she arched up, opened to him. Silently, she invited Mark—pleaded with him—to taste her.

His fingers on the back of her neck tightened. That was her only warning before he slanted his lips over hers, seized her mouth and invaded.

Suddenly, he was everywhere. The taste of creamed coffee and mint and something that could only be him flowed from his tongue to her with every caress. It blended with the scent and feel of aroused man. The elements exploded in her head, igniting a spark of need that made her knees go loose and wobbly.

Her ability to think—gone, burned away in a kiss that was three parts lust and one part Mark's determination to make her surrender.

He was thorough, methodical in his passion, ensuring no part of her mouth felt neglected. His tongue raked the roof of her mouth before he nibbled her bottom lip. Nicki whimpered, drowning in sensation. The man's kiss was a tender domination. Soft, yes, but no less in control. Persuasive, cajoling, yet Nicki knew—just as he did—who commanded it.

Having her control stolen away so quickly, so completely, was a new and unsettling experience—but one that only made her want him more.

Pressed against his firm chest, her breasts ached so badly. The idea of his fingers, his mouth, on her stiff nipples obsessed her. That thought alone gushed the pulsing place between her legs with moisture. At least one part of her was an optimist, hoping he'd be guiding the length of his impressive male anatomy deep inside her soon. But the length of his arousal pressed stiff and strong into her lower belly, far too north of her ache to alleviate any need.

Damn him.

She squirmed, her body seeking relief. Without lifting his mouth from hers for an instant, Mark fitted his hands beneath her arms and lifted her from her floor. Hands clinging to his shoulders, Nicki held on as he braced her against the wall and held her in place with the burning width of his chest. She felt seared with his touch, the need to get that evil shirt off his body and feel his flesh against hers.

Instead, satisfied that her mouth and torso were firmly under his dominion, Mark's hands glided down the sides of her body. The palms brushed her breasts, lingered, before outlining her waist and hips. Then he cupped her rear in his hands and bent until he could curl his hands in between her thighs, his thumbs toying for an instant with each of her cheeks.

Mark lifted her legs, parting them on either side of his hips, wrapping them around him. He slid every part of his body flush against her. The amazing ridge of his erection nudged her clit as he rocked against her once, twice.

Ohmigod! Nicki felt the ache inside her sizzle and spread. She clutched at the bunched muscles of his shoulders and cried out as the rhythm of his mouth and hips synched up, catapulting her sensations into overload, until she kissed him back in a frenzy, locked her ankles together at the small of his back, and arched into him, drowning in the sudden rush of desire.

Nicki felt him tugging at her tank a moment later, lifting it over her abdomen, up her ribs. He freed her breasts. Thank goodness! The cool air rushed over them, and she felt the jolt of the chill all the way to her toes. The impossibly hard pebbles of her nipples tightened more. As Mark angled his head, deepened his kiss yet again, the scorching heat of his palms enveloped her breasts, thumbs teasing their tips in a slow glide.

At the moment, she'd give anything to have his talented mouth on her. If he was this mind-blowing with a mere kiss . . . the other things he could do with that mouth would likely replace her concept of oral gratification with something she'd only vaguely imagined before.

Another pinch of his fingers on her nipples coincided with another bump of his cock against her clit as his tongue swept through her mouth, demanding surrender and conquering anything that resembled thought. Lust, thick and heavy, urged her to thread her fingers into the soft strands of his golden hair. The heat ratcheted up as he growled, and the sound reverberated through her body, ramping up the coil of want in her stomach. Breathing took a backseat to pleasure. The ache between her thighs turned sharp. A bell rang in her head. She was so close. Almost there . . .

Against her, Mark stiffened, lifted his mouth from hers, and set her on her feet.

No! He couldn't leave her like this.

Damn him!

He swore in a low growl as he whirled away from her and marched toward the door. Mark dug into his pocket, then she heard him wrench the door open. Nicki frowned, lost in a haze of pleasure-clouded senses. What was he doing?

The scent of hot pizza bombarded her brain a moment later. Food. The pizza delivery guy. Nicki released a pent-up breath. The bell ringing in her head had been the doorbell, not a signal of great sex to come.

She pulled her shirt down over her aching nipples and clapped a hand over her swollen mouth. That kiss had gotten totally out of hand.

Gee, what was your first clue?

Mark emerged around the corner and set the pizza box on her kitchen table. His heated green stare told her that food was the last thing on his mind.

God, it was tempting—the thought she could grab him by any and all protruding parts of his body and lead him to her bedroom mere steps away. Pizza could wait. Sanity could, too.

But now that she could breathe again, she just couldn't bring herself to conveniently forget her intelligence for the next hour or two.

She didn't need distraction, and Mark Gabriel was definitely a big one, with a capital *D*. He worked for her, so tangling the sheets with him didn't seem like something a reasonable person would do unless her common sense had flown off to Fiji for a vacation.

But that wasn't what stopped her.

The domination in his kiss, the easy and total mastery he wielded over her body from the instant he touched her—nothing in her experience had come even remotely close. In the past, men had always been easily led. A suggestion here, a sharp note there, they generally danced to the tune of her choice. She wasn't called Commando Bitch for nothing.

Mark was different. He wouldn't even dance unless he felt like it, much less let her pick the tune. Nicki wasn't prepared, had no defenses.

From the beginning, the attraction that flared so bright had been unsettling. She'd wanted Mark bad—faster than anyone else, ever. On some level, her body must have known he could give her something she'd always craved yet feared: A real challenge, a sexually dominant man who didn't *need* to control others but unconsciously asserted quiet authority because he *was*. The devastating skill of his mouth only served to further overwhelm her.

That's what scared her. She'd never asked herself this question before, and couldn't believe she was now, but what if she couldn't handle him?

"Why don't you take the pizza and go back to your place?" Her voice shook, and she didn't care. She just needed time alone, to sort this through.

"Nicki . . ." He raked a hand through his hair, as his brow furrowed with a frown. Wisely, he didn't step any closer. "That went farther than I intended. I didn't mean for it to get so . . . intense. But I'm not going to apologize, not when you were right there with me. Admit that."

Anger and embarrassment stung her. She felt her face flush. He could have let her off easy by taking the blame. He'd started it, after all. But no, he wasn't going to let her squirm away from it. Not a bit.

Damn him.

"Fine. You're the man." *And I apparently have all the spine of Gumby.* "Take the pizza and go."

"Truce," he cajoled. "Let's eat and talk about my costume. I swear I won't touch you again, not even if, by some miracle, you beg me to."

"You wish." Nicki snorted. But inside, she feared it wouldn't take anything near a miracle to make her beg. God, she needed to get a grip on herself.

"Yeah, I do." He shot her a rakish smile, complete with dimples, as he lifted the lid on the pizza box, grabbed a slice and handed it to her.

Nicki took it and bit into the crust and cheese concoction just to give her mouth and hands something to do.

Mark took another slice and followed suit.

"You got five minutes," she laid down the law—though she was painfully aware she had no way to uphold it. "What's the matter with your costume?"

He sighed. "I look like a vampire. And the silly horned helmet, are you serious?"

"The dancer you're replacing had a whole cowboy bit. It doesn't fit you. This does. If you're image-conscious, this isn't the right job for you. When you're here, you're a fantasy. Period."

In fact, he was a fantasy, in general. Not lasting, not really real, not something she could keep. Nicki knew she needed to drill that factoid into her head for her self-preservation.

But the unvarnished truth didn't stop her from aching for him. Everywhere.

True to his word, he didn't touch her again. Not even to shake her hand or hug her good night. Not even his eyes held remembrance or suggestion. That made her want him more, not less.

Damn him.

* * *

THE fact Zack had asked Mark to an emergency rehearsal on Thursday afternoon underscored the reality that his efforts to screw up his Viking routines had not gone unnoticed. The fact Nicki had been called in to observe delighted him.

Mark arrived a few minutes early, wearing the stupid-ass costume—except the helmet. He wasn't wearing that unless absolutely forced.

With a scowl, he tossed the offending headgear on a nearby trunk.

"You're not still pouting about your costume, are you?"

Nicki. Mark whirled toward the sound of her voice to see her entering the stage area from the left, dressed in a denim skirt that showed a long length of thigh and a white sleeveless top that gathered right beneath breasts, which he lamented that he hadn't gotten his mouth around when he'd pressed her between the wall and his raging hard cock three days ago.

She'd been avoiding him since.

"I don't pout," he returned.

Rolling her eyes, Nicki flashed him a kitten's smile. "All men do. Whether you call it brooding or contemplating or 'needing space,' it's pouting."

"So do you women have a name for that thing you do when you avoid us, like you've been doing to me?"

Her mouth tightened. "I have not."

"Isn't that code for 'needing to catch up on a few things'?"

"There's no code for being busy. It's just a fact of life. I have more to accomplish than to buff myself up at the gym by day and take my clothes off at night." She tossed the glossy curtain of her inky hair behind one shoulder. "Besides, I don't owe you an explanation. We're not dating."

Mark cupped his chin and pretended deep thought. "No, we're just almost having sex against your breakfast nook wall."

"It was just a kiss!"

He held in a laugh. "Okay, we'll go with your terminology. A kiss, as I knew it, was much less involved. But I definitely like your idea better. I'll be sure to win more bets from you so we can . . . explore that definition more."

Nicki's face turned several shades of pink. "Don't be a smart-ass. You cornered me, and we kissed. I let things go on a bit too long. Out of curiosity, more than anything else."

Curiosity? Yeah, right. Did she expect him to believe in the Easter Bunny, too?

"Hmm. So the hard nipples in my palms and the damp panties pressed against me, that was curiosity?" He grinned. "I like your way of being curious. I noticed that the more demanding I got, the wetter you got. What other burning questions do you have that I can help you solve?"

She drew in a harsh breath and stepped closer, blue eyes flashing. Oh, boy. Nicki had a temper, and Mark had no trouble guessing that he was pissing her off good. Too bad. He wasn't about to let her deny that their "kiss" packed all the punch of an X-rated Christmas and Fourth of July celebration rolled together.

He couldn't forget it. Why should she get off easy?

"Oh, and your reaction was so cerebral?" she shot back. "I doubt very much that was a . . . a lead pipe in your jeans."

Mark figured he could play this one of two ways. One, he could fess up to the fact she'd charged him up enough to supply Vegas's power grid for a month. Two, he could downplay, even deny, his intense reaction to her—and watch the fireworks.

He'd bet his second-degree black belt that her pride wouldn't stand for the latter.

Feigning a shrug, he said, "A hard-on is like a reflex for a guy. You're female, I'm male . . . It happens. It doesn't *mean* anything."

"Really? And you're just tossing my reaction up in my face to inflate your own ego?" Her glare was half disbelief, half fury.

Pretending to ponder, Mark wandered a bit closer. "I hadn't given it much thought. Maybe I am."

She gritted her teeth and closed her eyes. Mark swore she was counting to ten.

"This is why I don't date. No one in the asshole population appeals to me. You all feed us every line of crap you can think of and—"

"You think I'm lying?" Mark did his best to sound offended.

Nicki's eyes threatened to bulge from their sockets.

One-way ticket to Las Vegas: three hundred fifty dollars. A week's stay at the Bellagio while he convinced Nicki to give him this crazy job: eighteen hundred dollars. Cost of pizza to bribe his way into her apartment: fifteen bucks. Seeing her reaction to his claim that she didn't particularly affect him sexually: absolutely priceless.

Holding in his mirth, Mark regarded her with the blandest expression he could manage . . . anticipating the imminent pyrotechnics.

"Yes! You pinned me to a wall. You extended the kiss. You—you lifted my shirt and—"

"I enjoyed it. Don't get me wrong."

"But I personally didn't affect you? Any pair of breasts would do? You just had an erection that felt harder than granite for no other reason than the fact I'm estrogen-based?"

Nicki was winding herself up, and Mark was enjoying the view. Amazing that she hadn't stopped long enough to realize he was feeding her a line of bullshit just to yank her chain. His sister, Kerry, had ceased falling for his elaborate practical jokes when they were still teenagers and taken the fun out of everything. His sexy new boss was fresh game.

"I don't know," he said finally. "Not just any female gets me going, obviously. I doubt someone like Joan Rivers would get a rise out of me." Mark paused, pretending to consider the situation. "Come to think of it, I haven't really been interested in anyone for a while. Maybe it is you."

"Maybe? But you really don't know?"

Her feminine pride stung, he could tell. Poor baby. Next time, she'd know better than to write off the amazing chemistry between them. But today, he had a point to prove.

"Yeah, maybe." He shrugged. "How can I really know?"

Nicki's gaze, full of fire and challenge, skimmed his body, pausing over what he might politely call his lap.

"No lead pipe at the moment, it appears."

"Nope." Mark nearly bit the inside of his cheek to hold in a grin.

She slowly prowled toward him, hips swaying, those blue eyes glinting with an adult-style dare. No question, she was coming after him with both barrels.

He could hardly wait.

Mark expected the full frontal assault. It was her easiest and quickest shot to his libido. But no. She surprised him by brushing past him, her breasts barely grazing his arm. Stopping behind him, she ran a finger lightly down his spine—a mere ghost of a touch. Sensations shivered their way through his body, bursting out from his center.

His cock began to twitch.

Drawing in a deep breath, he waited, feeling Nicki ease to his left. Her hand trailed from his hip, over his ass and down his thigh, as she sidled up to his left shoulder. Once there, the lodging of her breasts on either side of his arm was clearly no accident. Damn, he wanted to turn to her, grab her, introduce her back to the stage floor for about the next two hours. Reminding himself that he was trying to convince her that he was unmoved, at least for now, he did nothing.

"You know," she whispered, her voice sex-filled and uneven, "it's important that the male dancers remain impervious to all the temptation presented by the club's female guests. If you have trouble controlling your reaction to women in general, we're going to have a problem. You'll need to practice resisting your . . . reflex."

He looked down, and Nicki's sultry smile nearly blasted a hole in all his plans. Half challenge, half invitation, that smile beckoned, communicated her power as a woman, taunted him with her self-confidence. She would do her utmost to turn him on.

Well, she was welcome to try. More than welcome.

"No . . . reflexes?" he asked.

Nicki slanted a saucy smile up his way. "G-strings don't leave much to the imagination. It's a no-no to show too much. Takes all the mystery out of things."

"I see. How do I practice resisting, as you suggest?"

"Let's see how much practice you need first."

Her game amused and thrilled the hell out of him all at once. He couldn't wait to see where this was going. "All right."

Blue eyes lit with mischief, she stood on tiptoes to whisper, "Pretend you've just finished your first number and you've approached my table. Let's see how you react to this."

Before Mark could even begin to guess her intent, Nicki nibbled on his earlobe, then brushed her mouth against the sensitive column of his neck. He shivered as the mounds of her breasts pressed against him, her warm breath heating his skin. Damn, she smelled good, like cinnamon and citrus all mixed.

But he managed to keep in control.

Nicki reached across his body. One of her hands founds its way into the disco-deep *V* of his black shirt and nestled against his skin. The feel of her touching him . . . wow. More than one of his fantasies in the last few days had been all about that.

He swallowed as she smoothed her palm down his bare chest

and abdomen. Her slow fingers journeyed back up, leaving tingles in their wake. That added to his rising temperature.

Might be a good idea to start thinking of Joan Rivers right about now . . .

As her slow, sure palm reached his chest once more, her thumb toyed with his nipple in teasing strokes, back and forth, back and forth. Both nipples stood at attention. Goose bumps broke out across his skin, along with a light sweat.

Nicki tossed him a teasing smile and licked those full red lips he hadn't quite forgotten tasting. At the sight, he sucked in a breath, as a jolt of desire radiated down toward his dick.

Gritting his teeth, Mark managed to keep his "reflex" under control. Barely.

"See," he said. "I'm good to go."

Liar, liar, liar. The strain in his voice proved it.

"Oh, I'm just getting started."

That sounded deliciously ominous.

"Nicki . . ."

The woman predictably ignored him and pulled him down to press a barely there kiss to the corner of his mouth, a series of kisses against his jaw. She pressed her entire body flush against him, and the feel of her nipples against his chest nearly drove him past his control. She was small and lush and fiery in his arms, and Mark clenched his fists at his sides to keep from grabbing her and letting his hands communicate his rapidly growing interest in the concept of having her naked on top of him.

Mark barely realized that Nicki was nudging him backward until he almost stumbled. She kept on, driving him back with her hands at his hips and her lips grazing his throat.

Holy shit, she smelled good. Noticing a woman's scent . . . he couldn't remember the last time he had unless, like with Tiffany, the store-bought musk made him sneeze. But this was all Nicki. A pinch of spice, a bit of tang—and a hint of her arousal, the scent he knew he'd wallow in once he had her naked and legs spread for his waiting tongue.

Oops, his "reflex" was kicking into gear at that thought.

She forced him back another step. He retreated the next pace on his own, hoping he could avoid contact with her lower body, especially the good parts. She would know she'd won then.

Time to think of . . . oh, even Joan Rivers wasn't killing his mood, mostly because he couldn't get Nicki out of his head. Damn it! Remember jail. Think of Blade Bocelli's ass nailed to a prison wall. Picture Barney Fife break dancing.

Too late.

The back of his knees hit a chair that doubled as a stage prop, and down he went. He landed on his ass with a thud in the metal chair. His bulk nearly sent it tumbling back, but he caught himself. He had no time for self-pats on the back, though.

Not when Nicki dropped to her knees before him.

Mark sucked in a harsh breath as she grabbed his hips and dragged him closer. He watched her in aroused amazement at she planted a kiss at the base of his neck. From there, she only moved lower. Her lips played at his collarbone, tongue nudging aside his Tom Jones shirt and laving over the swell of his shoulder.

Impatient fingers pulled at the silk garment's V. Cool air hit his nipple, turning it hard, an instant before her hot mouth enveloped it. Mark nearly lost it.

With a gentle nibble, her teeth sent pleasure careening from his nipple to explode in his gut. Blood rushed by the gallon to his cock when her fingers took up where her mouth left off—and said mouth started traveling south again.

"Nicki . . ."

Her only answer was to dip her tongue into his navel and push his knees farther apart with a wriggle of her shoulders.

He groaned.

And still, Nicki kept going south, low on his abdomen, lower still . . . Mark pressed his lips together to keep in a groan. Then he felt her hot breath cascade over his cock, now constricted by his tight pants and feeling swollen to the size of Mount Vesuvius.

What the hell would she do next?

"What's this I see?" she mocked, running one finger from the tip of his cast-iron hard-on to the base. "No, it couldn't be. Not you. Tsk. Tsk."

"I'm hard as fucking granite. Happy?" he managed to grit out.

A faint smile curled her mouth. A dangerous smile. She wouldn't, not again . . . Before he could finish the thought, Nicki ran a fingertip up the length of his erection. Her tongue followed. Only a very thin layer of fabric separated the wet heat of her mouth from him, and the knowledge was burning him alive. Suddenly he had a vivid picture of what Nicki would look like with her mouth wrapped around his naked cock. It burst across his brain and scalded his blood.

She repeated the process, a sweeping caress, a decadent lick. He felt everything. It was too much. Not enough.

He speared his hands in her hair and wondered if pleading would induce her to continue. The woman was killing him.

"On second thought, no," she said suddenly, her voice penetrating the haze of his lust. "I think you're just having a reflex to the fact I'm female. I don't play with boys who don't admit they want *me*."

"I want you," he groaned, wondering how she'd turned the tables so quickly, so thoroughly. "You know damn well I do."

Nicki licked the length of his cock one more time, then rose. "That's your problem. Mine is your behavior around the customers. Keep your 'reflex' under control."

She stepped back once, twice, her eyes sizzling, full of sparks and challenge.

Mark watched Nicki, struggling to restrain his reaction to her mocking seduction. They weren't done here. He hadn't had time for equal opportunity arousal. Where the hell did she think she was going?

A devilish smile turned up the corners of her lush, red mouth. "I'll leave you to deal with your . . . problem. Don't yank my chain again."

"Nicki, this isn't over."

As if he hadn't even spoken, she tilted her head and informed him, "Oh, Zack should be here any minute. He called to say he was taking his grandfather to the doctor, and he'd be a few minutes late. In fact, he should be here about the time that goes down." She gestured to his erection with a toss of her head, that smug smile still firmly in place.

"Damn it, Nicki—"

Anything else he'd been about to say disappeared in an instant as something big and black began falling from the rigging above the stage—and straight toward Nicki.

Adrenaline surged, powering his legs. Lunging out of his chair, he ran for her with every ounce of his energy and leaped on her. Her back hit the hard stage with a surprise gasp. He rolled her beneath him an instant before the something big crashed into the stage inches from his left shoulder—where her head had been just moments ago. Glass shattered, colored shards peppering the air. Mark closed his eyes and covered her face with his chest. Electrical sparks zapped, sizzled, then died.

A glance at the object told him it was one of the large overhead lights. The thing had to weigh at least fifty pounds. It would have more than likely killed her.

He tensed, then forced himself to relax. *Safe. Nicki was safe.*

Mark let out the breath he hadn't realized he'd been holding.

"What the hell happened?" Nicki asked, panting.

She sounded shocked. He didn't blame her. It was a good question, one at the top of his list, too.

Mark glanced up at all the metal rigging and lights overhead. He saw nothing odd. Nothing swinging loose. No one up on the bridge toying with the lights for the night's show or anything.

"I don't know." He raised up on his elbows and peered down into her face. "Are you all right?"

Nicki might think of herself as tough and gutsy, and she was— most of the time. But underneath it all, he saw glimpses of something else. Something more vulnerable. That had never been more obvious than now.

With an answering nod, she asked, "You saw it coming?"

He shot her a grim nod.

"And—and you got me out of harm's way." She sounded almost surprised.

"I wasn't going to let anything happen to you."

Slowly, she nodded, still panting. "I . . . Thanks. That would have been one hell of a headache."

"Any idea what caused that?" He stared up into the dark, silent rigging above the stage.

"No." Her voice shook. "We just had some lighting maintenance done yesterday. M-maybe they didn't secure everything when they were done."

It was possible. Accidents happened. If some*one* caused it, they'd somehow crept down and snuck past them, without either him or Nicki being the wiser. That seemed unlikely, and yet . . . what would have made that light fall suddenly at that particular moment?

"Mark?"

Nicki raised her gaze to his, clinging and wide. She trembled. The connection jolted him down to his toes. Damn it, the woman was as potent to his system as a bottle of tequila on an empty stomach. Beneath him, she was lush and warm. And safe, thank God. Mark wondered if she knew that her gaze shouted a need for reassurance. Denying that he wanted to touch her—hold her—was pointless. The fact his hips rested squarely between her spread thighs, and his still-hard cock was notched right where he wanted it to be wasn't helping his self-control.

Nicki took the decision from him and pressed her mouth to his with a cry, desperate fingers twined in his hair.

Mark met her and dove in ravenously, tongue dominating the inside of her mouth with one bold stroke. Lust pounded at him, as if he hadn't touched a woman for years. What was it about this woman? Something about her pulled at him. Thinking of Nicki without thinking of sex seemed beyond his capabilities. He needed one night with her, to fuck her and get her out of his system. She provided too much distraction for him to focus on his case, just by being herself.

Nicki threaded her hands into his hair and lifted her hips to his. She was wet. No mistaking the damp humidity of her seeping through her little panties as she pressed against him. The realization pumped any remaining blood from his brain and jetted it south.

All thoughts of focus and investigation ceased.

Shifting, Mark fitted his hands beneath her ass. Firm, bare cheeks? Sweet heaven, she was wearing a thong. The knowledge swept a fresh burst of lust through his system.

He rocked against her, notching his cock toward the top of her pussy, right over her clit. Her gasp, followed by the nails in his back told him he'd scored a direct hit. And still, he kept at her mouth, tasting her, drinking her essence, her passion.

More. He needed more of her.

Lifting one of his hands away from her mostly bare ass cost him, but he used it to push aside her flimsy summer top and her little lacy bra. He tore his mouth from hers to look. Her pert breast and beaded rosy nipple beckoned. He couldn't wait another minute. Another second.

Dipping his head, he captured the hard bud in his mouth and sucked her deep in his mouth, rasping the sensitive flesh with his tongue. Jesus, she was like heaven. Sugar and spice. Hot, sweet, all woman. He was going to combust if he didn't get inside her soon.

Grabbing fistfuls of his shirt, Nicki arched up to him, moaning, "Mark."

Hearing his name on her lips ripped lightning through his body.

"More," she moaned. "Now."

"You like it fast," he observed aloud, pressing his hips down right into her clit.

"Yes."

"Hard."

"Yes."

"And a little bit rough. Don't you?" He grabbed a handful of her hair and forced her to look at him.

"Yes." Nicki gasped for a breath, blue eyes sultry, dilated. "Yes."

Good damn thing he did, too.

Even better, since he knew he could get out of his absurd Viking getup in about four seconds. Time to find out how quickly he could get Nicki out of her annoying garments.

Caressing his way from her bare cheek to her hip, Mark found the delicate string that held the two triangles of fabric together and wrapped his fist around it.

Lifting his mouth from her nipple, he stared down into her flushed face and swollen mouth, brimming with satisfaction at her unfocused, dilated eyes. "I'm going to rip these little panties off you, Nicki, then taste you, get inside you . . ."

She groaned, grabbed his face, and pressed her mouth against his again.

The air around them exploded with sound suddenly—the buzz of an electric guitar, the vibration of rock music turned up to concert-loud levels. Nicki gasped. Mark nearly jumped out of his skin. Next came Joan Jett's mocking voice asking, "Do you wanna touch, do you wanna touch, do you wanna touch me there?"

The old song was a favorite at the club, particularly when the mood got raunchy, Mark had noticed. He'd never liked the taunting song. He liked it even less right now. Who the hell was playing it?

Nicki righted her top. "What is going on?"

Good question.

Mark rolled to his feet and looked toward the DJ's booth. Blade Bocelli exited the disk jockey's little space with a derisive glance before striding through the club and disappearing upstairs, leaving the snide, pulsing music on full blast.

That son of a bitch! How long had he stood there like a fucking Peeping Tom, staring at them?

Thoughts raced, suspicion danced through his nerves. Clearly Bocelli had been there long enough to play voyeur. What about longer? Perhaps long enough to send the light crashing down toward an unsuspecting Nicki?

"Damn it!" she cursed. "I'm screwed."

Mark fisted his hands at his sides and did his best to restrain his temper. Beating the hell out of the Mafia bastard right now would be pointless—enjoyable for a few minutes, but ultimately pointless. Mark's whole purpose for being here was to bring Bocelli to justice for his money laundering, and God only knew what other crimes. He doubted Blade was the guy's given name. Surely he'd earned it in ways the authorities would find interesting, and Mark vowed to give them the needed proof. The laws Bocelli had broken, coupled with what he'd done to Tiffany, ensured him a one-way trip to the federal penn.

But if Bocelli had anything to do with that light nearly falling on Nicki's head, there would never be a hole small enough for him to hide in. Anywhere. And Mark would make certain the asshole ended up being very sorry.

Suddenly, Zack bustled in from the right side of the stage, looking harried. "Did I miss anything?"

* * *

THE opportunity to get into both Nicki's panties and the club's accounting records hadn't panned out yet. Mark was determined that his luck, with regard to the latter at least, was about to change.

His luck with the former was anyone's guess. Nicki would have to stop avoiding him first.

Pushing thoughts of hot sex with his "boss" out of his head for the moment, Mark rose. It was before eight A.M. Today, the club was closed. Right now, most everyone would be in oblivion, sleeping off the effects of nights that didn't end until four in the morning.

Leaving his barren apartment, he slipped down the stairs and crept down the hall on silent feet, toward Nicki's office door. He expected to find it locked. That was fine. What guy didn't know how to pick a lock or two?

But he stopped short when he saw Bocelli sitting in a chair, staring at columns of numbers on a computer screen.

Crap! What was the Godfather gorilla doing here at this hour?

Easing closer, he peered over the thug's shoulder, scanning the columns of debits and credits for the month of April. He was *accounting*? Unbelievable. Talk about leaving the fox in charge of the henhouse . . .

Mentally, Mark began adding, gaze dodging from one column to the next. Last month, Nicki had a night where the bar had only brought in three hundred dollars? Impossible. Frigging impossible. A slow night at the bar wouldn't be less than a thousand. And yet she'd outlaid fifteen hundred dollars for janitorial services in a week? Mark scowled, skimmed numbers that seemed more fictitious than a novel. Two and two shouldn't add up to five. What the hell was going on?

Suddenly, Bocelli swiveled his chair around as if he'd sensed Mark there. He had no idea how, since he knew he hadn't made a sound.

"What the hell do you want, Viking?"

"What the hell are you doing here?" Mark shot back.

"My fucking job. And you?"

"If you're supposed to be her accountant, you know shit about it. The debits don't add up correctly, and alcohol expense doesn't belong in the office supply category."

"What? You work for the fuckin' IRS now? Mind your own business, boy toy. Nicki lets me take care of a lot of things for her, because I'm good at them." Bocelli's nearly black eyes mocked Mark. "Her accounting . . . among other things."

Mark felt his jaw turn to granite. His blood turned to ice. A nun couldn't mistake Bocelli's insinuation that he was fucking Nicki.

While trying to kill her by crashing a stage light onto her head?

He wanted to strangle Mr. Italian Stallion Macho all over again.

If Nicki was, in fact, having sex with Blade, it shouldn't be a surprise. If there was a bad girl in the crowd, Mark would find her every time. And want the hell out of her.

His first girlfriend in middle school had been expelled for selling the answers to a history test. From there, it only got worse. As a freshman in high school, his girlfriend had been caught giving a blow job in the boys' bathroom—to someone else. As a senior, his squeeze had a skull and crossbones tattooed on her ass—after having her nipples pierced. In college, the lust of the moment had been putting herself through school by subscribing people to her website so they could pay to watch her masturbate. Hell, his own wife had married him just to have him take the fall for her felony.

No one had worse taste in women than he did.

The fact he was sweating over a woman who wore thongs, had her naval pierced, and owned a strip club was just par for the course. Her spreading her legs for a Mafia thug shouldn't surprise him in the least.

It just pissed him off that he should feel let down. Some things, he reminded himself, never changed.

Regardless, he still had to get into Nicki's accounting records. And even though it was stupid, damned if he didn't still want to get inside her . . . just once.

Mark looked at Bocelli and sneered. "Well, you may have handled some things for Nicki in the past. But 'things' will change now that she's got competent help."

Chapter Five

MARK had the uncomfortable feeling that, if the old saying about someone's ears burning when others were talking about them was true, his would have been on fire.

After an unexpected voice mail from Nicki asking him to drop by her place at five, after Monday rehearsal, he arrived at her front door, just as Lucia was exiting. The look that passed between the sisters suggested he'd been the topic of conversation.

Uh oh.

"You are in so much trouble," Lucia whispered, a smile playing at her soft mouth.

"What? Why?"

Lucia continued on, down the hall to her own apartment as if he hadn't spoken.

Scowling, he turned back toward Nicki's door. Toward Nicki, now standing at the portal with a solemn face—and wearing a killer black dress. What the hell was going on?

Her hesitant posture only underscored the tense furrow of her brow. Clearly, she hadn't invited him here for the fun of it. With her low-cut minidress and sexy stilettos, Nicki looked good enough to eat . . . all the way to multiple orgasms, but he wasn't fooled by her outfit de jour. Since Bocelli had discovered them nearly having sex on the club's stage last Thursday, Nicki had done a masterful job avoiding him. He doubted very seriously she had invited him here for sex.

Damn shame, too.

"You called?" He held up his cell phone to indicate that he'd received her message.

With a jerky nod, she stepped back, opening the door wider. "Come in."

He paused, looking into Nicki's apprehensive oval face, the sharp, watchful stare of her upturned blue eyes. Whatever had prompted her surprising request to drop by her place wasn't something she was looking forward to.

Mark's mind raced. Why would she ask him here, at exactly five o' clock, on the club's only dark day? Either she wanted to talk about his lack of progress in learning his damned Viking routines or ask why he'd appeared in her office early this morning to peek at her accounting records and give her "accountant" a hard time. He was more than willing to bet Bocelli had already informed Nicki of their altercation earlier today.

Before or after he climbed between her legs? a snide voice in the back of his head asked.

It shouldn't matter. He and Nicki weren't going anywhere, relationship-wise. Since Tiffany, he didn't do relationships. But he couldn't deny that, for some head-scratching reason, he worried about Nicki. Yeah, it bugged the hell out of him that she might be fucking the hairy Italian jerk. But it concerned him more. Did she know she was sleeping with a guy who was probably a stone cold killer?

Resigned that he wouldn't get answers while standing in the hall, Mark brushed past Nicki and entered her apartment. Damn, she smelled good, like . . . tangerine but lighter, with a hint more spice. Whatever it was, that scent kicked his libido into gear every time.

Without meeting his gaze, she shut the door behind him, then led the way to the little Old World living room.

He sat. She also sat, then rubbed her hands together. Nicki didn't often display a demeanor other than her usual brass balls. Her tense, out-of-sorts gestures only confused him.

If this was about Bocelli finding him trying to get a peek at her books—and he suspected it was—he had to somehow convince her to keep her distance from the dangerous prick . . . without getting fired or blowing his cover.

The best way to fight fire was with fire.

"I'm glad you called me over here. I want to talk to you."

"I-I want to talk to you, too."

"I'm going to skip being a gentleman today and go first. Sorry." Mark plowed on, despite the fact Nicki looked taken aback. "Bocelli is more asshole than accountant. He doesn't need to be doing your books, Nicki."

She blinked several times. "You want to talk to me about my choice of accountants?"

"I know you have more sense than to hire that Stallone wannabe to take care of your money. Do you know anything about his background? Is he even qualified?"

Her frown reflected equal parts confusion and anger. "So he's not from H and R Block. What do you care?"

"I don't want to see him take you down the river. He could be cheating you, Nicki."

Holding up her hands to stay him, she said, "Look, you two don't like each other. I get it. He's made it really clear that he doesn't think you're qualified for your job, either. The two of you need to quit your macho posturing and stop telling me how to run my business."

"I think he's hiding something. I'm trying to protect you."

"That's crap. Both of you big he-men seem to think that I must have my brains in my boobs. This is so like every man I know." She gritted her teeth. "Listen, I started this club virtually on my own. You and Blade and my uncle all think you should tell me how to handle the operations because you got something dangling between your legs. I know why the other two think they have the right to boss me around. What's your excuse?"

Clearly, her uncle thought the familial connection allowed him to put his two cents in with Nicki. What was Bocelli's claim to fame here? Had Nicki just admitted that she was sleeping with him? Her words felt like a punch in the gut.

"Do I need an excuse to want to make sure he doesn't take advantage of you?" he countered, voice rising. "He's no accountant."

"And you are?" she shot back tartly.

Mark hesitated. "Yes."

Her stunned expression took some of the starch out of her spine. *Bingo*. "You're an accountant?"

"I'm a CPA, yes."

"Really?" The set of her full mouth showed her utter confusion. "Is that what you did in Florida when you worked for the bank?"

Not exactly, and not as Mark *Gabriel*, but why split hairs? "Yes."

"Why did you give it up?" Nicki's face softened, reflecting her confusion. "Why come here and take work as an exotic dancer?"

Actually, he'd finished his CPA shortly after leaving jail and going to work for Rafe. But Nicki couldn't know that, or it would blow his cover. She'd asked good questions that, if he didn't find good answers for fast, would make her very suspicious. Keeping his cover was paramount to catching Bocelli doing something illegal with her money.

"Long story. That life is behind me. It needs to stay there."

Ugh, did he sound like a bad soap opera, complete with cheesy angst?

"What happened before, the embezzlement allegation, it's unlikely to happen again," she said softly.

He shrugged. "Whatever. I just came here to warn you. You've worked too hard to let a jack off like Bocelli mismanage your money."

A hint of annoyance flitted across her face. "Hanging out here for a week and a half doesn't make you an expert on my business or the people here."

"Maybe, but being around Bocelli twenty-four/seven hasn't made you one, either."

Nicki rose and paced across the living room, agitation apparent in every stomping step. "Why are all men such arrogant bastards? They treat you like you're a moron, like you couldn't possibly make a decision more important than what to have for breakfast without their help. Even when you think you like one of them and want to have sex with him and call him over for that very purpose, you get some sort of speech—"

"What?"

Mark crossed the room in three steps and grabbed her arm. Nicki gasped, blue eyes flashing up at him with a mixture of fury and hurt.

"You called me over here to spend the night with you?"

She wrenched her arm from his grip and clapped. "Thanks for playing 'Jeopardy: The Home Edition.' You got Brilliant Deductions for four hundred correct *and* managed to phrase your answer in the form of a question. Someone get the guy an award."

"Nicki—"

Gesturing down to her outfit, she said, "Did you think I hung around here on my day off looking like this for the hell of it?"

With her sarcastic question, puzzle pieces clicked into place for Mark. Nicki despised talking business on her day off, but she'd invited him over. The last time he'd seen her on her day off, she'd been wearing yoga pants and a tank top with her hair in a ponytail. When he'd entered her apartment a few minutes ago, she'd been anxious and a little hesitant. Mark had assumed she dreaded reaming him out about bad rehearsals or asking suspicious questions about his interest in her accounting. In retrospect, Nicki would have been all for sinking her teeth into those situations. She thrived on solving conflicts and getting things done.

No, she was nervous, which meant he got to her. She'd been waiting for him to notice her appearance and do something about it.

Boy, when he screwed up, he did it right.

None of this changed the fact that Nicki was probably consorting with a suspected gangster. But now wasn't the time to talk about that. Now, he was going to make the most of this situation and try to influence Nicki's opinion of Blade Bocelli . . . all while indulging in this walking, talking fantasy.

"I'm sorry. I'm an idiot."

The sleek black brows arched up, and she crossed her arms over her chest. "At least you admit it."

With a half smile, he nodded. "You look great. What made you change your mind?"

She rolled her eyes. "If we have to talk about it first, just forget it. Clearly, I read the situation wrong."

Don't say a word. Grab her, kiss her, take her to the bedroom, sink into her for the rest of the night.

Mark sighed. Why did he have to be a nice guy? "We should talk about it. I don't want you to regret it later."

The starch left her shoulders. She uncrossed her arms. "I'm sure of this. I mean, you saved my life."

His lust deflated faster than helium from a popped balloon. "I don't want you to thank me like that."

"You're misunderstanding." She shook her head and looked around the room, apparently searching for the right words. "You risked your life for me. It was brave. Heroic."

"Nicki, believe me, I'm no hero. It was a . . . reflex."

"You have a lot of those." She smiled.

"Apparently so." He slowly approached her. "Look, I just did something that came naturally. You don't owe me anything."

"I didn't think I owed you." She glanced down, then lifted her chin and met his gaze squarely. "The fact that you had an instinct to save me tells me a lot about you. It's one of the things that makes me like you, even when I wish I didn't. Even when I shouldn't indulge. That's why I invited you here."

He squeezed her hand, then released her. "I'm glad you like me but . . . I like a lot of people I don't sleep with."

"You're not going to let me off easy. Damn," she muttered, then glared at him. "It's hard to admit the attraction is stronger than I am. I want you. You did something to me the first time I saw you. It's not going away. Happy?"

Her admission made Mark's heart stop. "Seriously?"

Nicki drew in a deep breath. "Yes. I was nervous, okay? I didn't want to have to explain it . . . I really hoped the dress would say it for me."

"Explaining it to me made you nervous? I can't picture you truly nervous."

"I'm not *all* stilettos and bad attitude, you know."

Once he stopped and thought about it, Mark believed her. Nicki could have tossed him out the night he'd snuck into her office to explain his "reasons" for needing this job. She didn't have to rent him the apartment down the hall from hers when he'd all but begged for help in finding a place. She worked around Zack's grandfather's doctor appointments. Nicki wasn't heartless. Driving, tough, determined, yes. But not a bitch.

Mark eased closer to Nicki. She watched his every move, eyes growing wider when he paused inches from her. The little pulse pounded at her throat. Mark felt his own desire rising dangerously fast.

He reached for Nicki, slid his hand underneath the wild curls she'd teased into her hair, to cup the sensitive skin at her nape. "That's true, but I like your stilettos and bad attitude, too."

A little smile played at the corners of her mouth. "Are you going to kiss me now?"

Splaying his free hand at the small of her back, he drew Nicki's small frame flush against him. "Kiss you, get you out of these sexy

clothes, get deep inside you so I can hear you scream. Any[...]
with that?"

"Yes." Nicki released a shaky breath. "What's taking so long?"

* * *

HAZEL eyes swirling with sultry green, Mark answered her question with a lazy, dimpled smile.

Excitement and nerves danced in Nicki's belly. Yes, it had been a long time since she'd taken a lover. And it was their first time. Their *only* time. She just couldn't justify taking needed energy away from her business to maintain any sort of relationship. And she didn't do friends with benefits. Too . . . tangled.

Still, something more put her on edge, something more than the fact he was built like a mountain.

"I suspect you're used to calling the shots and getting your way in bed," he murmured, his deep, masculine voice vibrating inside her. "That's not going to happen tonight."

Tension knotted tighter in her belly.

"You think you're taking charge?" she challenged.

"You think you are?"

His quick counter let her know he thought the idea ridiculous.

Quickly, Nicki realized his attitude was exactly what she'd resisted and feared . . . and secretly yearned for. He had the muscle and prowess to pull it off—but then, a lot of guys did. The question always became if a man had enough resolution and control to challenge her strong personality. That she'd never found. But Mark . . .
She sensed now—and had from the start—that he would.

The idea terrified and inflamed her at once.

What would it be like to just surrender? To put herself in his hands so utterly and give him total control of their mutual pleasure? To let him control her, just the tiniest bit?

"So you think you're the big man calling the shots?" She couldn't resist baiting him.

Mark tilted his head to study her. "I don't think anything, except that no man has ever really challenged you. They've danced to your tune, let you decide everything, thinking it would please you."

"Maybe it did."

"Maybe you're lying."

"You think I want to be pushed around?" She arched a dark brow at him.

He shocked her by grabbing her arm, spinning her around, and molding her back against his chest.

"I think you want to be taken, dominated, pleasured until you can barely think," he whispered in her ear and splayed his huge hand over her belly. "You have a lot of responsibility in life. I don't think you want to have it in the bedroom."

Nicki swallowed, searching for a comeback. She didn't have one. Everything he said was true. In fact, secretly, she fantasized about surrendering utterly. How did he know it? How did he understand something no other man ever had about her? Everyone saw her as strong and tough and brash. She hated admitting, even to herself, that she didn't want to be in charge of every single thing in life. And Mark knew.

It made her want him like crazy.

The solid length of his erection pressed against the small of her back. Holy cow, if he was as big as he felt, he was going to stuff her full and then some.

Her knees—and other parts of her—turned liquid just thinking about it.

"Prove it," she said finally.

Behind her, Mark laughed, something low and sensual. "If you insist . . ."

Nicki had no chance to say a word before he bent, lifted her into his arms, and started walking down the hall. It didn't seem to cost him any more effort than it would if she'd lifted a shopping bag or two.

The thought disappeared when he fastened his mouth on hers, tongue delving inside to alternately tease and devour. She drew in a breath, as a wave of desire slammed her. Dizzy, disoriented, she clung to him, fingers twining in his soft, shoulder-length hair.

The kiss shouted his desire, his intent to touch her all over, even as it claimed. She'd been kissed plenty . . . but not quite like this. He angled his head perfectly so he could fully penetrate her mouth. He scorched her senses as he nipped at her bottom lip, then made himself at home, his tongue tracing slow, caressing circles around her own. She moaned against him, aware of the arousal bubbling inside her, of her heartbeat picking up speed.

Mark stopped both walking and kissing, then eased her to her feet. Nicki opened her eyes to find herself in her bedroom, the back of her legs edged right against the bed.

The look he sent her was pure sex, half knowing smile, half wicked intent. Lord, that man could charm the sternest woman, even Sister Mary Anita, the witch with the evil ruler who had blistered the backs of her hands in the fifth grade.

Nicki wasn't nearly that tough. She felt herself melting perilously fast.

Twisting his fingers through her hair, Mark tugged, then bent to spread kisses across her jaw. He lapped his way back toward her ear, nipping, following up with a sensual lick here and there. His breath fanned down the sensitive skin of her neck. Nicki shivered.

"You look beautiful with your lips all red and swollen. I can't wait to see how the rest of you looks in that state," he whispered.

Then his mouth found hers again. His slow invasion made her toes curl, as he licked her lips, enticing her to part them. Cupping the back of her head, he swept into her mouth again, lingered, as if he had all the time in the world to drive her insane with his kiss.

It was working.

Most every guy she knew would be trying to rip off her clothes and put her flat on her back by now, whether she was ready or not. Not this one. Apparently, he intended to tease her until she couldn't remember her name.

Desire ratcheted up. Her patience dwindled. She hated to admit he was succeeding.

Breathing ragged, Nicki gripped the front of his shirt and used it to pull her way up to his neck. She wanted more. She needed additional contact, preferably without all this annoying clothing in the way.

Pressing her body flush against his, she absorbed his heat, gloried in the feel of his unyielding chest flat against hers. And the luscious length of his . . . equipment. Already she was aching to put it to good use.

Instead, he broke away with a laugh that dripped male satisfaction.

"Eager?" he murmured.

Wasn't it enough that her body sought his? Now she had to admit how much she wanted him out loud? "No, just thinking about the rules of Parcheesi."

Her panting made a liar out of her.

He flashed her a wide, heated grin, dimples and all. "That's too bad. I was thinking about how great it was going to be when I got my mouth on the rest of you, but if you'd rather play Parcheesi . . ."

"Maybe your idea is better." Nicki couldn't keep the husky tone out of her voice.

"Let's find out."

Mark's hand dropped from her hair to the tie at the back of her neck, holding up the top of her halter dress. Nicki's heart started racing as he grabbed the strings and gave a single pull. They slithered apart. The top gaped slightly, showing him a flash of cleavage. Apparently that wasn't enough.

He wrapped his hands around the sides of her dress at her neck and slowly—so damn slowly—slipped it down past her collarbones, down the swells of her breasts, down over her pebble-hard nipples.

That got a groan out of him.

Mark caressed the sensitive skin at her waist, then smoothed his hand up her body. He found her bare breast, cupped it, brushed his thumb over her nipple once, twice.

Nicki's knees threatened to buckle.

"Damn, you look sexy. No bra . . ." He groaned again. "You feel amazing."

Knowing she'd excited him aroused her even more. She couldn't wait to do it again.

"Want to guess what else I'm not wearing?" she whispered, taunting.

His hazel eyes flared with a lash of heat that burned her. "Sure, I'll guess."

That sultry smile of his dazzled her as he knelt down and lifted one of her feet onto his thigh, a breath away from his impressive bulge.

"You're not wearing a left shoe," he said, removing it, then setting her foot back on her Persian rug. He reached for her other foot and repeated the process. "Or a right one, either."

Before he could shuffle her foot back to the floor, Nicki scooted her foot a scant inch to the left. *Bull's-eye!* His erection bisected the bottom of her foot, hard and totally as advertised in those yummy jeans. She curled her toes over the swollen head and rubbed. He groaned.

"Who said you could do that?"

"I did." She proceeded to do it again.

Mark grabbed her foot and pressed it even harder into his steely shaft. "Every once in a while you have a damn fine idea."

Nicki laughed . . . but not for long. Drawing in a bracing breath, Mark set her foot aside.

"You're not in control here. Where was I before you ruthlessly sidetracked me?" he murmured, leaning in.

His hot breath was her only warning before he kissed her ankle, licked his way up her calf, nipped the back of her knee. No one had ever paid so much attention to her legs. Oh, they looked. But kissed like she was better than a centerfold fantasy? No.

"Mark . . ."

"Well, you're not wearing panty hose, I see." He planted an open-mouthed kiss just above her knee—on the inside of her thigh. His fingers grazed the back of her legs. Goose pimples broke out everywhere.

"I'm not," she choked. *Just a little higher!*

"Good. Never liked them." He nibbled on her thigh, just at the hem of her short dress.

Nicki felt herself tremble. Actually tremble, for Pete's sake. She was so wet, and he was so close to it that he had to scent her.

"Mark . . ." She heard the pleading note in her voice and just didn't care.

Then she felt a little tug on her dress, heard the rasp of her zipper. Nicki closed her eyes as the dress slid down her body, a sensual caress of black crepe. The cool air massaged her skin. But she felt Mark's gaze heating her back up.

"You're not wearing a dress. At least not anymore." His voice dropped a beguiling octave, and Nicki seriously contemplated jumping on the man and ripping his clothes off just so they could get on with getting it on.

"And what else do you notice I'm not wearing?" she baited, voice raspy.

"Hmmm." He pretended to ponder the matter.

But when Nicki looked down, his face was mere inches from the patch of dark hair between her legs.

"Why, Ms. DiStefano, where are your panties?"

"I left them off, just for you."

Holy cow, he had stripped her totally naked, but was still completely dressed himself—just like what was happening between them. She was laid bare, stripped of control, while he still had his completely intact.

The thought aroused and worried her at the same time. What if she didn't really affect him beyond his usual . . . reflex?

Doubts swamped her. Just as she seriously contemplated covering herself with the virginal white bathrobe Lucia's mother had bought her for Christmas, Mark planted his thumbs on either side of her vaginal lips and parted them.

"I like you without panties," he breathed against her. "Feel free to forgo them anytime you're with me."

Then his tongue sank into her slick folds, and he licked upward, settling right over her clit.

Tingles shot up her spine. Sensations bombarded her. Nicki gasped and blindly searched for his shoulders for support. He took another lazy swipe at her with his mouth, sucking her clit inside and rubbing the sensitive tip with his tongue.

Her head fell back, even as her fingers threaded through his hair, grabbing fistfuls, as if it would help her find her sanity. Oh, he was so orally gifted.

"Mark . . ."

He ignored her cries. Instead, he eased her back onto the bed, ensuring her ass rested on the edge. Nicki tensed as he lifted her legs and placed them on either shoulder. His every exhalation hit her right *there*. Oh, holy hell. He was getting comfy on the floor, as if gearing up for a picnic at which she was the main course.

Desire coiled tight in her belly. The ache he'd created swelled hotter and higher inside her. She couldn't hold out much longer . . . especially when he slipped a pair of fingers into the empty depths of her vagina and began a slow pump, which he augmented with that fabulous tongue.

"Mark . . ."

Nicki barely heard the hitch in her voice. She was too busy listening to her heart roaring in her ears. The orgasm was big already, and it was growing, swelling to epic proportions, twisting inside her like a living flame, threatening to incinerate her.

"Mark . . ."

Hooking the fingers buried in her slick flesh upward, toward her navel, Mark found that perfect spot. Nicki gasped as a whole new dimension to the pleasure zipped through her body, joining up with the mass of need congealing deep inside her. Oh, wow—this one was going to kill her.

But she'd die with a smile on her face.

The storm of need gathered, building, building. It descended down, anchoring between her legs right where his mouth moved over and over her clit, blowing her mind. Nicki held her breath, legs tense, back bowed.

"Mark!"

The mass of erotic tension exploded. She cried out again, convulsing, as pure red pleasure shot down her legs, ricocheted through her belly, zinged up to her head, then back between her legs, where Mark was still lapping at her.

Blackness danced at the edges of her vision as one peak flowed into another. She tried to brace herself for more, but there was no preparing for something out of her realm. Another spike of pleasure, another unbelievable pinnacle, another scream.

Finally, the tension began to ebb away. Nicki wasn't sure she could move, even if she wanted to. Vaguely, she wondered if he would mind setting her alarm clock for, oh . . . just before Thanksgiving.

Mark raised himself over her body, wearing a huge Cheshire smile. "So, are you still mad at me?"

Nicki tried to muster the energy for a glare. "I'll answer later, when my brain starts working again."

He laughed and dusted kisses along her jaw, over her neck, as he settled himself between her legs still fully dressed. The feel of his erection, still as thick and rigid as ever, perked her up far more than it should.

"You're wearing too many clothes," she complained.

With a shrug, he reached over his head, pulled at the back of his shirt, and yanked it over his head. And she saw the ripple of every bronze satin muscle in his shoulders, arms, and chest as he did. The Celtic knot tattoo on his biceps undulated when he flexed— and nearly made her sigh. Nicki wondered how he'd feel about a tongue bath over that incredible torso.

But he had more goodies to expose.

"The rest, if you don't mind," she prompted.

He hesitated. "I'd love to, baby. But I didn't come prepared."

Nicki lifted her hips to him, certain she'd coated the crotch of his jeans with her moisture. Served him right for hiding such a magnificent package from her.

"You feel mighty prepared to me."

Groaning, he ground into her. "Oh, I'm more than ready. But I don't have a condom. I'm so damned sorry." He kissed the tip of her nose. "If there's a next time, I promise to be better prepared."

So he'd planned to give her the most amazing oral gratification of her life and leave? No way. No freaking way! She'd never dated a guy who hadn't demanded something oral in return. Yet Mark had merely apologized.

"Is that your only problem?" With a smile, Nicki wriggled out from under him. "Up."

He was quick to frown, slow to respond. But finally he eased to her side . . . taking her nipple into his mouth as he did. It felt good, so good. Oh, too good. But if she let him continue, they'd still be here an hour from now and no closer to a condom.

That would be a tragedy.

Dislodging her nipple from his talented mouth, Nicki scooted across the bed and reached into the nightstand, where she withdrew a box of condoms she'd bought at the store earlier today—with this exact occasion in mind.

"I'm prepared, so I guess that makes me a better Boy Scout than you."

He glanced between her legs, his greenish-brown gaze reigniting the spark down there, not like flint to a piece of metal, but like kerosene to a bonfire. Instant and hot.

"You're missing an essential piece of equipment to be a Boy Scout."

Nicki tossed him a condom. He caught it with one hand.

"Why don't you share?" she shot back.

Mark glanced at the lone condom in his hand. "I could, but I'm going to need more than this."

She tossed him another out of the box with a smile. He merely caught it and sent her a pointed stare.

"Another?"

"I plan on being real busy tonight."

That dark, orgasmic voice reached into her and seemed to strum on all her senses.

"I like that idea," she said, sending a third condom his way.

He picked it up with one hand—and gestured with the fingers of his other hand to fork over more.

"Are you serious?"

"Am I laughing?"

Cautiously, she sent him another. "Will I be able to walk tomorrow?"

"If I arrange it so that you can't, it only means you'll have to stay in bed. What a shame."

His self-satisfied expression sent a little thrill shivering down her spine. Could he actually perform that many times in one night? A glance at his wide-as-a-doorframe shoulders, the hard ridges of his chest and abdomen . . . along with that tempting bulge she had yet to see in detail certainly convinced her that he was healthy enough.

Nicki pounced across the bed and tore into his jeans. Oh, button flys, her favorite. And as each button came undone under her dexterous fingers, she exposed bits of white cotton, all of which she eventually pushed down his hips.

He stepped out of them without any prompting, leaving him as bare as she was.

A mere glance proved his anatomy every bit as impressive as she remembered. More, even. Blue-veined and thick as her wrist, his cock sprang from a bit of light brown hair and heavy testicles. The mushroom head was so engorged, it looked purple. The last time she'd seen that many inches on a man it had been in a movie she'd watched at a bachelorette party.

"Do I pass inspection?" he teased.

Realizing she'd been staring, Nicki turned twelve shades of red. "Um, yes."

"Excellent." He grabbed a foil package, ripped it open and laid the condom on the bed beside him. "I'm dying to see how many other ways I can find to make you come."

"You first," she said in a sultry tone.

Leaning toward him, she dusted a series of kisses on his chest, across his abdomen . . . and down. The muscles of his abs clenched as she dipped her tongue in his belly button and started nipping her way lower.

She wrapped her hand around his cock. Oh my, every inch of him felt like heated velvet steel. Nicki stroked the length of him once, twice, grazing the responsive head with her thumb. Her gaze climbed its way up his taut, gorgeous body and stopped at his face. Eyes closed, jaw tense, he looked like a man lost in pleasure.

"Nicki, put the condom on." His voice broke on the last syllable.

Pouting, she grasped him tighter, raising her other hand and using it to glide up and down his length. "Not yet."

"Now."

Normally, Nicki didn't take orders. Mark's voice told her he was deadly serious. She grabbed the condom he'd laid on the bed and placed it on the tip of his sex. She used her fingers to roll it down the first inch. He moaned.

It was his turn to suffer a little. He'd said to put the condom on. He hadn't specified how.

Smiling, Nicki bent and wrapped her mouth around his cock, using it to roll the condom farther down his length.

A sibilant curse slipped from his lips as his hands slid into her hair. "That's cheating."

He stretched her mouth wide, and she couldn't possibly take him all in. But it was fun trying.

"Oh, yeah," he breathed. "Oh. Yeah."

Nicki anchored her hands on the outsides of his thighs and thrilled when they tensed beneath her like pure iron. She drew her mouth back slowly, then took him back in—a little more this time, all the way to her throat.

"Damn. Oh, Nicki. You feel . . ." He groaned, and his hands tightened in her hair. "So good."

If her mouth hadn't been so full, she would have smiled. Instead, she settled for rolling the condom down the rest of the way with her hands, then licking the underside of his shaft from base to tip with her tongue.

That earned her a hiss. Good, she *was* getting to him.

Determined to give him pleasure, she swiped her tongue across the soft-textured purple head, then sucked him into her mouth, down then up, down then up. Using a firm grip, she pumped the base of his cock in same rhythm.

Unbelievably, he grew even more, the blood swelling his shaft with her every movement. In the past, she'd performed oral sex to please partners, to rev them up for the main show, not because it gave her a thrill. This . . . wasn't the same. She liked the heavy feel of him on her tongue, liked the way he tensed and shuddered and muttered incoherent words of appreciation, liked the musky smell of him as she took him in her mouth.

She loved knowing he enjoyed the sensation of her mouth on him.

As her tongue wandered over every inch of his rigid flesh, Nicki found sensitive spots. She set her tongue to dancing over each one—just under the ridge, the very tip top—even as she let her hand wander lower, first cupping his balls, then shifting behind to rub against the smooth skin there. When she combined the two sensations at once, nearly every muscle in his body tensed, the delineation of each clearly, yummily visible.

"Holy . . ." He took a deep breath as he lifted her mouth off of him and scooted her farther up the bed. "Damn, baby. You're tempting fate."

"But I wasn't done."

"You are for now. We'll definitely explore that more later," he promised.

Mark followed her down to the mattress, covering her body with his. He eclipsed her, outweighed her by a hundred pounds, yet he held himself on his elbows, careful not to crush her. Positioning his cock right at her weeping entrance, he paused. The feel of him, hot and ready right *there*, charged her with the desire. Nicki drew in a ragged breath, every nerve straining toward him, desperate to feel him inside her, filling her, pounding at her, all hers.

The strength of her arousal stunned her. But now wasn't the time to psychoanalyze it. Instead, she lifted her hips, inviting him, silently begging him. He held her hips in place with his big hands.

"Right now, I have a driving"—he thrust forward in one great surge, trying to press his entire length deep inside her at once— "need to be inside you."

She gasped. Her body couldn't accommodate his girth fast enough—and she still had inches of his length to take. He'd stretched her wide, and her flesh stung, burned. Nicki dug her fingernails into his back and instinctively tensed her thighs against his intrusion.

"All right, baby." He panted, kissing her temple. "Just relax. I'll go slow."

Nicki heard the soothing note in his voice and tried to drain the tension from her muscles, tried to adjust. "I don't know if I can do this. You—"

"Shh. You can take me. We'll do this together." Mark drew in a long breath, then let it out. He stroked her hip. "It's going to feel so good."

That seductive promise in his midnight voice brought her gaze back to him. Nodding, she searched his face, the barely leashed wildness shining in his deep hazel eyes. Nicki felt connected to him by that hypnotic gaze that both seduced and revered her at once, as if she was the only woman in the world he wanted or needed—and he would have her, no matter what.

Her heart tripped when he placed a gentle, lingering kiss on her mouth, soft lips and a brush of tongue. Languorous. Light. Sweet. She exhaled, then opened wider to him.

He drew back, almost completely withdrawing, then eased back in, sinking in another inch—but still not completely.

"You're tight." He gritted his teeth.

After two years and a handful of months without sex, it was no surprise. But not for anything in the world would she tell him that. He'd only know how much power he had over her, the degree of surrender she'd actually given him. Just meeting his gaze now, she already felt as if she was giving him more than she should.

He was taking the rest.

"I'm not apologizing," she whispered.

"I would never ask you to." He smiled softly. "Just keep relaxing. It's going to be so good."

He pulled back, then sank down into her again. Another inch slid home. Nicki arched as his head dragged against a wonderfully sensitive spot.

"You like that?" he asked, repeating the process, entering her a bit more.

Answering "Yes" in a shaky voice, Nicki clasped his shoulders and tugged him back down so she could plant kisses along his neck and jaw, nibble on his lobe, glory in the musky scent of his skin, the murmurs of appreciation he made. She wrapped her legs around his waist.

"That's good. That's right. Open up for me, baby."

He grasped her hips and pushed himself the rest of the way home.

Nicki groaned and tightened around him. Now that Mark was in to the hilt, the feel of him buried deep amazed her. He left no part of her untouched—her walls, the very mouth of her cervix, and when he shifted and pressed down, he bumped her clit. She gasped, wanting more of him. Grabbing fistfuls of his silky hair, she tilted up to slide him a bit deeper.

He felt so right, so inevitable.

"Perfect," he groaned against her lips.

Mark started slowly, moving in and out as if he had all day, hesitating over that one spot guaranteed to drive her out of her mind with need. Pleasure built and multiplied with every lazy thrust, followed by the press of his hips, which put pressure right on her clit. Desire coiled in her belly, winding tighter and tighter with his every move.

Oh, yeah. He knew *exactly* what he was doing.

Without hurry, he stroked her until her breathing turned ragged, until she felt a sweat break out between her breasts, until pleasure gripped her like a fist, tight and ruthless.

"Mark, ohmigod!" She thrust up against him, urging him. "Faster."

"No rush, baby." He held her hips still with his unyielding fingers, thwarting her attempt to control the pace.

"Harder," she demanded.

"Patience." He forced her to lie beneath him and take the building pleasure as it spiraled beyond her comprehension, even bigger than before. Mewling, she felt herself swell and tighten. She couldn't breathe, couldn't think, as he continued to pump slowly into her hungry channel, scraping his head over the G-spot, then nudging her womb as he put pressure on her clit all in one smooth stroke designed to devastate.

Need began to center deep inside her as tingles tore through her body. Liquid fire danced in her blood like a fever that raged. She pressed desperate kisses to his jaw, the corner of his lips.

"Please. Please!"

"Please what?" he returned, lifting one hand to toy with a distended nipple.

That only added to the bliss her body found in his touch. She dug her fingers into his back. He seemed to know what she needed better than she did, and it amazed her. He ramped her arousal up with merciless precision. It rose inside her like a steep slope. Now she dangled over a precipice she couldn't quite cross. Instead, Mark just took her higher and higher with no end in sight.

"More. Harder. Now!"

He controlled the rhythm, the stroke, the depth, the angle— her and himself. Only a slight sheen of perspiration between his shoulder blades hinted at anything less than sheer calm on his part.

"You're not ready," he breathed in her ear, then nibbled on her neck.

Need zinged through her body. She shivered and moaned and clamped down on him.

"Like hell," she parted, arching up as much as the vise grip on her hips allowed. "I am ready. Beyond ready."

"Trust me. I want this to be good, baby."

His voice vibrated through her body as the latest in a series of effortless strokes overwhelmed her senses. Good? It was going to kill her. She was going to drown in the pleasure and never surface.

Above her, he tensed. Inside her, she felt him swell impossibly bigger. A glance at his face showed his clenched jaw, eyes closed in concentration. And still he kept on, ravaging her wits with every controlled surge of his hips, with every soft brush of his mouth over her skin.

"Mark, I'm ready! So ready," she panted between breaths. "Please!"

He opened his eyes, and she drowned in fiery green pools of pure need. *Bing. Zing!* Nicki felt that gaze deep inside her again, this time somewhere suspiciously near her chest, as he filled her again, going deeper than ever before. Their gazes connected them, as every nerve in her body converged between her legs, where they were joined. Her heart skipped a beat. Pleasure shimmered outward from the center of her need, pulsing, warning of the explosion to come.

"Mark," she sobbed. "I need—"

Suddenly, he thrust himself into her with a hard, pounding stroke, lifting her hips off the mattress. His fingers dug into her hips as his mouth fastened over hers until she felt completely invaded. Completely, wonderfully, taken.

She surrendered utterly for the first time in her life.

"Come. For. Me. Now," he demanded between relentless strokes deep, deep inside her as he captured her lips again for an wild, sweeping kiss.

Fast, faster. Ohmigod! Oh my—

Nicki screamed into his mouth as the fire burst inside her, hotter than a thousand suns. She pulsed around him, feeling him embedded within her so deep, so perfect. Just like heaven. The dizziness returned, as the orgasm continued to shake her with a pleasure even stronger than before. Sublime ecstasy knocked her breathless.

She squeezed her eyes shut, reveling in the feel of Mark, strong and powerful and so male above her, inside her. She encouraged him with an upward thrust of her hips.

Then Mark tensed and shouted with a hoarse cry. His cock swelled yet again, sending her up another impossible peak. Fingers digging into her hips, he held her tighter as he rode her through his climax.

Long moments later, his thrusts slowed, then stopped. Winding her arms around him even tighter, Nicki held him close. As orgasm subsided, emotions rose, new, powerful, confusing. At the top of the list was a troubling reluctance to let him go.

Mark lifted his head to peer down at her. Gently, he brushed her hair from her damp face. Nicki gazed back through half-closed lids. He really was so incredibly good looking. Add fabulous in bed. And tender afterward. No wonder she was experiencing a moment of attachment. It would pass, but at the moment it made sense. Who wouldn't want the complete package?

Why had she spent even thirty seconds resisting him? There was a reason; she just couldn't remember it now.

"Hmm." He planted a soft kiss on her mouth. "That was . . ."

"Beyond amazing. I think that registered on the Richter scale."

He laughed softly. "You may be right. Does that mean you don't regret calling me?"

"Fishing for more compliments?" she asked sleepily.

"If you'll take the bait."

"I'm pleading the fifth."

"You're mixing metaphors."

Nicki sent him an ironic but tired smile. "Whatever works."

A long moment passed in peace. Mark remained inside her, now semi-erect. He kissed the arch of her brow, traced her cheekbone with his thumb.

She could melt under that warm gaze, stay here forever, and not grow tired of that dimpled smile or the beautiful swirl of his hazel eyes.

"I want to stay with you, Nicki."

An odd relief slid through her—trying to melt away her wall of resistance.

Then Nicki frowned. What did he mean? Stay the night? Stay until tomorrow's show began? Maybe he only meant to be here long enough to use those three condoms he had left . . .

Suddenly, she remembered exactly why she'd been avoiding him. Funny how a killer orgasm or two could unclog all the lust from a girl's thought process and make things clear as crystal again.

If he wanted to stay the night, that suited her—as long as he left afterward and didn't expect a repeat performance some other time. Seriously. Mark was an employee and a distraction. She needed to be focusing on her business, not her love life. They weren't having a relationship. She didn't have time for one. This was a one-night stand. It had to be.

Why stress? More than likely, he'd last as long around here as a wooden toothpick after a steak dinner, anyway. Which shouldn't bother her. He wasn't the first brief fling; Nicki doubted he'd be the last.

Still, somehow Mark was . . . different. In light of the odd sense of connection she'd experienced tonight, Nicki feared it would be easy to get attached. And when he left, well, imagining her broken heart in his wake wasn't a stretch. His sense of humor, his sharp mind, even his bit of mystery all appealed to her. Not to mention the fabulous sex. That in itself was a distraction neither she nor her business could afford.

Putting a stop to this now was the smart thing to do. She just wished it didn't feel so crappy.

"I, um, have someplace to be at ten tomorrow," she lied. "But I'd love for you to stay until then."

Above her, Mark's shoulders stiffened. He cast a hard, narrow stare straight into her eyes. Nicki resisted the urge to cringe under his severe gaze. He knew it was a lie. Knew it.

But he just gave her a tight nod, withdrew from her body and rolled away in silence.

It was all Nicki could do to endure the aching emptiness she felt the instant he'd gone.

Chapter Six

NICKI fell asleep within two minutes. Muscles relaxed and sated, Mark rolled to his back with a sigh and stared at her faux-finished ceiling. He wished his mind felt half as much peace as hers must have.

What the hell had just happened?

One minute he'd been gearing up for sex with a woman who flipped his switch like no other in recent memory. The next, he'd been balls deep, sucked into the depths of her, into everything that made Nicki unique. He'd started in control—then lost it inside her and went completely wild.

Why?

True, he loved the fact she was orgasmic. Really orgasmic.

Tiffany had had difficulty reaching climax, so Mark had learned to be patient, had learned lots of little tricks to get her off, hopefully once for an hour's effort. Nicki had gone off like a rocket four times in twenty minutes, then pushed him right over the edge.

But it was more than that. Was it knowing he had overwhelmed such a strong woman with arousal, that she'd surrendered? Was it the way she cared about lots of the people around her, even if she liked to pretend she didn't? Was it those blue eyes seeming to stare right into him, as if she needed him?

He had no fucking idea.

And then, she'd brushed him off before he'd even left the bed. What the hell was up with her? It wasn't as if they were exclusive or dating or really involved. Still, it annoyed him. Irritated him, really. But the case had to come first. He'd figure out the odd workings of her female mind later.

Standing with another sigh, Mark disposed of the condom and stared at the clock. It was barely six in the evening. It felt odd to have the club two floors below them so quiet, without music rattling the windows. The parking lot around them looked so dark and empty. Usually the place teemed with noise and people.

The fact it didn't now made it the perfect time to look at Nicki's accounting records.

Mark glanced at Nicki sleeping peacefully and naked, all rumpled and curled up with a pillow and damp sheet. His heart skipped, and he hesitated. Nicki would be one pissed off woman if she ever learned the truth about why he'd pursued this job and the fact he'd taken advantage of her sexual satisfaction to further his agenda. Maybe he should wake her and tell her why he was here, rather than keep up this damned Viking charade.

Except she had no reason to believe him. Sure, he had a CPA but no proof to offer her of either Bocelli's involvement or the FBI's investigation. She'd already defended Blade, more or less, while telling Mark to butt out. He gritted his teeth at the memory.

Telling her about his mission wouldn't get him anywhere. Even if she believed someone was using her club to launder money and that he suspected Bocelli, what would prevent her from taking the knowledge straight to him, her lover? Her other lover.

That reality just sucked. Where was the nearest annoying Italian jackass when you needed someone to hit?

Part of him wanted to vow that somehow, some way, he'd convince Nicki to dump Mr. Hairy America and share her bed with only him. But his first priority had to be his mission, nailing Bocelli to the wall for his crimes, as well as for what he'd done to Tiffany and Mark's marriage.

Still, the need to totally claim Nicki didn't seem to be far down his mental priority list. And he didn't want to analyze why, didn't want to think about it. Maybe it was just the residual glow of good sex, and if he ignored it, the feeling would go away.

In the meantime, while Nicki slept and the club was closed, would be the perfect time to sneak down one floor into Nicki's office and start deciphering her accounting records, so he could complete his first goal and prove to her that Bocelli was dirty. That would free him to get on with the second, more personal task of being Nicki's only lover.

Stepping into his jeans and shrugging his shirt on, Mark padded his way barefoot to the front door, unlocking it on his way out.

Quickly, he stopped in at his apartment and grabbed a few blank CDs and a flashlight. Before he exited his apartment, he heard footsteps on the stairs leading up to this floor. Using the little peephole in the door, Mark looked out, only to find the object of his angry ruminations coming up the stairs.

Dressed in black, carrying a wicked, stainless steel .45 semi-automatic at his side and wearing a diamond stud in his left ear, Bocelli looked as if he'd earned his bad reputation with lots of blood—someone else's.

The asshole disappeared into his own apartment a few moments later, and Mark emerged quietly, carrying the blank CDs as he eased soundlessly down the stairs.

Sneaking into Nicki's office wasn't a challenge. Picking the lock didn't exactly require a master thief's talents. Mark made his way into the office.

As he entered, an exterior door to the club slammed somewhere below him. Who would be here? One of the dancers who'd stayed after rehearsal? Maybe Zack had been doing that stage and costume maintenance he'd mentioned. The guy worked damn hard.

A glance out the window of Nicki's office down into the club below proved no one remained inside. Whoever had slammed the door did so as they left. Good.

Shrugging, Mark booted up the accountant's machine. It was still warm. Apparently, Bocelli had just finish another day of screwing up Nicki's books.

With a shake of his head, Mark called Rafe on his cell phone.

"Hey, buddy," his brother-in-law greeted. "It's about time. Enjoying strutting your stuff half-naked?"

"Fuck off and get to work."

Rafe laughed. "Isn't that my line?"

"When you get your mind off humiliating me, yeah," he said. "Oh, and happy slightly belated birthday. What did you and Kerry do to celebrate your official welcome into the firmly over thirty club?"

"Ha, ha. Well, it's hard to dance the night away, since we have a baby due in two months and your sister has ankles that could double for the Goodyear blimp. So we went for sushi. Had any luck fishing out the identity of the Fed on location?"

Mark paused. He hadn't given it a lot of thought, to be honest. But then no one around him seemed like they could be FBI. Lucia? Not a chance. Zack? The very idea made him laugh. None of the other dancers seemed like good candidates, although he admittedly didn't know them well. But there was one other possibility . . .

"Any chance the Fed could be dead and the folks in Washington wouldn't know it?" he whispered.

The pause on the other end indicated Rafe was mulling over the possibility. "I guess anything is possible. What happened?"

"I hear Nicki's accountant was murdered in March. Supposed random drive-by."

"The time line fits. Norton said the agent hadn't been heard from in about three months."

"Exactly, and Marcy died just over two months ago. Not only that, if the Feds were going to put someone in here, why not undercover as the accountant, where they'd have access to all the financial figures?"

"I don't know what this agent's assignment is exactly, but that makes sense."

"And with Marcy out of the way, bet you can guess who's taken over the accounting."

"Bocelli? Seriously?"

"Guessed it in one. Now that I think about it, I wonder if Bocelli discovered that Marcy was a Fed and did her in. It would serve two purposes: remove the threat of an agent and get him one step closer to handling Nicki's money."

"You're right," Rafe said. "I'll talk to Norton and see if their agent was a female operating under the name Marcy and get back to you. But keep your eyes open just in case it wasn't Marcy. If the agent is rogue, he is one dangerous cat."

"Or she," Mark pointed out.

"Or she. If the agent is just deep undercover, we can't afford to be in their way."

"Got it. Thanks."

"No sweat. So, how's your boss? Have you managed to charm her yet?"

Rafe's suggestive voice crawled on Mark's exposed nerves. "Get your mind out of the gutter and off of Nicki."

Mark did his best to ignore Rafe's laughter in his ear.

A moment later, the Windows desktop on the computer appeared with pictures of a dark-haired woman about Nicki's age standing next to an older woman who had to be her mom. They'd tilted their heads together, each wearing bright red Santa caps and matching smiles.

Based on what he'd heard about the murdered accountant, the younger woman in the picture had to be Marcy. Mark felt a shiver as he stared at pictures of the dead woman, who couldn't have been much more than twenty-five, apparently gunned down in the parking lot in a random drive-by.

Random, my ass. The more Mark thought about it, the more he was sure the shooting had only been random enough for the current accountant to separate the previous one from her duties so he could gain control of the books and Nicki's money. In other words, totally premeditated.

The picture reminded him that his mission was no laughing matter. Bocelli was deadly serious.

"Okay, let's get on with this. Nicki doesn't know I'm here. Bocelli just went upstairs to his place," Mark said, all business. "No password protecting the machine as a whole." He explored around, found what he wanted, and tried to launch the file.

"What else?" Rafe prompted.

"There's a password protecting the main accounting files."

"Is the machine connected?"

"Yep." He clicked around, found the device manager. "Cable modem."

"What's the IP?"

Mark hunted, then found the series of numbers that identified the machine. He recited them to Rafe.

"Firewall?"

"Yeah . . ." Mark clicked and found the answer. "Just the usual Windows firewall."

"Damn it, after a week and a half, couldn't you at least give me a challenge?"

"I thought my sister was your challenge."

"Good point."

Silence. Mark knew better than to interrupt Rafe while he hacked. Less than two minutes later, he said. "Got it. The password is 'poodle,' followed by the number one, no space."

"Seriously? I'm not sure I want to know why."

Instead of questioning it further, Mark simply entered the password for the accounting files in question. The entire balance sheet emerged.

"I'm in," he said to Rafe. "Saving to CD right now. I'll study it later. Bank account numbers . . ." Mark tugged on filing cabinets, finding them locked. A few moments and a few handy pieces of metal later, they opened. In the second drawer, he found a series of bank statements. "Got it."

"Lay it on me."

Mark gave Rafe the name of the bank and all the associated account numbers he could find.

"Good work," his brother-in-law said. "Give me a few minutes and I'll e-mail the bank's records to you."

"I'll compare their records with the CD. I have an inkling that these records will be pure fiction," Mark said.

Maybe then he'd have some proof to take to Nicki, show her that her Italian stallion was cheating her out of her money. It would start a circumstantial case against the asshole for Marcy's murder. Maybe then he'd get sweet revenge and sweet Nicki all at once.

"Good work," Rafe praised. "Now get out of there before anyone sees you."

"Yeah. I'll be in touch when I find something."

"I'll wait. Your sister will, too, although a lot less patiently."

Mark laughed. "Kiss Kerry for me."

"You got it. Talk to you soon."

Mark flipped his phone closed. The CD finished writing the current imprint of the file, and he extracted it from the drive. Quickly, he shut down the computer and exited the office, carefully locking it behind him.

Back in his apartment, Mark booted up his laptop and found a nearby high-speed wireless connection that wasn't encrypted. He surfed on. Within moments, he'd launched his e-mail and downloaded three months' worth of the club's bank statements. Bless Rafe's pointy head, but he was a truly great hacker.

Mark opened both files and compared debits and credits for February. It looked good. Nearly every *I* dotted and every *T* crossed—except on the last day, very late in the day. On the twenty-eighth, a flurry of activity littered the bank's records, after five in the afternoon. Several sizeable credits from a corporation Mark had never heard of and would bet his eyeteeth was a dummy front for something else, followed by even more sizeable debits sent to offshore accounts. None of that appeared in the accountant's records. The monthly totals, however, ended up exactly the same.

Even so, Marcy would have seen the activity on the bank statements. If she hadn't already known about it, no doubt that would have incited her to start asking questions. Questions Bocelli wouldn't want her finding the answers to.

March started very much the same. After the nineteenth, the accounting records became incomplete. Some items weren't categorized correctly. Others had amounts that just looked plain wrong. Four thousand dollars for catering in a single night? Girls' Night Out served a whole lot of drinks, but not much in the way of chow. But payroll files looked good. Same for taxes and insurance. It just didn't make sense.

April and May looked a lot like March, whacked out and full of shit that struck him as totally mismanaged—or fabricated.

And at varying times in every month, the bank's records showed a slew of credits in large but not alarming amounts, all from obscure corporations. Inevitably, those amounts were transferred offshore on the same day, late in the day.

None of the accounting records reflected a dime of that.

At this point, Nicki's books were simply screwed. It would take Mark a solid week and access to every one of her records to even begin to sort it out. But more, it begged the question: How could Nicki be so unaware of what was happening in her business financially?

Frowning, Mark began to close the file with the bank's records . . . until something at the bottom snagged his attention—a series of deposits from more unheard of corporations totaling about a hundred thousand dollars, followed almost immediately by transfers to offshore accounts. Every one of these transactions had occurred today, after five in the afternoon. In fact, the transactions had transpired just under an hour ago. Where had Bocelli been then?

In Nicki's office, probably overseeing it all.

The bastard had to feel pretty smug in his position to pull a stunt like that under Nicki's nose. He couldn't have had any clue that she would be occupied.

Could he?

The thought stopped Mark cold.

While Blade had been playing musical bank accounts, had the wise guy known that Mark would be busy getting to know Nicki in the biblical sense?

No. Impossible.

But it was possible . . . if Nicki was in on the scam, too.

Mind racing, Mark sat back in his chair. The Feds thought it likely she was unaware of the money laundering in her club, but weren't certain of that. Could they be wrong?

Maybe he was jumping to conclusions. After all, why would Nicki allow her club to be used for illegal crap? And if she was, and if the light nearly falling on Nicki hadn't been an accident, why would Bocelli try to kill her?

Well . . . there was another possibility: The falling light might actually have been an accident—or a warning from a jealous lover, just like the blaring music. But the money laundering would, no doubt, make Nicki money. The question was, how far was she willing to go for it?

Mark closed his eyes, but couldn't escape that sick feeling, as if he'd been punched in the gut. Was it possible he had again fucked a woman who was just as intent on fucking him outside the bedroom?

He dialed Rafe again, who answered on the first ring.

"That was quick," said his brother-in-law.

"These records are all bullshit," Mark confirmed.

"We figured they would be."

"Yeah, it's just . . . Nicki is so smart and together. I don't see how she's letting this happen under her nose. So I'm wondering . . ."

"If she's involved? Why would you think that?"

Mark sighed, feeling dread slide through his gut. And something that felt suspiciously like hurt. Damn, he wanted to deny the possibility. But it *was* possible . . .

"She tried to avoid any personal interaction with me from the minute I walked in the door. I've spent some time with her, but not any quality time, if you catch my drift."

"Yeah."

"So, today the club is closed, and I get this voice mail from Nicki to come see her at her place at five o' clock. I go up there and try to convince her that Bocelli is no accountant and that he may not be honest. She basically defended him, told me to get my nose out of her business, then informed me that she had invited me over for sex."

Rafe choked. "Are you serious?"

"As a heart attack. Afterward, I get the subtle hint that this is a one-night thing, which is odd since she invited me and things went well. When she drifted off, I slipped out of her place to find Bocelli coming up the stairs, probably leaving Nicki's office, and all the bank records in a file cabinet that, I think, only Nicki has the keys to. Worse, a whole bunch of money changed hands while Nicki and I were busy. Coincidence . . . or by design?"

Mark shrugged, but inside denial raged. Fury grew. Would a woman that smart and successful participate in such a scheme? He wanted to say no. God knew he did. They'd connected in bed, not just sexually. For the first time since his marriage, he'd felt something with a woman besides the release of getting off. He'd felt *her*, the woman he sensed she didn't share easily. The wants she'd never told anyone. Her need to let go. Both her insecurities and her sexual confidence. For that, he'd wanted her fiercely, so deeply it scared the hell out of him.

And now this shit.

He shouldn't be surprised, he supposed. He had terrible taste in women. The badder, the better. After an ex-wife who'd been a thief and married him to frame him for her crime, why shouldn't he be interested in a woman with secrets of her own, like being a money laundress?

His temper soared until Mark wondered if the top of his head would pop off from the pressure. Had Nicki invited him over at just the right time, then spread her legs for him to distract him, to cover up the fact she was involved with Bocelli both personally and criminally?

"Maybe I'm answering my own question," he growled to Rafe, seething inside. "Maybe Nicki isn't unaware of what's going on with her accounting records. I can't see her being duped like that."

Rafe paused. "Wait. Look at this logically. If Nicki was involved, why would she imagine that she needed to distract you while Bocelli shuffled money around the globe? For all she knows, you're just one of the dancers."

"Until this morning, yes."

"What did you do?"

Mark held in a curse, mentally replaying this morning's scene in Nicki's office. "I got up bright and early to get a peek at Nicki's records while everyone else should have been asleep. But Bocelli was already there, messing with Nicki's books. He saw me peering over his shoulder while I was mentally adding numbers. I told the asshole he was doing it wrong and that things would change now that Nicki had competent help. No doubt Bocelli told her about the altercation."

"Maybe. Even if he did, if Nicki isn't involved in this scheme, why would she care what the jerk said?"

"Bocelli let me know that he's fucking Nicki."

"You sure he's not lying, just to jack with you?"

Mark wished like hell it was that simple. That Bocelli was just being his usual prick self and talking smack just to piss him off. That Nicki hadn't invited him over while Bocelli was breaking the law, and he hadn't fallen for it like a stupid panting sap . . . But he had.

No wonder she'd given him the proverbial nudge out of her bed before drifting off to sleep. Now that the damage was done, she didn't need to distract him anymore, at least not today. And she had to cool the sheets down before Bocelli returned to crawl between them.

Damn it! After the initial fury had worn off, Tiffany's perfidy had left him feeling numb and hollow. In retrospect, he'd been more disturbed that he'd been deceived than crushed that he'd lost his wife. This . . . was different. Hell, yes, he was pissed at Nicki's deceit, furious actually—but equally angry that whatever chemistry they'd shared, whatever could have been, was already history. He had no idea why he lamented that fact, but he did. He'd actually liked her.

But then she'd planned it that way.

"I don't think Bocelli is lying. Why else would Nicki defend the thug? Or let him do her accounting?"

"Any chance you could find some way to ask her, at least about Bocelli? One thing marriage has taught me, brother, is good communication is golden."

What he and Nicki shared wasn't a marriage—by any stretch. In fact, it was rapidly looking like a race to see who could fuck each other over the worst. "Tipping my hand at all could make Nicki suspicious and get me killed. Better just to assume that Bocelli telling me he's Nicki's main squeeze was the equivalent of a dog lifting its hind leg."

"True."

"Bocelli acted jealous *before* I touched Nicki. Why would he, unless he knew I was going to touch her? And how would he know that, unless they'd cooked up a scheme for her to distract me?"

"Hmm. Those are good questions. The situation looks a little shady. Just make sure you think everything through. Nicki isn't Tiffany, and I'd hate to see you jump to conclusions."

"Why would I?"

Rafe hesitated. "Tiffany hit you with some heavy shit, man. With the divorce and the trial and everything, it didn't seem like you spent a lot of time sorting it all through before you moved on."

"What was there to sort? She fucked me over, so I ended the marriage. End of story," he returned, teeth gritted. "Don't worry. I've got my head screwed on straight."

"Well, from what you said, it's definitely possible Nicki is involved. There's enough of a smell to make it all seem fishy. I'll get you a report on her from my local PI." Rafe sighed. "I'm sorry, man. Watch your back . . . and anything else that might get hurt."

* * *

NICKI woke to the sound of a slamming door. Groggy, she sat up and glanced around her shadowed bedroom, only to find herself alone.

Disappointment dragged her shoulders down. She frowned. What time was it? How long had she been asleep? The clock told her a little over an hour.

Had that slam been Mark leaving?

Gosh, she hoped he wasn't upset that she'd nodded off. It wasn't her fault that he'd pressed her into such amazing orgasms she'd practically lost consciousness. Or was he upset that she'd lied about having an appointment tomorrow morning? The thought made her wince.

Heavy footfalls coming down her hall alerted Nicki to the fact that someone had entered her apartment, rather than left. She had no time to be afraid of who it might be before Mark filled the door frame, eclipsing the light that spilled in from the living room.

He gripped the portal, shoulders tense. His mouth was a taut line. His hazel eyes were flat, hard, as he raked an abrasive gaze down her naked body.

Alarmed by his stance and stare, she gathered up the sheet and covered everything from the shoulders down. "Mark?"

"Feeling shy, suddenly?"

The edge of his voice sounded sharper than a brand-new razor. This wasn't the man she'd exchanged banter with a few hours ago, before amazing sex. This was a different man. A furious man.

A stranger.

"What's wrong?"

Every line in his body tensed at her question. His jaw clenched. But he said nothing, didn't move. Concern seeped through Nicki. What had happened? Not only did he look angry, but the anger seemed to be directed at her.

"Mark, are you all right?"

Again, he didn't answer, but his eyes . . . they changed. He stared at her, his gaze like a sexual crowbar. Desire thundered in those hazel depths, so intent she wondered if he thought he might be able to read her mind—or turn her on—if he simply glared long and hard enough.

Nicki couldn't vouch for the reading her mind part, but the turning her on . . . oh, yeah. A zip of thrill zinged through her at Mark's ferocious gaze. A discreet glance down proved that incredible anatomy of his all revved up and ready to go.

Pushing away from the door, he stalked to the bed and tore the sheet from her hand, ignoring her gasp.

"Why hide when I've already seen your body?" he taunted. "And touched nearly every inch of it."

Nicki bit her lip, torn between concern and arousal. "Do you want to talk? It looks like something upset you."

"Why would you think that?"

His sarcastic tone told her something was definitely wrong. That, and his cold eyes. Before she could say more, he continued.

"You invited me here to fuck. So let's get to it." Mark pulled his shirt over his head, toed off his shoes, and doffed his jeans in less than fifteen seconds.

Nicki gaped at him, torn between her worry for him and the shiver of desire that danced up her spine at the sight of him, huge, hard body completely naked and aggressively coming after her.

"Mark, I—"

Not another sound made it out before he leaped on the bed, pulled her under him, and covered her lips with his.

As his tongue slid into her mouth, deep and possessive, arousal slammed her, knocking the breath from her body. He commanded her kiss, demanded a response. He got both. After two years without sex, and longer than that without any worth mentioning, Nicki was embarrassingly charged up for more of Mark. And already he knew her body well.

With one hand, he grabbed her hands and hoisted them up

over her head, pinning them to the bed. Surprised at his move, Nicki writhed, testing his hold. It was solid, iron. No way was she getting up, unless she asked to be released. The hard glitter in Mark's gaze as he looked down at her with both challenge and authority told her that he knew she was utterly at his mercy.

Her breathing kicked up a notch. This was something she'd always wondered about, feeling helpless underneath a man who aroused her out of her mind. She'd never found a man strong enough to *try* to contain both her body and her will, much less succeed.

Until Mark.

In the back of her mind, Nicki knew that he was likely using sex to avoid talking to her about whatever had angered him. If she could just think beyond his desire-soaked mouth pressed against hers and his hand clamped around her wrists, she would confront him.

His other hand roamed her body in a fast, electric sweep, settling over her breast as if he had every right. He plucked at her pebbled nipple, pinched and rolled it between his fingers. Closing her eyes as need raged through her, Nicki arched and melted into his amazing touch.

"You like this." His voice was a deep rumble in her ear, vibrating inside her. "You like to be manhandled, don't you?"

She couldn't give up, give in, too easily. It was embarrassing. "Bite me."

"Eventually. But first I see something I want to suck."

Maintaining his grip on her wrists, Mark bent and took her other breast in his mouth. Voracious and unrelenting, his mouth settled over her, working the nipple with gentle scrapes of his teeth and the pluck of his lips. He hadn't paid much attention to her breasts the first time, but he sure was making up for that now.

The double pressure-pleasure of his mouth at one nipple, hand at the other, was unraveling her composure. Her skin heated until she felt like a furnace on overdrive. When his teeth nipped at her again and he soothed the little sting with a long swipe of his tongue, Nicki moaned.

His free hand left her breast, and she whimpered in protest. Nicki doubted she'd ever made such a sound in her life, but the sudden deprivation of stimulation made her nipple ache.

As if atoning for his abandonment, he eased to her side and tracked a pair of fingers right through her wet slit, then plunged them deep inside her. Gasping, Nicki arched up to his touch, wild for the new sensation, and looked at him with unfocused eyes, feeling so vulnerable yet so alive.

His tight smile and heated hazel eyes told her he was enjoying pushing every one of her buttons.

He proved he could—quite easily—when he crooked his fingers and scraped them right over her most sensitive spot. Again and again, he nudged and provoked that bundle of nerves deep inside her. Pressure, pleasure, swelled and grew. God, he was about to push her over the edge into a black abyss so deep . . . Nicki found herself short of breath, chest rising and falling with the effort to get more air.

"Do you want it?" he growled.

"Yes." She arched up to him, willing him to shut up and get on with it.

Gently nipping at her nipple with his teeth, Mark warned her to keep still. The sting only engorged the pleasure deeper inside her. Without conscious thought, she moaned and spread her legs wider.

Mark accepted her invitation.

"How do you want it?"

He was going to make her admit it. Make her completely surrender. Dented pride aside, she loved it. "Take me. Hard. Now!"

"I'm going to hold you down while I do."

"Yes!"

Quickly, he reached to the bedside table and grabbed another condom. Nicki watched as he tore the packet open and rolled the latex down his length in about three seconds, before she could think or move. Before the tingles could abate and sanity could return.

Jaw clenched, eyes glittering down at her with that swirl of anger and challenge, Mark pushed her legs wider with insistent hands, settled into the new space as if he belonged there, then grabbed her wrists and pinned her down again.

He slid inside her in one fierce thrust.

Her body stretched to accommodate him a lot more quickly, but he still filled her beyond full. The tip of him pressed against the mouth of her womb in a piercing pleasure that had her crying out and wishing she could dig what was left of her fingernails into his back. Instead, he held her still, eased back most of the way out.

Before plunging into her with a ferocious, heavy stroke.

Nicki had thought the pleasure couldn't get any more intense. She'd been wrong.

Already swollen with arousal and slightly sore from their first tango between the sheets, Nicki discovered her body was even more sensitive. She closed around the hard length of his insistent cock, as it drove into her again, a third time, a fourth, and then . . .

"Ohmigod! Mark!"

He eased up, prolonging her agony, controlling it. "Does anyone else make you feel this good?"

Bucking her hips up to him, Nicki silently pleaded with him to fill her full and fast again. She soon learned Mark would not rush unless he want to.

"Anyone?" he barked, even as he tortured her with slow strokes that dragged the head of his cock over that one spot . . . ramping up her pleasure but not giving her enough to fall over the edge.

"Mark," she breathed, pleaded.

"Who else makes you feel this way?"

Another slow thrust, another slide of his erection just where it pushed her to the limits of her sanity.

"No one," she whispered, trying to catch a breath. "No one."

"Remember that."

Then he became a wild man, plunging into her with rapid-fire hips that sent her soaring high, then higher still, until she was holding her breath against the mounting pleasure.

Her heartbeat resounding in her ears, Nicki surrendered to the ecstasy. She convulsed around Mark's hard flesh, squeezing, pulsing—totally losing her mind as he continued to pound into her and took her to yet a higher peak. This one had her screaming incoherently.

As the pleasure slowly subsided, Nicki became aware that Mark's strokes had slowed as well. She opened her eyes to see a rivulet of sweat running from his temple down his neck, to find his eyes raging with lust, anger, need, fear. Nothing in his expression made sense.

Since she couldn't free her hands from his grasp, she lifted her mouth to his and placed a gentle kiss over his lips. "Mark?"

He didn't answer.

Instead, he quickly withdrew from her, flipped her over to her stomach and shoved a pair of pillows under her. Grabbing her hips, Mark positioned her exactly where he wanted her, then thrust deep inside her again.

It was like unleashing a man possessed.

The control he'd maintained to that point unwound. He laid his body over hers and nipped at her neck, hot breath making her shiver with welcome delight as he began to hammer into her. Nicki drowned in all the new sensations. His heat on her back, his wide cock stretching her channel, which felt narrower in this position, then, oh yeah, his fingers swirling over her swollen clit.

One hand held her hips in place, fingers digging into her as he pumped his way inside her, again finding just the right angle to hit every spot guaranteed to set her off. But the arousal climbed up over her head so fast, rushing her like a tidal wave until she couldn't breathe, couldn't think. The telltale bubble of aching need began expanding inside her, even as her vagina closed around him, gripping until he had to push his way inside with each thrust.

Deeper, faster, hotter, higher, Mark pushed her, his incessant strokes inside her unrelenting. She had no place to hide from the enormous swell of her own desire, ready to sweep her away like a strong undertow. Inside her, he engorged, pressing against her very walls until she was sure she couldn't stretch any more.

"Mark . . ."

"Come for me," he urged in a gravelly voice in her ear. "Come!"

His raspy demand and that last relentless plunge inside her pushed her over the edge. Nicki exploded in a tangle of light and colors, of breaths and sweat and fire. As she did, Mark groaned in her ear, an urgent, hoarse sound that bordered on pain as he released.

A minute passed. Heartbeats slowed. Breathing regulated. Neither said a word.

Mark might have spent himself twice tonight but he held himself above her, tense and still. Nicki just knew he wasn't in the mood to chat.

But he hesitated, seemingly reluctant to move. Nicki had no idea what to make of his behavior. Now that she could think rationally again, she couldn't help but wonder why he was mad. Especially at her.

Why did it matter? So they'd had sex. Amazing, earth-shattering, heard-the-bells-ringing sex, yes. But it didn't mean that she had to care about him. In fact, it was better if she didn't.

Too bad she wasn't getting her way on this one. Denying that she cared about his odd mood was pointless. She'd never been good at self-delusion. Why start now?

It mattered, because *he* mattered.

Nicki turned her head to find him hovering over her, still inside her, with a stark face and haunted eyes.

"Mark, talk to me. Is something wrong?"

He blinked once. When he opened his eyes again, all expression had disappeared. His face was a harsh, flat landscape, barren like the unforgiving desert.

Tensing, he pulled away from her, out of her, and stood. In thirty seconds, he'd disposed of the condom and dressed. He didn't look at her again. Nicki found herself grabbing the sheet to cover up, somehow wanting to hide. Tears stung her eyes. She blinked them back.

This was not a good sign.

"Damn it, Mark. What is going on?"

He finished tying his shoes, then looked up at her with a dismissive glance. "Thanks for an . . . interesting evening."

Nicki didn't have a chance to say a word before he left her bedroom and slammed her front door behind him.

Chapter Seven

THE cold light of the following day told Mark one thing: He'd fucked up big.

He paced the bare little living room of his apartment, trying to decide how to repair the damage he'd done in his stupid ass fury. He ignored the ache in the center of his chest and forced himself to review the facts.

One, Nicki most likely knew what Bocelli was doing with her accounts and those phony books. Wishful thinking, more than logic, made him hope otherwise. Nicki had so much going for her, looks, wit, guts, smarts. Why would she throw it away on a jerk like Bocelli and help him commit crimes that jeopardized the club she'd worked so hard to build? Was she in financial trouble? There had to be a reason she was willing to take such risks.

Two, Nicki apparently didn't let people into her life easily. She'd let him in, likely for her own purposes, yes. But he'd bet she opened up far more than she intended. So chances were good that she'd fire him and throw off his whole investigation if he didn't atone fast.

Three, whatever he thought he'd felt for her last night couldn't mean anything. Period. He didn't get involved with women on a meaningful level. Not anymore. He had no business trying to put together any sort of relationship with Nicki, especially now that she was a suspect. Romance never worked for him. If he was hot for a woman, he could guarantee there was something shady about her.

He was on fire for Nicki, even knowing the laws she'd likely broken.

Mark stalked to the kitchen and poured himself another cup of coffee, his fourth since five this morning. If he'd slept more than three hours last night, he'd be stunned. Unfortunately, the coffee wasn't curing what ailed him, only making his mind race faster.

Memory flashed him an image of Nicki in her bed, using the sheet to cover the essentials, when he'd entered her bedroom after making his discoveries. He hadn't meant to touch her. Really. He hadn't meant to strip the sheet from her hand, get deep inside her and fuck her until neither of them could breathe. Somewhere in his head, he'd imagined he would restrain his fury, ask her a few questions while she was feeling open to him and a little vulnerable. Unfortunately, his brain had stopped doing the thinking once he'd seen Nicki mostly naked.

Another memory streaked through his mind, this one of her face, stricken with shock and hurt as he rose and dressed before leaving. His gut tightened with something that felt stupidly like regret. He pushed it away. The expression, the maidenly clutch of the sheet—it was an act. A damn good one, yes. In the moment, though, he'd nearly caved, sunk to the bed beside her, and asked her to explain away everything he'd found.

But he couldn't afford to give away his cover—and questions like that would. Besides, Tiffany had taught him that if it looked like a duck, walked like a duck, and quacked like a duck, chances were good it was a damn duck. When they'd been married, he'd known something was wrong. Something . . . but he'd had no clue what. He had ignored his gut, written it off to newlywed adjustments. What a fucking idiot he'd been.

A sudden pounding on the door made him jump. Hot coffee

sloshed over the rim of his cup and onto his hands. With a curse, he tossed it into the sink, wiped his hand on his jeans, then opened the door.

He mentally prepared an apology. Nicki would be standing on the other side of the door, expecting one. He'd need to deliver it quickly and find enough sincerity to get back in her good graces—while he held in his suspicions. While anger bubbled like acid in his gut.

Instead of Nicki on the warpath, Lucia stood in her place, looking as infuriated as a soft woman with warm chocolate eyes and a curtain of loose auburn curls possibly could. Even the pink bow of her mouth couldn't be condensed to a thin line.

Despite being about five feet, three inches, she barreled past him and slammed the door behind her, then did her best to glare at him. Since her gaze had to travel up over a foot to reach his, the glower lost a little of its impact.

Then Mark realized she had to be here on her sister's behalf. He sobered.

"Good morning, Lucia."

"For you maybe," she tossed at him. "For Nicki, not so much."

Holding in a grimace, he determined to play this right, since he'd screwed up last night so damn bad.

"Coffee?"

"No. If you'd like to offer me answers, I'll take those."

"Let's sit." He gestured to the lumpy blue couch against the far wall, bypassing the kitchen area he used as a portable office. "If you'll tell me the questions, I'll do my best to give you answers."

Lucia clenched her small hands into fists and shuddered with an annoyed sigh. "You don't even know?"

"I have an idea, but let's make sure we're on the same page, hmm?"

She marched across the living room, full breasts swaying, and seated herself on the sofa. Mark sat next to her. Even furious, she looked warm and soft and so honest. Like a great friend. Like someone a man could really talk to. Without makeup, she looked incredibly young and innocent, and he'd bet a month's salary she was a virgin. Why couldn't he be attracted to *her*? Why always the glossy femme fatales with something to hide?

His fatal flaw, he supposed. He sighed.

"My sister called me near midnight, slightly tipsy and ranting about you."

That wasn't a pretty picture. "What did she say?"

"Just that you were a raving jerk. And something about letting you keep your reflexes to yourself next time. What is she talking about?"

"An inside joke." Mark massaged the back of his neck. "About last night . . . We argued."

Lucia sent him a skeptical glare. She might not be able to convey anger in a way that frightened anyone, but she sure had scorn down pat.

"That's one way of putting it. I went over to her place after she called. She was drinking Chianti and eating brownies." The accusation in her tone told Mark that happened as often as a full planetary alignment or the Dolphins winning the Super Bowl.

He frowned, but before he could get a word in, Lucia plowed forward.

"Her bedroom was a sty. So I started picking up. I knew immediately she hadn't created that disaster alone. The two used condoms in the trash pretty much confirmed what I'd suspected. So, what did you do, the male version of a hit-and-run?"

Well, at least Nicki hadn't told Lucia that he'd gone all Conan, held her down, screwed her into the mattress, and left. At least not in so many words.

"Let's say I wasn't using my brain to the best of my ability last night."

She snorted. "I don't think you were using your brain at all, unless it's south of your waistline."

He felt a wry grin creep up his face. "So you're smart about more than books, I see."

Her answering expression was anything but amused. "You're

not going to charm me. Don't waste your breath. But let me warn you: You upset my sister, and you have me to pay. Obviously, I don't have the ability to beat you up, but I have a vicious tongue and a mean vocabulary, and I won't hesitate to use either."

Mark believed her. The bigger question in his mind was what was it about Nicki and her behavior with the wine and brownies? Was her unusual behavior guilt? Part of the act? Would she go so far as to pretend heartache for her sister? Lord knew he wanted Nicki's confusion and hurt to be genuine. If it were, that would mean Nicki was innocent. And if she were . . . well, he'd apologize right now and offer himself up as her punching bag.

But since he had solid reasons to believe Nicki was involved, he was going to have to consider her a suspect until proof to the contrary arose.

Nicki had likely feigned misery with fermented grapes and chocolate for some reason he would never fathom. He and the female mind had never synched up, so his success in deciphering her rationale would likely be on par with his success at debating Einstein on physics.

Instead of Nicki's Oscar-level performances, he had to focus on his first priority, his mission to put Bocelli away. He didn't want to take Nicki down with the bastard, but if she was guilty of assisting a felon . . . he wasn't going to be able to help her. And he shouldn't. A crime was a crime.

His maddening infatuation with the accomplice couldn't matter one whit.

"I've been warned," he told Lucia. "I came this far to escape my sister's uncertain temper. The last thing I want to do is rouse yours. So how about you help me out? Maybe you can tell me where I went wrong with Nicki and give me some suggestions on how to patch it up."

"And maybe you can go to hell."

Both her fury and her language took him aback. Hmm, the soft little kitten had claws.

Lucia stood, fists clenched. Given his height and her lack of it, she barely got to look down at him. That didn't seem to faze her in the least.

"Lucia—"

"Shut up. You may work here," she cut in, "but that doesn't mean Nicki has to see you outside the club's hours and rehearsals. Stay away. I swear if you break her heart, you'll get an up close and personal view of this 'nice' Italian girl turning into your worst nightmare!"

* * *

MARK was supposed to strut to the end of the stage, turn his back toward the audience, shake his ass, then look over his shoulder with a wink. Instead, he staggered into position—not quite like a drunk with a hangover, but close—forgot to shake, then turned and greeted the empty seats of the audience with a glare.

Thank God this was just a rehearsal!

Behind her office wall of smoked glass, Nicki winced. Where was the sexy smile, the fluid moves that had attracted her during his audition? This man didn't just look like he had two left feet, but rather like he had them and couldn't find them. After two weeks of practice, Mark was no closer to being ready to perform than he'd been the day she hired him.

"And just what was that, Mister?" Zack demanded of Mark, which she heard through her intercom speaker. "I've seen elephants with more grace."

Shrugging, Mark cast an apologetic glance at her stage manager. From the petulant set of Zack's mouth, Nicki could see that her stage manager was quickly losing patience.

"A shrug of those pretty behemoth shoulders isn't going to save you from my mood today. We're going to stay here until it's right!"

With an impatient snap, Zack made Mark repeat the move, which produced no better results.

Nicki took back her last thought; Mark actually looked less prepared than the day she'd hired him. What the hell was she going to do?

"You're lucky the boss-lady likes you. If it was up to me, I'd have tossed you out on your tight ass after Monday's awful rehearsal."

Zack had a point, Nicki conceded. She probably should fire Mark. He wasn't ready to perform for the crowd; she wondered if he ever would be. His Viking costume had mysteriously disappeared, forcing her to order another one, which wouldn't arrive for at least another week.

On the other hand, he served drinks diligently enough. And apparently made good tips. He wasn't lazy or slow. He wasn't unreliable or intentionally difficult. The ladies liked seeing him strut around in tight black pants, a bow tie—and nothing else. He'd paid his first month's rent on time.

Oh, just admit it. He was fabulous in bed. You're mooning over him and don't want to let go, no matter how big a butthead he's been.

The truth hurt.

At Zack's cue, Mark tried the sequence again. This time, he damn near tripped on his own two feet. Nicki winced again, as her stage manager stomped his foot, a loud boom resounding through the club.

"I told you to spend the last three days practicing. From what I can tell, you've spent them glowering. You've got that look down. Now you'll be all prepared to imitate Clint Eastwood in a thong. Too bad no one asked for that."

"How's it going?" Lucia asked, easing into her office.

Nicki turned to greet her. "Not well."

Together, they watched the stage.

Mark glared at Zack, looking half a heartbeat away from telling the smaller man to go fuck himself. Apparently, Mark did not care if he made friends and influenced people, at least where Zack was concerned.

"His mood looks almost as bad as yours," her sister commented.

"I am not surly."

"So you regularly chew out the pizza guy for taking twenty-two minutes to deliver? And you know, I've never seen you pounce on either of your bartenders for failing to clean a lone glass. You snapped at my mother when she called to check up on me, I'm told."

Guilty as charged. Nicki sighed. "Okay, so I'm feeling a little bitchy. It's not totally new."

"You've just taken it to new heights the past few days. Why don't you just get rid of the man? He can't do the job, and he's making you miserable."

Her shoulders drooped. "I know."

"But he's still here, because you're not ready to let him go." It wasn't a question. Lucia knew her too well.

"It's just . . . There was something between us, like this click. I felt good with him. He can make me laugh. He's one of the few men who really sees me and hasn't run screaming. My bitchiness just rolls off his back. For the first time in more than two years, I was with someone who made me feel good and sexy. With him, I knew it was okay to be smart and strong and vulnerable all at once. Or I thought so, until he got up, dressed, and slammed the door on his way out."

Lucia wrapped her arms around Nicki's shoulders. Dropping her head back against Lucia, Nicki tried not to succumb to the stupid tears she'd been battling for days. Why cry over the man? He worked for her, and she'd made the mistake of having sex with him. It wasn't as if they'd tried for a lasting relationship.

All of that was true, and yet . . . Nicki wanted more, missed him even now. She couldn't even say why exactly.

Back onstage, Zack put his hands on his hips, then wagged a finger at Mark. "My grandfather with Parkinson's can do better than that. Let's put a little effort into the move this time, shall we?"

Mark tried again. The results were about the same as before—disastrous.

"Has Mark tried to talk to you since his abrupt departure?" Lucia asked.

She nodded. "Tuesday morning, he did his best to ply me with bagels and an apology. I was still so mad, I slammed the door in his face. Then, before the club opened, I found a box of chocolates in my office chair."

"Did you eat them?"

Nicki turned to give her sister a *duh*-style glance. "Were they chocolate?"

"Good point. Did you say anything to him?"

"Not yet. I was too mad until this morning."

"And now you just want to cry." Another statement. Lucia really did know her. "Anything else?"

"Yesterday afternoon, he left a nice bottle of chilled merlot on my doorstep, along with a note asking if we could share it so he could grovel appropriately."

"Where is the bottle?"

"In my fridge."

"Darn, I was hoping you'd use your landlord key and pour that nice bottle all over his bed. Maybe give his tighty whities a nice dousing so they'd wash up pink."

"You're evil," Nicki said with a weak laugh, which morphed into a sigh. "This morning when I woke up, I really wanted to talk to Mark. I mean, like, so bad it hurt, which probably makes me ten kinds of stupid. I know what he did was crappy."

"At least you're clear on that."

"But I keep thinking that something went wrong so suddenly. His behavior the second half of that night was so weird. He was like Jekyll and Hyde, perfect and charming one moment, and an intimidating but sexy ass the next. I keep wondering if I did something . . . He was mad. And it seemed like he was mad at me."

"You wonder if *you* did something?" Lucia incredulity rang in her voice. "No."

"I know. I'm making excuses for him. Maybe he suddenly felt odd about sleeping with his boss."

"So odd that he did it again?"

"Okay, so that's not it. But something happened."

"Like he got off and was done with you?"

Nicki glared at her sister. "Who's telling you this stuff?"

"I'm a smart girl, remember. You are, too. Don't make more excuses for Mark."

"But maybe . . . he's bipolar."

"Maybe you have it bad."

Her shoulders drooped again. "I know."

"I shouldn't tell you this; it will only encourage you. But I hate to see you mope." Lucia sighed. "If it makes you feel any better, he has asked me how to get back into your good graces."

"Really?" That sounded at least somewhat promising. And he *had* left gifts. Geez, she was sounding pathetic. "What did you tell him?"

"To go to hell."

Sighing, Nicki rolled her eyes. "Great."

"I may have done you a favor." Lucia crossed her arms across her ample chest. "I think he's hiding something, to be honest."

Nicki frowned. "Hiding something? Like what?"

"I don't know. But I went to his apartment on Tuesday morning early to cuss him out for upsetting you—"

"You didn't!"

"Oh, trust me, I did. He got the message. But while I was there, I got a peek around. No sprucing up the place. I doubt he'd been to the grocery store yet. But he had an apartment full of electronics. Not TVs and stereos, like a normal guy, but a laptop, a BlackBerry, a portable printer, a few CDs, a video camera. He had papers and file folders stacked on kitchen table, and all that equipment was humming. Mind you, it was barely five-thirty in the morning. It just made me wonder what he's up to."

Nicki's frown deepened. Lucia had a good point. What did an exotic dancer need with all those gadgets?

* * *

A few minutes later, the lights in Nicki's office went out. Through the smoked glass, Mark could see that she and Lucia had left the room.

Behind him, Zack switched off the music again and shoved his hands on his hips in a pose that couldn't be interpreted any way except annoyed.

"That's it! I'm talking to Nicki and telling her to fire your ass. I don't even see effort on your part."

Zack was very passionate about the club and the show . . . and maybe, Mark thought, he could use that to his advantage.

"I . . . I'm just distracted."

"Distracted? My grandfather who practically raised me is slowly dying, and my last relationship just ended. Talk about distracted! You don't see me bringing it here."

"You're right." Mark did his best to stroke the other man's ego. "You've got it together. My problem is, my distraction is always here." He glanced up to Nicki's empty office.

"You and the boss lady?"

Mark shrugged. Not for anything would he give away the truth about the extent of his interaction with Nicki. Even if she had deceived him, used her body to distract him. He wasn't the advertising sort of guy when it came to his sex life. Even telling Rafe for the sake of the case had gone against his grain.

"I'd like that, but so far . . . I'm not having a lot of luck. I did something the other day that apparently made her mad, which wasn't my intent. I feel really bad about it."

Well, at the time he hadn't given a shit what Nicki thought. He'd quickly seen the error of his ways, given the fact that being on Nicki's bad side was not helping his case. Her refusal to deal with him now that she apparently didn't need to distract him from her accounting records at the moment also pointed to her guilt. If he didn't have this case to work, he would cut her loose and get her out of his mind. Or do his best, anyway.

Though it was likely an act, he also couldn't get her hurt expression and wide, wet blue eyes out of his head. However, getting back on her nice list was about the case. It had to be.

"And?" Zack prompted.

"I want to make it up to her. What does she like? How can I

make her see me so I can say I'm sorry?" For good effect, Mark added an extra measure of brooding.

"You're not going to be able to wipe away bad performance on the stage by buttering her up." Zack wagged his finger at him.

"I wouldn't try," he assured the stage manager. "The reason she's mad isn't my performance; it was something in a conversation."

One conducted horizontally in her bed in which her amazing body closed around him in a mind-blowing welcome and clung until every dip and curve fit perfectly to him. He could still hear her cries of pleasure in his ears. He'd had the marks from her nails on his back for the last three days. And when he'd had his mouth on her, the taste of her rippling over his tongue . . . so sweet. Addicting. Guilty or not, Mark wanted her again. Given what he knew about her accounting records and the manner in which she'd arranged the first time they'd had sex, partnered with her cold shoulder since and the urgency of his desire even now, Nicki was probably as guilty as sin.

He sure knew how to pick 'em.

"Hmm. Let me think." Zack cocked his head and stared at the cavernous metal rigging above. Suddenly a broad smile split his smallish face. "I'll make you a deal. If you can finish the first half of this routine without stumbling or glowering, and finish it well, I'll help you out."

Mark perked up. Finally, an accomplice. With Zack's help, he could get this case back on track, and while he was finishing his investigation he'd get Nicki out of her clothes and preferably impaled on his cock.

"Really? Great!"

"This isn't a gimmie," Zack warned. "You have to do the routine right."

"Absolutely." Mark nodded. "I'll do my best. I just appreciate the help."

"You help me by learning, and I'll help you with information. Besides, Nicki needs a little diversion. She works too hard, fixates on this place. Getting her mind on something else would do everyone good."

Sporting a big smile, Mark asked, "So where in the routine do you want me to start?"

Zack reached over to the boom box and fiddled with the CD. "From the top. Remember, it better be good."

With a nod, Mark got into position upstage. Gritting his teeth, he waited for the music so he could start counting the beats, like Mario, his instructor in New York, had taught him.

He hated this. Really. Was their anything worse than embarrassing oneself in public like this? He just loathed practicing all this strutting on the stage, knowing that, unless he finished this case fast, he would be doing it in front of total strangers wearing less than the average pair of underwear real soon. He was going to look like a football player in butt floss. Rafe would surely laugh his ass off if he could see. Not a comforting thought.

On the other hand, he needed Zack's help pronto. Which meant he had to show that he was, in fact, capable of performing the routine.

Damn!

The pulsing music began, filling the air with a deep, sexy beat that seemed somehow ancient and modern at once, in keeping with his Viking theme. Mark began counting the beats until his cue arrived. At the appropriate throb in the music, he strutted downstage, doing his best impression of a cross between a gigolo and a runway model, the one that always made him sure he was going to lose his lunch. Cursing under his breath, he stopped, shook his ass in a manner that would surely do a pro cheerleader proud, then glanced over his shoulder with a wink. Not directed at Zack, thank you. He wasn't going to flirt with a gay man who was already clapping and whistling.

With another pivot, Mark threw off his horned helmet. Too bad he couldn't seem to dent the damn thing. He'd already tried breaking the horns off. No luck.

Next, the shirt came off with a quick tear of Velcro. He got appropriately down and dirty with the makeshift costume, his original still missing, thank God. If all went according to plan, it would stay that way. Finally, he finished up the sequence after a few more turns, facial expressions that made him want to plow Zack's face with his fist for dreaming up this crap, then the ripping off of his pants. A few hip thrusts later, which truly made him wonder if he could perform this in public, and he was done.

Zack jumped up and down, clapping like a little kid who'd received his favorite present for Christmas.

"You did it! And that was stunning. Positively yummy! I had no idea you really knew the routine and could move like . . ." Suddenly, he frowned. "Hey, wait. You could do it all along!"

Busted. Getting back into Nicki's good graces was worth it—barely, but it was.

Mark merely answered Zack's accusations with a smile.

"Lucy, you got some 'splainin' to do!" He wagged his finger in Mark's face.

He shrugged. "I didn't have the right incentive before."

Zack glared at him, but Mark could tell that, deep down he was amused. Finally, a conspiratorial smile crossed his face. "Oh, you are a devil. Nicki won't know what hit her. Sweep her off her feet!"

Too bad sweeping her off her feet just might mean carrying her off to prison. That is, if she was as guilty as she appeared to be. Instead, he just nodded. "That's the plan. Now, tell me everything I want to know . . ."

Chapter Eight

IT was a damn long day. After reams of tedious paperwork, a visit to her masochistic aerobics instructor's class, a flat tire, errands all over town, and an unwelcome message from Uncle Pietro, saying he'd be in town over the upcoming Memorial Day weekend, the last thing Nicki expected as she walked toward her apartment door was to be abducted.

Carrying a fast-food salad with low-fat dressing and a wedge of chocolate cake for comfort, she dragged her way up the stairs, judiciously avoiding looking at Mark's door—wondering what he was doing and why he'd gotten so angry with her and if she should try to talk to him about his abrupt departure from her bedroom—and walked across the landing toward her apartment.

Out of nowhere, an arm curled around her waist and dragged her back against a big body, holding her so tightly she couldn't turn and fight. Panic flamed in her blood. It flared higher the instant she struggled and realized she was trapped. The man grabbed the fast-food bag from her hand and dropped it to the floor. Then he raised his palm to cover her eyes, plunging the corridor that was drenched in early evening sunlight into darkness. Her heart crashed against her chest.

Oh, God!

Refusing to panic, Nicki tried to remember her self-defense training, reinforced by an occasional watching of *Miss Congeniality*. He anticipated an elbow to the stomach, and she encountered only air when she thrust hers back. Next, she went for his instep, lifting her leg to stomp down as hard as she could on his foot. But he predicted that move, too, and managed to move out of her way. With her back against his hard chest, she had no way of reaching his nose or groin. Frantic now, she tried a head butt, but only managed to bang the back of her head against a muscled pectoral.

Now what? She wasn't willing to be some psycho's entertainment for the evening.

Then his scent hit her. Musky. A pine forest, earth, and man thrown together with a hint of spice. Definitely male. Definitely familiar.

Mark. *Oh, no!*

"You scared me to death! Why didn't you tell me it was you?"

"Because I knew you would figure it out and you wouldn't struggle any less if I told you."

Bastard! As she continued to wriggle against him, straining for freedom, Nicki felt his erection at the small of her back, the one that had haunted her lonely nights lately with remembrances drenched in devastating pleasure. She thrashed and squirmed . . . until she realized he was only getting harder, bigger.

"You're exciting the hell out of me, baby. Is that what you intended by wiggling all over my cock?" He growled in her ear.

No. Well, maybe. It would serve him right. The man was confusion on legs. "Let go, damn it! You work for me—"

"Not until seven o'clock, I don't."

With that, he lifted her from the floor, turning her so he could sling her over one of his linebacker shoulders. He palmed her bare thigh beneath her miniskirt, which suddenly felt way too small for this occasion. His hand crept up, dangerously close to her ass. That, combined with her gripping the stunning muscles of his back as she looked for a way down, only made her blood begin to heat and her panties a bit more damp than they should be.

"Don't be a Neanderthal!"

That remark merely earned her another grunt as he walked three steps, slammed a door, and set her on her feet in front of him.

Nicki nearly fainted. Mark looked enormous in the small, low-ceilinged foyer of his apartment. In a body-hugging black T-shirt that emphasized the green of his eyes, which drew her gaze like a beacon, he hovered over her with shuttered eyes and an expression she couldn't quite read. Something about it, about him, made her retreat a step.

Her back hit the wall.

"I'll stop being a Neanderthal, if you stop being a preschooler," he murmured, his low voice vibrating inside her.

She loved the sound of that voice, rich and smooth, like chocolate over good sex. In fact, she loved it so much, it took her a minute to process his actual words.

"A preschooler? What the hell does that mean? You're the one who stormed out—"

"I did. I know it. And I've spent four days trying to apologize. The preschooler part came when you refused to listen, ignored my messages and peace offerings, ducked out of any room I entered, and watched my practice from the safety of your little second-floor perch."

He'd known she was there? Oops . . . "I wasn't interested in hearing your apology."

"You were afraid to talk to me. Either way, it's childish."

Tired of looking up at him, Nicki put her hands on her hips and rose to her tiptoes. Even so, she couldn't compete with Mark's towering height.

"I resent that."

"I resent being ignored when I'm trying to tell you that I know I fucked up. I really am sorry. Can't you just hear what I have to say?"

She hesitated, her mind turning his request over. Sighing, she glanced up into his hazel eyes, fringed by thick, dark lashes. Just gorgeous. But she wasn't a sucker. She didn't cave in just because someone had their feelings hurt. She did, however, try to be reasonable.

Besides, she was curious.

"Fine. You've got three minutes. I'll listen. I don't think it matters, but whatever."

"Back to being Commando Bitch, huh?"

"Why are you making this about me, when it's your lousy behavior we're supposed to be discussing?"

Mark shrugged, then leaned in, anchoring one massive palm on the wall next to her head. "Because we can't get there until your attitude improves, and your cinnamony scent is driving me out of my mind."

Seriously? Another glance into those mysterious eyes of his revealed banked lust, a hint of teasing, of promise.

The look told her without a word that if she didn't get some space between them fast, Mark would do everything in his power to get her naked and on her back. And she'd likely comply, given the fact that her determination that their one-night stand had reached its expiration date was getting shaky. His expression was slow-cooking her, and without distance, she'd soon agree with his ideas and sort out everything else later. Much later.

Nicki ducked under his arm and shimmied away from the wall, heading for the relatively open space of the living room.

A glance back at the breakfast nook proved that the computer equipment Lucia mentioned Mark having was nowhere in sight. But it did point her nose in the direction of the kitchen and make her aware of the heavenly smell of Italian food, ripe with oregano and hot sausage.

She also saw that Mark was bearing down on her fast.

"Damn it, Nicki."

"You've got two minutes left, and you're wasting your time."

Cursing, he shoved his hands into the pockets of his jeans. "Fine, you get the Cliff's Notes version. I freaked. Okay?"

"Freaked?"

Mark sighed. "Being with you was . . . mind-blowing. It was beyond sex. I realized it would be too easy for me to fall for you." He looked down, then away. "I knew you liked the sex, but that doesn't translate to you liking *me*."

"You knew I liked the sex?" Gee, most guys usually asked if it was good.

A little smile tipped up the corner of his mouth. "I guessed so, anyway, since I still have the imprints of your fingernails on my shoulders."

Good point . . . A flush crept up her face, which he was polite enough to ignore.

"Why would you think I wouldn't like you?" she countered. "Contrary to whatever is running through your head, I don't go to bed with guys I don't give a damn about."

Mark nodded, his eyes unreadable . . . "When I stopped and thought about how sex had been between us, about you in general, I figured you weren't the kind of woman to just nail anyone. I knew I'd screwed up royally and started trying to apologize the next morning. In fact, I didn't sleep that night at all, I felt so damn stupid."

Well, that made her feel better, but still didn't answer her question. What had set him off in the first place?

"But I was angry, too. You didn't have any place to be at ten the next morning, did you?" Nicki didn't know what to say, and her silent pause shouted her guilt. "So why tell me you did, unless you wanted me gone? I wasn't in a hurry to go."

Nicki bit her lip. Had she been the culprit? Gosh, in trying to keep things simple between them, maybe she'd done more harm than good. "When you said you wanted to stay, I wasn't sure what you meant."

"So you thought you'd get rid of me first thing in the morning, just to make sure I didn't overstay my welcome?"

"Sort of." Guilt filled her, thick as the smoke in an old casino. "It's just a bad time for me to be distracted. And you're a huge distraction!"

Mark flashed her a dimpled, heart-melting smile. Damn, did the man have to be so yummy all the time?

"My business consumes so much time and energy," Nicki pressed on. "I haven't had a real date with a guy who doesn't work in this building in over two years. I-I enjoyed our night together. It definitely meant something to me." *More than it should.* "I just don't think it's smart to continue this . . . fling."

"Ah. But a one-night stand is okay?"

Nicki winced at the sarcasm that edged his voice. "Is that a problem? I don't remember any exchange of commitments before we hit the sheets."

Why was he angry? Most guys would love a woman who just wanted a night of great sex and then just walked away. Except he'd confessed that he felt like he could fall for her. That made a bevy of tingles take up residence in her belly.

She didn't want to want him, but she still did. And it wasn't just about sex.

His insecurity made no sense. Seriously, why would a guy as gorgeous and great in bed as Mark worry that she wouldn't fall for him? Nicki was uncomfortably aware that Mark could easily— probably too easily—persuade her to allow their one night to melt into many. It seemed surreal that Adonis in a G-string would worry about her not reciprocating. He had to have women coming out his ears. Instead, his being "freaked" seemed like the act of someone who . . .

Wait a minute! She remembered a comment he'd made before she'd hired him that had her rethinking the whole situation.

"Some stupid bitch hurt you."

Mark's gaze zipped to hers. Sharpened. He blinked and stared, clearly surprised that she had figured it out.

Face taut, eyes wary, he nodded.

Apparently, Mark had been the dumpee, rather than the dumper, and he'd "freaked" the other night in her apartment because he'd been hurt before.

"Back in Florida, just before you left, right?"

He nodded again and turned away this time, meandering across the room.

If Nicki had a pair of Elvis's blue suede shoes, she'd bet them that this dumb-ass woman was one of the main reasons Mark had left Florida. She'd love to say that the other woman's loss was her gain, but Nicki wasn't having a relationship with an employee—or anything other than her fledgling business or her vibrator.

Still, she couldn't resist asking, "Want to tell me about it?"

"No."

His soft, swift reply somehow made his point more emphatically than if he'd yelled. He did *not* want to discuss it.

Nicki tried to be mature and understanding. Of course the man didn't want to spill his guts. They weren't dating. In fact, she was trying, however halfheartedly, to end the fling. Mark had only known her for a few weeks. Guys weren't into sharing emotions unless forced. She shouldn't expect otherwise.

But a part of her did. She was expected to happily take a man into her body, even if it was temporary, give of herself, and he didn't have to share anything in return except an erection and a little semen?

"Any chance she's back in your life? Or coming back?"

"No."

Well, that made her feel better . . . and worse. Based on what Mark said and the bit of digging she'd done about him, this relationship had to have ended a year ago, give or take a few weeks. He still wasn't letting anyone near him, at least not more than physically. Nicki knew she should be happy about that. Thrilled, even. Now was not a good time for her to be preoccupied by romance, even if the sex was wonderful.

A loud electronic beep filled the room a few moments later, startling her.

Mark, on the other hand, looked really relieved. *Saved by the bell* . . .

"What was that?"

"Dinner." His voice came out in a low rumble. "It's ready. I made lasagna for you, along with salad and garlic bread. I really want you to stay so I can prove that I didn't mean to insult you."

Lasagna. Her favorite. How had he known? Lucia? No, she wouldn't spit on Mark if he was on fire right now. Blade? The idea was so ludicrous, she nearly laughed. Had to be Zack.

Damn. She didn't want to stay. Trying but not succeeding to mentally relegate him to the onetime-fuck category made her feel spineless, a feeling she just hated. But Mark had gone to the trouble to ferret out her favorite food and—had he made it himself?—so that she wouldn't feel hurt or slighted by the fact he'd shut her out in self-defense, and it only made Nicki want to kill the bitch who'd made him gun shy.

Then she wanted to slap some sense into Mark.

But he wasn't ready to hear it today. It really wasn't her business, anyway. Even if, despite everything logical, she wanted it to be. Still, she knew her stubborn streak too well. She wouldn't keep her feelings about this to herself for long.

"Okay, I'll stay," she assured him. "It smells great. Thanks."

The set of his shoulders visibly relaxed. Gosh, he really didn't want her mad at him. Was he interested in more than one night? If he was, it didn't matter. If he wasn't, that didn't matter, either. But she had no reason or desire to hurt his feelings. He apparently had gone to a good deal of trouble to soothe hers.

Against her will, Nicki was touched.

"If you want to wash up in the bathroom, I'll get everything out," he said into the awkward silence.

Her smile felt stilted, but she flashed it at him anyway. "Beats the hell out of my fast-food salad."

Mark hesitated. "That's what was in your bag?"

"Along with a gooey piece of chocolate cake." She smiled sheepishly.

He turned toward the apartment door, opened it, then returned a few moments later with her bag. "Thanks for bringing dessert!"

Laughing, Nicki headed to the bathroom, realizing that was the first time she'd done more than snarl or cry in days. Lucia had called her surly. Even Blade had been taken aback by her sour attitude. But Mark . . . Fifteen minutes with the man, and suddenly she was wearing a smile, forgetting about the fact she was still short a dancer, still had her finances in a jumble, still worried she wouldn't finish her second year in business successfully. Why did he always manage to cheer her up?

Nicki walked into the bathroom and looked around. He'd done absolutely nothing with the place. White walls, white soap. He hadn't done anything beyond hang a blue plastic shower curtain. No pictures, no candles. He didn't plan to stay, obviously. That fact shouldn't bother her.

But she felt the smile sliding into a flat line. A glance in the mirror reflected her own disappointment. She looked away.

Turning the stainless tap, Nicki ran warm water and washed with the soap gracing the pedestal sink. It was only after she'd rinsed and turned off the taps that she realized he didn't have a towel handy.

Cursing, she turned to the hook on the back of the door. Empty. Spinning the other way, she spotted the little linen closet that was a replica of the one in her bathroom. Hands dripping as she made her way across the room, Nicki opened the accordion-style door and found a towel.

She also found Mark's "missing" Viking costume shoved underneath. She didn't have to be a member of Mensa to know that he'd hidden it on purpose, because the idea of dancing in public made him anxious.

As she stared at the silky black shirt and the thigh-high boots, the ones that made him look like a walking wet dream, Nicki knew she should be furious with his duplicity. Absolutely pissed beyond description.

Instead, a smile curled up the sides of her mouth. Poor guy. He really was afraid.

"Chow is on!" he shouted.

Drying her hands on the little towel, she set it aside, debating what to say to Mark about the costume he'd clearly stashed where he hoped no one would find it. Mentioning it now, as much as she wanted to, wasn't her best plan. They had bigger fish to fry at the moment, and it would likely turn into another confrontation. While that might be great in helping her keep their fling down to a single night and trying to forget the exact feel of him buried deep inside her, she neither needed an unhappy employee nor wanted to hurt a man who'd already been hurt before.

Thoughts racing, Nicki wandered back to the kitchen nook. She wouldn't keep the knowledge to herself long; it wasn't in her nature. In fact, remembering his initial audition for her gave Nicki an idea . . . for later.

Back in the apartment's main area, Mark set a pan of lasagna—homemade, there was no question now—on the table, lit a candle, and turned to her with a wide, sexy smile.

Nicki gulped. Someday, some woman was going to fall madly in love with Mark Gabriel. The kind of love she would never recover from. Nicki was so glad she wasn't that woman.

Mark held out her chair, grabbed a bottle of wine, and sat across from her. The scents of basil and tomatoes wafted in the air. Candlelight glowed between them, as he took her plate and dished up a he-man sized portion of the layered pasta. He treated himself to a helping double that size. A leafy, vegetable-laden salad rested on the table between them. Garlic drowning in butter scented the air around them, wafting from the foil-covered sourdough in the middle of the table.

She took one bite of lasagna . . . and nearly died. Could a woman have an orgasm from sausage, cheese, noodles, and tomato sauce alone?

Lord, Mark had charm, was great in bed, and could cook like a master chef? He was the complete package, and for a moment, Nicki resented Girls' Night Out and what a demanding mistress she was.

"Good?" he asked.

"You don't ask about the sex but you ask about the food?"

He shrugged. "Guess I don't share the usual insecurities of my brethren."

That got a laugh out of her. "Obviously. It's wonderful!"

"Glad to hear it," he said, smiling smugly.

"But there's a problem," she said, unable to resist toying with him and that grin.

"Oh?"

"Did you fail your Neanderthal lessons? Last I heard, you're not supposed to drag a woman back to your cave to feed her. Or is this the modern version?"

"Any Neanderthal worth his salt wants a woman well fed before he has his way with her. If he's doing his job right, she'll need the energy."

Nicki arched a brow. "So the meal is just to butter me up for sex?"

The idea that he'd try to use her taste buds to manipulate her should piss her off, be unappealing, at least. Nope. She liked the idea that Mark wanted her enough to pull out all the stops to impress her, even if feeling that way was on par with walking across a Manhattan street blindfolded.

He took a sip of the heavy red wine, then set his glass aside, his hazel eyes suddenly serious. "No. It really was to apologize. If fringe benefits follow, I wouldn't turn them down. But I have no expectations."

Mark smiled. Dimples creased the sides of his face. Only his slash of a nose and blunt, square jaw saved him from being pretty. Nicki found herself far more interested in the fringe benefits than was wise.

Don't go there! They'd had their one night. Beyond the tumultuous end, it had been amazing, orgasmic, devastating in its pleasure. Nicki didn't think she'd ever been so sated.

But good things weren't meant to last, especially with heartbreakers who would distract her from keeping her business afloat and growing.

"That's probably wise," she said finally, hoping he would drop the matter there.

He didn't.

"You know, I understand why you think continuing to sleep together is a bad idea. I don't like it. But I understand it.

"One of the things that first drew me to you was your independence. You do things your way. I hear you argued with your family over starting this place. You followed your vision, made yourself a success. I'm sure you sacrificed to make it happen, gave up time and money and energy that could have been spent elsewhere."

Their knees bumped under the little table. A jolt of fire screamed its way up her leg, right to where it counted. She nearly choked on the bit of salad in her mouth. Damn it.

"I did use most of my inheritance to open this place. I've also had to do without some autonomy since I took Uncle Pietro on as a thirty-percent owner. And I gave up the rest of the family's approval." She shrugged. "My stepmother is still in shock, I'm afraid. When Lucia told her mother she was coming to spend the summer with me, I got two hours of lecture over the phone about protecting her baby."

Nicki didn't touch his intimation that she'd given up men and dating and hours of sex in order to open the club. Truth be told, it hadn't bothered her much. Until Mark.

Right now, he was bothering the hell out of her. He gave her an itch she really, really wanted to scratch.

"And you started all this at twenty-four. It took guts and intelligence and, if you don't mind me saying, it took balls."

Dangerous pleasure suffused her, both from his words and from the tasty pasta sliding down her throat. He didn't seem to judge her for her choice of business and recognized that it hadn't been easy. Yes, Mark likely had ulterior motives for his pretty speech that involved parting her from her clothes, but she liked the words all the same. At least he knew her better than to try to seduce her by saying she was pretty or had a nice rack.

"I couldn't go from party to party like my mother. I wanted to *do* something. But I'm not like my genius sister. I barely finished high school. After my upbringing, the only thing I could be a professor of was partying. So I used it. I knew people in New York,

Paris, and London. I used the connections to come up with a place I thought would cater to women's fantasies. So, here we are."

"You've done a great job. Not every woman has the vision and the determination to make something like this happen. I love my sister to death, but Kerry would never do this. She's a helper and a pleaser. She'll have her teaching certificate soon, and it will be the perfect job for her."

Nicki heard the love in his voice, and she was envious. Not in the way that she might be jealous of another lover. Instead, she suspected Mark would never share his feelings as completely with anyone else as he did with his beloved sister. Women like Nicki . . . he would fuck her if she let him. He might even respect her determination and independence to a degree and like her a little.

He would never love her.

The sadness that elicited all but drowned out the voice in her head that said it didn't matter. She knew it didn't, not in the long run. But tonight, that fact bothered her for some reason.

"I often wished growing up that I was more like your sister. Forging your own path just tends to piss everyone else off."

Hoping the subject—and the mood—would pass, Nicki drowned her odd sorrow in a swallow of the rich, dry wine and another bite of lasagna. She looked down to find her plate nearly empty.

"I'm sure it does. Do you ever bend?"

"Not easily," she admitted. "I'm stubborn. Growing up, my mother often called me Mule."

"Now I know why I find you such a delicious challenge." He flashed her his million-megawatt grin.

Nicki nearly swallowed her tongue.

"Don't try to tame me or conquer me—or whatever verb it is that runs through a Neanderthal's head."

His knee brushed hers again, and she started, first at the contact. Then at the blaze that zipped right up her leg once more, to deepen the ache between her thighs.

This was not good. Not good at all.

Mark's smile merely widened. "Baby, that's like asking me not to remember you naked and writhing underneath me. Impossible."

"Try to forget. It's not going to happen again."

His hazel eyes sparkled, as if he relished the thought of making her eat her words. Apparently, Mark liked being challenged. Lucky her. Nicki wished she'd known that before she opened her big mouth.

"Whatever you say," he answered in a breezy voice that held just a hint of laughter.

Clearly, he didn't believe she had the willpower to resist him. Unfortunately, Nicki wasn't sure she did, either.

* * *

THE Saturday night crowd over Memorial Day weekend had been a terror. Mark swore he'd never seen so many drunk women under one roof in his life. While that might be a frat boy's fantasy, it had become Mark's nightmare. His feet hurt from waiting tables all night, and his ass hurt from being pinched so much.

But finally, they'd shut the doors to Girls' Night Out.

Now the fun stuff began—cleanup.

Mark began picking up empty cocktail glasses and lipstick-smeared napkins from the tables. Around him, some of the others did the same. One of the dancers, Josh, left immediately after closing, one hand lifted in a halfhearted wave, the other clutching his stomach. Not twenty minutes later, another dancer, Ricky, did the same. Mark had to wonder how much of it was a stomach bug and how much of it had to do with the fact Vegas was one huge party during Memorial Day weekend.

Behind him, Mark heard Nicki enter the main room of the club from the door behind the bar and greet the bartenders. Against his will, he turned to stare. A short red dress hugged the curve of her breasts and hips, lay against her flat belly, dipped low to show downy cleavage. A pair of black heeled sandals graced her feet, complete with laces that wound around her ankles.

A glance—that was all it took for Nicki to have him standing at attention. Damn it.

Prying his eyes away, he wiped off nearby tables and willed his erection away. Why her? Why, even knowing that she'd most likely deceived him, that she'd probably whored herself to assist in a crime, did he want her so bad he clutched a chair in a white-knuckled grip?

There was only one answer: He was a stupid bastard.

All of her chatter at his place last night about putting an end to their night together because he was a distraction? Bullshit. How could he be so desired one minute, then be in the way the next? None of it added up, not her excuse, not her behavior . . . not his insane need to bury himself inside her and pound away until she confessed and swore not to do it again. Until she promised not to lie to him anymore.

Yeah, the lying bothered him most. Mark winced. Her deception actually hurt, if he was entirely honest. For the first time since Tiffany, he'd wanted something besides a female body to help him relieve the tension. He'd wanted Nicki's mind and her laughter. He'd wanted to make her smile.

And she'd probably been playing him.

Moving to another table, Mark cleared away the glasses, then wiped the surface down.

Unable to resist, he snuck another peek at Nicki. And caught her staring. For an instant, their gazes locked, and Mark felt the connection like a punch to the solar plexus. Nicki sucked in a breath, and her gaze skittered away.

Damn, he wished they were alone. It was probably for the best that they weren't. No telling how many milliseconds before his feigned indifference would crumble. He might even set a new world record for undressing and begging.

Several dancers finished putting away their equipment and signed out, waving as they went. Zack ran past.

"My grandfather has fallen—"

"Go," Nicki told him instantly.

Zack squeezed her shoulder in thanks, then left.

Mark shook his head. Not only did she look good, but she clearly wasn't all bad on the inside. He knew she loved her sister. She seemed to care about Zack's issues with his grandfather. Though she ran a tight ship, she did her best to make the people who worked here feel valued—except him.

Maybe he just had a KICK ME sign on his back.

Both of the bartenders locked up and headed out, followed by the waitstaff. Other than Lucia, he and Nicki were alone.

After glaring a dagger or two his way, Nicki's sister said, "I'm off to bed. Lots of research to do tomorrow. I want to wrap up early in case my friend Ashley can visit in a few weeks. You don't mind, do you?"

Before Nicki could say a word, Bocelli breezed in the side door, dressed head to toe in black.

He looked like the *GQ* model of the thug underworld, sporting a hundred dollar haircut, two days' growth on his jaw, and a black leather jacket to ward off the desert wind. And all that money had come from somewhere, starting right between Mark's ex-wife's thighs.

When the asshole spotted Nicki, his strut became a stride as he crossed the room.

Much to Mark's satisfaction, Nicki turned her back to the jackass. Maybe there was trouble in paradise . . .

"Heck, no, I don't mind!" she answered Lucia. "I think it's great that Ashley wants to leave her sheltered existence and visit Sin City. The two of you could do damage," Nicki asserted.

"A history professor and a librarian. Won't we set all the men on fire?"

"What if you do, Doc?" Bocelli drawled. A challenging smile curled up his mouth.

As if she couldn't resist a moment longer, Lucia's gaze slid to the resident Goodfella. Her expression said he both fascinated and scared her. Finally, a frown creased her forehead, and she looked away.

Nicki's face tightened at the exchange. Was she jealous at Blade's subtle flirtation with her sister? The man had to be doing it to piss Nicki off.

Purposefully not looking at Blade, Nicki hugged her sister. "Good night, Lucia."

"You look tired, Nik. Go to bed soon, huh?"

"I will, Mother." She laughed.

Lucia took herself upstairs, leaving behind an awkward silence. For about two seconds.

Then Blade turned and took two aggressive steps forward. "Nicki, I wanna talk to you."

"Not now," Nicki barked before Bocelli even reached her.

"When? Hell will fucking freeze over before I let this go another day. We gotta talk about this, Nicki."

"Not at three in the morning!"

Bocelli grabbed Nicki's arm and tugged her closer.

Mark felt his fist closing around the dishrag he held. The sight of Bocelli's hand on Nicki made Mark's blood pressure soar.

"Ten minutes. Maybe fifteen, tops. You got that much time," Blade challenged.

"I'm tired, and I'm not in the mood to deal with you. Take your hand off of me."

In typical thug fashion, Bocelli ignored her. When he tugged her even closer and towered over her, Mark nearly lost it. If the motherfucker hurt a single hair on her head, Bocelli was going to die painfully.

"You forget who you're talking to. Don't screw with me."

Nicki ripped her arm from his grasp, then flashed him a narrow-eyed glare that impressed Mark with its meanness.

"Ditto that for me, buster. I'm sick and tired of your attitude. You don't own this place, and you don't own me."

Bocelli took a menacing step forward.

Mark had had enough.

He threw down the dishrag and dropped the plastic bin of

glasses on the nearest table. They rattled in the tense air. Both Nicki and Blade both turned to him in surprise.

"You're not going to be alive long enough to worry about this conversation if you don't get the hell away from her," Mark told Bocelli.

"What, are you her fucking bodyguard?"

"I'd like to be the one to teach you some manners."

"Mark—" Nicki pleaded.

Blade cut her off. "Yeah? How? You gonna fight me?"

The Italian thug's insolent pose made Mark gnash his teeth. He crossed the room, grabbed Nicki by the shoulders, and shoved her behind him. Then he glared down at Bocelli. The other guy was only a handful of inches shorter than him, but Mark relished every bit of it.

"I've got a black belt, and I spent six years boxing. Pick your poison or leave her the hell alone."

It occurred to Mark belatedly that he was defending the very woman he'd been cursing just minutes ago. That aside, the fact remained that he hadn't liked bullies on the playground when he'd been a kid, and he didn't like them any better now.

"Mark," Nicki said from behind him, slender fingers latched on to his biceps. "You don't have to do this."

He heard her utter the words, but a quick glance over his shoulder showed her wide blue eyes filled with equal parts fury and fear. She might not need him here, but she wanted him.

"Well, ain't this sweet," drawled Bocelli. "So, Gabriel, what's the price of chivalry these days? A piece of ass? She give you some?"

The urge to taunt Bocelli that he'd had more of Nicki's ass than the son of a bitch ever would leaped to the tip of his tongue. The only problem was, it wasn't true. He swallowed the bitter lump, and Blade smirked, almost as if he knew what was going through Mark's mind.

Fury rose inside him, like an elevator careening to the top floor. As if bursting through a glass ceiling, his control shattered. If someone had told Mark steam was coming out of his ears, he wouldn't have been surprised.

"That's it. I'm going to pound your face."

"Mark!" Nicki screamed and grabbed his right arm.

Fine. He had another arm that worked, which led to a fist itching to plow Bocelli's smug smirk.

His left hook connected with Bocelli's jaw. Satisfaction poured through Mark when the asshole's head snapped back and he staggered. Mark wrenched his right arm from Nicki's grasp and followed with a fist to Blade's stomach.

He set up to punch the thug in the nose when Bocelli retreated and flung back one side of his jacket. He withdrew a stainless semi-automatic from his shoulder holster and pointed it right in Mark's face.

Chapter Nine

CONTEMPT dominated Blade's expression. "You better watch yourself, dancer boy."

Holy shit, would Bocelli really mow him down with bullets here and now? Mark's heart pounded like a jackhammer. Nicki was so close and could easily be hurt. That thought made his blood ice over.

Nicki gasped, and before Mark could tell her to take cover, she jumped in front of him.

"Get out of here!" Mark grabbed her and tried to shove her aside.

She wasn't having any of it.

Nicki jerked away from his hold and glared at Blade. He had to admire her courage—even if it was stupid as hell.

"Put the damn gun down!" she snarled at Bocelli. "What is the matter with you? I told you I didn't want you carrying that thing around here. You want to talk? I'll talk to you tomorrow."

Blade slid a rude stare from Nicki to Mark and back again. He tucked the gun back in its holster and grumbled, "Fine. Neither one of you is worth having to clean up the blood and make excuses for doing everyone a favor."

With that, Bocelli stomped past them, disappeared up the stairs, slamming the door behind the bar in his wake.

Cold fear and even colder fury deflated from Mark faster than an overstuffed balloon stabbed with an ice pick.

"Thank God," Nicki whispered, one hand raising to clutch his forearm for support. "He scared the hell out of me."

She trembled. Mark felt her as that one hand clung to him. Shoving aside his questions, he pulled her against him and folded her into his arms. "You okay?"

"Yeah." She eased back and looked up into his eyes. "That's twice now that you've come to my rescue. Confronting Blade like that was so dangerous! You scared me to death."

"Likewise, baby. Why the hell are you jumping in front of him when he's got a gun?"

"He isn't going to hurt me," she assured him.

Privately, Mark disagreed. Tonight put a whole different spin on Nicki's relationship with Bocelli. Was the asshole abusive? And did she put up with it? Or could it all be part of the act?

"Nicki, why are you going to give him the time of day after he threatened you?"

She sighed and stepped out of his arms. "I have to."

"You don't have to do anything with him you don't want to. Like you said, he doesn't own this place, and he doesn't own you."

"It's more complicated than that."

Mark gritted his teeth. Complicated how? Did she think she was in love with the guy? Why else would she would put up with his threats and bad behavior—and allow her club to be used to launder Mafia money? Was that how she'd gotten involved?

Nicki in love with someone else . . . The thought was more painful than serrated knives carving into his gut. Which made no sense. Mark had no claim on the woman. But he couldn't lie and say he didn't want to kiss her, taste her, plunge deep inside her until she acknowledged otherwise.

The realization sucked the air from his chest, leaving him gaping, blown away.

What a stupid ass. The last thing he needed was a woman as any sort of fixture in his life, especially one like Nicki. He had a case to complete—and she was a suspect.

What a fucking nightmare.

Maybe she just didn't see a way out of Bocelli's clutches. Maybe if someone showed her an exit, she'd take it.

"It doesn't have to be complicated." He grasped her shoulders. "I can help you."

Nicki stood on tiptoes and laid a soft kiss on his cheek. "My hero."

The feel of her mouth on his skin jolted Mark with both lust and frustration. "Nicki—"

"Let's not talk about Blade, okay? I have something else I want to ask you about."

Mark let the subject of Bocelli drop—for now. They weren't nearly done talking about this. But getting back in Nicki's good graces had to be his top priority, and arguing with her wasn't the way to get there. If he could win her trust, convince her to let him help her, maybe he could get her out of this mess she'd dug herself into . . . provided she actually wanted out.

"Ask away," he said finally.

"So, the other night when you invited me to dinner, which was wonderful, by the way, I went looking for a hand towel and found your Viking costume."

Shit! He'd forgotten he'd stashed it there. Luckily for him, she didn't look angry as much as she looked amused. Evidently, she enjoyed the thought that she'd foiled him all by her little, clever self.

"You caught me." He shrugged and smiled.

"And then, Zack informed me just today that you actually can perform the routines. That you know them, haven't really developed the grace of an elephant on roller skates since I hired you, and can shake, wink, and gyrate with the best of them. How do you plead to that?"

Damn Zack! Mark had half a mind to strangle the blabber-mouth the next time he came through the door.

Wincing, Mark said, "Guilty."

"So I'm guessing the issue is stage fright. Am I right?"

This he didn't have to lie about in the least. "Kind of. I'd never been in a male strip joint. It's different than guys watching a woman take it off. Touching there is discouraged, other than slipping tips in a G-string. More than that can get you tossed out on your ass. Here . . . there's a lot of touching. And kissing. I didn't expect that. I didn't expect the leering, the clapping, the suggestive comments, and propositions."

Nicki burst out laughing. "Did you think we sat and watched in silence, legs crossed like perfect ladies, and hands folded in our laps?"

"No, but I expected something more restrained than women trying to cop a cheap feel and asking how many inches a guy has."

"You've got something against a woman who knows what she likes and goes after it?" Her gaze challenged him.

"I like assertive women . . . just not five hundred in the same room, most of whom have had too many kamikazes and wine spritzers. After that, they start demanding their screaming orgasms—and not the kind they pay the bartender seven-fifty for. The decibel level in here starts at earsplitting and only gets worse."

"It is loud," she conceded with a smile. "But I don't think that's what's stopping you from performing the job I hired you to do, nor do I recall you having a specific problem with screaming orgasms. So spill it. I want the truth."

Mark hesitated. He couldn't exactly tell her that he hadn't wanted to do this job in the first place. It had been a way to buy time and proximity to pry into her accounting records. To his frustration, nothing had happened recently with the accounts. Less than zero. If it took weeks before Blade and Nicki made another move, he'd be forced onto the stage. Probably sooner rather than later.

"If you can't tell me," she said, "I can't help you. And I'll have to let you go."

Her clear blue-sky eyes said to Mark that was the last thing she wanted. She all but begged him to give her something so she could help him. Keep him.

That expression really begged the question, why did she want to have him around if she felt the need to distract him with sex so she and her lover could commit a crime? Maybe Nicki was innocent. It was possible. Mark didn't have a solid answer. Or hard evidence. Until he did, she was a suspect. Period. He couldn't let his guard down until he had proof one way or the other.

But now, he had to respond to her—fast. The only thing he could think of was the truth.

"I don't like crowds. I really don't like being the center of attention. It's . . . embarrassing to know so many total strangers are looking at you."

"You mean when you're taking your clothes off?"

"Even if they were watching me do nothing. It's the crowd and the staring. It just makes me freeze."

"Hmm. Most guys who come to work here love the attention. This is a new one for me." Nicki blinked and cocked her head to one side, as if in thought. "What if you weren't dancing onstage alone?"

"Maybe it would be easier. I could at least tell myself the crowd had something else to focus on."

A mischievous smile crossed Nicki's face. *Uh-oh.* She grabbed his hand before he could protest.

Climbing up on the stage, a dicey proposition in a very short skirt, Mark followed, guided by the tug of her hand on his and the amazing view of red silk inching up her thighs.

"I have an idea," she announced, then released his hand to cross the stage.

She sorted through a nearby box of CDs, then held up one in triumph and slid it into the portable player. The already dim lights played on the inky hair that hung in a sleek, glossy fall nearly to her elbows.

In his chest, Mark's heart started doing the samba against his ribs.

Nicki DiStefano was the full package: gorgeous, smart, determined, assertive, unique.

And very possibly involved in the planning and execution of a felony. He couldn't forget that.

A soft jazz tune filled the air, lilting over him in a smooth, suggestive rhythm. Rich with sax and piano and a faint tinkling of bells in the background, this was music meant to seduce.

"Dance with me." She held out her hand, eyes beckoning.

"Now?"

She nodded. "We're going to dance together on this stage, so that every time you stand up here, you can picture dancing up here with someone else. With me."

Mark took hold of Nicki's hands, more because he couldn't resist the opportunity to touch her than because he believed she could cure him of stage fright in a night or less. But her attempt to do so confused him. Why was she trying to help him, especially if he was just in her way while she was trying to commit a crime? Why not just fire him and hire someone oblivious?

The questions evaporated when Nicki stepped into the circle of his arms, one hand on his biceps, the other held up as if waiting for his hand. Close but not too close. Mark ignored her invitation and took more. He erased the space between them immediately by gathering her against his chest and winding his arms around her waist. He hadn't thought it possible, but he got harder—again.

Cinnamon and citrus blended together to tantalize him with memories, fantasies of what they could have together if he didn't believe in upholding the law . . . and he knew for sure that she wasn't trying to break it.

At the moment, he almost didn't care—almost. Her laughter, intelligence, and sass drew him like metal to a magnet. Memories of her tight flesh closing around him, sucking him back in with every thrust, pervaded his memory. The way she'd looked the instant before she'd exploded around his cock, blue eyes wild and blurred, cheeks pink, throat arched and bared for him. Her expres-

sion in the first few seconds afterward, soft and sated and worship-
ping.

You can have that again, have her again, whispered the devil in
his head.

"Obviously, I'm not alone up here." He sidled closer still, molding them chest to chest, belly to belly. He had no doubt she felt him—
every inch of him. "Being alone doesn't make me the human
equivalent of steel pike."

Nicki tsked at him. But she also wriggled closer, brushing her
center right against his throbbing erection, as if testing the waters,
before backing away.

"This isn't about your penis; it's about your stage fright."

"Right now, with you this close, I don't know that I can concentrate on anything but how you make me feel—and the way my
penis and I would like to make you feel."

Mark felt her smile against his chest. "Then let me go and focus!"

He'd give her focus . . . He notched his cock right against her,
where she could feel the heat and need for herself. God knew he
could barely think about anything else.

He whispered in her ear, "I get within five feet of you, and logic
goes out the window. Your smell alone drives me beyond rational
thought. When I get my hands on you . . ." He slid one of his palms
down the smooth line of her back, all the way to her ass. Curving
one broad palm around her cheek, he lifted her against his cock,
resisting the urge to hiss at the contact. "Any brains I have give way
to sheer need."

At the feel of her against him, lust streaked through him like
an addiction. She wasn't immune, either, based on the way she
wriggled against him, her breathing hitched.

He'd uttered the words so that Nicki would let him back into her
life. Too bad every syllable was true—and then some. He didn't just
want to touch her; naturally it couldn't be that simple. He wanted
the *right* to touch her.

He wanted to possess.

"Mark . . ." she warned, her voice satisfyingly breathy. "Let me go and dance next to me. You need to concentrate on dancing on-stage, feeling the rhythm—"

"The only rhythm I want to feel is the one we make together as I'm pounding deep inside you, baby."

Nicki trembled. Mark smiled in wicked satisfaction as he felt a shiver stir her small frame. At least he wasn't feeling this fever alone.

"Sex is not the point of this exercise." She tried to steer him back on course. It might have worked if her thin voice hadn't sounded as if she'd just run a marathon.

Lifting his free hand from her mid-back up to wind around her neck, Mark stared down at Nicki, gratified to see her pulse pounding at her neck as solidly as the beat of a hip-hop dance song.

The previous night all through dinner, Mark had looked across the table at Nicki's exotic, flushed face and fought a terrible urge to clear the table with one swipe of his arm, prop her on it, and feast on her instead. But he'd managed to hold out. Somehow.

Tonight, with their proximity and his restraint pushed to the limit, there was no resisting. He wanted. Period.

Nicki molded around him, yielding, soft. Her nipples poked his chest, as if daring him to touch them. He could feel the heat from her body all over his cock. And her expression, yearning, wary, was delicious.

She wanted, too. But she was fighting it.

"One dance," she whispered. "Please."

At times like this, he wished he was the kind of heartless bas-tard who could just seduce a woman without regard for her wants and feelings. Life would be simpler, anyway. But he wasn't built like that.

Everything below his waist protested when he eased some space between them. He wasn't about to release her, so he simply held her close, swaying to the music, until the first song ended. Another began with a flare of violins.

"Thank you," she murmured, trying to push discreetly at his chest.

"You're welcome." He ignored her attempt to put distance between them.

"When you're up onstage," she whispered, her lips a breath away from his neck, "don't think about the audience as a whole. Think about being somewhere else. Or being alone in the club. Or focus on whatever you were thinking about when you auditioned for me. That was perfect."

"Dancing for you was easy. You looked at me like a starving woman cases a buffet."

"You made me feel hungry for you," she confessed. "Whatever you did that day, it was like magic. Can you do it again?"

"Maybe. If you're in the audience, watching, it might work."

"I will be. I promise."

"That day I auditioned for you, I imagined getting my hands on your body, giving you pleasure."

Nicki sucked in a breath. "Mark . . ."

"I still imagine it every time I see you."

She didn't respond for a long minute. The music cascaded around them, lilting, a caress to the eardrums, a soft seduction. The dim golden lights beamed a spot on the stage to Mark's left, leaving him in shadow with a warm, cinnamon-scented woman in his arms.

The way she pumped his libido up with a steady stream of lust wasn't smart. It made no sense, how badly he wanted to taste Nicki. To claim her. But Mark couldn't wait another second.

Cradling the back of her neck in his hand, he tilted her face to the perfect angle and stared down at her. Her red lips parted, her breathing grew shallow. Reading her breathless anticipation only made his gut tighten again, his erection that much harder.

Damn it, why this woman?

He stopped cursing, stopped questioning, when he slanted his lips over hers. He didn't ask for entrance or cajole. No patience. He simply took full possession of her mouth. Nicki opened for him without hesitation. Her fingers clawed their way up his shoulders.

She stood on the tips of her toes to press her lips into the kiss. And she moaned. God, the sound was like heaven as it sang down his spine, and then directly into his cock.

A haze of lust fogged his mind. He had to have her. Now. No more waiting, no more wondering why she scorched him like a desert brushfire blazing a hundred thousand acres.

It just was—and he was done questioning it.

His hand at the back of her neck found the zipper to her sexy red dress on the first feel. As he guided it down the length of her narrow back, the metallic glide accompanied the music.

Nicki stiffened. "Mark . . ."

He answered by capturing her mouth again and sliding his hands to the clasp of her bra. As he nibbled on her lower lip, he swept into her mouth with a melting kiss meant to drown her in the lust he felt. Mark swept away the top half of her dress with insistent fingers until it pooled around her hips, ready to come off with one tiny tug. Her bra followed, and he dropped it to the ground as he broke the kiss to fasten his hungry gaze to her nipples. Rosy nipples. Hard, swollen nipples.

An instant before he leaned down to seize one with his mouth, Nicki raised her hands and covered her breasts. She did a really lousy job, though. Her palms barely covered the essentials. Lots of pale, rounded flesh beckoned him between her fingers. God, he'd love to have a picture of this. Arousal itched just under his skin, distracting him from everything except scratching it. The only thing sexier would be to watch her stroke herself.

In fact, the idea made Mark smile. He moved that to the top of his priority list.

Nicki retreated a step. "Mark, this isn't a good idea."

He snapped his gaze up to her face. She said the words, all right, but her voice, breathy and uneven, along with her dilating blue eyes, told him it was her head objecting. Her body wanted him just as bad as he wanted her. Until she stopped lying, he wasn't listening.

"Put your hands down."

"I think we should talk. What if Blade—"

"I don't give a shit about Bocelli. This is between you and me. Put your hands down before I tie them down," he growled.

She blinked, hesitated. But her chest rose and fell with a shaky breath, then another. Her lips parted, flushed and moist. Her hands began to tremble. Arousal had to be creaming her slit, because he smelled her in the air between them. It nearly brought him to his knees.

Oh yeah, the rational part of her was fighting it. Too bad that part of her wasn't going to win. Even without his seduction, Mark sensed her lust growing faster than she could fight it off.

"Now, Nicki."

Mark was relishing the thought of making good on his threat to tie her down when she slowly lowered her hands, exposing the hard peaks of her nipples and the gentle slopes of her breasts to his greedy gaze.

"Good girl. Now take the rest off—dress, panties."

She closed her eyes. "Nothing good can come from this."

No doubt, she was right. After all, Nicki was a suspect.

But with every word, every scrap of resistance, she tested the unraveling thread of his patience. He'd never found himself so hungry, so demanding of a woman, felt such a deep need to have her full cooperation in her own surrender. Something about Nicki . . . She had to submit utterly; he wouldn't accept anything less.

"Orgasms aren't tragic." His voice sounded like something rubbed raw with sandpaper. "Don't lie to me. Don't lie to yourself. Do you want me?"

Nicki hesitated, bit her lip. "Yes," she finally whispered.

"Then take everything off."

Biting her lip, Nicki opened her eyes on a sigh. But the truth now darkened her upturned blue eyes. She did want him and she accepted that fact.

Mark's heart pounded like a hundred horses circling the track at the Kentucky Derby as Nicki raised her hands to the dress about her hips, wriggled once, twice, then let go. She stood before him wearing nothing but black, wraparound stilettos.

A surge of lust had his hands clenching into fists. Desire burned his blood. He never remembered feeling anything as strong as the demand pounding at his body, the ache pooling in his cock, the need to have her open to him, accepting him, taking everything he could give.

"Are you wet?" As if he didn't know the answer. Still, he asked in slow, controlled tones, fighting off the urge to rip his clothes off and fuck her until he didn't know his own name.

"Yes." She swallowed.

"Prove it."

Nicki's gaze clung to his—wide, uncertain, confused. Then she looked down, past her flat stomach, all the way to her pussy, and hesitated. Her gaze, now shimmering with heat, climbed up his body, to his waiting stare.

Taking a deep breath, Nicki covered her dark, shadowed mound with her hand, fingers sinking slowly between her slick, pouting lips. As he watched, Mark felt a jolt of lust as potent as a live wire.

She spread her legs slightly, brushed her clit with her fingertips.

"Deeper," he urged. "Get inside."

For once, she did as he asked without pause. Her fingers sank deep, and a moan slipped from her parted lips. Then she eased them out to toy with her clit again, rubbing in small, whispering circles until her eyes slid shut and she arched her neck on another moan.

God, she looked hot, wanton—a woman seeking her own pleasure, baring it to him. It enticed the hell out of him, made his erection swell yet again against his leather pants. She likely knew she affected him, and he didn't care. At the moment, he was her adoring audience of one.

Her moans shortened to panting mewls. Her fingers swept over the swollen bud of her clit more rapidly. With her free hand, she grasped one breast and pinched her nipple.

Desire surged through him, trapping the breath in his chest, stopping his heart.

Damn, a man could only take so much teasing. Mark had always enjoyed spectator sports, but when given a choice, he'd rather be a player. This was no exception.

"That's enough."

Nicki's eyes fluttered open. The lost-in-pleasure haze in her eyes was like a Bruce Lee kick to the gut, potent, disarming.

"But . . ."

"You still haven't proven to me that you're wet."

Squeezing her thighs together, Nicki winced. "I'm so close . . ."

"Tonight, any orgasm you have comes from me."

Her fingers started moving again. Oh, it was subtle . . . but Mark wasn't blind.

"It's my body. If I want an orgasm—"

"You'll let me give it to you." He grabbed her wrist and pulled her hand away from the wet flesh he couldn't wait to explore, to possess.

"Damn you!"

"Prove it to me, Nicki."

Swallowing, she jerked her wrist from his grasp and held up her fingers. Glossy and thick, her juices coated her skin and all but dripped to her palm. Mark smiled in savage satisfaction.

"Very nice. Feed them to me."

Time seemed to slow to a crawl as she led her fingers to his waiting mouth. Still she trembled, watching with wide, dilated eyes.

Nicki reached him finally, and he opened his mouth to her approaching fingers. Her spice dripped onto his tongue, along with the taste of her skin and her trembling want. The combination exploded in his mouth. He sucked hard, drawing her in farther, tracing the crease between her fingers with the tip of his tongue. She closed her eyes and let loose a delicious moan. Oh yeah, she was ready for anything he gave her.

And he was burning to give her everything he could.

Taking hold of her wrist, he guided her arm around his neck and drew her flush against him. At the feel of her, naked and eager against him, everything inside him gave way. Restraint—gone. Patience—vanished. The only thing left was this woman and his insane need to have her as completely as he could.

Mark took hold of her chin with his free hand and forced her gaze right into his eyes. "If you don't leave now, I'm going to get inside you, Nicki. Deep inside, where you cling to my cock. I'm going to stay there, hammering at you, until you don't care that you can't breathe, and you'll use your last bit of air to scream my name."

Nicki's eyes widened, darkened. Mark swore he could see the endless ocean under moonlight swimming in her face. He wanted to drown.

She didn't move a muscle except to say, "Yes. Now!"

Her raspy whisper flared over his skin with the intensity of a third-degree burn.

Frantic, wild-eyed, Mark scanned the stage, looking for any place to spread Nicki out and lay her down beneath him.

Nothing but a dusty black floor and a flimsy chest of props likely to give her splinters on her ass. Besides, he wanted her alone, where no one could find them and interrupt, especially with a blare of loud, taunting music.

Growling, he lifted her against him and fused their mouths together. He found his way offstage, blindly stomping through the club, to the door leading to the upstairs apartments.

"Wrap your legs around me," he demanded.

She complied instantly. Gratified with her response, he fisted his fingers into the sleek waterfall of her hair and tugged. Angling his mouth over hers, he thrust his way inside to taste the addictive honey of her kiss. Her moan vibrated deep inside him, rasping against his urgency to get inside her again and make certain she knew he would send her clawing over the edge of restraint.

Barely aware of his ascent, Mark climbed the stairs, Nicki's sweet mouth submitting to his, her bare ass cradled in his hand. With every step, her oh-so-wet pussy rubbed against him, right where it counted—right where he could barely tolerate another moment outside her wet, silk walls.

Mark resisted the urge to kick his door in. Instead, he slid her down to her tiptoes, pressing her against his door, while he fished out his keys with one hand and stroked his thumb over her nipples with the other.

Nicki clung to him, her lips nibbling their way down his neck, to the sensitive seam of his shoulder. As she lifted one leg over his hip again and gyrated against his nearly exploding cock, he jammed the key in the door, shivered as she nipped at his lobe, and wondered if he could get her on her back and put a condom on in three seconds or less.

"Hurry," she pleaded in between raw, panting breaths.

In a flash of movement, he wrenched the key in the lock, shoved the door open, and slammed it behind him. Nicki only took that as a sign to lift her other leg over his other hip and make sure in her own way that he didn't divert his attention elsewhere.

As if there was any chance of that.

He swore his vision was nothing but a passion-hazed red as he cupped her ass, devoured her mouth, and carried her into his apartment all but impaled on his cock.

His round kitchen table was the first smooth, flat surface he found. He laid Nicki down on its spotless Formica top. She hissed at the chill on her back and arched up to him like an offering.

Mark had every intent of receiving.

Throat tight, he fished a condom from his pocket and yanked his pants down to his hips. Fingers fumbling in haste, he thrust the condom on his engorged cock, gathered Nicki's slender thighs wide into the crooks of his elbows and drove his way home.

She parted around him like melting butter, hot, pliable. Mark sank deep, fingers pressing into her hips as he pushed his way inside, deeper, deeper, until he was in to the hilt. Nicki's walls quivered around his cock, and pleasure gushed over him, so utterly complete. God, he'd never known its equal.

Nicki lifted her hips to him with a whimper. "Mark!"

He couldn't wait, had no control. Instead, he gave her everything he had in long, frantic strokes. Hell, she was so damn tight, every push in rasped with the wet, velvet friction. It teased his cock and had him tensing to hold back.

No, damn it. Not that quickly. Not that easily. He might not have Nicki all to himself, but before tonight was over, she was going to know that he understood the secrets of her body and could give her pleasure like no one else could.

She was not going to simply fuck him and forget him.

Drawing in a deep breath, he stilled, pushing out the insistent feel of his throbbing cock, and focused on finding his calm, his center.

He found only a modicum of control before Nicki wriggled her hips. Ecstasy careened through his body, made him grit this teeth. She responded by grabbing his wrists and dragging his hands over her breasts.

"Now!" she demanded with a wild-eyed growl as a flush spread across her neck and shoulders.

Refusing her was impossible.

A quick pinch of her nipples had her gasping. Then he unleashed his lust. With punishing strokes, one after the other, he impaled her. The head of his cock rubbed her G-spot, dragged up her entire channel to nudge the mouth of her womb with every thrust. Her nails dug into his biceps. She swelled around him, clamping down on him even more, and she closed her eyes against the sheer ferocity of the sensation. Mark fought not to lose his mind, too.

"Look at me, damn it!" he demanded.

Her eyes flew open, blue gaze connecting with his, locking.

Pushing into her again, he growled, "Don't look away."

Nicki did as he demanded and watched as he lifted his hand from her breast, licked his thumb, settled it right over her distended clit, and circled. Her eyes widened as if in distress as the blue darkened to endless pools of need.

Three strokes later, she exploded with a guttural shout of primal pleasure, as her silken slit milked him. But it was her expression that pushed him dangerously to the edge of his restraint, so focused and yearning, as if he was the only man in the world who'd ever made her feel this way.

God, he'd love that to be true.

Rededicating his efforts, Mark rubbed at her clit again. The harsh strokes of his cock abraded her swollen, slick channel. In seconds, Nicki rewarded him by squeezing him even tighter inside her. The quivers became pulses, hard and constricting as she released again and screamed his name until her voice cracked and she ran out of air.

And still she looked at him, as if he alone could undo her and remake her like this. As if he alone could save her.

As if she loved him.

Mark's restraint broke into a million pieces. The tingles brewing at the base of his spine detonated through his body, rushing pleasure and the thick honey of satisfaction through his blood.

He leaned over her, shoving his arms under Nicki's slender back and lifting her against him, fusing them together. Gasping for breath, he babbled hoarse words beyond his own comprehension and pumped everything he had into her during an endless climax that left him dizzy and spent and somehow raw inside.

Slowly, he came to a stop. Only their harsh breathing punctuated the silence. And still he couldn't look away from her eyes, now so warm and blue, like the sky on a perfect summer day. Mark wanted to stay and bask here, pretend nothing else mattered or existed.

Duty warred with the feelings pressing at his chest. The conflict felt like a thousand-pound weight sitting on his ribs. Why? She was just a woman he'd shared the sheets with. Now, it was over.

He ignored the voice in his head reminding him that, since his divorce, he'd never been inside any one woman as many times as he had Nicki. One-night stands—that's it. Occasionally he went back for easy seconds, never thirds. Never. And he'd never taken a moment to get to know any of them, much less like them the way he liked Nicki's velvet-encased steel personality.

Worse yet, he began to rise again, his body was already telling him that he wasn't nearly finished with her. The tight squeeze in his chest as he looked at Nicki again, now glowing and soft. Oh, God.

This was a bad sign. Very bad. With Nicki . . . he could get in way over his head. Forget completely that she was not just a woman, but a suspect. He wouldn't lose himself again to another pretty, dangerous face.

Mark shut his eyes, breaking the connection with Nicki, and withdrew from her warm, clinging body. She gasped, but he didn't turn back as he went to deposit the condom in the trash.

In the next room, with a wall separating them, he leaned into it, his forehead against the cool plaster, and drew in a shaky breath. What the hell was he going to do?

On the other side of the wall, he heard Nicki shifting, rising.

Then she appeared in the entrance to the kitchen, and he straightened to meet her.

"Another hit-and-run, huh?" She crossed her arms over her bare breasts.

"What do you want, Nicki? Like you said last time, it wasn't as if we made any commitments before we hit the sheets. We have great sex."

"And that's all it is?"

"What else do we have?"

Pain lanced Nicki's face, tightening her mouth. "I'd love to say something smart ass, like 'thanks for an interesting evening,' but I won't. You told me not to lie to myself earlier. Take your own damn advice."

She turned away and headed to his foyer before pivoting back suddenly. "God, I'd love to know what that bitch did to you. I got the message that it's none of my business. Fine. She screwed up your life once. Ask yourself if you're going to let her do it forever."

His stomach plummeted to his toes. "What the hell are you talking about? It was just sex."

Nicki raised the black wing of her brow. "If that's true, then re-member that when you're coming, and don't tell me you love me."

* * *

AFTER finally finding sleep at five in the morning, the last thing Nicki needed was to be back up at nine to meet Uncle Pietro's plane.

Clutching her cup of piping hot Starbucks, she loitered in the baggage claim, clutching her aching head.

She did her best to ignore her aching heart.

No, she wouldn't think about Mark. Again. It would only upset her more. Still . . . Was there any chance that the declaration of love he'd shouted during his climax had been true—even a little?

It didn't matter. She shouldn't want it to be true. She wasn't looking for the lasting bond that came with love. But when he'd said it . . . she couldn't deny her heart had leapt in response.

After she'd reminded Mark what he'd said last night, he denied saying it, turned a sickly shade of white, and apologized. Apologized, of all things! Clearly, he didn't recall saying it. Nicki supposed that was his way of saying it wasn't true.

God, why hadn't he just stabbed her in the chest? It would have been more humane than the way he'd cut her heart out with his words.

And her pain only told Nicki that she cared far more about Mark than was wise.

Whatever that woman had done to Mark had been painful, deep, and lasting. Even if, by chance, he did feel anything for Nicki, he'd bury the feeling and deny it until the end of time.

Whatever they'd had was over.

Having major sex with a hunk who could make guys posing in calendars envious and was beyond stellar in bed was fabulous, yes. He could make her smile, laugh. He never failed to make her feel sexy, to steal her self-control and replace it with his will. And she loved all of that. Right up until the climax was over, when he realized they were getting too close and he withdrew both physically and emotionally. Completely.

Girls' Night Out was not just time-consuming but mentally

demanding. She couldn't afford to divert time to healing Mark . . . if he could even be healed.

Though Vegas was a betting town, Nicki wouldn't lay down money that he could be. Whatever he'd let slip in a moment of passion, whatever he might feel, he'd spend all his formidable will burying.

Tears stung her eyes.

"What's the matter with you, huh?"

Nicki blinked away her tears, then glared at her uncle, who looked so polished in his gray double-breasted suit, despite the early hour, that it set her teeth on edge.

"Some of us run a business that doesn't close until two in the morning. Being at the airport a few hours later doesn't put me in a good mood."

"No one made you get up. Blade had my flight information. I was expecting him."

"Well, you got me instead. I wanted to talk to you. Alone."

"Nicki," he chided with a sigh. "I barely got here, you know."

"Yeah, you've been off having a great time in Italy, but you left without giving me key pieces of information, like the fact you'd told Blade he could be my accountant."

"You need help, Nicki." He patted his slick salt-and-pepper hair. "You can't do it all, and math was never your thing."

"I never said I could do it all or that I was good at math, but I am capable of hiring someone to do my accounting."

"Blade was supposed to find out if you can afford a new accountant."

"I managed to pay Marcy before—before she . . ."

Nicki bit her lip, unable to go on. Marcy had been her friend. They'd been opposites in personality, but always on the same side in business. Her death had been a huge shock. And on top of her ragged emotions, thanks to Mark, Nicki was having a hard time staying collected.

She cleared her throat. "Look, I don't think Blade is qualified.

I can hire someone temporarily to get it into shape, then take it over myself."

"Blade is a smart guy. He'll fix your books and keep them up. You stick to meeting and greeting people. And looking pretty. You're good at that."

His patronizing attitude ripped the thin thread of her temper. "Damn it, I own most of this business. You can't tell me who to hire! Why don't you—"

Pietro grabbed her arm and squeezed, not hard, but enough to get her attention. "Keep your voice down. We don't need all the nice people at the airport to know we're fighting, right?"

It pissed her off, but he had a point. She nodded.

"Good. Now, listen up. I own thirty percent of your club. Unless you can pay me back in cash today, close your mouth. Blade is your accountant, because I said so. End of conversation."

* * *

MARK leaned down to serve three thirty-something women their drinks when he saw Zack zip through the club, race behind the bar, and launch himself through the doors and up the stairs leading to Nicki's office.

Whoa! That was beyond unusual. Zack never left the backstage area unless he was onstage himself. Something was definitely wrong.

Besides you blurting to Nicki that you love her? He still couldn't fathom why he'd apparently done such a thing.

Pushing the thought away, Mark absently took the ladies' money and smiled. He glanced upstairs, through the obscured glass. Sure enough, Zack was talking rapidly, gesticulating all over the place. Nicki was pacing. Not a good sign.

Maybe this was his chance.

For what? the voice in the back of his head asked.

He had to get back in Nicki's good graces since he still had a case to solve. It was a no-brainer to say he'd screwed up by professing his love, then insisting it was just sex. She was still pissed. Hell, if he'd told Nicki she was cheap and easy, he couldn't have made things worse.

Wincing, Mark deposited his tray with Leon behind the bar, eased behind the counter, and headed for Nicki's office. Halfway up the stairs, he stopped.

He'd never allowed himself to indulge in denial before—not when his mother had died three days before his fifteenth birthday, not when he discovered he had cancer at twenty, not when Kerry had told him about Tiffany's perfidy. He would not start now.

Clenching his hands into fists, Mark stopped on the stairs, short of Nicki's office. The truth . . . Knowing she was furious with him didn't make his top-ten list of happy events. But seeing the pain that had darkened her eyes when she'd left his apartment completely naked this morning made him feel just like that snake in the grass she accused him of being.

What he still didn't understand, though, was why she'd acted upset. Why pretend that his lack of feelings for her mattered? Did she need to keep him occupied so that her lover could continue committing crimes? Or maybe she simply needed an alibi and he would do.

Was there any chance she was upset because she actually cared about him?

Stupid, wishful thinking. Nicki was a case; she couldn't be a woman to him.

Now if he could only keep that straight in his head the next time she came near him . . .

"Do you see now why it won't work?" Zack's voice drifted down the stairs.

"You're right. He could never change in time."

"Never. And then we'd be short one person for the finale."

Nicki sighed and began pacing again. "Why tonight?"

Mark trudged up the stairs and hovered at the threshold of Nicki's office. He didn't know exactly why he was here, only that he felt compelled to be. If he could win her back, keep his personal feelings out of this case, maybe he could solve it and be out of here before he got any more addicted to Nicki.

"What's wrong?" he asked her. "I saw Zack run through the club like he was on fire."

Zack rolled his eyes. "Fire would be easier. This is a real disaster!"

Turning to glare at Zack, Nicki barked, "No drama. I'm good at creating my own without yours, too."

"What is the drama about?" Mark asked again.

"We're short a dancer. Ricky is still out with the stomach flu, and Josh reported this afternoon . . . but he can't do it. He's not well yet."

Wrinkling his nose, Zack shuddered. "He tossed his cookies backstage twice. I had to send him home when everyone else nearly got sick."

"Which leaves us short an act for the evening and minus a performer for the finale."

Zack was looking at him expectantly. Nicki wasn't looking at him at all.

Silence descended, heavy and awkward. Sweat broke out all over Mark. Chest, back, neck—everything turned damp in an instant, then chilled. Tension claimed his back, rippled through his arms. He knew what they wanted.

"He's ready," Zack finally said to Nicki.

"He's not. Not mentally," she argued.

"Sweetie, the show must go on!"

She sighed, and with it, her shoulders and face fell. He'd never seen Nicki look defeated. Angry, annoyed, spitting mad, even hurt, yes. Never defeated. Her expression twisted the knife she'd already somehow managed to lodge in his gut.

Mark grabbed her hand, cursing himself. Why couldn't he be an asshole? Why did her concerns matter?

"Why is it a disaster?"

Nicki shook her head, looking a heartbeat away from tearing her hair out. "It's Memorial Day weekend, and the place is packed. My uncle is here watching everything like a greedy jerk waiting for a rich relative to die. A single screwup, and he's going to lord it over me and demand I pay him back his thirty percent, pronto."

"Would he do that?"

Her laugh was mirthless. "He already did once this morning. It's his way of ensuring I run the business to his satisfaction."

Mark already disliked the man he'd never met. One thing he knew about Nicki: This club was important to her. For her uncle—a member of her own family—to come in suddenly, put pressure on her, and tell her how to run her show . . . The guy sounded like a class-A bastard.

"I'll do it."

At his words, she blinked. Her gaze sharpened, then a smile broke out on her face. "Really? Will you be all right?"

God, he was a sucker. He'd love to tell himself that agreeing to this was just a ploy to win back her trust. But he'd only be lying.

"I'll be fine."

"Thank you." She kissed his cheek, still beaming at him like he was a superhero.

Mark sank into her smile, knowing he'd consented to a night of utter torture just to see it.

* * *

AS Zack had insisted, the show was going on, all right. Women cheered, drinks flowed, all the guys made enormous tips.

But Mark was the undisputed star.

Gritting her teeth, Nicki watched from behind the bar as he held court on the second stage. The line of women waiting to see him stretched nearly to the back of the club. Patiently, he smiled, flirted, posed for pictures, flexed various muscles as requested. And kissed. He didn't give tongue baths the way some of the guys did, thank God. But more than one of the locals slid business cards and cocktail napkins with scrawled phone numbers his way. Each time, he flashed his dimples and nodded as if he were flattered.

Nicki wanted to vomit. Wondering if he'd call any of them only intensified her nausea.

A bride-to-be, wearing a "veil" of condoms approached, egged on by friends who gave her a not-so-subtle nudge in Mark's direction. With a gentle yet still sexy smile, he cradled the woman's head in his big hands and placed a soft kiss on her lips. He lingered, a heartbeat, two.

Unable to watch more, Nicki turned away.

"He's very popular," Lucia said, joining her in the corner, near the second stage.

"At least I was right about that."

"But you were wrong about something else?"

Nicki turned a tired smile to her half sister. "I can't watch him with other women. I never imagined it would bother me. It's supposed to be business." She frowned. "It's crazy. He's not mine. But it's like someone's pouring acid on my heart when I see him flirt and smile and—"

"And kiss other women. Is that it?"

Nodding, Nicki smiled bitterly. "I knew I couldn't handle a fling with him without being distracted. I just can't sleep with someone without caring. He doesn't owe me anything, and he's free to see anyone he wants."

"And it's killing you."

Nicki wanted to lie. She really, really wanted to. "I almost think I'd rather someone put a gun to my head than be forced to watch this again."

Lucia cocked her head, her auburn hair flowing across her shoulders. "Do you love him?"

She risked another peek at Mark. Head thrown back, he laughed as a forty-ish woman cupped his ass and said something undoubtedly naughty. Apparently he'd gotten over his stage fright, because he looked like he was having the time of his life.

"Unfortunately, I think I do. And what crappy irony that I'm the one to give the commitment-phobic hottie what probably amounts to his dream job. Here's an endless string of women willing to screw him so he never has to worry about anyone getting too close. He and his adoring public ought to have a great future."

"It's not like you to just give up."

"Look at him." She gestured Mark's way. "He couldn't look more pleased if someone told him he'd won the Megabucks Jackpot. There's no way I'll get him to quit."

There were other obstacles to a future together, namely, her lack of time to devote to a relationship and the ice encasing his heart that made the likelihood of him having any lasting relationship with her on par with meeting an alien life-form tomorrow.

Lucia smiled like the cat who ate the cream. "Don't be so hasty. If you really want him, I think I might have an idea or two you'll find interesting . . ."

Chapter Ten

Waiting for Mark to answer her summons on Wednesday afternoon, Nicki figured she was about to take brazen to a whole new level.

Before she had time to think about everything that could go wrong and lose what little bit of lunch Lucia had forced down her, Mark appeared. He ducked to enter her office. His shoulders strained against a green T-shirt that made his guarded, sooty-lashed hazel eyes look mesmerizing. The jeans that fit snug in all the right places only distracted her more.

"You wanted to see me?" His voice rumbled across her senses.

"Thanks for coming in. Have a seat."

Mark glanced around and found the rarely used office chair Marcy had once procured for her. It sat in front of the computer that her former accountant had insisted she have. Nicki had barely learned how to turn it on. After Marcy's death, she hadn't even tried. He folded his length into the chair that looked two sizes too small for him and looked at her expectantly.

More than anything, Nicki wished she had any idea what Mark

was thinking, feeling. Did he miss her? Would he laugh at her suggestion? It had seemed so plausible coming from sensible Lucia. As she'd mulled it over last night, her wicked mind had clutched on to the idea like a child with a new toy. She'd become very fond of the new concept . . . until now.

"What's up?" he asked into her silence, looking anything but relaxed.

Having no idea where to begin, Nicki took the roundabout route. "Sunday night went well. How did you feel about performing onstage?"

He snorted. "I made a fortune. Who knew there was so much money in this?"

Or so many women. He forgot to add that part. But then, he likely wouldn't say that to her face. Nicki's heart fell. She chewed on her bottom lip, considering her next tactic.

"So you want to keep performing?"

Mark shrugged. "I was surprised when Josh and Ricky came back that you didn't put me into the show so it would be fully staffed again."

Nicki did her best not to wince. He'd noticed that. Of course, only a fool wouldn't, and Mark wasn't a fool.

"I wanted to talk to you about it first. A few days ago, you confessed to stage fright." *Right before you stripped me bare, rocked my world, and told me you loved me. Did you mean any of it?* Nicki cleared her throat, trying to clear her head. "When you performed on Sunday, did you feel nervous or awkward?"

Mark frowned. "Did I look like it?"

"No," Nicki was forced to admit. "You looked great."

"I did my best."

Oh, he had, all right. He'd scored a hit onstage. Nicki couldn't help but wonder if he'd scored afterward as well, given the volume of phone numbers and propositions he'd received.

"You were everything I'd want a dancer to be."

"Why do I sense 'but' coming up? Out with it, Nicki."

She drew in a steadying breath. Fine. He wanted the truth; he was going to get it. "But I want to talk to you about doing something else for me, instead."

Nicki waited, trying to decipher his facial expressions. No luck. Given Mark's success as a dancer, she expected he would protest. Surely he would. All the money, all the women, even if he didn't care for attention, had to be a lure.

Rather than spewing an expletive, Mark merely cocked his head. "Really?"

"I need a dancer, and I know that's why I hired you. But I also need an accountant."

"Do you?" he leaned in.

His expression changed and seemed . . . almost pleased. What was that about?

"My books . . . I'm pretty sure they're messed up. I can't do them myself. I've never been stellar at math, and I'm not too fond of the computer, much less the software Marcy picked for the accounting."

"What about Bocelli?"

"I've been thinking that you're right about Blade not being qualified to keep my finances. You are. I also need someone I can trust."

Someone who could find out if there was a reason her uncle was so insistent that Blade and no one else do those books.

"And that's me?"

"Yes. You've always been honest with me . . . even when I wished you weren't." She sighed. "I know you're here for the money, and that Sunday night must have been killer in the revenue department. I can offer to let you live in your apartment for free, but I can't afford to pay you a lot. Marcy only worked part-time, so I don't think it will eat up all your days."

"Besides free rent, what's in it for me?"

Damn it, she knew he was going to ask that question. In his place, she would have.

"Well, not having to be the center of attention onstage again, assuming it still bothers you." Dredging up her courage, Nicki looked right into those hazel eyes that never failed to make her melt. "And me."

Mark leaned in closer, narrow-eyed and intently focused on her. "Did I hear you right?"

"I'm yours, if you still want me. You told me not to lie to myself, so I'm not. Like you said, we have great sex. If you're after more money, the best I can offer you is to let you wait tables and keep your tips."

"Forget the tables." With a dig of his heels into the tile floor, he rolled his chair across the room, closing the little bit of distance between them. "Are you offering me unlimited access to your body?"

Desire darkened his expression, and her heartbeat revved up accordingly. God, she hoped this wasn't a mistake. But she wanted him. Bad. Lucia was right. Hell, so was Mark for that matter. Trying to ignore what has happening between them wasn't getting her anywhere. Yes, Mark was an employee—but a temporary one, most likely. The truth was, all her rhetoric about not being distracted was crap. It was her heart she feared for, deep down in places she didn't want to admit.

But the kind of chemistry they shared was totally new, felt strong enough to launch her into space, seemed deep enough to wet the vast desert they lived in. As her sister had so kindly pointed out, trying to deny how badly she wanted to explore this . . . thing between her and Mark just wasn't working.

Time for a new approach.

So for now, the best Nicki could do was shove aside the fact he could break her heart. She'd do her best to stay strong, not fall totally in love with him. Maybe she'd care just a little. And if she failed at that . . . well, she'd worry about her broken heart later.

"I'm yours anytime, anywhere, any way. Yes," she said finally.

The room fell so silent, she could have heard the smallest intake of breath.

Nicki could see instantly from his heated expression and the bulge in his jeans that the idea intrigued him. Thank goodness.

Every day without Mark made her feel like an addict going through withdrawal.

"Why? Last I heard, you were too busy to be distracted by me. You wanted to leave it at a one-night stand . . . that happened twice. I haven't always been great to you afterward."

"No, you haven't," she admitted softly. "But I realized when I saw you perform Sunday that I was so busy trying not to be distracted by you and denying myself that I was actually wasting more time and mental energy than if I just went with it. When I'm with you, I just feel . . . revved up. Connected to you. Trying to pretend that's not true is a waste of energy."

Slowly, he stroked that square chin of his and studied her with steady eyes. "I don't do commitment, Nicki. If you're looking for—"

"I don't, either. Maybe this is a one-month stand, you know? I'm not quite done with you yet, but I don't have any forever sort of expectations."

"If I say yes, I'd have the right to do this?"

Before Nicki could brace herself, Mark dragged her onto his lap, positioning her so that her legs straddled his thighs and the arms of the office chair. No question he was aroused. For the first time ever, they were eye to eye, and he used the opportunity to claim her mouth in a kiss that completely devastated her senses in two point two seconds. With a nip to her bottom lip, he cajoled admission, then swept inside for a gentle, methodical tasting. The tip of his tongue brushed behind her upper lip, loved hers in a slow circle, then dragged along the roof of her mouth. She tingled everywhere, as if she'd popped a whole box of cinnamon red-hots on her tongue at once.

That quickly, Nicki arched into Mark and clasped her arms around his neck. Grateful and somehow more centered now that he was with her, touching her, she buried her fingers in the golden silk of his hair. He was hard everywhere, chest, abs, shoulders, cock— but his hair was so touchably soft, she moaned.

His thumb brushed across one pebbled nipple, shooting darts of pleasure all over her body. But before she could encourage him more, Mark eased away.

"Is that a yes?" she asked once she managed to find her voice again.

"Most definitely." Mark smiled, his grin so brilliant and bright, it could nearly compete with the summer sun.

Nicki gasped. Of all the things she imagined he would say in response to her question, she'd anticipated that one the least.

"Seriously?"

Mark nodded. "Trust me. I'd rather be your accountant any day, and have these fringe benefits, than to prance half-naked on a blindingly lit stage for a bunch of strangers."

"Even though you'd make more money dancing?" *And have throngs of women falling at your feet?*

"Yep."

Shocking. "That's good. Great! But . . . I do have one request."

"Oh?"

The sharp syllable almost took her aback. It sounded almost suspicious.

"Nothing big. I just don't think it's a good idea if the others know we're, um, involved."

"The others? Your sister? Zack?"

"Lucia knows." She could feel the flush climbing up her neck and cheeks. "But the other dancers . . . and employees. It's probably not a good idea."

"You mean Bocelli."

His hard-eyed glare made Nicki wince. "Telling him only makes my life very complicated."

Everything she did went straight to her uncle through Blade. Who needed the headache, the browbeating about the shame of not being a good Italian virgin?

With a shrug, Mark said, "All right. I won't tell the people around here. Hadn't planned on it, anyway."

"Thank you."

Relief wound through her that she'd managed to convince him, both to have a fling with her and keep it to themselves. Maybe by tonight he'd be all hers—at least for the duration of their great affair.

Today, she would not worry about later—which she usually did quite well—and wonder if it would hurt when her books were in order and Mark chose to leave. She could only think about now, focus on the pleasure he would give her, the temporary right she had to touch him.

And she'd have to guard her heart. No matter how tempting Mark was, how smooth his words, how apparently sincere his eyes, how deep the adoration in his voice, she could not fall for him.

That would be a bad, bad move.

* * *

"SO she asked you to be her accountant, huh? You must have really sucked as an exotic dancer." Rafe laughed his way through the comment.

"I couldn't have been too bad. I made twenty-five hundred dollars in tips in four hours."

Rafe stopped laughing. "Are you serious?"

"As a heart attack. Shocking, isn't it?"

Mark wrinkled his nose as he looked out his apartment window at the morning sun beating down on the club's parking lot. Today would be a scorcher in Vegas, and it was only the first of June.

"Holy shit. I'm in the wrong profession."

"No. The last thing I want to see is you without clothes."

"Your sister likes it," Rafe shot back. "When she's not big and pregnant and complaining about having Beeky-Ticks or Braxton-Licks—some sort of contractions."

Mark frowned. "She okay?"

"These are normal. Just a little early, I guess."

Mark could hear his concern and tried to distract him. "Well, you without clothes is just a mental picture I don't need!" He laughed. "Seriously, the night I danced, the whole scene was insane. I collected twenty-eight phone numbers. I lost count of the number of propositions after an hour or so."

"Wow, that kind of job could keep you up to your eyeballs in horny women. There are worse things for you, my friend. Take any-one up on their offer?"

Being propositioned should have been like a fantasy . . . but it had left him cold. Instead, he seemed stuck, fixated, on Nicki. Since when did a healthy, single heterosexual man lose interest in most of the opposite sex?

Damn it, he needed to solve this investigation before he lost sight of his reason for being here.

"No."

"What's up with that? Since your divorce, you haven't been the type to stay at home on a Saturday night."

"It's Nicki." Mark sighed into his cell phone. "I just can't figure it out, man. One minute Nicki is distracting me away from her books and won't give me the time of day. The next, she's asking me to be her accountant, promising me free rent—and get this—bribing me with a fling."

Rafe whistled. "Are you for real? She asked you to make getting down and dirty a regular thing?"

"A temporary regular thing, but yeah. I'm not sure what's going on with her. Whatever it is, I worry it's not legal."

"But if she's up to something she could do hard time for, why would she show you the books? Why not hide them?"

"I don't know. Unless she thinks she's going to sweet-talk me into doing her dirty work for her, setting me up to be the fall guy, or planning to use me as some sort of alibi. I'm baffled."

"It's looking pretty odd."

"And feeling that way. The kicker to all of this is she asked me not to tell anyone about our fling. What she really meant, I think, is that she didn't want me telling Bocelli. Why would it matter unless they were a regular item, both personally and criminally, and she was stepping out on him in both ways?"

That thought was like a machete to the gut. Not only was she tied up with a thug, but also cheating him while cheating on him. It didn't seem like the Nicki he knew, who was usually straightfor-ward, not manipulative and sneaky. But then, he knew firsthand that when someone wanted to hide their true nature, they usually could—at least for a while.

"Good question," Rafe conceded. "I have another one: Why doesn't she do her own books? As you say, she's not a stupid woman."

"According to Nicki, she's lousy with both math and computers."

"Do you buy that?"

He'd bought a similar excuse with Tiffany, and it nearly landed him in Leavenworth.

"It's possible, I suppose. She's got a relatively new computer in her office, near her former accountant's, and I've never seen her turn it on. But her sudden change of heart raises red flags. The last time we talked about her books, she refused to hear that Bocelli wasn't competent. Now she's telling me that she doesn't think he's capable. As if this is news to me?"

"Any chance she's just now seeing the truth about the thug? Maybe the fact she invited you to her place when the money transfers were going on was just one of those weird things."

"It's not impossible, but what are the odds? If she was getting a clue about Blade, why not just cut him loose altogether and tell him to take a hike? It seems more likely to me that she's trying to cut Bocelli out of the action and keep whatever profit they've been making for herself."

"What are you going to do?" Rafe asked.

"I already said yes. What else can I do? I'm here to get into Nicki's books and figure out what's up, find the source of the illegal shit going on around here, and see that it stops."

Yes, he'd had to agree to her proposition in order to stay close, earn her trust, so he could dissect Nicki's accounting records and find the truth. But he couldn't deny that he'd also agreed because it allowed him to touch her whenever and however he wanted. The thought was dizzying—and dangerous. He was aware that it wasn't terribly ethical, but couldn't bring himself to care.

Rafe hesitated. "Mark, I know Tiffany messed you up. I—"

"I don't want to talk about it."

"Too bad. I'm just reminding you, watch yourself with this woman."

Mark tensed. "What does that mean?"

"How do you feel about Nicki?"

"I don't feel anything." Mark squeezed his cell phone in a death grip.

"Bullshit. I know you too well, and it's not like you to lie to me, much less yourself. There's something in your voice, man. You care about her."

So much so that he'd apparently babbled that he loved her in the heat of passion.

He sighed. "It's one of my flaws. If there's a very bad woman up within fifty miles, I'll get really hung up on her. I'm such a fucking schmuk."

"Not necessarily. She might not be guilty of anything more than having crappy timing and changing her mind about wanting to be with you. Don't assume she's Tiffany revisited. What if you just asked Nicki some of these questions?"

It was Mark's turn to hesitate. "I can't rouse her suspicion and jeopardize the investigation. If she thinks I'm here to probe her business practices, she'll throw me out on my ass with supersonic speed, or have Bocelli gun me down, if she's guilty."

A long moment later, Rafe finally said, "Don't get in too deep with this girl without getting some answers, man. I don't want to see you with another broken heart."

Yeah, he didn't want that, either. He just hoped the advice didn't come too late.

* * *

WHEN Nicki answered the door after Mark knocked on it around noon, she wore a mostly sheer white baby doll nightie that had his eyes bulging from their sockets. He could clearly see the outline of her rosy-tipped nipples. The garment parted down the front, and her diamond navel ring winked at him. Her matching thong left almost nothing to the imagination, except between her shadowed thighs, where he ached to see her most.

His heart stopped. But a vision of Nicki with her legs wrapped around him, pleading in shattered screams for more, set his heart pounding again, into a fierce rhythm against his chest, like a boxer on steroids.

"Hi," she muttered, voice throaty, smile wicked. "You're right on time."

Swearing his tongue had grown to the size of a football field, Mark tried to swallow his lust so he could answer her.

"You look amazing," he managed to get out.

"Are you going to stand there all day and stare, or come inside and touch me?"

As nice as the view was . . . it wasn't a contest. Mark shoved his way inside her apartment, slammed the door, and threw the dead bolt home. Then he propped Nicki's back against a convenient wall and seized her mouth. He dropped the little bag he'd brought with him. That freed his hand to tilt her head in the perfect position to take the ravenous onslaught of his lips. Smoothing the other hand down her body, he aligned her hips with his and pressed his erection right against her soft, damp spot.

She wound her arms around him and opened her mouth to him, receptive, so damn welcoming, he felt a groan building in his chest. Her tongue danced slyly with his, spreading the sweet taste of her all over his senses. And her smell . . . cinnamon and citrus tang. Spicy. Fresh. His.

God, where did that thought come from?

Thoughts fled a moment later when she grabbed handfuls of his shirt and gathered them up his body, tracing every contour of his abdomen and chest with the heat of her palms. He began to sweat. Blood rushed to his cock by the gallon when she lifted his shirt over his head and tossed it away. Then she set her sweet lips about torturing him, gliding a seductive path down his jaw, to his shoulder. Her teeth nipped him there, jolting him with a little bite of pain before she eased it with her tongue. And her fingers . . . drifting over his nipple with a little scrape of her nail made the man inside him start to itch to feel her hot and wild and yielding around him.

"I can't get you out of my head," she whispered.

Before he could reply, she dipped down and took his other nipple between her lips and drew the flat male disc inside. The suction beat a path straight to his groin. The ache throbbed with every pull of her mouth. He'd never been sensitive here before, never remembered this affecting him so much. Now it was driving him insane, and it was all he could do not to push her to the floor and thrust himself inside her. He hungered so bad for her, he was about to crawl out of his skin.

"Nicki . . ."

Her little teeth teased his nipple. He responded, tensing, as her fingers traced his navel. The combination of sensations was nearly his undoing. And her fingers kept moving south . . .

She unsnapped the button of his khaki shorts.

"Yes?" Her whispered question and blue eyes taunted. The vixen in her had come out to play, with a vengeance.

The smooth slide of his zipper filled the air next as she freed his cock from the tight confines of his shorts. Eyes clenched shut, head bowed, he panted against her neck, breathing in the aphrodisiac of her skin over and over. Why was it he'd been in the door less than two minutes and already he had no fucking control?

He had even less when she slid his underwear down his hips and took his steely erection into her hands. Her thumbs glided over the sensitive head in alternating strokes designed to drive him insane while she squeezed him tight with her palms.

"Baby . . ." He groaned. "You're killing me."

She smiled against the bare skin of his pectoral.

"Not yet, but soon."

Her whisper rasped over his senses, even as her teeth scraped his nipple again. The incessant stroke of her fingers over his solid length had his breath coming hard and fast.

Mark could barely process how badly he wanted her. Was it only this morning he'd tried to reassure Rafe he'd keep his head on straight when he was with her?

Nicki's every move made a liar out of him, especially when she slid down the wall and to her knees. Suddenly, her hot breath cascaded over his cock. He felt dizzy from the want storming him.

He gripped the door beside him for support, praying for a miracle. He'd need it if he had any hope of maintaining his self-control.

Nicki parted her lips, stretching wide to accommodate his cock, and took him inside the hot, slick cavern. As she enveloped him, he felt the back of her throat, her tongue swirling around him. After the first downward stroke of that beautiful mouth, shards of pleasure scraped up his shaft, then exploded in the rest of his body.

By the second, he could barely remember to breathe.

Oh, God . . .

Nicki moaned on his cock, licking and sucking as if sampling a favorite dessert. The soft stroke of her fingertips climbed up the back of his thighs before she settled one palm at the base of his erection. The other held his testicles and scraped with the light abrasion of her fingernails. His hands clenched into fists. The woman knew exactly what she was doing.

His eyes flew open and met hers, now looking up at him with brazen sexual challenge. Cheeks hollowed, lips dragging up and down his cock—Mark relished the view, the torturous heaven of Nicki on her knees before him.

"Oh, yeah," he moaned.

Ecstasy rushed up hard, fast—undeniable. Again, she took him deep, deep inside and sucked, as if she could draw out his very soul. Then she hesitated, lingered. His need spiked. Sweat gathered between his shoulder blades, filmed his chest.

A tortured moment later, Nicki's mouth enveloped him again. Pleasure so intense he could barely form a coherent thought—not that he truly cared—bombarded him. His lungs pumped air like bellows, as every muscle in his body tensed. His balls tightened, as tingles zipped like electricity up his spine and the moist sound of her sucking brought him right to the edge.

"Can't. Hold. Out," he panted, his hips flexing toward the sweet heat and snug temptation of her mouth.

Instead of stopping, Nicki merely moaned and laved the head of his cock with her hot little tongue, before sliding him all the way back inside with a suction that had him gritting his teeth and trying to hold back.

Groaning, desperate to beg her to suck him faster, but unable to find the words, he slid his hands into her hair and grabbed fistfuls of the wild strands that filtered like inky silk over his fingers. He guided her to the deep, mind-blowing pace he needed now, before he lost his sanity completely.

The coil of desire wound tighter and tighter, squeezing at his gut. More blood rushed to his cock, and still she pulled at him, moaned. Still the utter body bliss climbed, sharp as a butcher's knife.

Then her tongue teased a little spot just under his crown, so sensitive a blast of heat shot straight to his belly, uncoiling all his self-control. He unraveled completely as she wrapped those sweet red lips around him one last time.

Mark tried to pull free from her mouth. As much as he wanted her to take him completely, he wanted it to be her choice.

Nicki simply took him deeper and held on tight.

Then he was oblivious to everything but the pleasure that jolted up his cock and burst in his belly, expanding until it nearly swallowed him whole. He felt like it detonated the top of his head. With a harsh cry, he came, reveling in the feel of the warm haven of her mouth until the pulsing in his body came to a slow, jagged stop.

Spent and shaky, he swayed as Nicki rose and faced him.

With unfocused eyes, he took her in. She looked beautiful, triumphant, with swollen lips and flushed cheeks and glittering blue eyes. Her scent was stronger, sharper with arousal. He swallowed. Nicki clearly yearned to be touched now.

He was nothing, if not accommodating.

To his shock, interest stirred deep in his belly, despite the mammoth orgasm that had just eradicated half his brain cells. What was it about this woman, that he could never seem to get enough?

Within moments, Mark kicked off his shorts, hustled her back to her bedroom, and proceeded to kiss her senseless until she melted onto the bed. Sweet and slightly salty, her mouth opened under his so completely, he couldn't imagine wanting anything more than to stay here and take all she had to give, to sink deep into her silken heat and plunge into the pleasure over and over, hearing her gasps in his ear, feeling her nails rake his back.

It was possible she'd invited him to her bed to deceive him—but she could never deny that he knew exactly how to make her moan. Or that when he touched her, he felt more than her flesh. In some odd way he didn't understand, he felt *her*.

Suddenly impatient, he pulled on the lone bow holding the front of her baby doll nightie together. The gossamer sides parted, the cups falling away from her breasts, revealing swollen, hard tips that rose up and begged for his touch.

He gave in immediately.

Rising above her on his elbows, his hips spreading her thighs, Mark dipped his head and took one of those juicy nipples onto his tongue. At the first firm pull of his mouth, Nicki clutched his head and arched, offering herself to him. It inflamed him; she inflamed him. Already he stood at full staff again, aching, impatient, dying to get inside her.

But not until she was wet, aroused. Not until she could only breathe long enough to beg.

Mark curled his tongue around her other nipple, giving it equal attention. Her gasp shot straight to his cock, engorging it even more. Shifting his weight over her body, he laved attention on both her nipples, back and forth, sucking, nipping, tormenting. Soon, the rigid peaks were red and wet from his mouth. He felt her thighs tense against the building pressure of orgasm and smiled against the underside of her breast.

Need inflamed him, heating him up from the inside out. How

could the urge to get near her, share pleasure with her again, be riding him so hard and so fast?

Desperation clawed through him as he lowered his hands to the side of her thong and yanked. Blessedly, the little white string holding the gossamer triangles together came apart.

"That was Victoria's Secret," she protested weakly.

"Now it's out of my way."

He peeled away the damp strips of material, totally baring her pussy to his hot gaze. A dusting of dark hair covered her secrets—but couldn't hide the slick juice of her arousal. The scent of her exotic flavor rising from her needy flesh tempted him, more today than the last time he'd had her. Far more than the first time.

Consumed by his craving for her, Mark shifted down her body to part her nether lips with his thumbs and taste her swollen vulva. Arching, Nicki opened her legs wider to him in silent invitation.

"Yes. So fucking sexy."

He barely got the words out before the fact that she was spread out like a banquet compelled him to partake again. Firmly planting his head between her thighs, he eased his tongue across her sensitive skin, flirted with the opening that seeped for his attention, then teased her distended clit.

Her thighs went from tense to trembling. Her breath came in short, deep pants.

"Ohmigod! I-I . . ."

"What do you need?" he taunted, circling her swollen red pearl with his tongue again.

"You inside me," she gasped, grabbing fistfuls of the blanket beside her and lifted her hips to him in silent supplication. "Hard. Deep."

"Soon," he promised.

Then he sucked her clit into his mouth and drew on it. Nicki cried out in a sharp gasp that nearly bought a purr of male satisfaction to his chest. He loved the way she responded to his every touch. So sensitive. So revealing.

"Now. Please now!" she pleaded.

In response, he merely flicked the tip of his tongue over the hard bud in his mouth. With the core now peeking above the hood, the gesture had her arching, screaming—an instant from coming.

She lifted her hips in a renewed plea, and Mark relished how close she was to the edge of rapture. The trick now was to keep her there as long as he could . . . then shove her into ecstasy and listen to her scream his name. He looked forward to that especially.

Easing his way up her body, Mark trailed his mouth across her abdomen, suckling her breasts, nibbling at the sensitive crook of her neck. A flush suffused her cheeks, the creamy skin between her shoulders. Her mouth was a provocative shade of red that had his cock tightening. Her panting and restless movements, the moaning as he pinched her nipples or rubbed his thumb over her needy clit, all told him she was teetering at the edge of control. Her responsiveness amazed him.

But the vise grip of need squeezing his balls and urging him to get inside her tight, sweet channel told him that he was at the edge of his as well.

Realizing that he'd left his bag with his condoms in the entry, Mark held in a curse. Too far away. He wanted her too much to leave the bed for anything. Damn! Then he remembered . . . The first time he'd come here, Nicki had been prepared with a box in her nightstand.

Crawling across the bed, he yanked open the drawer. He found the condoms, all right, and grabbed one. But that wasn't all he found.

Mark looked over at Nicki, who realized what he must be seeing and gasped, a fresh flush darkening her face.

"Leave it alone, Mark."

"I don't think so, baby." He smiled and grabbed the surprising object. This was going to be fun.

Ripping open the foil packet, he quickly gloved up and lay on his back. "Come here."

Nicki crawled across the bed to him, aroused and wary. As soon as she got close enough, he grabbed and lifted her, settling her astride him. Holy hell, she looked like a goddess above him, slick, flushed, dark hair a riotous tangle, framing dilated blue eyes. Her nipples beckoned. The curve of her hips fit perfectly under his hands as he lifted her over his cock and guided her down slowly.

Gasping, Nicki tightened around him, tossing her head back at the exquisite sensation of her flesh parting to accommodate him, welcoming him deep inside her. Like silk so hot it nearly scalded, she surrounded him, gripping him snugly. Seated to the hilt, Mark gritted his teeth at the tingles screaming through his erection and fought for control.

He had at least one weapon in his favor.

Smiling, he held up the item he'd found in her drawer, a pink slimline vibrator, which was about five inches tall and barely an inch thick. He flipped the button at the base and a faint hum punctuated her audible breathing.

"Mark . . ."

"Does this little thing do a man's job?"

He set the buzzing wand on her shoulder, then let it drift down her collarbone. Waiting for her answer, watching her body tense, he glided it over her distended nipple. She tensed and grabbed his shoulders. Nicki tried to lift her hips. Mark held her down with one hand.

"No," she gasped in answer to his question finally.

"Does it make you come?"

Nicki wriggled on top of him, rubbing the sensitive head of his cock right against the mouth of her cervix. He hissed at the sudden sting of pleasure.

"Sometimes," she panted.

"It can't possibly fill you up."

"It doesn't." She gyrated on him again restlessly, clearly searching for relief.

Mark smoothed the vibe down her abdomen, traced her navel. Her belly clenched.

"Do I?"

"Yes. God, yes!"

She tried lifting her hips again. Again, he held her still. He had a point to prove.

"A vibe like you've got is only good for this," he growled, then set it over her slick clit.

In seconds, she began to jerk, buck. Her vagina fluttered around his dick. Pulses gripped him every few seconds, making him sweat, as she gasped above him.

When she slowed, he turned the vibe off and tossed it across the bed.

"Did that ease your ache?"

Nicki writhed above him and lifted her hands to squeeze her nipples. The sight just about set him off. But when she tried to lift her hips and stroke down on his cock yet again, he held her hips immobile with both hands.

"Did it?"

"No. Please. Stop teasing me. I need you now!"

Seeing her naked? Great, but he'd managed to hold on. Feeling the orgasm generated by the vibrator? A real treat, but he hadn't lost control. Hearing that she needed him now? Those four words sent him into overdrive.

Grabbing her shoulders, Mark brought Nicki down until they were chest to chest. He buried his face in her neck, grabbed her hips and pumped up into the suctioning heat of her body, lengthening his stroke and focusing on her G-spot. Once, twice, again and again, he pounded into her tight channel, pouring the desire that clawed at him into every thrust.

Wrapping his arms around her, he crushed her against him. What was it about her? He loved her expressive face when she was laughing or angry, or like now, aroused. He loved the sound of her hitched breathing, the little keening cries in his ear as her orgasm approached. He loved her stubborn grit, starchy sass, and commando-bitch ways. He loved the scent of her skin, spiced and clean and female—and the way her desire enhanced that scent. He loved her quick mind and the fact she wasn't afraid to use it. He loved the feel of her against him, holding on with trembling thighs as she clamped around his cock. Oh, and those hard, demanding pulsations as she came that drove him beyond rational thought. He loved that about her. He loved . . .

Her.

Mark had to bite his lip to keep from shouting it out, as rapture exploded in his belly, melted his brain, and squeezed his chest full of something he'd hoped never to feel again . . . and yet something he'd never felt before. Not like this.

Above him, Nicki clung. His ears rang with her cries, "Oh, yes. Ohmigod. Mark!"

And still he kept pumping into her, giving her everything he could, everything she could take, until she finally collapsed over him, sweaty, spent.

Knowing it was stupid and still compelled anyway, Mark kept her close and dragged a palm up her back, aligning their hearts together, now both beating in crazy rhythms, yet oddly in synch.

He loved her. How the hell had it happened? Why?

Man, he was so fucked.

Struggling to catch his breath, Mark realized that his choices were limited. Either he continued to deceive her and hide the truth, knowing he'd have to walk away from her in the end. Or he confronted her without giving his secrets away and hoped she was in a confessing mood—and that he could help her somehow if she was as guilty as she looked.

"Nicki, why don't you want Bocelli to know about this? About us?"

Tiredly, she raised her head enough to look into his eyes. "Why do you ask?"

"Humor me."

She groaned and rolled to her side. Before she could get away, Mark pulled her back against his body, face-to-face. He stared right into her eyes, his chest tight as he willed her to answer, wished like hell that she wasn't guilty of anything.

"He's my uncle's watchdog. Everything I do, Blade reports back

to him. If I sneeze, Pietro knows. If I sleep with the hired help . . .
he'll know that, too."

"So you're saying that Blade is here on your uncle's behalf to . . .
what? Protect your virtue?"

Nicki sighed. "You're not from a traditional Italian family, so
you can't understand. We should all be good virgins who attend
Mass regularly, enjoy saying 'yes, sir' and 'no, sir' and love cooking
so that when we get married, we know our place."

Maybe that was the truth. Mark couldn't say definitely yes or
no. It was possible, if incredibly old-fashioned. To her credit, she had
said previously that her uncle was overprotective and that he lorded
his investment in the club over her whenever he didn't like her behavior. But that could also be part of the scam . . .

"So Bocelli was doing your books because your uncle insisted?"

"Absolutely. I really meant to hire a new accountant after Marcy's death, but when I didn't do it fast enough to suit my uncle . . .
well, he let his little lapdog have at it."

The bitterness in her voice sounded so genuine. Mark steeled
himself against hope.

"What made you suddenly change your mind and defy your
uncle?"

At that, Nicki looked away. "I just thought about what you'd said.
You're more qualified. You don't like the dancing. It made sense."

"I don't think that's the whole story."

Her gaze zoomed back to his, moist lips parted.

Mark tamped down the crazy urge to seize her mouth and kiss
the truth out of her. Wouldn't do any damn good. Instead, he rolled
on top of her and grabbed her face, locking her stare with his. He
was uncomfortably aware of jealousy clawing at him, of how damn
bad it would hurt if she answered in the affirmative to his next
question.

"Are you sure it doesn't have anything to do with the fact you've
been fucking Bocelli? And then what happened? Did he piss you
off? Is this your way of getting back at him? Or dumping him?"

"What?" Nicki bucked underneath him, trying desperately to shove him off.

Mark held firm.

When she realized she couldn't displace him, Nicki glared at him, mouth tight. "Damn you! The first time we have sex, you treat me like a meaningless one-night stand afterward. The next time, you tell me it's just sex and to get over it. Now you think I'm some kind of manipulative whore. Get out!"

"Not until I get some answers."

"You're not entitled to any when you insult me like that. Every time I think I like you, you do something thoroughly shitty. Your afterplay sucks."

She gave him a mighty shove, her knees moving missiles beneath him. Forced to protect his assets, he moved aside. Nicki climbed from the bed and made for the door to the bathroom.

Mark grabbed her by the wrist. "Did you fuck Bocelli?"

"Never, you dumb prick. I've grown up loathing Italian machismo. Why would I voluntarily sign up for more of it?" She tried to yank her wrist free.

Her eyes shone like blue jets of fury and truth. Mark found he was inclined to believe her.

But just like the money-laundering scam . . . he didn't know for sure.

"I'm sorry," he soothed, rubbing her wrist with his thumb. "Blade led me to believe that you were. I couldn't think of a reason why he'd lie."

"Because he's a deranged bastard! I don't want him around here. I never did. And the fact you accused me of sleeping with him . . ."

Her chin trembled. A sob tore at her chest. Seconds later, tears fell. Mark felt her pain and anger tearing through his gut. If this was an act, she ought to be getting twenty million a picture.

He gathered her close and wiped her tears away. "I'm sorry, baby. I didn't like the thought of you with him."

"I know this isn't forever, but I thought we were sharing something special. It meant something to me." She drew in a shaky breath. "I don't sleep around. Before you, I hadn't had sex in over two years."

With those words, she may as well have kicked him in the gut with cement shoes. But some things made sense now. Why she'd had to open a new box of condoms that first time. Why she'd been so damn tight he'd had to fight his way inside. He'd never seen Bocelli come or go from her apartment, or her from his.

It seemed a little more likely Bocelli had been lying about him and Nicki. Except . . . why would he?

"Nicki, I'm so sorry. I didn't mean to hurt you. I was just trying to understand why you suddenly wanted me doing your books and touching your sweet body." He brushed her dark hair away from her face and looked straight into her eyes, willing her to tell him more. Tell him everything.

"Because I trusted you." Her whisper was broken. "Because I needed you. I couldn't stand the thought of sharing you. When I saw you dancing last Sunday, saw how many women wanted you and slipped you both their phone numbers and their tongues . . . I-it bothered me. Apparently I'm really stupid."

The man inside him roared with triumph. She was tangled up in him, as much as he was in her. But it made the investigator in him pause. Just because it appeared as if she wasn't inserting Bocelli's Tab A into her Slot B didn't mean she wasn't a criminal. There was still the matter of the books and her initiation of sex during the exact time the illegal transactions took place. Coincidence? God, he wanted to believe so. But she could still be playing him for a fool.

"No," he assured her, soft-voiced. "I'm the stupid one."

That was the truth. Hell, what could he do now?

* * *

MONDAY morning came, and finally Mark started on his new gig as Nicki's accountant. And he purposely started early, at 6 A.M. Vegas time—while his "boss" was still fast asleep after a night of managing the unusually rowdy club that had likely ended about three hours ago.

Alone and focused, Mark locked Nicki's office door behind him. Now he'd get to the truth—one way or the other.

Mark turned on the former accountant's computer and spent hours reconciling her records against the receipts and bank statements in front of him. By three that afternoon, he could only be assured of two things: Nicki made good money at this business, and Blade was one shitty accountant. Unfortunately, the books in recent months were convoluted with items often categorized so incorrectly they should have been the punch line to a joke. Marcy had been better at the job but not perfect. Still, the books balanced to the penny.

But they completely lacked any reference to the frequent incoming and outgoing money that came in from all over the world and inevitably wound up in Eastern Europe.

Shit.

The real accounting records, the ones with the truth about every deposit and transfer, dates, times, amounts—the works—had to be here somewhere.

After scouring Marcy's computer and finding nothing of the sort, he had only one option that he could think of. It was the simple, obvious, not-going-to-happen one. But what the hell?

Mark rolled his chair across the narrow little office and booted up the computer that belonged to Nicki. She said she didn't know how to use it, and maybe that was true. He'd never seen her type even a single letter or number into the sleek black machine.

But he'd heard this song and dance before, courtesy of Tiffany.

He encountered a password screen before he even reached the Windows desktop. Clearly, he wasn't going far without help.

Swearing, he quickly took out his cell phone and punched the speed dial key to ring Rafe.

"What's up, buddy?" he asked.

"There's another computer here. It's Nicki's. I need help getting in."

"No problem."

Mark gave some info so Rafe could start his preliminary search. "So how's Kerry?"

"Complaining that her back hurts. Still having those damned contractions."

Concern niggled at Mark. "But she's going to be okay, right?"

"She has a doctor's appointment tomorrow. We'll find out then what's up."

"Keep me posted," Mark insisted.

"Will do. Okay, your password for that machine is JimmyChoo, all one word."

"Who the hell is that?" Mark demanded.

"Hmm." He paused. "According to Google, he makes fabulously expensive shoes."

Figured. Nicki had a thing about shoes.

Grunting, Mark typed in the password, and the computer played the annoying little Windows song, signaling the fact the computer allowed him access inside the system.

When he launched the accounting software, he encountered another password. Again, Rafe had to bail him out by deciphering the password Ty Pennington, all one word.

"Who?"

"The dude on *Extreme Makeover: Home Edition*. The show that makes your sister cry every week when they're rebuilding a house for someone in need? He's the ass with the megaphone."

"That guy? Ewww."

"Someone needs to talk to Nicki about her taste in men, if she likes both him and you."

"Shut up," Mark growled, typing in the password.

Mark wasn't sure what he expected to find . . . but this wasn't it.

"What do you see?" Rafe demanded.

"One file. One lousy file."

"Launch it."

He did . . . only to be greeted with yet another prompt for a password.

"What the hell is going on here?" Mark demanded. Why all the security? This computer was beginning to make Fort Knox look like a cakewalk.

Rafe hacked away and discovered the next password. Frank29.

"Who the hell is Frank?" Mark wondered aloud.

"That I can't help you with. If this is Nicki's machine, she's seriously obsessed with men."

It sure looked that way. A sour ache ate at him. It didn't jibe with the story she'd sobbed to him just a few days ago. She'd looked so earnest, stripped naked, both in body and soul. He'd believed her when she said she wasn't fucking Bocelli, hadn't been with any man but him in the last two years.

Did you believe it because you wanted to?

Shoving the thought away, Mark put in the latest password and waited.

Chapter Eleven

IT took Mark three seconds to realize he'd hit pay dirt.

His stomach plunged down toward his toes. "Oh my God."

"What?" Rafe demanded.

Scanning the columns, the dates and numbers, glancing at the bank statements to ensure accuracy, Mark realized they all matched. Every fucking number. His belly tightened, even as fury chewed at it. The pain in his chest . . . sitting a city bus on it would certainly hurt less.

This file had every appearance of being the real accounting records. And it was on Nicki's computer. Protected by her passwords.

The realization opened a gaping wound in his chest, and betrayal gnawed it, reducing him to a moment of pain he had to shut his eyes against.

Either Nicki and Blade were in this together and they had dragged him into it to make the fake books look good, or she was trying to cut out her partner in crime. It didn't really matter. In either case, she was using sex to distract him from the truth.

He'd nearly been sucker enough to fall for it.

God, was it possible to have worse taste in women? Even a twisted S.O.B. like Hitler had managed to find a loyal woman who loved him. So Mark wondered how it was possible that he just continued to fuck up his love life with the worst women possible.

"What?" Rafe demanded. "Clue me in here!"

"I found a file. It's got everything," he forced himself to say. "Perfect categorization of income and expenses. Correct lists of *all* deposits and withdrawals, even the shady ones."

"On Nicki's computer? Hmm. When was the file last updated?"

A few clicks later, Mark bit back a curse. "A little after three this morning."

Apparently, she'd ridden him to the edge of exhaustion that afternoon, then updated this file after the club closed and the staff departed. After she had known he would be sound asleep.

"Three A.M. is an interesting time to balance your books. You sure this is Nicki's file?"

"It's on her computer. She probably felt safe keeping it here. I'm sure she thought no one would seriously challenge her."

The evidence all pointed to Nicki being involved, perhaps even as mastermind. But Mark still paused. How could a smart, assertive woman be involved in something so criminal? She appeared to have a genuinely warm heart, despite her often prickly armor. Yet . . . her involvement in the crime made all the sense in the world. She was bright enough to do this, and she liked calling the shots. There'd been plenty of whispers that her uncle Pietro was connected to the Gamalini crime family. Maybe she'd undertaken this operation for him. Or for someone else, to spite him. And who didn't like money, especially when breaking your back to get it wasn't required?

"What do you mean that no one would challenge her?" Rafe asked.

"This has been going on almost since she opened her doors, and no one has caught her yet, right? Bocelli is the only other person who's seen her records. If he's involved in this scam, he's done a great job pretending to be a damn lousy accountant—too good a job, maybe. If he's not involved, he doesn't have the skill to figure out Nicki's game. Her uncle . . . he might be involved. But he's absent so often that she had to feel relatively secure. Unless . . . What about the FBI agent? Did you get any info to corroborate my theory that it was Marcy?"

"The only thing Norton would say was that they had no reason to believe their agent was dead."

"That doesn't tell me anything."

Rafe snorted. "I'm pretty sure that was the point. Anyone else there a possible G-man? Or woman?"

Mark mentally skimmed the possibilities. "Who? Lucia? Zack? Neither seems to have the skills. Maybe one of the other dancers, but I've got to be honest, if any of them are investigating anything, they're not here often enough to do a decent job."

"Any word from your private investigator yet? Does he have a report on Nicki?"

"Just got a preliminary report today. It doesn't give any obvious indication of your girl's guilt, just a lot of background. Average grades. Party-girl mother. Distant father, with ties to the Mafia— bumped off a few years back, likely by one of his underlings. Names of guys she dated, but no one who sends up a red flag. I'll send you a copy."

Less than he'd hoped for . . . "Damn! Thanks, anyway."

Turning back to the balance sheet, Mark scrolled to the bottom. And scowled.

"Holy shit! I haven't seen the May statement from Nicki's bank yet, but this is wild. Deposits by the dozens. All moderate amounts that would pass right under the government's radar. And they're coming more frequently."

"Really? Where are they coming from? Going to?"

"I can't tell from this file. But they never stay in the account long. They disappear almost immediately."

"And we can't call the bank to ask questions, or they might call Nicki, who would get suspicious. I'll see about getting you some transactional records and e-mail it."

"Good. Damn it." Mark sighed, then frowned. "Wait. What's this?"

Mark saw a tab in a menu to the side of the balance sheet marked RE. A click on the RE tab only proved to be as confusing as hell.

"What's what? Dude, your description today sucks."

Peering closer to the screen, Mark tried to decipher what the file was trying to tell him. "I see nothing but dates, addresses, dollar amounts—row after row of them—on this sheet. A laundry list of places. Like an address book of places listed in different cities all over the world."

To the left of the dollar amounts, every row had a column of three-digit numbers, arranged in an ascending order. He had no idea what they meant.

Rafe said nothing for long moments. Mark could almost hear his brother-in-law's brain turning over the phone.

"One common money-laundering scheme is real estate transactions. Dummy corporations buy, then sell to the laundering agent, who funnels the money to another dummy corporation through a shell account, usually in the Caribbean or Eastern Europe. Then it just . . . disappears."

"R.E.? Real Estate. That must be what the tab stands for." He scanned the numbers again. "Damn, if you're right, someone is making a fortune at this. Condos in the south of France worth millions. Houses in Hawaii, London, Buenos Aries, Italy. This is big-time stuff."

"Very. Have they sold already, or are they currently for sale?"

He peered at each row, trying to discern some marking that might tell him. He found nothing. "I can't tell. Let me e-mail these to you. Maybe you can do a little research."

"You got it, brother. I'll figure it out."

As Mark cut and pasted the numbers into an e-mail, Mark had

no doubt Rafe would do just that. The idea made worry burn like a raw wound in his chest.

"Nicki, what have you gotten yourself into?" he muttered to himself. And why did he care that a criminal had voluntarily submerged her own ass in hot water?

His hand tightened on the mouse. If he kept digging, what other morass might he find Nicki to be neck deep in? Still, he had to know. Running away wasn't going to make it go away. Or make this nightmare of an investigation end any sooner.

Wincing, he looked at the contents of the bank account again.

Ninety-eight lines, all with dollar amounts of less than ten thousand individually, but totaling more than three-quarters of a million dollars altogether.

"What's it looking like?" Rafe prompted.

"I don't know. It just . . . I don't get a good feeling about this. Something big is about to happen. The operation is picking up steam. It seems to be building toward something . . ."

Heavy footsteps on the stairs alerted Mark that he likely wouldn't be alone for long. He closed the accounting program and quickly shut down Nicki's computer as the footsteps drew near.

"Got company," he whispered.

"Call me," Rafe demanded as Mark flipped his phone shut and maneuvered back in front of Marcy's computer, where he pretended to be baffled by the collection of receipts on the desk.

Blade slapped a hand on his shoulder. "So, Nicki wasn't bullshitting me. Dancer boy thinks he has a brain."

Mark tensed, torn between treating Bocelli like bacteria in week-old puke or suggesting something anatomically impossible. In the end, he merely fixed the thug with a stare.

"This dancer boy has a CPA, and it's clear you can't add without using your fingers. I suggest you move your hand if you want to be able to count all the way to five in the future."

Bocelli shifted, reclining in the doorway of Nicki's office. He looked less than happy. "That doesn't mean that Nicki's other investor approves of you in the club's records. I suggest you leave it to me, if you know what's good for you. Capisce?"

"Have you watched every gangster movie ever made and decided to become a walking cliché? Or are you really that unoriginal?"

His brows slashed down above his eyes in angry black slants. "Last time I restrained myself from introducing you personally to my Beretta Brigadier Inox." He patted the bulky side of his jacket where his shoulder holster rested. "Shut your mouth, or you might not be so lucky this time."

Mark watched Blade, dissecting his aggressive stance and cocky smile. The look was all right for someone ass-deep in the Mafia. He appeared to be exactly what he was—a midlevel player on the rise with his hands in multiple pies, which, until recently, included the one holding Nicki's money.

Yet he couldn't help but wonder why Blade simply didn't shoot him.

After their last altercation a little more than a week ago, Mark had taken to sleeping with one eye open, half-expecting Blade to break into his place and finish him off. But he never appeared.

"Don't threaten me, asshole," Mark shot back. "In fact, why don't you tell me why you lied about sleeping with Nicki."

Nothing but the merest tensing of his body betrayed a single thing Blade thought. Then the Italian stereotype in black leather laughed.

"What? She told you you're the only one, and you believed her?" Blade shook his head. "There's a sucker born every minute . . ."

"Don't fucking lie to me!" Mark stood, shocked to find himself shouting.

He'd sensed Nicki's sincerity when she told him she hadn't had another lover in two years, felt the tightness around his cock that a woman couldn't easily feign. Lord knew he didn't dare believe another damn word out of her mouth, but he wanted to believe that.

Every single thing they'd shared couldn't be a lie.

Bocelli shrugged. "You think what you want . . . Sucker."

Mark took a deep breath. *Think, Sullivan.* Nicki was going to jail if the evidence kept stacking up against her. It didn't matter if everything between them was a lie. Hell, it probably was. It shouldn't matter if Nicki had fucked Bocelli—and half the Gamalini family. And losing his cool with Bocelli wasn't going to solve anything.

It was some flaw in his genetic makeup that made him want a woman who was likely only using him for a despicable scam.

"Nicki is now paying me to keep her accounting records current and clean. If her uncle has an issue with my competency, he's welcome to call me. I'll list my qualifications, and provide him proof of my abilities. But until I hear objections from his mouth, get the fuck out of my face."

"Boys!" Zack chastised, sliding past Blade and into Nicki's office. "As yummy as the testosterone display is, all this fighting isn't necessary. I'm sure that Nicki and her uncle can solve this matter without you two making hamburger out of each other's faces."

Mark scowled at Zack, who turned away and peered down at Nicki's desk, looking all around. A quick glace at Blade told Mark the Italian ruffian was equally baffled.

"Do you need something?" Mark asked Zack.

Zack turned back. He stood next to Blade, and they looked very alike with their short dark hair, olive complexions, and six-foot frames . . . but the attitudes were so different. He'd love to see how Mr. Macho would feel knowing that he could almost be mistaken for a flamingly gay man's twin.

A smile tipped up Mark's mouth at the thought, before he realized that Zack was blushing.

"I met someone and got his phone number. I set it down here last night when Nicki and I were discussing the show." The stage manager braced his hand on the computer tower and turned back to the desk to search for the scrap of paper, scouring behind the monitor.

And Mark was done playing with both of them. "I'll look for it in a few minutes. I need to wrap something up so I can discuss a few things with Nicki. If I find it, I'll let you know."

Zack shot Mark a pissy glare but reluctantly allowed himself to be shepherded out the door. Blade scowled as Mark crowded him out of the doorway, too. Then he shut the door in their faces—and locked it for good measure.

Quickly, he searched Nicki's desk. When he didn't find a bit of paper with a phone number on it, he shrugged. Not his fault if Zack's love life would suffer. Zack shouldn't have lost the number in the first place.

Pushing the issue aside, Mark sat back in Nicki's chair. He had a little more research to do before he questioned her in some clandestine way he had yet to fathom.

But an hour later, he could make no more sense of the accounting records on Nicki's computer than before. But his gut told him that something big was coming soon . . . and that something was likely to take Nicki down with it.

* * *

DRAINED, yet still furious, Mark stomped up the stairs toward the third-floor apartments. Early evening sun slanted in bold golden swaths through the window, casting lazy shadows on the wall. Outside, the usual tumble of Vegas tourism bustled below. He hadn't eaten since dawn, Rafe had left a message an hour ago, and his buddy Jason, from his old days at Standard National Bank, had called to say he was getting married.

Right now, he didn't give a damn about any of that. He couldn't get his mind off of Nicki or his head around the fact she looked so guilty, even the comparison to sin was too mild. He didn't even want to think about the fact that her betrayal crushed him just north of the ribs, until he wasn't sure where his next breath would come from. Since it was Monday night and the club was closed, Nicki had the night free from responsibility, so they had an appointment to rendezvous and screw each other breathless. Not that the thought didn't have all the pertinent parts of his anatomy rising in interest . . . but he had questions that he wanted answers for even more.

Such as, could this all be real? Why would she deceive him like this? Why would she choose him to scam? And did she feel any-thing for him at all? It hadn't escaped his notice that the one time he'd apparently shouted his love aloud she hadn't said a word in return. And then there was the ever-popular question, how long would it take him to get over her once this case was done so he could go back to his mind-numbing one-night stands?

The answer he had at this point: No idea.

With a heavy sigh, he approached her door. They'd agreed to meet at six, and he was half an hour early. What the hell. Given everything he'd discovered today, he wasn't inclined to give a shit if being a bit early would piss her off. No, that wasn't the whole truth. He'd be lying if he said that he wasn't as eager as a six-year-old on Christmas morning to touch Nicki, sink into her. In her arms, he could forget—for a few precious moments—about her deception.

After a quick knock, Nicki answered the door wearing a sizzling blue corset that matched her uptilted eyes and didn't require him to stare too hard to define the outline of her hard berry nipples. A barely there matching thong and sheer nude thigh-high stockings added to the erection-inducing getup. A stray silken lock of her hair nestled itself right into that enticing cleavage. He started to sweat.

Wow, if he showed a lot of willpower tonight, he might manage to restrain himself from ripping her clothes off long enough to greet her.

"Hi."

Her breathy voice and sultry smile went straight to his cock. They said *follow me to the bedroom, and let's get busy*. He wasn't about to argue.

Mark swallowed, fighting dual urges to question her about her secret files and get her flat on her back with her legs open wide for him.

Clearly, he was going to have to pick—quickly.

No contest, really. Not with an investigation in the balance and the opportunity to put Bocelli the home wrecker behind bars, he couldn't tip his hand too quickly.

"Hi." Tempting fate, Mark smoothed a hand down the curve of her waist, over her hip, and settled it on the sweet curve of her ass. "You look edible in that shade of blue, baby."

She flashed him a wicked smile. "Glad you have eating on the brain. Come with me . . ."

Grabbing his hand, she turned and led him into her bedroom. She'd turned the bed down and adorned it with white satin sheets. Candles glowed all around the room—on her nightstand, her dresser, the cedar chest in the corner. Perched on a TV tray next to the bed was an array of fruits and pastries, along with two glasses of wine.

When Nicki set her mind on seduction, she did it right.

"You're way overdressed for the occasion," she chastised.

Then she peeled off his shirt, sliding warm palms up his abs and his chest as she did. Her hands against his bare skin made him shiver. Then, smiling like a naughty kitten, she unbuttoned his jeans. The lowering of his zipper was a seductive rasp in the silence. Slowly, she released the zipper and dragged the back of her finger over the outline of his engorged cock, still shielded by his underwear. Her fingertip swirled over the sensitive head. Mark sucked in a breath, bit back a groan, and wondered how she could get to him so damned fast—and how the hell he was going to keep his wits long enough to keep his heart from sinking deeper.

* * *

"HUNGRY?" Nicki shot him a cheeky grin at her silly double entendre.

Mark sent her an answering grin that dazzled her, despite the fatigue around those beautiful hazel eyes. "What do you have in mind?"

Gosh, do you want the list?

"Giving you a full belly so you have plenty of stamina. I'm pretty sure you skipped lunch."

"Guilty."

"Here." Nicki reached behind her and snatched a fresh cream

puff with strawberry glaze, topped with powdered sugar. She'd tried one—just enough to know they were to die for and that if she made them a habit none of her clothes would fit for long.

As she approached the sculpted curves of his mouth with the confection, he opened wide. Oh, she could hardly wait until he did that to her nipples. Nicki pressed her thighs together to relieve the sharp, sudden ache at the thought.

Food first, girl! Feed him, then *jump his bones. All the while wondering if he loves you . . .*

No. Scratch that last thought. This was sex. Just sex. Surely that wasn't too hard to remember.

Placing the pastry on his tongue, she watched as he bit down. And groaned. Even the sound of his pleasure seemed to drive her crazy. Not just in the arousal sense—though if he didn't get her out of this thong soon, it was likely to be doused—but also crazy in an entirely new sense. Some part of her wanted to find fifty new ways to make him smile or groan or any other indication of happiness she could think of. It was like a special gift she wanted to give him . . . something that would make him glad every day to be with her.

Dangerous territory. Very dangerous.

But when he licked the powdered sugar off her fingers, she couldn't exactly remember why.

"Very sweet, baby. But I think you've got something sweeter hidden somewhere in here." He traced a pattern over the swells of her breasts with his finger.

Nicki bit her lip to restrain the urge to rip the garment off for him and offer him anything he wanted.

But the shuttered look on his face troubled her. She wanted nothing more than to soothe whatever was troubling him, replace that disquiet with a happy light that permeated him all the way up to those hypnotic eyes.

"Strawberries?" She plunked one into his mouth.

He ate it, seeming to consider its flavor. "It's great . . . but surely you have something even more satisfying."

That dangerous finger of his traced the valley between her breasts, bisected her stomach, toyed with her belly ring and glided over her mound, barely there. A phantom touch that left her aching.

Gritting her teeth, she continued to tease him, tease them both. "Wine, maybe."

Mark took the glass from her hand, drained it in a few hearty swallows that showed off the sexy cords in his neck—and made her want to plant her mouth all over him.

With a sigh, he set the glass aside. "Lovely, but lacking. Take it off, Nicki."

She sucked in a breath. She knew that voice, the soft one that resonated inside her body with steel-edged command. He meant it. And he meant for her to do it now.

Staring right into his eyes, where she was sure she could lose herself for at least half an eternity, she pushed one strap off her shoulder. Her body lit up like an out-of-control brushfire, as the heat in his gaze notched up a few degrees.

Then the cell phone clipped to his jeans rang.

Yanking it from its holder with a curse, he looked at the caller ID. He cursed again and flipped it open. "This really isn't a good time, buddy. I'm hanging up now."

"No," said the voice on the other end. "It's your sister. I left you a message earlier . . . She's in the hospital."

Nicki stood so close, she couldn't help but hear the conversation.

Mark suddenly gripped the phone so tightly, Nicki was stunned he didn't crush it. All the dancing, seductive light in his eyes evaporated. She held her breath as he sat on the edge of the bed, stunned.

"Why? What's going on? Is she hurt?"

"Those damn contractions. Your niece-to-be is trying to come six weeks early. They're afraid her lungs aren't fully developed. We've been here for a few hours. They're trying to stop Kerry's labor . . . But she's—shit." His voice broke. "She's bleeding."

"Which hospital, Rafe? I'm on the next plane."

"It'll be over before you can get here. The doctors . . . they're trying. But they've got her hooked up to so many tubes and monitors, she looks like an alien. Damn, I—" He sighed. "I've never been so fucking worried in my life."

Mark's heart all but stopped. Cool, in-control Rafe sounded on the verge of tears.

"I know." Hell, he was worried, too. Terrified. Kerry was the only family he had left, and after everything she'd done to prove him innocent of embezzlement . . . God, no. "I'm coming back to New York. Can Kerry talk at all?"

There was a pause, then Rafe returned. "The doctors want to talk to me. I'll call you back."

Flipping the phone closed, the sudden silence assaulted him. He stared at the wall, in shock. Suddenly, Nicki approached and threaded her fingers through his hair, soothing him with her gentle touch.

"I'm sorry," she whispered. "If the doctors are trying, there's every chance they can save the situation."

Possibly. But what if they couldn't?

He looked up at her, at the gentle concern on her face, and wondered why the hell she cared. And why her touch made him feel better?

"I've got to go." He stood and buttoned his pants, searching for his shirt.

"Absolutely. The books can wait a few days. Or more, if necessary. Do you need money for a plane ticket?"

In the middle of donning his shirt, he paused. Nicki was offering to help him get home to his sister? Even as she was committing a felony behind his back?

"Why?" He hadn't realized he'd said the word aloud until it rang in the air between them.

"What do you mean? I know how important your sister is to you. And you look . . . apprehensive. You want to be with her, set your mind at ease, I know. Take whatever time you need off, but if you need the money—"

"You'd give it to me?"

Not that she didn't have it to give, but someone greedy enough to commit a felony and screw a bunch of people over for greenbacks just shouldn't be the sort who'd offer a guy a plane ticket to visit family.

Even more odd, she looked confused by his question.

"Of course." She stood on her tiptoes and kissed his cheek. "You pack. I'll find you a flight. JFK or LaGuardia?"

Forgetting the hundred reasons why getting close to Nicki in any sense but the physical wasn't smart, Mark clutched her against him. He stopped lying to himself about how comforting she felt against him. How right. He just held on to her for a few brief seconds. Despite the fact he knew everything was wrong in his world, holding her made it somehow bearable.

"I don't need the money. But thanks."

He finally pulled away—and felt somehow empty the instant he did.

"Call me if you need anything. I'll be thinking of you and your sister. I'll even drag out my rusty rosary beads and offer up a prayer." She put on a weak smile, but he saw the concern shimmering in her eyes. It kicked him square in the middle of the chest.

How the hell was he going to fall out of love with her if she kept acting like she cared?

* * *

TWO days later, Mark walked back into Girls' Night Out. He hadn't called to let anyone know he'd returned. In truth, he'd wanted to surprise Nicki, both with the fact Kerry had been released from the hospital yesterday, baby safely in her tummy, and that he'd come back.

Now, at four in the afternoon, he could barely wait to see her.

Ever since knowing that Kerry and his soon-to-be-niece were going to be just fine, he'd been wondering about Nicki and her behavior before he'd left. She'd been tender . . . concerned. Offered to help him get to New York. Even though she had the money, he just kept wondering: Would a greedy criminal really give a shit if an employee, even one she was sleeping with, needed the money to see to a family emergency?

The only known criminal in his past was Tiffany, and she wouldn't have lifted the phone to dial 911 to save Kerry. In fact, Tiff had tried to kill his sister. And Tiffany had been stashing away money in the Caribbean, while he'd been nearly crushed with medical debt following his episode with melanoma.

In short, Tiffany wouldn't have offered him a dime for any reason that didn't benefit her.

From where he was standing, Nicki had no reason to offer him money . . . other than out of the goodness of her heart. That didn't sound like a criminal. So what was her story?

Climbing the stairs to the third floor of the club, Mark cursed. Did Nicki have a good heart? Or was it just something he wanted to believe?

He was so damn confused. But the fact remained that, as long as he had no hard evidence to clear Nicki, she had to remain a suspect. And he had to treat her like one. Somehow.

Well, he was back in Vegas, so it was game on. He'd have to answer his questions . . . and gather the proof Rafe had sent him here to find. For his sanity's sake, if nothing else.

Mark knocked on Nicki's door. No answer. No stirring inside. He didn't hear the clink of the pipes to indicate she might be in the shower.

An indrawn breath of frustration smelled like . . . natural gas. Was it coming from her apartment?

Alarm jolting his system, Mark pounded on her door. No answer. "Nicki!"

Silence.

Where was the gas smell coming from? Why was it so strong? What if . . . No, he couldn't think about Nicki being hurt—or worse.

Then damn it, why the fuck wouldn't she answer the door?

Alarm turned to panic. Mark threw his weight against Nicki's door, shoulder plowing into the door. Nothing. Damn it, he had to get inside!

"Nicki! Baby, can you hear me?"

Still no answer.

Fear racing through his blood, Mark forced a calming, centering breath and reached into his years of karate. He could kick the door down. He'd broken bricks with his foot. It was a matter of focus, of channeling energy.

He set up for his kick.

"What is going on?" Lucia demanded, opening her apartment door, which was across the hall from his.

He whirled around. "Do you have a key to your sister's place?"

"Yes." A concerned frown furrowed her brow.

"Get it. Now!"

Lucia hesitated only an instant before she raced away. Mark turned back to Nicki's door and clobbered on it again. The sickly odor of gas was stronger now. Terror ratcheted up in his system. Adrenaline roared inside him until he was sure he could break down the walls with his bare hands.

Thankfully he didn't have to. Lucia sprinted to the door with the key.

"This better be something more than she's not speaking to you and you're wanting me to let you in so you can invade her privacy."

"Inhale deeply."

Lucia did—and she paled. "Oh, no!"

Mark snatched the key from her hand, shoved it in the lock and cranked it to the side. A click signaled the bolt retreating from the portal. He flung the door open.

The smell of gas nearly dropped him to his knees.

"Stay out. Call 911!" he shouted to Lucia as he stormed inside, placing his forearm over his nose.

He raced through the apartment, looking for her. "Nicki!"

Not in the kitchen, not in the living room. He rounded the corner, but did not find her in the bathroom.

Stepping into her bedroom, he prayed she wasn't home at all. Maybe that's why she hadn't answered, why he couldn't find her . . .

Barreling into her bedroom, he found her sprawled across her bed sideways, facedown and hanging over the edge of the bed.

"Nicki!"

Mark raced to her side and scooped her up in his arms. She didn't respond to his voice or his touch. Instead, she lay limp in his arms, head dangling over one arm, feet over the other, as if she was . . . *No!*

Swallowing, his heart racing, Mark darted out of her apartment. Lucia met him on the landing, gasping when she saw Nicki was asleep, unconscious or . . . No.

Sprinting down the stairs, he raced for the club's door.

"Follow me!" he shouted.

Shouldering the door behind the bar open, he dashed into the club and out into the sun-drenched parking lot. He sank to his knees ten feet outside the club's doors and cradled Nicki in his lap, beneath the shade of a palm tree. Immediately, he placed two fingers over her carotid artery. Her heart was beating, thank God. But it pumped double time, like a marching band on fast forward. She looked pale. Even the red lips that always tempted were a waxy yellow with a tinge of blue.

What the hell had happened?

Panting and pale faced, Lucia made it outside and knelt beside him. "The Fire Department is on their way. They're sending an ambulance."

"Good. Go call the gas company. They need to shut this off and figure out what happened."

"There's a phone inside. I'll just—"

"No, the gas is worse than I thought, and it's unpredictable. Any spark or current, and this whole place could blow. Even my cell phone could set it off. Is there a phone nearby?"

Lucia shrugged, hands shaking. "I guess . . . I've only been here a few weeks."

"All right. You'd better shout into the club and make sure no one else is in there. Everyone ought to know this place could turn into a fireball at any moment. Maybe someone in there can help you find another phone."

"Yes." Then Lucia looked back at him and said, "Take care of my sister."

Mark looked away from Nicki's pale, unresponsive face to gaze at Lucia. Tears now seeped from her dark chocolate eyes and tracked down her smooth cheeks. Her chin trembled as she fought more tears. Clearly, these sister shared a deep bond—a bond he understood, sharing something similar with Kerry.

Sirens began to wail, coming closer and closer.

"As if she was my own," he vowed.

Lucia sent him a shaky nod. "Thank you."

A few minutes later, she appeared with Zack and Blade in tow, along with a few of the other dancers who had arrived early for their shift.

"What's going on?" Zack shouted as he jogged next to Mark. "Why is a fire truck pulling into the parking lot?"

Mark looked up to respond and saw Bocelli standing beside Lucia, as the Vegas heat shimmered off the blacktop.

"Doc?" Blade said softly to Lucia. "Do you need something? Help?"

Never had he seen Bocelli be anything other than threatening or sarcastic. Apparently even the thug had a little compassion somewhere for Lucia's pain and worry.

"Nicki . . ." She trailed off, looking back toward her limp sister's form in Mark's lap.

She sobbed quietly into her hands.

Bocelli glanced at Nicki and squared his jaw, as if he was angry. Then he wrapped his arms around Lucia.

Mark had no time to ponder the Italian's reaction before he barked to Zack. "Get over there and see if they have any EMTs."

"But—"

"Don't fucking argue. Now!" he growled.

Petulant, Zack stomped away.

Then he turned to the other man. "Bocelli, will you take Lucia somewhere so she can call the gas company? We need to shut the flow of gas off to Nicki's place immediately."

Nodding, and without any smart-ass comment or argument, Blade slid an arm around Lucia's waist and led her away. She looked back at Nicki until she was out of sight.

Bocelli seemed surprisingly gentle for a Mafia heavy.

Finally, Mark was alone with Nicki. He didn't even want to think that fate might force him to do without her.

"Baby, can you hear me?"

Chapter Twelve

"Heard anything yet?" Zack asked as he darted into the hospital's stark waiting room just before midnight.

"No," Lucia whispered, looking up at Nicki's stage manager with damp, red-rimmed eyes. Blade sat next to her in utter silence.

Sitting in an uncomfortable chair the color of baby vomit across from her, Mark was every bit as distraught as Lucia looked. He rubbed his cold palms together, absently wondering why hospitals were always cold enough to double as meat lockers. Mostly, he wished he could say something to comfort her. Nothing came to mind. No one knew how severe Nicki's gas poisoning was yet.

No one knew if she'd live.

What the hell had happened?

God, he'd seen enough of hospitals the last few days to last him a good decade, at least. He only hoped that the ending to Nicki's stay in this hospital was as happy as Kerry's had been in hers.

"Damn it," Zack cursed, sliding into a chair next to Mark's. "I got here as fast as I could. The gas company turned off the gas in Nicki's apartment and checked out the rest of the building to make sure it's safe. When I closed the club early for the night, the other dancers had a lot of questions, we had an irate thirtieth birthday party . . ."

"Thanks for coming. You're important to Nicki." Lucia did her best to smile.

Zack shuffled his feet and looked at the ground. Apparently, he was as uncomfortable with praise as a kid wearing shoes two sizes too small.

"Did the gas company have any idea what caused the leak?" Mark asked.

"They suspect a broken pipe at the stove."

Mark nodded. What else could he say? Those pipes were reportedly easy to break, so it was possible Nicki had accidentally endangered herself. It was also possible the broken pipe was planned. This incident just a few weeks after a light nearly crashed on her head made him wonder . . . Still, he couldn't prove anything.

Either way, the last thing he'd expected when he returned from New York was to see the woman he couldn't get out of his head slumped across her bed, near death. Sitting here, watching Lucia huddle in the seat across from him, struggling to keep herself together, he wondered if this incident was going to extinguish the bright light Nicki shined in all their lives. It was surreal. And terrible.

Zack fell into the same somber silence as the other men.

Lucia covered her mouth with her hand, trying to stifle a sob. The anguished sound ripped through the silent room, occupied only by the four of them and some dusty artificial plants.

Wishing he could do something—damn it, anything—Mark clenched his teeth against the rising frustration and reached out to comfort Lucia. Blade shot him a fuck-off glare and tucked her against his shoulder, murmuring soft assurances in her ear. Apparently, she preferred to receive her comfort from someone she knew, someone who hadn't driven her sister to a chianti-induced crying jag. But Bocelli was no Boy Scout. Clearly, Lucia had no idea he was a Mafia thug who knew murder intimately. Mark made a mental note to warn her if things began to look any cozier between them.

"It's okay, Doc. Nicki's a fighter. She'll come out," Bocelli whispered.

Nodding as if she wanted to believe more than she actually did, Lucia sobbed again. Blade rubbed her back, stroked the long auburn tangle of her hair. She clutched his shirt and hung on as if he were a life preserver in a raging sea.

"How could something like . . . like this happen?" Lucia wailed. "How is it possible I-I was right down the hall and never n-noticed anything?"

Mark shrugged, wishing like hell that he had answers. Nothing made sense. None of it.

"I-if you hadn't come back." Lucia looked up at him from the tangle of Bocelli's arms. "Hadn't smelled the . . ." She pressed her lips together, unable to go on.

"Don't worry about that now," Mark murmured. "Focus on Nicki pulling through. While my sister was in the hospital, Nicki offered to get out her rusty rosary beads and pray. Maybe you should do that for her."

Lucia smiled through her tears. "Hers would be rusty. She probably hasn't been to confession since eighth grade. She's always teased me that I'm the good sister."

On that note, she cast a furtive glance at Bocelli, then straightened away from him. Blade gritted his teeth, but he let her go.

"Did you notice the smell of gas in her apartment when you were there earlier in the day?" Blade asked Zack.

The stage manager shook his head. "No. I was really only there for a minute to talk through a costume problem and run a new idea past her. She said she'd just come back from the gym and was going to shower." He shrugged. "I left and . . ."

Something horrible had happened. Zack didn't have to say it. They all thought it, Mark was sure.

"Ms. DiStefano?" a white-coated doctor called from across the room. "I'm Dr. Halstar, the resident on duty. About your sister . . ."

Mark held his breath. Every second that passed in silence was like a rusty blade to his insides.

"Yes?" Her voice trembled. She squeezed Blade's arm, as if he alone kept her upright.

"It was close, but she's going to be fine." His kind smile softened his young face.

Collectively, they sighed in relief. Mark heard his roaring heart slow, finally stop kicking his ribs like a kung fu master on meth.

"Thank God," Lucia sighed. "Can I see her?"

"Briefly. She's being moved to a bed where she'll be watched very closely tonight. I expect she'll sleep quite a bit for the next few days, but she should recover quickly and have no lasting effects. Come this way."

Lucia stepped forward to follow the doctor. Before they disappeared around the corner, Dr. Halstar paused, then looked back at the trio of men remaining in the waiting room.

"Is one of you Mark?"

"I am." Full of relief and washed-out adrenaline, his voice scratched like steel wool as he stood.

The resident smiled. "She's been asking for you. I'd prefer that she only have one visitor at a time, so I'll take her sister first and come back for you."

Swallowing against a jolt of shock strong enough to light up Girls' Night Out on a swinging Saturday night, Mark nodded. Nicki had asked for *him*? "Please. Thank you."

Lucia and the doctor disappeared, then. Twenty minutes ticked by, and Mark found himself pacing. He knew why family got to visit first, but the waiting made him want to pound something. He watched the clock, ticking. Slowly. So damn slowly. Was it broken? Was he in the Twilight Zone, where five minutes suddenly took two years?

"Could you sit down?" Zack rolled his eyes. "You're making the rest of us nervous."

Mark zipped a glare at Zack, who was tapping his foot on the yellowed linoleum. Bocelli, on the other hand, lounged in his chair with an arm draped across the one beside him. A smile flirted at one corner of his mouth. Yeah, he looked stressed, all right.

Before Mark could tell Zack to take a flying leap, Dr. Halstar and Lucia reappeared. She was pale and teary, but wearing a tremulous smile that tugged at his heart.

The doctor motioned at Mark to follow, and he fell in step beside him.

"Lucia tells me you saved Nicki's life."

"I just happened to show up in time." Mark shrugged.

"Lucky, indeed. She's a pretty girl. Very pretty."

"She's taken," he growled.

Mark stopped, stunned by his own assertion. Nicki wasn't *his*. Somewhere in his head, he knew he couldn't afford to think of her as anything more than a suspect, not while he was investigating her, not when he suspected her of felony behavior. Not when there was any chance he'd be helping to ship her off to prison.

But tonight, when her life had hung in the balance, when his heart had all but stopped as he carried out of her gas-riddled apartment . . . none of that mattered.

The doctor laughed. "I figured by the way she called for you that you weren't her brother or a gay best friend."

Doing his best to keep his scowl to himself, Mark followed Dr. Halstar down a series of twisting corridors, through a few double doors, up a story in the elevator.

Finally, they reached Nicki's room. Mark charged in with all the subtlety of a wrecking ball. Then stopped dead when he saw her lying there, eyes half open, still pale, tubes sticking out of everywhere. The heart monitor beeped in the background. The IV dripped into her right arm. The sight hit him like a barreling semi to his abdomen.

"I'm alive," she croaked. "So you can stop scowling."

He nodded, feeling his throat tighten. "For a while, we wondered, baby. You okay?"

Sinking down into the chair beside her bed, he reached for her hand, then thought better of it.

"I won't break," she assured him and fitted her hand in his.

He held on tight. "How do you feel?"

"Other than wishing for a whole bottle of aspirin to make my head stop hurting? I'm fine."

He squeezed her fingers in his palm, relishing the warmth and life pulsing under her skin. "What happened?"

"Don't know. I worked in the office when I got up, then went to the gym."

She took a deep breath and wheezed. Mark flinched.

But she went on. "I returned, and Lucia came over for lunch. Then Zack dropped by to talk. I took a shower, laid down. Felt really sleepy."

Nicki had run out of breath, and Mark couldn't stand to hear her tax herself anymore.

"Rest," he ordered.

A tired smile flitted across her face. "Thanks again. My hero."

Frowning, Mark let go of her hand. He didn't feel like a hero. He felt jumbled and torn. Too weak to resist her, too uncertain about her innocence, too committed to ending the criminal behavior that shattered the life he'd once led in Florida to give up investigating her, Mark had no damn idea what to do next.

* * *

THREE long days later, Mark didn't know whether to thank God that Nicki was back home safely or kick himself for caring so damned much.

Oblivious to his dilemma, Nicki sat propped up in her bed with a bottle of flavored water in one hand, a romance novel in the other.

"Oh." She smiled and brushed an errant strand of inky hair from her face. "Listen to this: 'She raised her slender hips to his every savage thrust, her eyes wide with astonished pleasure as his engorged wand of passion parted her womanly folds relentlessly.'"

She laughed, and through it continued with, "'Desire swirled in her belly as she clasped her long, slender legs around his muscular hips, capturing him deep inside her. Her fingernails raked the strong muscles of his broad back and shoulders. Whimpers of pleasure and frustration escaped her cupid's bow mouth as she climbed ever closer to achieving a woman's pleasure and—'"

"Why are you reading this?" Mark asked, frowning.

She'd clipped her hair in a haphazard twist that left skeins of the dark silk caressing the back of her neck. Even with a scrubbed face and simple striped cotton pajama pants and a tank top, Mark couldn't escape the fact she was one of the most beautiful women he knew. And one of the most interesting and vivacious. She lit up from the inside, face glowing with equal parts intelligence, moxie, and sex appeal.

Mark hated how much he wanted her at this moment—at every moment, if he was honest. But it didn't surprise him.

Nicki shrugged. "Bed rest doesn't provide enough mischief. If the doctors won't let me out of bed tonight and you claim you're too busy fixing my books to be in bed with me, well . . . A girl has to get her kicks somewhere."

Her smile teased. Mark didn't smile back.

Nicki had to bring up the subject guaranteed to confuse the hell out of him—her books. How could she flash that eye-catching grin if she was involved up to those pretty blue eyes in felony money laundering? It seemed impossible . . . but Tiffany had taken him on a similar ride. He knew all too well it was possible.

Shaking his head, he wished it hadn't occurred to him to check her electronic banking and accounting records while she'd been in the hospital. But he'd hoped—prayed, even—that some spark of activity while she was clearly laid up and unable to see to that "business" would at least hint that she wasn't involved. If she had cut Bocelli loose from the operation, as he suspected, and someone else started moving money in her absence, that would say something about Nicki's lack of involvement, maybe even her innocence.

Instead, all records had been more silent than a roomful of monks. Money had been transferred in, and none of the accounting records or real estate transactions had been updated—a definite departure from the previous behavior, where frequent updates had been the norm.

From that, Mark could only conclude that the operation was waiting on Nicki to proceed.

And she was guilty as hell.

"Mark?" Nicki folded her purple prose onto her lap and stared at him.

He forced a smile. "Sorry. I'm tired. I've had a lot on my mind."

"Between your sister's pregnancy and my terrible accounting records and the gas line accident, you've been hopping. Have you talked to Kerry today? Is she all right?"

He wondered why it mattered to her. "She's fine. Bed rest is doing her a lot of good. So is laying off the ice cream."

"I'm glad she and the baby are going be all right. Honestly, when you got that phone call, you turned twenty shades of pale." Nicki grabbed his hand and squeezed. "I'm glad you got to see her."

Mark extracted his hand and settled the blankets around her. "What about you? How do you feel?"

"Much better today. I'm not tired anymore. I have my appetite back. My skull-piercing headache is gone. Must be all this wonderful care I'm getting." She shot him a warm smile, which Mark did his best to ignore.

"Lucia informed me that taking care of you is my job, especially while she's gone to the airport to pick up her friend Ashley."

Her smile wobbled for a moment, then righted itself. "They'll have a nice time together. They've been friends since college. Because college for Lucia started at fourteen, it was hard for her to find friends, but Ashley has been one of the best. I think she kept Lucia from drowning in academia and made my brilliant sister remember that she was still a young woman. I'll always be grateful to Ashley for that."

Mark peered at Nicki, doing his best not to frown. Could a woman care so much about the people in her life, then use others as if they had no meaning or value? With no concrete proof to convict Nicki, no way to absolve her, a slow burn of frustration flared in his gut. Before he said something stupid, something revealing, he rose from the edge of the bed and walked to the window.

"They'll have fun," he said absently, looking at dusk settling over the tourist-drenched street below.

"Mark? Is something wrong?"

The better question was, was anything right? At the moment, he couldn't see it.

"I had a repairman replace the broken hose to your stove while you slept yesterday," he answered. "The gas leak shouldn't happen again. He said you need to be careful not to move the stove too much, particularly not close to the wall. That's an easy way to break those hoses."

"I've cleaned behind the stove before without problems. Guess I didn't do well this time. I'll be more careful in the future."

Sheets rustled, and a moment later Mark felt Nicki at his back. He stiffened as she wrapped her hands around his shoulders and placed a soft kiss on his back. Her lips burned him, even through his shirt, through the armor he fought to trap his desire in.

"Thank you—again. You came to my rescue once more."

"I would have done it for anyone in that situation." He shrugged, turning to face her.

"I know you would. That's you."

Her smile was so genuine and lit with warmth, Mark nearly staggered. How could she seem so caring when she could be so dangerous?

"If you hadn't come to my door when you had and carried me outside . . . I wouldn't be here to tell you how much I appreciate you," she murmured.

Mark nodded. Yeah, if he hadn't come by . . . He could barely think about the consequences. In the moments he'd seen her pale and limp, heart beating too fast, he'd been more than shaken. The weight of fear had damn near crushed his chest like a two-ton block.

How much would it hurt if he had to put her behind bars?

He wrapped gentle fingers around her wrists, removing her hands from him. He couldn't stand her soft touch, wondering if it was a lie. She might appreciate his rescuing her, but she could still be using him to tidy up her false books so that they'd look nice and legal if the FBI or IRS came sniffing around. And she might be using his desire for her to keep him from the truth about her accounting. Why? Who knew? If she got caught, would she claim the manipulation of the books—and the money laundering—were all his doing and throw him under the bus?

Despite her dislike for Precious Moments dolls, was she as guilty as she appeared and, in the end, just like Tiffany?

Or was she a victim of something sinister?

Releasing her wrist, he stepped around her. "You should get back in bed."

She stopped him with a hand on his arm. "Come back to bed with me. I missed you."

Mark did his best to shut down, shut her out. Pain seeped in around the edges anyway, mixed with searing desire. He still wanted her, still loved her.

Damn, he was a stupid bastard. Maybe it wasn't that he was attracted to bad women as much as to wounded doves, to women he thought he could save. Maybe he had some twisted hero complex he wasn't aware of and didn't understand. Or maybe deep, deep down, he got off on emotional pain. Mark couldn't think of any other reason he would turn to Nicki, drag her against him, and seize her mouth as if his next breath of air could only come from her.

As he parted her lips beneath his with a moan, Mark sank into her sweetness, tasting, taking, ravaging. This was the one place she couldn't lie to him, couldn't pretend he didn't matter or didn't affect her.

Nicki might have a calculating heart . . . but she also had a very responsive body. He planned to make sure she understood just who had the power with only bare skin and shared sighs between them.

And he planned to make his point starting now.

Cradling the back of her head in his palm, Mark kept her mouth captive as he pushed farther inside, swirling his tongue around hers. Not that she was shy—never Nicki. She melted against him, seeming to give everything, as her own tongue slid in a sensual dance against his and, wriggling against him in invitation, set his blood boiling.

Pulling her with him, their mouths still connected, Mark twisted around and lay Nicki down on the bed, then followed her there. If she was going to be his downfall, by damned, then she wouldn't escape the encounter without a scar or two. By the time he was done with her, she'd know what it meant to want until her gut cramped with it, she woke in a cold sweat, aching with need, her heart clutching every time she looked at him and wondered why.

Turnabout was fair play.

Beneath him, Nicki arched, pushing erect nipples into his chest. She parted her thighs in invitation.

"You shouldn't have pushed me, Nicki," he whispered, voice thick. "You offered, so I'm taking. And taking, and taking. This isn't over until you've come so many times, you've lost count."

"Mark," she breathed. "I missed you. Touch me. Take me."

Then she stripped off her tank top, leaving nothing but the smooth satin of her olive skin that rolled into the hills of her firm breasts, topped with tight rosy tips.

He swallowed, steeling himself against the sight. If Nicki wanted to control him and drive him out of his mind, she was off to a great start. But not today, damn it.

Not ever again.

"My pace, my way," he growled. "You don't lift a finger unless you're told to."

"But—"

"Not a word, either."

She stared up at him, blue eyes dilated and confused—and aroused. Their blue invited him, like a calming pool. But he knew if he went there, he would drown.

Her arms came around him, fingers smoothing down his spine, leaving a swell of tingles in her wake. Then her palm cupped his ass and squeezed, and she lifted her hips beneath him, grinding her damp heat right against his cock, which began to throb in time with his quickening heartbeat.

Damn her.

"Stay there."

He lifted himself up from the bed and felt her stare glued to his back as he searched the drawers in her dresser. A few moments later, he found a bright red scarf. Then he flung the door of her walk-in closet open and prowled inside, past the miles of clothes and organized rows of shoes. Finally, he found a silky black robe and removed the belt. He turned back to her with a devious smile.

Nicki'd had him tied up in knots for weeks. Now it was her turn.

"Mark?" She looked at him with uncertainty, eyeing the items draped across his palm. But he saw excitement on her face, too.

He didn't answer. Before she could speak, he wound the red scarf around her right wrist and affixed it to her slatted headboard. He repeated the action to her left wrist, using the belt of her robe.

"Mark?" Her voice turned breathy. "What are you doing?"

He ignored her again, transfixed for the moment. Lean arms tapered down from her slender body. Her breasts had already swollen just the barest hint, her nipples as tight as ever. Her pajama bottoms rested low on her hips, revealing the dip of her waist to his hungry gaze.

But he wanted more. He'd bet she was already wet. Since Vegas was a gambling town, he decided to call his own game and find out.

Gaze fixed on the flimsy little bow beneath her navel, he gave a single tug, unraveling the whole thing.

"Answer me," Nicki demanded, her blue eyes flared with equal parts uncertainty and arousal.

Using his palms, he slid the garment down the sweet swell of her hips, smiling as he realized she wore no panties. He trailed one thumb over her cleft, pushing between the plump folds, grazing her clit. She gasped.

When he pulled his hand away, Mark found his thumb coated in her thick juice. He licked the pad of his thumb and smiled darkly, then wordlessly pushed her flimsy cotton pants over her thighs and past her feet.

She was naked.

"What—"

Placing a hand over her mouth, he sent her a razor-sharp smile. "You look pretty all bound and at my mercy."

He'd never given much thought to tying a woman up during sex. Immediately, he could see that his priorities needed adjusting.

Peeling off his shirt, Mark tossed it behind him and set to work on his button flys. Nicki watched his every movement, gaze glued to his fingers as one, two, three . . . all four buttons came undone under his insistent fingers. He pushed his jeans and underwear down, away, and kicked them aside.

They were quickly forgotten as he stalked closer to the bed, arousal boiling in his blood. Had he ever been this hard? Seeing his cock standing straight at attention and seeming to flirt with his belly button, he didn't think so.

Turning back to Nicki, he reached down to palm her breast and flicked his thumb over the turgid nub of her nipple. Her eyes widened. She stiffened. He did it again, this time not just smoothing his digit over the tight kernel, but rolling it between this thumb and forefinger. He squeezed, then rolled again. Squeezed and rolled. Nicki closed her eyes and pressed her thighs tightly together.

"Open them," he demanded.

She frowned. "What?"

Mark smiled at the raspy tone in her voice. "Your eyes. Your legs. I want all your secrets bare for me."

Slowly, she lifted her lids. Blinked. Then she settled her gaze on his face, somehow solemn and flush-cheeked at once. She appeared to be excited and wasn't sure she wanted to be. He related to that sentiment.

"Don't stop there." He dropped his gaze down to her legs, still firmly closed. She glistened with her arousal now. He could barely tear his eyes away.

Still, he sensed her stubborn resolve not to surrender . . . and found it totally unacceptable. She'd had him enthralled since the moment he'd seen her picture. Time to help her appreciate what he'd been going through.

Inserting one of his hands between her feet, he tapped on the inside of her ankle, gently nudging. Her thighs parted a fraction. He tapped again. She opened a degree more, swallowing as she did. Lust? Apprehension? A bit of both, judging by her expression. But she relished the uncertainty, if he could believe her taut body.

Feral need tore through him as he patted her other ankle and she inched it away from the other slowly. Now he could see more than the dark dusting of her pubic hair. Suddenly, she revealed a peek of the plump folds of her wet sex. And he was dying to get his mouth on her.

Lowering himself to the bed, he covered Nicki's legs with his torso, his mouth hovering over the valley between her straining breasts. Again, he palmed each, toying with her nipples, manipulating the hard nubs with his fingers and thumbs—a hard squeeze, a gentle brush—for endless minutes he did nothing more than tug on her nipples, soothe them. Beneath him, she began to squirm, moving her hips as if looking for the relief of the pressure building inside her. That wasn't happening until he was good and ready.

"Mark . . ." Her voice had a pleading, breathy quality that both pleased and aroused him.

In answer, he lowered his head, took one of her aching peaks in his mouth, and swept it with his tongue, curling, laving. He kept his fingers relentlessly fastened to the other nipple for long minutes.

Nicki writhed with more determination. Her juices dampened his belly. Poor baby. Too bad she wasn't even close to finding release . . . yet.

"Mark," she said firmly.

Hard for him to take her seriously when her demand sounded more like a moan.

In answer, he only switched nipples, orally fixating on the other one while he massaged its slick, rigid mate.

She gasped as he nipped at her with his teeth, then soothed her with his tongue. Beneath him, her breathing turned shallow and fast.

"Don't tease me."

"If you want something, stop demanding. Start begging."

* * *

WRITHING beneath Mark, Nicki couldn't decide if she wanted to tackle the arrogant hulk and show him a few things about teasing, or give in and beg . . . and revel in the pleasure he was so gifted at giving.

And as much as she'd love to contemplate what might be causing his he-man behavior, the ache he created was making thought so not possible.

But begging? It went against her pride, her independent nature.

Unfortunately, it was hard to care when her blood scalded her insides so thoroughly, Nicki felt sure her skin would soon start peeling from her bones. And he hadn't yet touched anything besides her breasts.

Pride wasn't what stopped her from begging, however.

"C'mon, Nicki." His rough voice scraped over her defenses, slowly wearing them down. "What do you like, baby? What do you want?"

"For you to play fair," she managed to eek out.

Mark laughed. "Another time."

He traced a fingertip in the valley between her breasts and dragged it down her abdomen. She sucked in a sharp breath, watching the Celtic knot around his biceps ripple with every movement. Then he veered away, circling her hipbone, before gliding down the seam between her abdomen and thighs.

Heading straight for her wet center.

Nicki squeezed her eyes shut, desperate to block out the sensation, to stop this crazy game. She wanted him—God, so much, in so many ways. He was about to fulfill one of her favorite fantasies. For once, her heart and her body were in sync. It just wasn't the best timing. And he wasn't the best guy with whom to lose her head.

What began as a fling had morphed into something that made her heart soar when they laughed together, something that clenched her chest with pain when they argued. And something that cut her like a dull knife when she sensed Mark holding back, as he was now.

Unfortunately, he had learned her body. Very well. Learned that when he inserted a pair of fingers inside her and pressed up while thumbing her clit she could not keep herself from crying out for him and reeling heart-first into the orgasmic pleasure he gave her. Like now. He'd learned that when he spoke to her in those soft, rasping tones and told her how beautiful she looked when she came that she almost always fell over again. Like now.

Damp everywhere with perspiration, Nicki strained against her bonds. Not because he frightened her. Mark had saved her life twice. He wasn't going to hurt her. She yearned to be at his tender mercy, in fact. But not when he was using her desires to control her. Not when he kept his heart distant . . .

"Untie me," she panted. "Please."

In answer, Mark wended his way down her body. He positioned his head between her legs. She felt his hot breath against her, right where she ached. She began to tremble.

"God, I love to have you spread out like this, so wet and ready for my mouth or my cock. But you know that."

The ache between her legs tightened unmercifully at his words. Looking down her body at Mark lounging between her thighs, Nicki watched as he gathered her hips in his big hands. The lust in those dark-lashed hazel eyes was easy to spot. A fiery green seemed to dominate whenever he was aroused, highlighted by a stain of flush on his cheeks.

But he hid everything else behind that fierce expression of desire.

Trapped between the fantasy of her bonds and the reality of Mark's distance, she tried to wriggle and thrash from his grip. He was far too strong, too determined to simply let her go.

"I don't want you when you're like this."

"Clearly not true." He slid a finger through her humid center. Her juices coated his fingers in seconds. "I see the resident commando bitch has a submissive streak."

Frustrated by her own arousal and his sheer stubbornness she hissed, "Fuck you!"

Mark just smiled, something cold and glittering, that made the woman in her both pant and worry.

"I plan to do just that. And enjoy myself thoroughly."

It wasn't politically correct, and it made no sense to her, but Nicki couldn't deny that the crude, dominating streak he was displaying now turned her on despite the warning bells in her head. But she also knew this conversation, odd as it was, couldn't be anything less than serious. She had to keep her wits . . . somehow.

Easier said than done, particularly when he bent to her and raked his tongue over her clit in a long, lapping stroke that had her thighs tensing against the pleasure.

"Is this some sort of game to you?" she croaked out.

Mark froze, then seemed to force himself to relax. He distracted her by strumming his thumb over her clit once, twice. He followed that with another lazy swipe of his tongue. So sensitive now after a pair of demanding orgasms, Nicki couldn't stop herself from gasping and arching.

"You tell me, Nicki."

"Of course it's not a game," she managed to get out.

"You've never tried to control me with this pretty pussy?" Mark sucked her clit into his mouth and teased the hard bud with the tip of his tongue.

Her entire body clenched as sensations ricocheted through her, bouncing off her nerve endings, swelling her with blood and need. God, she *had* to reach him, but the air between them seemed almost combative. Emotionally, he'd never been more distant.

"No," she managed to gasp out, even though her body really just wanted to end this verbal distraction and encourage him to lick her to orgasm with a resounding *Hell, yes!*

"Then a little harmless play between lovers shouldn't put you off from begging for what you need," he purred.

Then he bent his mouth to her in earnest. Tongue sliding up her folds, dipping deep into her core, taking a lazy lash against her clit. Pleasure didn't just climb like some leisurely stroll up to the peak. No, it soared, consuming her, keeping her hot, taut as he circled the throbbing little bud between her legs and massaged her nipples with firm strokes of his thumbs.

Her body established direct connections between her aching breasts and her swollen clit, every time he pulled on one, the other jumped. Which only darted the pleasure back up her body. Damn, she couldn't breathe. Her entire field of vision had been reduced to a pair or challenging hazel eyes that burned every time he settled his mouth on her flesh. A buzzing began in her ears.

"Do you need something, Nicki?"

She gasped. A plea weighed on the end of her tongue. It was so simple; a few little words, and he would take her to a euphoria likely higher than she'd ever known. Nicki wanted to say it so bad, to give in and relieve whatever demon was eating at him.

Giving up just wasn't in her nature.

"Give it to me," she panted. "Or get out."

He lifted his head for a moment, glancing up her body, silent, watchful. But his thumbs never ceased their exquisite torture of her nipples. Now slightly sore from his insistent fingers and mouth, the coil of desire inside her corkscrewed tighter every time he touched her.

"Big words for a woman who's all tied up." He shrugged. "Okay, we'll play it your way."

Mark settled his mouth back over her clit, his fingers still focused on the taut peaks of her breasts. He flicked the hard nubbin between her thighs with the firm tip of his tongue and pinched her nipples.

Nicki fought and fought . . . but she was no match for his insistent touch. She exploded with a cry, convulsing fast, so hard her shoulders left the bed and a moment of dizziness brought her crashing back to the mattress.

"Pretty," he murmured. "Let's see if we can do better."

Before she could question that, Mark climbed his way up her body and inserted a pair of fingers as he went, immediately pressing up on the sweet spot that always had her screaming. She expected his mouth to settle over her nipples, but after a gentle nip that made her back arch, he moved away in a flurry of kisses that strung up her neck so he could whisper in her ear.

"Come for me, Nicki. Scream. Surrender, baby. There's nothing that turns me on more than watching you give everything to me."

He settled a thumb over her clit and nibbled on her lobe, breathing hot and insistent in her ear. Tingles chased one another up her body. The ache ramped up again, twice as fast, twice as fierce, as before. *No, no, no,* her head screamed.

Her body screamed *yes, yes, yes* and released again—a long, drugging climax that made her cry out with an incoherent please, turned the edges of her vision black. She struggled to catch every breath.

"That's it, baby. So fucking sexy," he whispered. "Give me more."

"No," she said weakly.

"You ready to beg?"

She gritted her teeth, anger stirring her up. Or was that more arousal?

"Not in this lifetime."

"See? You still got plenty of spark in that lush body. And I want it all. I'm going to have you all sweet and docile before we're done."

He worked his way down her body again, mouth trailing soft nibbling kisses down her skin. With no idea what he might do, Nicki tensed. Another orgasm like the last one, and she'd likely lose consciousness.

Still, she wasn't going to let him win. Showing him weakness would be the worst thing possible.

"You want docile," she said between harsh breaths, "get a dog."

"You're pushing me, Nicki," he growled.

Glad to see him fraying around the edges of his control finally, she snapped, "Just like you're pushing me, over and over."

"And I'm not done."

With no warning, he pulled his fingers from her seeping folds, trailed one down. He circled it around the rosette of her ass. Nicki's eyes widened as she saw his mouth hovering over her breast, the feral intent on his face.

Never had she allowed anyone to touch her there. She'd never even given it much thought. Yet as he inserted the tip of his finger and began to slide the digit fully inside, she couldn't deny that the thought suddenly made her burn.

"Mark," she groaned, her body pushing against him of its own will.

"That's it, baby. God, you're sexy. Feel good?"

He lowered his head and took her aching nipple into his mouth. Nicki answered with a keening cry.

He inserted another wet finger inside her ass and pumped them in and out. Nicki arched into the stretching, burning sensation he created. So new, so forbidden. Arousal rocketed up, churning in her gut until she clawed at her binds. Her entire body grew taut, trembled, as she held her breath, waiting for the mammoth orgasm to send her over. Instead, he pulled back.

"You win, damn it. I can't wait, not another second," he growled.

It was not a happy admission.

Scrambling across the bed, Mark grabbed a condom and ripped it open. Nicki watched with wide eyes, heart pounding, skin damp. By all rights, she should be spent, have absolutely nothing left to give him. But watching Mark sheath that long, strong cock of his with the angry purple head . . . desire swamped her again, fresh and fierce. She felt empty, aching. Only he could cure that.

"We win," she corrected. "Once you're inside me, we both win."

He paused and stared with a look she couldn't decipher. Then he reached back inside her nightstand and grabbed her slimline vibe.

As he placed it on the bed, he smiled.

Oh, what did he have planned?

Then edging back between her legs, he bent her knees up to her shoulders and plunged inside with one deep stroke.

Nicki felt her swollen flesh close around the burning column of his cock, now buried to the hilt inside her, nudging the mouth of her womb. She gasped as he flexed his hips, piercing her with an extra fraction of an inch, touching her someplace that set her aflame.

Then he eased back, slowly, so slowly she bit her lip to keep a cry inside. Her body, with a mind of its own, did its best to suck him back in.

He groaned. "Nicki, baby . . ."

In answer, she whimpered.

"Oh, yeah. I feel you all around me. Give me everything."

His sandpaper voice echoed between them, firing her nerves, as he reached across the bed and grabbed her vibe. Flipping it on, he looked down at her, watched her reaction as he lowered it between them, gliding it over her clit. She tightened around him as the unbearable need in her belly clenched. *Ohmigod, what will he do next?* And still he kept on, rolling the wand lower, where they lay joined, teasing her dripping folds and the base of his cock, until the vibe was slick with her juice.

"Mark . . ."

"Push down, baby."

Nicki had no idea what he meant until he nudged her anus with the vibe. Pleasure speared her as it pulsed around her nerve-laden entrance.

With a little push, the tip of the vibe entered, stretching her a bit. A new burn seared her, both pain and pleasure.

He withdrew it to tease the seeping opening of her sex with the vibrating toy, until the pleasure pushed her past coherence. She whimpered as he lowered the vibe again.

"Push down," he growled.

Helpless, with all the resistance of melted butter, she did as he demanded. This time, the slender toy slid all the way inside, throbbing inside her, jangling her nerves, her needs, with something she'd never experienced before. Panting, she molded herself around him, as if he was her life raft in a drowning sea of pleasure. And every breath they shared, every heartbeat, gonged inside her body, multiplying her arousal.

Suddenly, Mark pinned her to the bed with a glowing green stare. Teeth clenched, bared, Nicki felt him trembling. He wanted something, and he was fighting it. No, not something, someone. *Her.* Suddenly, she got that. Her heart flipped over in her chest.

That love he'd inadvertently confessed to two weeks ago seemed to swirl along with the rage in his eyes.

Oh, Mark.

To let him know she was safe, that she wouldn't hurt him, she slowly wrapped her legs around him and invited him back inside her.

He hesitated, then with a groan, he accepted, plunging deep. He'd lodged the vibe firmly within her and held it there with a finger, making her passage that much tighter when he tilted her up to him with insistent fingers bracketing her hips and pounded into her. The first stroke scraped her G-spot. The second bumped her clit. The third did both . . . and the little vibrator throbbed inside her ass, providing extra fuel for every other sensation tearing through her. Already beyond stimulated and emotionally on the edge, she reached another pinnacle on the fourth thrust, convulsing around him so hard, she screamed.

She arched off the bed, as black spots did a slow waltz in her vision. Mark's arms came around her, under her, clutching her to his massive chest. She could hear the rapid *bang, bang, bang* of his heart, which matched the pace of his wild strokes. Tingles detonated on the sides of her tongue—a first for her. Pinpricks of pleasure suffused her skin, infecting her blood. It was excruciating, exquisite, unlike anything she'd ever felt.

And she knew without a doubt that she could only give that much to a man she truly cared for. She'd lost her battle with herself.

She loved him.

"Nicki." His voice, low and harsh, almost sounded like something out of an alien movie.

But when she forced her eyes to open and focus on him, desperation clawed at his face, along with a need so strong, Nicki sucked in a breath against its power. And love, spinning in a kaleidoscope of emotions in those green eyes drew her under his spell and persuaded her to return everything he felt.

Despite being sore everywhere and her inner thigh muscles screaming for relief, Nicki spread her legs wider and kissed the side of his neck.

"I love you," she whispered into his ear.

Shock dominated his expression as he lifted his head to stare. Then he swelled, hardened, slammed into her with breathtaking force . . . and ecstasy took over. With a roar, he came, pumping endlessly into her, as he muttered something muffled against her shoulder. Nicki would have paid her last dollar to hear it.

But he sent her careening over the edge one last time instead, until she swore she saw stars. Lord knew, she was already over the moon for Mark.

A silent moment later, he caught his breath. Quickly, he rose, extracted the vibe, untied her hands, and gathered his clothes. Nicki held her breath, hoping he'd say something—anything. Instead, he disappeared to the bathroom, shooting her a fierce frown.

Nicki knew then that whatever he might feel for her, that thick skull of his would never let her defrost the wall of ice he'd packed his heart in.

* * *

"YOU look like hell." Lucia slid into the diner's red vinyl booth, looking annoyingly well-rested and dewy after a morning walk.

Nicki scowled. "Damn. Nothing is supposed to be too matchy-matchy this season. Guess I'll have to change my look. My mood isn't going to improve anytime soon."

"Red-rimmed eyes usually say hangover, lack of sleep, or jagged bouts of tears. Which one?"

"Mostly the second, with a little of the third thrown in."

Lucia shook her head and sighed. "This has to be about Mark Gabriel. Everything else just pisses you off. Only that man can incite you to tears."

"You always were the smarter sister," Nicki said bitterly.

After they both ordered coffee and pancakes from the teenaged waiter, Nicki asked, "Where's Ashley?"

"Sleeping. The time change has thrown her for a loop. It's four hours earlier in Hawaii, remember. But that's not important." Lucia crossed her arms over her chest. "What is important, is Mark Gabriel. I'm forever grateful that he saved you, but why do you keep that man around when he only tears you apart on a regular basis?"

"Because the sex is beyond amazing?"

"I could have done without hearing that."

"You encouraged me, if you'll recall, suggesting that I practically offer myself."

"When I thought what you were feeling was mutual, it made sense. Besides, that's not the issue. Even if you had great sex with Jack the Ripper, you wouldn't keep him around if you didn't care about him."

"You're right." Nicki felt every instant of the eight hours of sleep she hadn't gotten last night. "Somehow, somewhere along the way, I fell in love. I even told him that, and I've never said those words to any man except Dad."

"What was his reaction?"

"After he came? He got up, disappeared into the bathroom, dressed, and left. All without a word."

And that hurt the most. He had nothing to say to her after she'd admitted she loved him.

Lucia reached across the table and squeezed her hand. "You know I can't offer you much advice, since I don't have any real experience with men, but I'm here for you."

"I appreciate it. I really have no one to blame but myself. The timing is lousy. Sometimes Mark is so secretive. He'll never stay in Vegas. And he's never going to admit he loves me, even though I think he does."

"Too macho?"

Nicki shook her head, almost wishing it was that simple. He'd be easy to write off, then. "Too broken, I think. There's a woman in his past."

"What did she do?"

"I have no idea. Mark has made it very clear that's not a topic open for discussion."

The waiter set down their pancakes, and Nicki sighed, half-heartedly buttering her breakfast. "Whatever it was went deep. He's scarred. You know I'm not a quitter, but I think banging my head against a wall actually has more purpose than trying to reach his heart."

Lucia winced at her words. Then she took a bite of pancakes, chewed. Suddenly, her expression smoothed. An idea lit her face.

"What?" Nicki demanded. "I see you're cooking up something. Spill it."

"You know, I realize that nearly five hundred years isn't irrelevant, but I'm not sure that the dynamics of male-female stuff has changed all that much, not deep down. Granted, knights weren't hooking up or making friends with benefits for a booty call . . . but maybe you ought to take a page from Anne Boleyn's book."

"Anne Boleyn?" Nicki poured syrup and took a bite.

Lucia nodded. "Henry the eighth's second wife. The daughter of a mere knight, though her uncle was a duke. Anyway, King Henry fancied Anne and wanted to make her his mistress. He even sent away Anne's main suitor. Anne refused Henry. Her sister had already been his mistress, and it had gotten her nothing but discarded. Anne was smarter. She refused Henry time and again, insisting that he marry her before she gave him any. Eventually, she prevailed. He not only married her, he split from the Catholic church and created a church of his own so he could do it."

"The vagina is mightier than the sword?"

Lucia laughed. "Something like that."

"After advising me to sleep with him, now you think I'm giving Mark too much sex?"

"Let him miss you a bit. If he doesn't have his every desire granted every time he snaps his fingers, he might talk to you, listen to you, find out that you're not the kind of woman who will break his heart. Hard to come to that conclusion when you're only focused on orgasm."

Nicki frowned. "You can't possibly have read *that* in a book!"

"You'd be surprised what history can teach you."

"Okay, so Anne and Henry got married and lived happily ever after because they knew each other so well and were ga-ga in love?"

"No," Lucia sipped her coffee, then admitted with obvious reluctance. "Henry beheaded Anne three years later."

Nicki gaped. "Pass! I'll take being brokenhearted."

"Stop. Mark isn't likely to off you because he demands to have a male heir you're not providing."

"True." She popped another bit of pancake into her mouth.

"Think about it. My mother always said 'why should a farmer buy a cow if she's giving away the milk for free?'"

"Are you calling me a cow?"

"It's an analogy. Work with me, here."

She sighed. "I'll try."

An electronic chiming had Nicki diving for her purse. She dug through all her junk, then snatched out her cell phone. Caller ID flashed the number for the club. *Damn!*

"Yeah?" she answered.

"Nicki, honey," Zack started. "Your uncle is here, demanding to see you pronto."

"Before ten in the morning?"

"Yes, ma'am. And none too happy that you aren't here."

"I'm eating."

"Fork it down fast. He's got all the charm of a six-headed snake, and I'm not in the mood to pet sit."

"This blows." She sighed. "I'll be there in fifteen minutes."

"What's going on?" Lucia asked as Nicki disconnected the call.

"Pietro is at the club and wants to see me now. This will be about Mark being my accountant, want to bet? Blade told him, no doubt. He probably also told Pietro that Mark and I are sleeping together, so I'm sure I've got that lecture coming, as well. Never mind that I damn near died."

"Dad's choice of brothers left something to be desired . . ."

Slapping a twenty down on the diner's faux Formica counter, Nicki rose. "May as well get this over with. After dealing with him, what could be worse?"

Chapter Thirteen

NICKI entered the club to pandemonium. With the first floor devoid of dancers or customers, hearing the shouting going on upstairs was as easy as reciting her ABC's.

"I don't care what Nicki said," Pietro shouted. "Blade is her accountant, not you."

"Are you aware, Mr. DiStefano, that Bocelli is not qualified? He categorized cleaning supplies as food and beverages."

That was Mark. And he sounded pissed.

"Oh, that doesn't sound good," Lucia whispered.

Wincing in agreement, Nicki climbed the stairs, her sister right behind her. They hovered right outside the door.

"Did the totals match the bank statements?" Pietro demanded.

Mark sighed. "By some miracle, yes."

"Then it don't matter. Get your ass back onstage and start shaking it so you make this place some money. Nicki don't got no sense to be thinking you belong in this office instead of in a G-string. What am I saying? She don't got no sense, anyway." He spoke as if that fact should be obvious to everyone. "Her queer stage manager tells me she gassed herself to incoherent with her own stove."

"My name is Zack," he protested petulantly. "And I prefer not to be called queer."

Pietro ignored him.

Outside the door, Nicki stopped and gritted her teeth. Sometimes she hated that man. Yeah, blood is thicker than water and all that, but he could be such an asshole.

"Actually," Mark's voice soothed after Pietro's annoying diatribe, "she has a great deal of sense. She hired an experienced CPA to do her accounting: Me. She runs a tight ship, takes care of her customers and employees, understands what her patrons want. She runs her ass off taking care of this place. More than once, I've seen her go for twenty-four hours straight just to make sure this club and its employees are properly cared for."

Did he really think that? Nicki wondered. Gosh, he sounded almost . . . proud of her. The mere possibility made her smile.

"That's true," Zack seconded.

"So?" Pietro's voice let everyone know he wasn't impressed.

"So how does you dropping in once in a blue moon and issuing orders that make no sense make you an expert on this place?" Mark challenged. "You discount Nicki, when you have no idea what she does or just how smart she really is."

Nicki's mouth dropped. *Go, Mark!* He'd just had the balls to tell her uncle everything she'd been trying to say for years. Not because she wanted to keep the peace—little of that between them. And not for the sake of family harmony. She'd kept it to herself only because she knew it would be a waste of breath.

But Mark had said it to Pietro—a virtual stranger—just to defend her. Damn if that didn't warm her heart.

"She's a woman. What the hell can she know about running a business?" he scoffed. "I need to find some nice Italian boy to put her in her place. Marry her and knock her up. Shut her up for a change and get her out of my hair."

"Apparently he's forgotten that most of his remaining hair is on his chest," Lucia grumbled.

Nicki nodded, fuming. Why did having a vagina somehow make her stupid?

"Are you blind?" Mark asked, his tone indicating that Pietro was more likely insane than visually impaired. "Nicki deserves so much more. She's too vital to be married to some chauvinist whose primary goal in life is to get her pregnant, keep a mistress, then piously attend Mass every Sunday. She's extremely smart—"

"Lucia is the one with brains. Nicki's assets are in her bra."

Both she and Lucia gaped at Pietro's rude comment. Nothing should shock her at this point, Nicki knew. But her uncle had reached a new low.

"Lucia is bright with books and learning," Mark conceded. "But Nicki knows people. She knows how to make sure they have a good time in this place. She's efficient and clever—"

"You keep taking up for her, and I'm gonna start suspecting you of banging my niece. That won't make me happy."

Blade hadn't flat out told Pietro about her fling with Mark? Shocking. Or maybe he just hadn't had time yet.

"Whatever sex life Nicki and I may or may not have is absolutely none of your business."

"I'm her guardian."

"She's twenty-six years old," Mark reminded him. "Trust me, Nicki is totally equipped to live her own life without your interference. That includes running her club."

"So you are banging her. Since you're not Italian, I won't have you in the family. You're probably not even Catholic," Pietro spat.

"Again, none of your business." Mark's voice had gone from hard to implacable. Not a good sign.

"Do you want your arms or legs broken first?"

Ugh! Mr. Old School had been watching gangster movies again. Having heard more than enough, Nicki set to burst in. Bad-news Bocelli interrupted her.

"Look, dancer boy. You heard the boss man. Turn the books back over to me and no one gets hurt."

"That's Nicki's decision. If Nicki says you're the man, fine. Until then, I'm here to stay. Now excuse me."

Nicki heard Mark's double-edged tone. Was he warning Blade that her choice applied to matters beyond who did her accounting? The thought pleased her.

A moment later, footsteps told Nicki that Mark intended to leave the room. Time for her to intervene before things got really ugly.

"Let's drop in on the overgrown boys," she whispered to Lucia.

"Amen," her sister shot back. "If you don't, He-Man and the Hulk will start fighting right there in your office and reduce it to rubble in ten minutes.

"Yes, but my money is on Mark to win." Nicki smiled.

Their mere appearance at the door to the office had Pietro scowling, Bocelli staring, and Mark pretending not to look relieved.

Poor guy, having to put up with the Italian version of Tweedle-Dee and Tweedle-Dum. Mark had earned a little backup. Everything he'd said to her uncle thrilled her. He'd defended her abilities, her intelligence, her right to make her own decisions. If he didn't believe in her and didn't give a damn, he wouldn't have said anything. Oh, he might have fought for his job, but not by reciting a laundry list of her capabilities.

Gotta love a man who knew it didn't take a penis to ensure an IQ larger than one's shoe size. And while not all men were sexist pigs these days, she knew enough to realize that Mark's willingness to put himself on the line to defend her was something just a little special.

Somewhere, deep inside that man, beat a heart that cared about her. Even if he denied it and hated it and was even now trying to carve it out with the rusty edge of a tin can.

The only thing between her and having the man she loved devoted to her in some way that didn't involve sex was to find out what that bitch in his past had done to him and prove she would not do the same.

* * *

MONDAY morning, Nicki knocked on Mark's door at an obnoxiously early hour, for her anyway: nine-thirty.

Mark opened the door. Surprise washed over him to see Nicki standing there, wearing a casual white sundress with a flared skirt, and thin, lacy straps that allowed a bare hint of cleavage to show, and carrying a wide-brimmed straw hat. Her hair fell down to her shoulders in soft curls that matched her soft smile. This was a whole new side of Nicki, feminine, a hint of sweet lace and innocence.

If he hadn't known her better, he'd be tempted to believe it.

"Hi," she murmured. "I've come to surprise you today."

"I'm already surprised. This is early for you."

She shrugged. "You're worth losing a little sleep. After all you've done for me, I wanted to give something back to you. And you've been edgy lately. Worried, I guess, maybe a little . . . down, so I wanted share something with you. Come with me?"

She held out her hand, face hopeful, blue eyes sparkling with warmth. There was nothing sexual about it, which stunned him. She wasn't here fishing for orgasms. Or asking him about the books. Nicki wanted to . . . cheer him up?

Or did she have a hidden agenda?

I love you. She'd whispered those three potent words the last time he'd been deep inside her. As soon as she'd uttered them, his trip through Pleasure Central had zipped at light-speed straight to Orgasmland. Yeah, in the cold light of day, he had to face the fact she could be lying, playing a game with him to cover her illegal activity, distract him from digging too deep and asking too many questions.

But in that moment, he'd wished desperately that she'd whispered the truth.

Today, who knew? Was she here out of obligation for pulling her out of her gas-ridden apartment? To pull the old bait-and-switch while something else with her accounts went down today? Any chance she actually cared?

Whatever her motivation, he had to play along. Not that spending the day with Nicki, who looked like a cross between a white daisy and a southern belle, was a hardship.

Mark reached out and put his hand in hers.

"Whew! I was beginning to wonder if you were going to turn me down," she bantered playfully. "Couldn't imagine why. I showered and everything this morning."

"You look great," he said softly, knowing it would likely be the only honest thing he was able to say to her all day.

She reached up and planted a quick kiss on the corner of his mouth. Intoxicated by her citrus-cinnamon scent and the pouting curve of her mouth, Mark shifted to move in and capture her lips.

Nicki had already turned around and tugged on his hand, dragging him out into the landing. "C'mon. I want to get there when the . . . well, when it starts."

Shutting and locking the door behind him, Mark allowed Nicki to lead him down the stairs and to the parking lot.

The heat was already shimmering off the blacktop. The incessant Vegas sunlight assaulted him with piercing brightness and oven-like temperatures. Gosh, and it wasn't even ten in the morning. But he had to admit all the people who'd said over the years that the dry hot of the desert was easier to bear were right.

"Where are we going?" he asked.

"It's a surprise, silly."

She smiled and . . . was she batting her eyes like a flirt? Sleek, stiletto-wearing Nicki was wearing a modest dress and giving him the Scarlett O'Hara routine? Okay, what the hell was up?

With a laugh, she pulled him over to her car. He stopped dead in his tracks.

"You're kidding, right?"

"You don't like my Crossfire Roadster?" The furrow of her brow conveyed confusion.

"Uh . . . It's very you."

The compact glossy red convertible with the black leather top sat low to the ground. She pressed a button on her key fob. The car beeped, lights flashed. She opened the door with flourish. "This is a great car. Speedy, reliable, responsive."

Mark cleared his throat. "And built for someone well under six feet tall. I'm almost six-six. Nicki, If I get in there, I'll have to duck my ears between my knees . . . if I even manage to squeeze in."

"I'll fix that. Gimme a minute."

She hopped into the driver's seat, started the engine, pressed a button . . . and down came the top. Nicki reached into the glove box, grabbed out a hairclip with plastic teeth, then twisted her hair on top of her head. A squeeze of the clip later, and the dark curls bobbed in the breeze, attached to just below her crown.

"How about now?" she asked. "The seat slides back a bit more, so you shouldn't have to do your imitation of the fetal position just to get to . . . where we're going."

"And I take it you're not going to tell me where that is?" he asked, climbing into the passenger seat.

A playful smile curled up her pillowy red mouth. "I always knew you were smart."

With that, Nicki flipped on the radio, something peppy and light and pop-oriented Mark had never heard, considering he tended to favor Nickelback, Nirvana, and classic rock. Not awful actually, the catchy little tune.

"How long is this drive?"

"Oh, no. No fishing for information. In fact . . ."

She reached over the middle console and grabbed her purse, which he hadn't noticed until now sat between his feet. From inside the overstuffed, tiny bag, she pulled out a red scarf. He instantly recognized it as the one he'd used to tie her right wrist to the bed two days ago. Between that bright red reminder and the sight of her leaning over his thigh to reach her purse—and a potent whiff of that tangy spiced fruit scent of hers—he became hard as an iron post in three seconds.

Had he last touched her a mere two days ago? Felt like two damn years.

To his shock, Nicki then folded the scarf, all but climbed into his lap, and placed it over his eyes.

"No." Mark grabbed her wrists, forcing her to lower the scarf.

"I'm not going to hurt you." She scoffed. "As if I could."

True, but . . . "I don't like not knowing what's going on. And I'm not thrilled at the idea of looking like a jackass."

"Well, certainly you can make one teeny exception for the sake of a surprise. I'll be driving, so my hands can't wander to your . . . person and disturb you. I'll be looking at the road, so I won't be staring at you when you can't see. I'll be in my own seat, so I can't do anything with my mouth you might disapprove of."

If the issue was merely about what she'd be doing with her hands and mouth . . . bring it on. He could take her—again and again. It was wondering what locale she'd drive him to and what would happen when they got there. He didn't think Nicki would chauffeur him straight to a lair of thugs set up firing-squad style, but he didn't want to bet his life on it. Even if it seemed out of character, Nicki could well be laundering money for someone who probably had no aversion to violence whatsoever. Both Pietro and Bocelli fit that description.

Still, Rafe had always advised him to use his gut. It told him that Nicki wouldn't harm him physically.

Emotionally, all bets were off.

Now she was looking at him as if his refusal and hesitation really hurt her feelings. Damn it, he either had to upset her or trust her. The hell of it was, he hadn't been good at trust since Tiffany.

"Look, it's not that big a deal," Nicki uttered as she backed away. But she sounded disappointed. "I wanted to surprise you, but if it makes you uncomfortable—"

"Just do it," he growled, grabbing her wrist.

Damn it. He'd deal with whatever came his way.

Hesitantly, Nicki leaned over and knotted the scarf at the back of his head. When she straightened away, he couldn't see a thing except the general impression of sunlight all around.

With that, she backed out of her parking space and zipped out of the lot. Soon out of the traffic, one upbeat pop song followed another, punctuated by the occasional ballad or offbeat eighty's hit. Most of it was drowned out by the wind stirring all around them, blowing his hair into his face. Her speed picked up, signifying open highway beneath the tires.

Otherwise, they rode in silence. Not comfortable, not awkward. Without his sight, he sensed a tension in Nicki he hadn't seen in her flirty expression. His own thoughts kept whirling with possibilities. He could be headed for an afternoon of danger at gunpoint or hot sex.

About an hour later, she slowed to a stop and put the car into park.

Nicki took a deep breath. "I wanted to bring you someplace away from the bustle of Vegas, hopefully someplace where you could forget about your sister's recent problems . . . and whatever else might be troubling you. I'm hoping that you'll just relax and enjoy yourself today."

Mark was still pondering where the hell she might have taken him when he smelled her mouthwatering scent looming close, felt the brush of her breasts, the warmth of her body, despite the rising temperature of the June day. The erection that had abated during the drive returned with a vengeance.

The blindfold fell away. Instantly, Mark realized there were no gangsters ready to fit him for a pair of cement shoes or use him for target practice. Just a few senior citizens milling in the parking lot and a young couple holding hands. In fact, the last thing he expected to see when he blinked and his eyes grew accustomed to the streaming sunlight was two white buildings basking in the perfect, cloudless day, one resembling a multistoried bell tower. The other structure was square and high-roofed with arched windows and a large sign welcoming them to the award-winning winery in the desert.

"Well?" Nicki prompted.

He turned to her hopeful expression, watching at she bit her lip nervously.

"A winery?"

"It's a pretty place. They have a great restaurant and tours, along with a neat little gift shop."

He said nothing; he didn't know what to say. He'd never been a big wine drinker, on the one hand. But the place was crisp and pristine, rising into the desert sun with the mountains as a majestic backdrop. The more puzzling thing, however, was Nicki. Had she really brought him here for no other reason than to cheer him up?

"Or if you're not interested, maybe I'll just buy you a bottle, get you drunk, take you home, and strap *you* to the bed for a change."

Mark recognized the acid impatience in her tone. And he burst out laughing.

"Wow, difficult choice. A day of culture with a pretty woman or hot, sloppy sex I'm not likely to finish before passing out. Hmm, guess I'll take a chance and go with door number one."

The smile dancing at the corners of her mouth kicked up again. "Good choice. Let's go." She climbed out of the car and called back to him, "The first tour starts at eleven."

Within moments, they joined the seniors and the couple drooling all over each other for a leisurely stroll around the grounds that looked like a lush green oasis rising from the desert. Green lawns, palms, and willows swaying in the breeze fringed the larger building that housed the equipment used to ferment and bottle the wines. Nicki slipped little tasting cups up to his mouth. He wasn't terribly interested in fermented grapes . . . but Nicki's blue eyes pleaded. He relented, if for no other reason than to see her smile, to feel him touch her as she lifted the cups to his lips.

God, he had it bad.

They sipped wine of all varieties, Mark gravitating to dry ones with a bit more body, Nicki to light, fruity ones with emphasis on sweetness. By the end of the tour, they marveled at the winery's workings. They also laughed with one of the seniors who'd done a bit too much tasting, then tucked the length of her skirt into her waistband and imitated Lucille Ball during the winemaking episode on *I Love Lucy.*

More relaxed than he had been in weeks, Mark linked Nicki's fingers with his and led her outside. They emerged on the other side of the building, into the sunlight again, on a long white porch. Slender white columns held up the porch, dotted with climbing ivy. Wicker rockers welcomed visitors to sit and stare at the vineyards beyond that stretched to the base of the mountain.

Mark had to admit it was beautiful here. Peaceful.

The seniors lingered inside, asking the tour guide all manner of questions about making wines . . . and several trying to talk the one into righting her skirt. The young couple clutched one another's hands. Mark overheard them discussing their upcoming wedding on this very porch. They looked deliriously in love as the man leaned over to kiss his bride-to-be, and she responded with a soft sigh.

They walked away moments later, murmuring about the rose garden, leaving Mark to stand in a suddenly wistful silence beside Nicki. Had her purpose in bringing him been strictly romantic, rather than nefarious?

"So, you hungry?" she asked. "After the vineyards below, we can grab a bite of lunch—"

"Are you looking for what they have?" he nodded toward the retreating couple.

He could have shot himself the minute the words were out. Why ask? It didn't matter—at least not to him. It couldn't.

Nicki hesitated, staring at her naked fingernails. "Not necessarily. They look honest with each other. Open. I'd like that."

Yeah, so would he. Starting with some information about who was laundering money and if she was involved.

Having been naive about Tiffany, Mark looked back on those months of their marriage and winced. In retrospect, the way in which she'd set him up had seemed obvious. She'd had access to every tool needed to frame him. If he'd asked a few key questions about her dirt-poor background, he could have pieced together her motive. Almost from the beginning he'd suspected something wasn't right. She kept secrets, insisted on her "privacy," only responded to sex after a lot of patient manipulation. Often she'd cried afterward. Still, he'd been infatuated by Tiffany's seemingly wide-eyed simplicity.

With Nicki, he hated to use a cliché, but at times the comparison felt like apples to oranges. She was neither wide-eyed nor simple. Sharp, slightly cynical, self-reliant, deliciously naughty. And he wasn't the same trusting chump he'd once been.

Still, his . . . relationship with Nicki felt different. Being with her—flirting with her, having sex with her—was easy. He got no sense that she kept secrets or had anything to hide. She definitely responded to sex and never with tears or guilt. When he really focused, his gut told him she was innocent.

But was that his heart telling him what he wanted to hear? His head shouted that he was making the same mistake twice.

Mark wondered if he had again failed to ask the right questions. So many puzzle pieces with so few answers.

"Mark?"

Nicki had spoken of being honest in the emotional sense, and part of him was dying to ask if her declaration of love, shouted in the moment of passion, had been real.

God, he was confused. His thoughts jumbled around like baby food and toxic waste tossed together into a blender. Every day, it got more difficult to separate his investigation from his personal feelings. They blurred. One affected the other, until he wondered if he had any prayer of getting out of it unscathed.

"I don't know if I can give you that," he said honestly.

"I don't know that I can give it, either." She shrugged. "I've never tried."

Just then, the tour guide and the seniors, still full of questions, emerged. The comedienne of the bunch looked again like a regular tourist, complete with a slightly staggered walk. They lingered on the porch, and Mark sensed Nicki's frustration that their conversation had been interrupted. Hell, on some level it chafed him, too. Not that he was looking for any kind of forever after. Never again. But maybe if they settled this dust and got some things out in the open, he could focus on this case and stop fixating on the fact that, with every heartbeat, he pined for Nicki.

Mark led her toward the vineyard and saw the young couple. The group of seniors were following them into the rows and rows of grapevines. No privacy there. He saw a sign for the rose garden that pointed to the side of the building and led Nicki that way.

Surrounded by a profusion of roses in yellow, red, and pink, he led her toward a small gazebo painted a crisp white. Its little blue roof pointed toward the noontime sun. Once inside, he sank down to a little bench and settled Nicki beside him.

"What do you mean, you've never tried?" he asked. "There have been other guys, Nicki."

She shrugged, looked around at the roses, seemingly entranced. Mark didn't buy it for a minute. Nicki didn't want to answer.

"You said open and honest," he reminded her.

Sighing, she extracted her hand and stood. "I've never let a man get really close to me. My dad loved me, I guess, in his Italian macho way. And you've seen my uncle." She wrinkled her nose, then turned away. "I can't wait to pay him his three hundred thousand and get him out of my club!"

"I can see why. He's a real charmer."

"Isn't he? Anyway, my mother had a string of worthless boyfriends, all of whom seemed to delight in breaking her heart. She was so emotionally needy. She gave and gave and gave. They always took and left. I can't tell you how many Sunday mornings I woke up to find her nursing a bottle of vodka, still drinking after Saturday night's dismissal." Facing him again, she did so with a bare expression of both desire and confusion. "I didn't want that."

"Smart girl."

"Not so smart, really. I thought I could just be casual about sex. Everyone else seemed to be." She shook her head and focused on her shoes. "In the end, pleasure for the sake of pleasure only seemed to make me more . . . lonely. After a wild beginning, I figured out that being on someone's booty call list wasn't what I wanted, either. After my dad was murdered, I cleaned up my act and opened the club. I was so busy that I gave up dating, men, and sex. I didn't really miss it. Isn't that weird? I mean, I was lonely, but I felt so strong. At the ripe old age of twenty-six, I've had never had a broken heart. But I've also never really had a real relationship. I've already opened a business on my own, and it's slowly succeeding. That's been my focus, so things were looking good." She looked up with a frown. "Then came you."

Mark winced. "I know I haven't been easy to get along with."

Nicki scoffed. "You're the king of understatements today. You flirt, you back away. You kiss me, then run off. You—"

"Make love to you, then make your life miserable by leaving or accusing you of crap." Mark sighed. "I know."

"Why? Did I do something to earn your distrust?"

Yes and no. So many signs pointed to her masterminding the felonious activities going on at the club and distracting him so she could complete them. But the evidence was circumstantial. The setup really didn't make sense. First, why did she keep him around? To add legitimacy to her phony books in case of an IRS audit or an FBI raid? Or maybe she strung him along to act as a buffer between she and Bocelli, now that it appeared she'd cut Mr. Mafia loose from the operation? He didn't know.

She had access to the tools needed to commit the crime, yes. But the more compelling question was, why would she do it? He couldn't pinpoint a motive, a reason to explain why she would do something to jeopardize the club she'd worked so hard to build. Revenge against her asshole uncle was a possibility, but Nicki didn't seem the type to cut off her nose to spite her face by committing a crime that could demolish all her hard work simply for retribution. He didn't see her doing it just because she was greedy enough to want extra cash—but he couldn't rule it out for sure. Was it possible that her uncle, who had forced her to allow Blade to be her accountant, had also forced her to launder money for him—and threatened with loss of his financial support if she didn't play nicely?

No. Raking a hand through his hair, Mark acknowledged that Nicki wasn't a woman who played games with jackasses. She cut them out of her life—

That was it! Now something made sense. This was Vegas, and Nicki was taking a short-term gamble by laundering money in order to take her cut and, along with the profits from the club, buy her chauvinistic uncle out of her business, out of her finances, out of her life as soon as she was able.

Mark had always known Nicki was a gutsy girl. But if his theory was right, this just proved it.

In an odd way, he admired her for taking charge of her life, clearing her own roadblocks to the life she wanted, being fearless, and just doing. But a crime was a crime—and if she was guilty, it was his responsibility to make sure she did the time. He knew of no other way to let his past die the ugly death it deserved.

And he couldn't say a word of this to her, not until the investigation was over and his findings were delivered to the FBI.

"Mark?"

The hurt in her voice sliced through his thoughts. When he looked up, tears welled in her eyes. Maybe she'd never had her heart broken before, but the two-ton stone sinking in his gut told him he likely qualified for her first. If he wasn't cautious, Nicki was going to be his second. And despite her criminal activities, he still felt for her—way more than was wise. And he didn't think she was faking what she felt for him.

"Damn it, talk to me! I've laid everything out on the table," she pointed out. "I know you've been hurt before, but I'm not her. I'm trying to open communication—"

"Nicki . . . I don't know what to say." He sighed, raked his hand through his hair.

This sucked. He didn't want to talk about the past, didn't want to risk his heart anymore and give her the means to cut him off at the balls. And he couldn't breathe a word about his investigation with the hope that in her "open communication," she'd just tell him all the reasons she was "innocent." He'd want to believe her too badly—even if she was ready to slit his throat. He knew his history too well as a stupid sucker who fell for a pretty face.

"Say something. Anything!" A tear dampened her dark lashes, ran down her cheek. "I told you I loved you two days ago, and you left without a word."

"Because you scare the hell out of me. I don't let women get to me. But you do. I don't need that."

He frowned, fighting conflicting urges to clutch Nicki to him and to run away. In the end, he couldn't do either. He had to stay and play this dangerous game that had already claimed a life, a marriage, and a heart. And it wasn't over yet.

"I would never hurt you. If you'll open up a little—"

"Nicki, it's not that simple." He sighed, paced. "My divorce was final a year ago today."

Chapter Fourteen

*D*IVORCE.

Nicki gripped the steering wheel as they rolled into the heart of Vegas in silence. The afternoon waned, golden sunlight blistering. She didn't know what to say. Clearly, his hurt went far deeper than a bitchy girlfriend could inflict.

Mark had stood at an altar and promised to love another woman until death parted them. And she knew him well enough to know that he wouldn't make such vows unless he meant them.

For all she knew, he still loved his ex-wife. True, he'd said she wasn't coming back, but that hardly mattered if the heinous woman held his devotion.

To feel betrayed by the fact he'd been married was irrational; Nicki realized that. But that didn't make the feeling go away. It wasn't as if she'd entertained the notion of getting married any time soon, right? She'd never even been serious about a man.

Despite telling herself to focus on the success of Girls' Night Out, Nicki had poured her energy into Mark. Stupid, stupid, stupid. And based on his behavior, the hot buttons of his she'd inadvertently stepped on over the last few weeks, she'd bet money his ex-wife cheated. Then most likely lied while pretending to adore him. Maybe she'd even left him, too.

I'm doomed. She gripped the steering wheel and fought the urge to cry.

"Are you hungry?" he asked.

They were the first words he'd spoken in nearly two hours, since putting the verbal nail in her coffin by telling her the details of his divorce were none of her business. And he thought she might want food?

"No."

Ahead, the club beckoned. With it dark on Monday, Nicki was grateful she would find her domain quiet tonight. The last thing she wanted now was to deal with loud music, demanding patrons, temperamental dancers, and general self-employment headaches. She could go to her apartment, lock the door, grab a spoon and a gallon of ice cream, then crawl into a nice case of sugar shock.

She'd figure out how to shut Mark out of her heart tomorrow.

Pulling into the parking lot, she slowed the car, then put the gearshift in park. She wanted her purse . . . but it lay on the floorboard between Mark's feet. She wasn't leaning over his thighs again, no way, no how. He aroused her just by being. Touching him . . . That was like inviting the devil to come play in her panties.

Cursing under her breath, she closed the convertible top, yanked the keys from the ignition, then got out and slammed the car door. And to think, she'd started this day with the hope that telling the man she loved him wouldn't send him screaming. Ha!

It would—for the rest of their lives. Just hopeless. Why did it take knowing that he was likely forever angry and closed for her to realize that somewhere in her heart she'd begun hoping for white lace and promises?

Stupid, stupid, stupid.

"Nicki," Mark called, unfolding his tall frame from the car and shutting the door. "Damn it, don't be this way."

She turned and raised a brow. "I'm merely silent, like you."

"Your silence has all the subtlety of a sonic boom," he called to her back.

"Since my mood disagrees with you, all the more reason for you to run along and play with yourself."

With that, she pressed the lock button on her key fob. The car beeped as she sashayed toward the club's side door.

Mark was right behind her. "Play with myself? Funny. I have a better idea; why don't you help me?"

"Why don't you take a flying leap?"

Nicki lifted up the section of the bar that led to the club's upstairs and ducked inside. Quickly, she tried to shove the makeshift flap back into place. Mark stopped it with a broad palm. He flipped it back up, walked through, and let it slam behind him.

"I told you when we started that I didn't have commitment in me," he reminded her.

Yes, he had. Shoving open the door to the stairs, Nicki did her best to ignore him. It beat the hell out of her nonexistent comeback. Instead, she marched up stair after stair, feeling Mark mere paces behind her, his gaze burning her back.

At the third floor landing, he grasped her arm and swung her around to face him. "Damn it, I told you I didn't do forever."

"But you were willing to do it for some unworthy bitch who . . . did what? Cheated? Left you?"

Mark merely stared at her with tormented eyes of green fire. Clearly, he wasn't going to tell her a damn thing.

"Whatever it was, she broke your heart," Nicki went on. "And where does that leave me? Outta luck? You're acting like a child who refuses to play checkers again because he lost the first game."

"The stakes are a little higher than a board game, baby. You can't even understand—"

"Because you won't tell me. Why? Do you still love this woman?"

"No." He shook his head, face solemn. "I'm just not making the same mistake twice."

"What? All women are liars and whores?"

"No," he assured—but didn't elaborate.

In the distance, a phone rang. Lucia's. Nicki could hear it behind her door and the angry course of blood pounding in her head.

Mark's face hardened, and he shoved his hand into his pocket and jerked out his keys. Forcing one into the lock of his apartment door, he opened it, pulled her through, and slammed it shut—all with one hand. The other stayed firmly on her arm.

"I'm not arguing with you on the landing where your sister and anyone else up for good gossip can hear," he growled.

"It's not gossip. It's history." Nicki tried to pull away from his grasp, to no avail. "Damn it, if you'll let go, I'll leave. Then there'll be no argument for anyone to overhear."

"No. I told you at the onset I didn't do—"

"Forever. Yeah, yeah, Mr. Broken Record. I heard you the first twenty times. You're all about the short term. We've had ours. I got the picture. Guess it's over. Buh-bye." She tried to jerk her arm free again.

Mark didn't budge an inch. "Why does me not wanting to rehash a shitty past change things between us? You agreed to be mine totally when I assumed your accounting. You said anytime, anywhere, any way. You backing out or firing me?"

"Don't go there. I'm tempted to do both."

"But you don't want to," he whispered, using her arm to drag her closer. "You're no more finished with me than I am with you. We sizzle together. I've never felt anything so hot as when I'm deep inside you, and you tighten on me, screaming in pleasure."

Nicki figured it wasn't a good sign that arousal curled through her belly and moisture gathered in some inconvenient places at his words.

"You're dreaming." She tugged on her arm again.

His grip tightened. "I'm remembering."

"Well, hang on to those memories, sweetie pie. From now on, that's all you'll have."

"We're not finished," he rumbled as he stepped in, invading her personal space.

Nicki refused to back down—even if her heart began to pound with all the gentleness of a sledgehammer against her chest. She really, really hoped he didn't test her resolve on this one. It was so weak, the comparison to Play-Doh came to mind.

"Oh, I think we're more than finished. You said yourself you're not a forever kind of guy. Consider this the official means to make sure we don't barge into your comfort zone."

"I'm not done with you, and you're not immune to me."

"Don't delude yourself." She raised what she hoped was a cool brow.

"I won't if you won't."

Mark leaned closer, eyes narrowing. She'd couldn't miss the sexual intent in his gaze. He was all body heat, all determination to make her scream his name. And damn it if everything inside her didn't respond with a tight ache of desire.

Bad girl! Down—and I don't mean flat on your back!

A smile that shimmered sex curved his full mouth a moment later. Maybe something in her eyes had given her interest away. Or maybe it was her stiff nipples poking desperately against the thin white dress. Those would be hard to miss.

He leaned in, forcing her against the wall. Damn if her nipples didn't get harder still. And her thong . . . well, much more of his unrelenting nearness and she might give Lake Mead some competition for the wettest place around. The realization didn't get any better when she remembered that two little ribbons were the only things holding up her dress.

Suddenly, Mark seized the sides of her face with both hands and his mouth crashed over hers. He plundered inside, tongue thrusting with ferocious hunger, swirling around hers, refusing to give quarter until she not only opened to his kiss, but welcomed it, participated in the damp pleasure of his mouth mastering hers. On this stolen handful of moments when he was solely devoted to her.

Nicki's spine melted, her resolve going straight from Play-Doh to thin air in the span of a heartbeat. He pressed her hips to the wall and aligned his perfectly to her, leaving no question about the size and strength of his erection. She already knew well the things he could do when fully aroused and focused on having her.

She was screwed here—literally.

The air left her lungs in a hot rush as he devoured her. One kiss tangled into the next, punctuated by the warm slide of his lips, the hot sweep of his tongue, the clenching of her thighs as she tried to stop the ache. Instead, heat prickled across her skin and seeped into her belly as Mark groaned into her mouth. The sound vibrated through her body, all the way between her legs.

This was going to end like the last time—and the time before, and the time before that—with her submission and his withdrawal. She had to do something if she didn't want him to keep chiseling away at her heart a chunk at a time.

Remember Anne Boleyn!

When Mark came up for air and pressed his heated lips to her throat, she took a deep breath, trying to filter out his woodsy-pine scent and gain control of her wayward hormones.

"I don't want it, not like this." She pushed at his shoulders. "You always trying to prove something with my surrender." Nicki wriggled, gaining a little space between them. "Sex isn't going to solve anything right now. You use it to avoid talking to me. And that's what we need most now, talking."

He stepped away, turned his back. "I don't want to talk about Tiffany."

Tiffany. Well, now she knew the bitch spawn's name—not that it made her feel any better. Tiffany even sounded like a class-A bimbo, like a selfish snot who'd ripped out the heart of a decent guy and replaced it with rage and mistrust.

"We don't have to talk about her. Tell me anything."

Nicki placed a gentle hand on his biceps. He tensed under her touch and said nothing. Long moments slid by. Finally, she dropped her hand. Biting her lip to hold back tears, she feared this effort was futile. He'd never agree to tell her squat. And she was too smart to count on him changing. Maybe she should simply make love with him one last time, then let him go.

"What do you want to know?" he croaked into the thick silence.

She lifted her head to stare at his stark, taut features. Mark didn't look happy, but at least he wasn't shutting her out completely. Relief gushed into her like water from a fire hose. But how far was he willing to go with this talk?

"We'll start easy," she assured. "How about your birthday?"

"October twenty-sixth. Yours?" He turned to face her.

"February third. Don't change the subject," she chastised. "We're talking about you."

Then she reached for his hand. This time, he didn't fight her; he let her touch him and wrapped his fingers around her in a death grip in return.

"Any siblings besides Kerry?"

He shook his head.

"Do you like her husband?"

"After a rocky start, yeah. He finally won me over when he married her. Before that . . . Hard to like a guy who's broken your baby sister's heart."

"True. So how did Kerry meet her husband?"

A grin eased the tension of his face. It was so sudden, the expression took Nicki by surprise.

"She kidnapped him."

Kidnapped?! "What? That's how they met?"

Mark nodded. "Rafe is an electronic security expert, with a background in hacking. I'd been accused of electronic embezzlement at the bank I worked for, and Kerry knew the charge was crap. Before my trial started, she tried to call Rafe and get him to help me. When he refused . . . she took matters into her own hands."

That blew the sweet schoolteacher image Nicki had of Mark's sister all to hell.

"So Rafe figured out that a coworker framed you?"

The smile slid from his face. "More or less."

"Which is it? More? Or Less?"

He sighed. "More. My coworker knew that Kerry was working to uncover the truth and tried to kill her. Thanks to Rafe, the police were there to save the day and overhear the confession."

"Wow, what a story!" She squeezed his hand. "Thanks for telling me."

"You're welcome." His strained voice suggested otherwise. The tense line of his shoulders had returned. "What else do you want to know?"

"You told me once that both your parents are gone. Are you up to telling me how your parents died?"

"Can we sit?"

Without waiting for an answer, Mark crossed the room to the lone, battered couch in his apartment. Nicki followed.

He sat, then looked across the scant inches separating them with sad eyes in a wary face. "My dad died in a car accident shortly after I turned six. I don't remember much about him, except that he was a tall man and he smiled a lot." He paused. Sighed. Struggled with the words. "My mom was shot and died in a convenience store robbery three days before my fifteenth birthday."

Nicki gasped and leaned over to wrap her arms around his neck. He didn't reciprocate, but he buried his face in her neck and eased his body against hers. It was enough of a sign for now.

"Oh, that's terrible. I'm so sorry, Mark. I can't even imagine how awful that was." She stroked the golden silk of his shoulder-length hair.

"It was," he whispered in her ear before he backed away enough to look into her eyes. "What about your mom?"

"Living in London. I haven't seen her in probably four years. She calls on Christmas day and on my birthday, most of the time complaining about the latest man to rip out her heart." Nicki couldn't help but wonder if trying to open Mark to her wasn't a lost cause and if she would follow in her mother's footsteps.

Not a comforting thought.

"Don't change the subject," she chastised again.

"But I'm good at it." He wrapped a hand around her nape, a smile tugging at the corner of his mouth.

"So I've noticed."

The smile slid into a serious line. "You ought to make up with your mom. You never know when something might happen."

Nicki nodded. He was probably right. She'd thought the same thing a time or two. In truth, her mother had coped as well as she knew how with her life. Being treated like a commodity in her profession had clearly affected her thinking in relationships. She was forever looking for signs of being important to everyone. It couldn't have been easy to be a model and have a baby out of wedlock, especially when the man came from a traditional Italian family and married a good Italian virgin shortly after she'd birthed his child. Mom had always been bitter about that. She'd never gotten over Nicholas DiStefano.

In the past, Nicki had never had much empathy for her mom's behavior. Now that she was pretty sure Mark was going to break her heart and getting over him seemed as likely as her becoming a gourmet chef tomorrow, she understood much more.

"I'll think about it," she whispered. "But we're talking about you."

"Damn, you're like a bulldog with Dracula's teeth. I just can't keep you from sucking all the blood out of this topic."

"I've barely scratched your skin." She sent him a give-me-a-break stare.

Mark sighed. "All right. What else?"

"What made you pick accounting?"

"I'm good with numbers. I like solving puzzles." He shrugged. "It seemed to go together for me. Besides, it was the business-related major that got me out of school the fastest."

"That's fair. I'd be all for getting out of school fast. What's your dream job?"

A thoughtful expression furrowed his brow. "Hmm. I'd have to say being your personal sex slave."

She rolled her eyes. "Seriously."

"Who says I'm not serious?"

Nicki swatted his arm. "One that doesn't have anything to do with sex."

"Well, if you want the dull answer . . . I think someday I'd like to be self-employed. Keep people's books. Do their taxes. Maybe some financial planning."

"You'd be good at it."

Sunlight slanting through Mark's apartment window and highlighting the golden strands that brushed his shoulders made her remember something Mark had told her long ago. "You want to talk about your bout with cancer?"

He drew in a deep breath. "Not a lot."

"Will you talk to me about it at all?"

He tried to shrug it off. "I never used sunscreen as a kid and it caught up to me just before I turned twenty-one, when the doctor told me the growth on the back of my neck was stage two melanoma."

"You must have been shocked."

"And then some."

"I can only imagine that diagnosis felt like a punch to the stomach. What was your treatment like?"

"Uncomfortable. Shitty." He sighed and turned to rest his elbows on his knees. "I had surgery to remove the tumor and nearby lymph nodes, followed by the chemo and all kinds of other crap. It took a good three years, but I beat it."

"I'm not surprised." She sent a gentle smile his way. "I've always known you're brave and strong."

A flush crept up his face as he turned to her again. "No, just too stubborn to give up."

Nicki laughed. "I believe that, too. You told me once that you wore your hair long so no one would see your scars. Would you show me?"

Immediately, he tensed. "Why?"

"Since I wasn't there, I'd like to understand what you went through. Will you share them with me?"

"They're not pretty."

That sounded like an excuse to Nicki's ears. "Hey, I'm not too happy with the shape of my thighs, but that hasn't seemed to bother you yet."

"You have great legs," he assured her, anchoring a hot, heavy palm on her knee—and inching upward.

The warmth of his touch seeped into her. It would be easy—so easy—to let go of difficult topics and let him deep inside her body again, deeper inside her heart.

But it would only give him more opportunity to hide—and hurt her.

She splayed her hand over his and clamped down. "You're trying to distract me again."

Mark merely shrugged, not even having the good grace to look sheepish. But he didn't move his hand.

"Look if you don't want to show me . . ."

Nicki knew she should say she was fine with it. He hid his scars from the world because he didn't want to show everybody. But she wasn't everybody. She loved him. And somewhere deep down, she was pretty sure he loved her, even if admitting it gave him a Ripley's-sized case of the hives.

Then again, his not sharing this only told her what she needed to know: He wasn't ready to share anything—a life, a love, a future.

"If you don't want to show me, I'll understand," she finally whispered.

He said nothing. Absolutely nothing. He stared—didn't even blink.

Nicki bit the inside of her lip so hard she nearly drew blood. His silent refusal shouldn't hurt. It certainly didn't surprise her. The only thing that did was how crushing her disappointment was.

Crying in his face wasn't an option. If he wasn't ready for more between them, no amount of crying would change that. And she might have lost her heart, but she could at least hang on to her pride.

"Look, I should go. I have paperwork . . ." She stood.

Mark latched on to her wrist. "Don't."

With a deep sigh, he eased her back down to the sofa. He turned away and gathered his hair in his hands.

Hope flared bright in her. Maybe he would share. Maybe he was ready for more.

His hands covered the back of his neck. And then . . . he hesitated.

The hope that in her belly flickered and began to die.

"This is harder than I thought," he admitted. "No one but Kerry has ever seen them."

Not even Tiffany? She wanted to ask him that. Now wasn't the time.

"What's the worst that can happen?" she asked.

That made him pause. "I don't know. Nothing. I'm not afraid of you running and screaming. I guess . . . I'm afraid of letting you in my life."

"I would never hurt you."

Nicki waited, tension coiling in her belly. The ball was in his court; she couldn't answer the volley for him.

"I believe you'd never mean to."

Before Nicki could ask what he meant by that cryptic statement, he turned to face her again. Mark took her face in his hands and stared deep down into her eyes. He frowned, the furrow between his brows conveying regret, torment. His endless hazel eyes looked glossy with unshed tears and rife with pain.

Suddenly, he covered his mouth with hers. Not harshly. He made no attempt to overpower her. Instead, he gripped her tightly against him, tasting of sweet desperation.

Nicki's heart wilted even as it answered his needy call. He wasn't ready for her, for them to be an "us." A year wasn't a very long time to recover from a divorce. Even as she understood, she mourned.

But she couldn't let go of him just yet.

"Stay with me tonight," he whispered against her mouth, eyes silently imploring.

It was reckless, crazy, sending her straight into heartbreak. Yet she needed him now, for closure, to say good-bye.

"Yes," she whispered.

Mark stood and lifted her, supporting her shoulders under one arm, tucking the other under the crooks of her knees, as he carried her to his bedroom like a man carries his bride. And he kissed her. Despite being long and eloquent, his kiss didn't offer the promise of tomorrow. Nor did it ravish. Instead, his lips offered an apology wrapped in tender seduction as he brought her over the threshold to their last consummation.

Soon, Nicki found Mark's bed at her back, the rumpled white sheets soft and comforting as he set her down and closed the blinds to the sinking afternoon sun. He approached the bed again, peeling off his shirt to reveal the body that had first attracted her to him. But now he was so much more.

He was her heart.

Nicki felt her throat close with emotion at the stark look of longing and tangled regret in his features. He wanted her—more than sexually. But his heart, which had endured a beating at Tiffany's hands, wasn't willing to risk, would not let himself be a part of them.

Thinking about that now was only going to make her cry. And there would be plenty of time for that later . . . after he had gone. Instead, she tried to focus on his slow saunter to the bed.

"You know I want you, Nicki." He lowered himself to his hands and knees, hovering over her, hazel stare penetrating. "I've never wanted any woman the way I want you."

Yes, he wanted her . . . just not enough.

She held tears at bay as he molded his lips to hers. The soft kiss caressed and worshipped. A sigh, a gentle brush of his mouth over hers, and Nicki opened under him, inviting him into her mouth. Slowly, he sank down into the kiss, laving her lower lip in sober acceptance.

Like honey, like ambrosia, the sweet flavor of his kiss lured her. He'd never been so tender, cajoling with his mood and his mouth.

She wanted to stay here forever, lock her arms around him, filter her fingers through his silken hair, and convince him of her love, of their rightness together.

Even as a distant part of her mind screamed at the futility of her desire, she looped her arms around his neck, parted her thighs so he could sink between them, and poured her heart into the kiss.

With a desolate moan, he swirled his tongue around hers, stroking the inside of her mouth, building her need.

His trembling hands smoothed back the hair from her face as he adored her with another silken kiss. Gentle fingers skated down her shoulders, leaving a trail of tingles in his wake.

Then he rolled to his back, bringing her above him, without disturbing the inescapable connection of their mouths. His hands skimmed her back, grazing her skin in the lightest caress. Nicki moaned, arched. He encouraged her with a more soulful kiss. And he plucked at the ribbons holding up her dress—the first at her neck, the second across her back—beckoning her to succumb to his tenderness.

His touch down the line of her spine was like a secret whisper. Nicki answered by pushing the straps of her dress down her arms.

Mark sat her up so she straddled his hips. Their gazes connected. Soft yet conflicted, alive but so hopeless, his stare drew her in even as his smooth fingers drew her white dress down her body. Slowly, he revealed her breasts as he eased the garment down to pool about her waist. Then he cupped her breasts in reverent hands, brushing their tips with his thumbs. Pleasure swirled with her love and sorrow, thick and inexorable.

With an urging palm at her back, her drew her down again, until she lay against his chest, skin to skin, heartbeats mirrored. He trailed kisses in a warm line up her neck, toward her ear. Nicki melted against him, eager for the succor his touch provided—even if, like a pool of water in the desert sand, it was a mirage. In his arms, she felt as if she belonged. As if he knew her, passionate temper and all, and still wanted her.

Nicki realized she'd never had that in her life. Her mother ignored her, rather than dealing with the daughter who puzzled her. Her father always told her to control her feelings and curb her tongue, despite finding it discomfiting and often pointless. Even Lucia, with her ability to play it safe and keep her opinions to herself when necessary, didn't get that need for empathy.

Mark got it. And for that, she would always love him.

"Nicki," he breathed as he rolled her to her back and slid her dress down her legs, to the floor.

With a snap and a zip, his pants and briefs followed. A rip of foil and a moment's pause later, she felt Mark sliding between her legs. He joined their mouths in an anguished kiss that had no beginning, no end, as he slid inside her with one velvet stroke.

Crying out at the feel of him deep, so much a part of her, Nicki arched up to Mark.

"Yes, baby. That's it. You're so beautiful." He took her hips in his hands and pressed into her again. "I love the way you feel."

He withdrew and glided into her again and again, whispering words of praise. He dotted her cheeks and mouth with kisses tasting of sweet urgency and gathered her up in his arms until they touched at every point from lips to thighs. Emotions crowded her, tangling in her chest, building up, up . . .

"Mark!"

"I'm here. Right here," he vowed, sinking deep into her, brushing the bundle of nerves inside her, bumping against her womb.

She cried out as the sugary build of pleasure sifted deep in her belly, spinning itself to something spiced with heaven. He swelled. She tightened. Their heavy breaths mixed every time they became one.

"Fall into my arms," he encouraged into her ear.

His rhythm became faster. His body grew tense. Nicki gripped him tighter with her arms, her thighs, her very body, imprinting everything about him—the smooth texture of his woodsy-pine scent, the silken slide of his hair on her neck as he thrust, the fire of those hazel eyes turning green just before—

"Oh, Nicki. Nicki!" he cried out and swiveled into her, as if he could pump every bit of his seed, his need, his life into her. The idea he might want to sent her straight into bliss, fluttering around him, gripping him tight as if she'd never let go.

Even though, all too soon, she knew he'd give her no choice.

* * *

MARK rolled a sleeping Nicki onto her back. Eyes closed to the anxiety and sorrow he'd seen in them, she looked much more peaceful.

But the damp, silvery tear tracks down her cheeks told him the peace was temporary.

His gut clenched at the sight, though it was no surprise. She'd loved him like it was the last time. Deep down, he'd known it, too. They couldn't go on like this. She wanted more from a man than his mistrusting heart could give. And he couldn't go any deeper with a woman he suspected of being a criminal, one who held the power to shatter him at a whole new level.

He had to finish this job now. Tonight. Be done. Be out of here. Before he stopped caring about what was legal and right in order to keep her . . . or she accepted a broken man who could never make her happy.

Sliding from bed, he quickly dressed and headed to her office. By the light of the computer, he saw the notes for Lucia's research paper in one corner. Setting them aside, Mark eased into Nicki's chair and turned on her computer. Blade's leather jacket was draped across the back, bulging into his back. Mark flung it to the ground.

Bastard. Bocelli had been in here, jacking around with the accounting records, he'd bet. Ever since Pietro DiStefano had come to visit, he'd been secretive, cocky. Lord knows what he was doing. He couldn't wait to nail the asshole who had helped Tiffany frame him and now had likely lured Nicki to take up crime.

A sticky note from Zack covered the keyboard, reminding Nicki to pick up the costumes from the dry cleaners. Damn, had Nicki's office turned into everyone's dumping ground or what? Sighing, he thrust it aside as well and pulled out his cell phone.

Speed dialing his brother-in-law, Mark wished he could imagine Lucia or Zack being viable suspects. Lucia was too wrapped up in her research paper, as Zack was consumed by caring for his ailing grandfather. Beside, he'd seen a picture of Tiffany with her legs wrapped around Blade's hips, hands clutching his leather-clad back. He was ass-deep in the money laundering operation, no doubt. And while Mark would like to think Bocelli acted alone in laundering money, he feared it would simply be wishful thinking.

"Hello?" Rafe answered, groggy.

"Hey, buddy. I know it's late there. Did I wake Kerry?"

A pause. Mark heard the rustle of sheets before Rafe said, "No. What's up?"

"We've got to solve this. Now."

The bed creaked, and Mark assumed Rafe got up. A few footsteps and a minute later, he heard Rafe's computer humming.

"I've been working on the real estate files you sent. I can't directly trace any of them back to Nicki. One shell account after another, from Eastern Europe to the Caribbean to Switzerland, nothing has Nicki's name on it. She might be innocent . . . and she might not be. This security is so tight, as if someone knows exactly how I could watch their transactions. I'm sorry I don't have jack to give you."

Sighing, Mark logged on to Nicki's computer, launched the accounting software, loaded the files. And stared at the screen. The accounts had been updated early this morning. Had Nicki awakened even earlier than he'd suspected and caught up on her criminal activity? Row after row of deposits had been put into her account over the past week. Each day a little bigger, each day a little more brazen.

Frowning, Mark clicked onto the tab marked RE. The real estate transactions had been modified as well. The previous addresses had been tagged with three-digit numbers in red in a column to the left. 142, 145, 151, 157. Other newer entries, about a dozen, had a different three-digit number, 164, in black in that same column. The amounts beside each entry were staggering.

What the hell did it mean?

Mark explained what he was seeing. "Got any clue what kind of code this is? These three-digit numbers are stumping me."

"Let me use Google . . ." A few keystrokes and multiple sighs later. "No. Nothing that makes sense in this situation."

Staring at the wall, fighting the rise of futility, Mark was tempted to wake Nicki and make her explain. No more clandestine shit. She wanted to talk, force him to share? Her first.

The calendar on the wall swam in his vision. June eleventh. He'd been here more than a month and had nothing to show for it except the prelude to another busted relationship, another fucking broken heart, this one worse than the last.

He stared at the date—it was better than staring at the screen that held nothing but mysteries. According to the little number under today's date, he'd just about finished one hundred sixty two days of this year and already managed to fuck—

Wait!

One hundred sixty two . . .

He grabbed the calendar off the wall. "I think I'm on to something. Can you dig up information on this address and see if it sold recently?" Mark recited an address with 142 in red beside it.

About two minutes later, Rafe shouted, "Bingo! The property sold—"

"May twenty-second?"

"How'd you know?"

Mark smiled. *Finally*, he was getting somewhere. "All the transactions on this spreadsheet give a Julian calendar date that represents its closing date. May twenty-second is the one hundred forty-second day of the year."

A quick pause and a few keystrokes later, Rafe said, "You're right. Good job, man!"

"Today is day one hundred sixty-two. A whole bunch of properties have the notation of one hundred sixty-four beside them, which means—"

"That in two days, something big is going down."

"I think you're right." Mark sighed. "But what?"

"I've hit a brick wall here. Every place I turn here is buried in offshore accounts, shell companies, and all kinds of red tape. You don't have any theories?"

Mark took a mental inventory of everything he knew . . . and came up empty. "Nope. But I have an idea."

"Yeah?"

He sighed. "I've been putting this off, but I think it's time I searched Nicki's place. Maybe I'll find answers there."

Heaven help them both if he did.

Chapter Fifteen

NOTHING could have told Nicki that her arrangement/fling/affair—heaven forbid she use the *R* word—with Mark was over more plainly than waking up in his apartment naked and alone.

Other than in the bed, the man had no staying power.

In the past, Nicki had wondered how smart women did stupid things like fall for a guy who was never going to commit. She always thought she'd see the trap coming a mile away and run in the other direction. Instead, she'd done an Olympic sprint right into Mark's arms.

Now her heart was paying the price.

Closing her eyes against tears that crushed her with the force of her despondency, Nicki rose—and refused to give in. Oh, no doubt, she was going to cry. But not here. Not now. Not when he might come back and see the kind of damage he'd done. He'd apologize, most likely. Deep down, he was a good guy. But his apology wouldn't change a damn thing.

They were over, it was done, and she couldn't see him anymore, for any reason. Not if she wanted to keep her sanity.

Gathering her clothes, Nicki sniffed to keep pesky tears at bay and quickly donned her dress. She stuffed her panties into her shoes and took a deep breath.

She was about to do one of the most gutless things in her life in the name of sanity and self-preservation. It wasn't something she'd tell the grandkids or write into any memoirs she might pen some-day, but she couldn't think of a better way to do it.

She had to ask Mark to leave.

Never in her life had she imagined herself writing a Dear John/Dear Employee letter all at once. But it severed both parts of their . . . interaction simultaneously.

Hell. Why was she stressing? He'd probably mourn the loss for all of five minutes, then move on without a backward glance.

It was exactly what she needed to do.

Groping her way up the lamp on the bedside table, Nicki found the switch and turned it. The sudden light, while subtle, burned her eyes. She stared at the bed, rumpled from her tangle with Hurricane Mark. Now only devastation remained, as evidenced by her decimated heart.

Nicki resisted the urge to grasp the sheet to her face and bury her face in it, smell Mark's unique scent and imprint it on her memory, leave behind the tears he'd never know or care about.

If she started crying now, when would she stop?

Paper, she needed paper. And a pen. *Remember your mission!*

Resolved, she turned away from the bed and glanced around the Spartan room. The bed took up most of the space. The closet door lined the opposite wall. He'd purchased a plastic tub, which held some of his clothes. Most garments, however, still sat in his open suitcase that lay sprawled near the bed. Clearly, he'd never planned on staying long.

She dug her fingernails into her palms at that reminder, stag-gering at the power of her pain. If this was being in love . . . it really blew chunks.

Swallowing her tears, Nicki pushed on in her search. The clothes didn't provide her anything on which to write a note.

The closet door stood ajar. Just inside, she spotted a leather briefcase. A very nice one, in fact. Briefcases usually had paper. She would simply write him a note that indicated she'd enjoyed meeting him but it wasn't going to work out anymore, and to please vacate the premises in the next twenty-four hours. She'd find another accountant. Auditions for replacement dancers were already under way. In a few days, it would be like he'd never come here at all.

Yeah, and pigs would sprout wings and start clucking like chickens, too.

Nicki crossed the room and grabbed the briefcase. It was heavier than she expected, but with a tug and a groan, she managed to lift it onto the bed. What the hell did he keep in here? Bricks would seem like a feather in comparison.

After unzipping the middle pouch, Nicki found a laptop computer and a portable printer, along with a tangle of cables and cords. Definitely not what she wanted. *If* she could figure out how to turn it on—big if—she'd have little idea what to do next.

With a tug on the zipper, she closed the middle section, then moved to an outer flap sealed shut with Velcro. It lifted to reveal a flap to a section that looked the size to hold business cards. To the right of that, two pens sat threaded through canvas loops made just to hold them.

Absently grabbing a pen, Nicki couldn't resist opening the flap and digging inside. Curiosity may have killed the cat, but since she felt half-dead already, what the hell.

Her fingers closed around a stack of business cards. She pulled one out. White. Made of thick, expensive cardstock. Charcoal lettering coupled with a sleek, contemporary graphic that contained a hint of red to create an eye-catching logo in the upper right corner. A Manhattan address and phone number. But the words . . .

Dawson Security Enterprises
Mark Sullivan, CPA
Vice President and Chief Financial Investigator

What? Chills slammed down Nicki's spine. Mark *Sullivan*, not Gabriel? And he'd said he'd worked for a bank in Florida. He'd never mentioned a security company in New York, much less being a vice president. And what was a chief financial investigator?

Another look at the card indicated the firm specialized in electronic security and services related to electronic commerce. Huh?

At the moment, Mr. Secretive-Gabriel-Sullivan-Whatever-His-Name-Was smelled like a rat. This card definitely meant something. Had he been hiding more than a bad medical past and a failed marriage? Or, God, had he made all that up?

She was going to find out. Right now.

Scowling, Nicki tore into the briefcase. Another zippered pocket produced a pad of legal paper with a local phone number, no name. A bad feeling brewing in her gut, she wrote the number down on a separate piece of paper and tore it out of the pad. Then she moved onto the final pocket of the briefcase.

Ripping it open with all the finesse of a kid with a stack of Christmas presents, Nicki plunged a hand in. Papers, file folders, a calculator. She yanked them all out.

The calculator turned out to be a handheld device she didn't recognize. BlackBerry, it said. Damn! It was probably loaded with information, but she really didn't know how to use it any more than she did the laptop. She set it aside and turned her attention to the papers. A computer printed receipt from the Bellagio hotel for nearly two thousand dollars, charged to Mark *Sullivan*. The last day of his stay coincided with his move here.

Nicki turned her attention to three file folders next. The first had the name of her bank on its tab and contained the last year's statements. Some entries were highlighted in yellow. She frowned. Why were these here and not in the office? He was a chief financial investigator, and having her stuff all in his briefcase, unbeknownst to her, was like being . . . investigated.

The next folder had the words *Real Estate* written in bold block writing on the tab. It contained a list of addresses, dates, and dollar amounts, none of which meant a thing to Nicki. Shrugging, she set that aside.

The third folder had nothing written on the tab. She flipped it open to find a cover letter from a private investigator here in Vegas. The phone number at the top matched the phone number she'd lifted from Mark's legal pad. Why would Mark have hired a PI here in town?

Scowl deepening, she scanned the letter.

Dear Mr. Dawson,

   Enclosed you'll find the requested report. To summarize, the subject has no criminal history, despite associations with suspected Mafia.

   Regarding the matter at hand, my field studies were inconclusive as to the subject's involvement.

   The full report follows this letter.

   Please don't hesitate to call me if you have any questions or would like to take a different avenue of inquiry.

                              Sincerely,
                              Jacob T. Lane
                              Private Investigator

The name didn't ring a bell. Again, Nicki felt as if she was groping in the dark. The subject? Inconclusive as to the subject's involvement? What the hell . . . ?

Flipping the cover letter aside, Nicki felt as if she was prepared to see anything—information about her uncle, who the authorities wanted to label Mafia because he was all Italian all the time. Or one of her dancers, incriminating pictures maybe. Who knew? The last thing she expected to see was her very own birth certificate, school records, documents showing the club's establishment, copies of her father's will, deeds to a house her father had left her and Lucia together on the shore in Atlantic City. Scanning the attached report, Nicki saw the investigator had delved into her childhood, social and dating history—the works.

She was the subject?

The last page Mark had clearly ripped from the legal pad. It was filled with his notes.

5/11—Nicki said Zack has worked for her since the club's doors opened, but has only been her stage manager for a few months. Relevant?

5/11—Lucia here for summer working on paper. Involved?

5/21—First peek at accounting records. Messed up. Changed while we had sex. Bocelli's doing? Sex a ploy to distract? Records fake?

5/25—Per Nicki, Pietro owns 30% of Nicki's club. She wants him out.

5/30—Why did Nicki ask me to be her accountant suddenly? More reason than realizing Bocelli is not qualified. Did they have a partnership? Did she sever it? Did he?

6/1—According to Nicki, Bocelli works here because her uncle demands it. Also says she's not having sex w/Bocelli. If not, what was the basis for partnership? Money?

6/4—Discovered real accounting records on Nicki's computer. Password protected. JimmyChoo, TyPennington, Frank29. Made CD of records. Deposits and transfers match bank statements. Rafe tracking down source accounts. Who's pulling the strings? Or is Nicki in charge?

6/11—Motive: Get enough money to buy out Pietro DiStefano. Major jerk. Underestimates her. Did she and Bocelli collaborate to screw her uncle over? Or is Blade trying to kill her?

He'd written something today? When? After nailing her? Nicki could picture it now, him crawling out of the sheets that were still hot from their friction and writing down his suspicions that she . . .

what? Clearly, he thought she did something for money that involved Blade in order to buy her uncle out of the club. She'd bet her one and only Prada purse that whatever Mark thought she'd done, it was illegal.

Unbelievable.

Pain sliced her brain, while fury diced her stomach. How *dare* he deceive her! How *dare* he become an employee and her lover for the exclusive purpose of investigating her! She'd meant nothing to him, she'd bet. Nothing! While she'd given him . . . her heart, her soul. Thrown away two years of carefully preserved celibacy and dedication to Girls' Night Out to be with him. Hell, she would have given him the rest of her life if he'd been interested in it.

Nicki knew she should probably be surprised by this revelation. But she couldn't exactly muster shock. Mark had been conflicted since the day she'd invited him into her bed. Well, this explained why.

Cursing, Nicki glanced down at the paper in her hand and the phone number written on it. It matched the number of the private investigator. One mystery solved. Just one more mystery remained: How long would it take to get him out of her hair? Out of her life? Out of her heart?

Nicki crumpled the paper in her fist. Oh, never mind taking the coward's way out. Forget leaving the bastard a note telling him to get lost both personally and professionally. The son of a bitch! She couldn't wait to tell him herself.

* * *

WITH a little finesse and a little luck, Mark picked the lock on Nicki's apartment door. He didn't dare return to his apartment for her keys and risk waking her, not until he had some answers or lack thereof. If no evidence to convict or clear her materialized during this search . . . well, he'd think about that later.

But he had to believe that somewhere around here something that would fill in the missing pieces of the puzzle existed.

The door unlocked with a soft click, and Mark pushed it open to reveal a dark room, vaguely shadowed by Vegas's lights streaming in through the open blinds.

What will you do with the information you find here? a voice inside him asked. *What if you learn she's guilty?* If that was the case, Mark saw prison time in her future. He ignored the anguish that clenched his gut at the thought. *What if you learn she's innocent?* Apologize, he supposed. Beyond that, he didn't know.

Stepping into the gray room and shutting the door behind him in near silence, Mark fished his keychain from his pocket. Thank goodness for the small attached flashlight he usually carried. He couldn't risk turning on lights, just in case. Nicki couldn't know he'd been here . . . looking at whatever she might be hiding from him.

A quick search of the drawers in her kitchen revealed the fact she was no Rachael Ray. Lacking much in the way of equipment, it was clear Nicki chose to spend her time engaged in activities other than preparing foods to please her palette. But he also found no personal papers in the drawers, just a stack of take-out menus, some dry cleaning receipts, a gift certificate to a local spa, and Zack's cell phone number.

Cursing softly, Mark retreated from the kitchen and stepped into the living room. Nowhere here to hide anything, really. He searched under the furniture, inside the sofa cushions, peeked into the entertainment center. Nada.

Which left only her bedroom and bathroom. And he'd at least conducted a cursory search of Nicki's dresser and closet the night he'd tied her to her bed and loved her until they were both exhausted—something he'd kill to do again. Gritting his teeth, Mark forced his mind back on task.

Hope bit into his gut as he made his way down the hall. A scented air freshener with a nightlight was plugged into the outlet in the hall. Using the faint light to help him guide his way to the end of the corridor and into the bedroom, Mark entered the nearly pitch-black room and paused.

Something wasn't right. Little hairs stood up on his arms. His insides prickled with alarm. Heartbeat roaring in his head, Mark listened. He couldn't hear anyone moving or breathing.

But a gut feeling told him he wasn't alone.

No one appeared to be in the bed or in the corners, though it was too dark to tell for sure. Nothing rustled. Nothing looked out of place, but he knew . . .

Acting purely on instinct, Mark ducked. A split-second later a flash and a blast exploded in the little bedroom. He heard the bullet whiz over his head and bury itself in the wall above his right ear.

"Die, bitch!" rasped a gravelly voice to his left.

Mark's blood ran cold. Someone was in Nicki's apartment, waiting to kill her. And if he hadn't left her sleeping in his bed, she might be dead right now.

Knowing the would-be assassin couldn't see any better than he could, Mark used the only element of surprise he had—he flashed the concentrated beam of light from his small flashlight right in the asshole's face.

Crouching in the closet, the man, clad entirely in black, tried to shield the slits of his eyes visible through the ski mask. Fury burst through Mark, hot, lethal. Who the hell would be in Nicki's apartment, shouting at her to die?

He dropped the light to the floor and jumped at the assailant, smashing the scumbag's smaller body against the back wall of the closet. Clothing fell on top of them. A high-heeled shoe dug into Mark's arm as he struggled to subdue the thug under him.

"What the fuck!" the other man shouted. "Who are you? Get off me, man!"

Ignoring him, Mark concentrated on pinning the asshole to the floor. He seized the smaller man's wrists and slammed it against the carpet until the assailant released his death-grip on the gun. The light Mark had dropped earlier now illuminated the fact the scumbag's sleeve had ridden up the length of his arm, revealing a heavy, angry set of needle tracks.

Mark grabbed the gun and pointed it at the man's temple, then ripped off the ski mask with his other hand. The pale, bony face below belonged to a stranger. His gaze seemed to bounce all around, like the slight tremor of an earthquake's aftershock. Mark smelled the odor of the man's fearful sweat.

Great. Someone really, really into meth. He could tell by looking. Unpredictable bastards.

"Who are you?" Mark barked. "Why are you here?"

"Fuck off. I'm not saying a word." The man's voice quivered.

"Silence makes me nervous. My finger might twitch." Mark prodded the barrel of the gun into the man's temple.

"Okay. Chill, dude." His face, surrounded by a mop of mussed, greasy dark hair, looked even paler. Little pale scars littered his skin where he'd spent time peeling off imaginary bugs. "I didn't do anything. I didn't even take anything."

"You came to rob this place? How the hell did you get in?" Mark growled.

"No. I wasn't planning to rob her. The dude who hired me left a door open and gave me directions."

A stab of suspicion needled Mark's gut. "Hired you? Who? To do what?"

"Some guy with dark hair. I don't have a name. Someone who hires me to do a job doesn't exactly give me all their personal info."

Dark hair? Blade. Was Mr. Mafia retaliating against Nicki for cutting him out of their money-laundering deal? Or had she been innocent all along? Of course, that assumed the twitchy criminal below him was telling the truth. "What kind of job?"

The stale-smelling assailant started to tremble even more. "I was supposed to, you know . . . bump her. Make it look like a home invasion gone bad."

Fury didn't just ignite at his words, they erupted like a spewing volcano. He'd known Blade was dangerous and an asshole. He'd suspected the guy was a killer, too. This just proved it.

"Kill her? You were going to kill Nicki?" Mark struggled not to choke on his words.

"Just doing my job," his voice bobbled. "Look, man, I need the money. If I didn't do it, he'd just hire someone else. He said he'd been trying for a while to get the bitch out of the way."

Trying for a while? How? She hadn't been mugged. Or attacked outside the building. No one else had snuck in. No one had shot at her or kidnapped her.

But Blade lived right here under the club's roof and had plenty of time, opportunity, and motive to try to take Nicki out. And maybe he'd been more subtle previously. What about the "loose" stage light nearly falling on Nicki's head? The gas leak that would have killed her if Mark hadn't arrived in time? Previously, he'd wondered if those two events were connected. Now their significance slid into place like pieces from some sickening puzzle.

Some of her "accidents" had been planned. By Bocelli.

And now, she was in danger.

Blade was trying so hard to kill Nicki and make it look like anything but an outright murder. It seemed unlikely Blade would go to that much trouble for revenge. No, he wanted Nicki out of the way. Hadn't Tiffany's contact, no doubt Blade himself, told Tiff that he'd have control of the money pipeline by this summer? Maybe that meant getting Nicki, the business owner, out of the way first. And if that was the case . . .

Nicki had been innocent all along.

He didn't have all the facts now, but enough to justify listening to his gut, which told him Nicki wasn't in collusion with anyone or the mastermind of any grand scheme.

But he'd sort out the hows and whys later. Now, Mark reached for the cell phone at his waistband when he heard a noise coming from the apartment's front door.

Hell, did the scumbag have an accomplice who'd just arrived?

He turned to glance over his shoulder and found Nicki standing in the shadowed living room, body tense. She dropped her shoes to the floor with a thud.

She gasped softly, and dread settled in his gut. Adrenaline rocketed through his system, setting off every one of his protective instincts. He could get Nicki the hell out of here and to safety, letting the foul-smelling meth freak have a chance at escape. Or he could stay and fight and hope that in the scuffle the smelly bastard wasn't able to finish his job.

No contest.

The thug below him struggled and tried to reach for his gun. Mark applied his knee to the guy's balls and pressed. The meth freak gasped.

"I better not ever see or smell you near Nicki again. I swear I'll kill you with my bare hands."

Grunting, Mark slammed the butt of the gun into the assailant's head, rendering him unconscious. He rose to his feet, breathing hard, trying to find inner calm. The urge to hog tie the murderous bastard roared. Then he itched to call 911. He couldn't afford the time for either. He could not have Nicki near the man who wanted to kill her. They'd call for help from the car.

At the moment, he had to get her to safety.

Mark crossed the room to Nicki, grabbed her wrist and started heading for the front door. "Where are your car keys? We've got to get out of here."

"Who is that?"

Shaking his head, Mark dragged her toward the front door. "It's not important now. What's important is that we've got to get you to safety."

Nicki dug her heels into the ground and yanked her grip from his. "Just call the police and have him carted out of here."

Frustration mounted. Damn stubborn woman. "It's not that simple. We have to go now."

"No. You go! I'll hold the door open for you. But don't think for a second that I'll go anywhere with you again, Mark. Or should I address you as Mr. *Sullivan*, vice president and chief financial investigator?"

Chapter Sixteen

To Mark's credit, when Nicki hurled the words at him, he barely flinched.

"We have to get you out of here." He grabbed her wrist again. "Now!"

Nicki yanked from his grasp, anger bubbling up like boiling acid. The man had invaded her life, deceived her, made her fall for him, and didn't have the decency to own up to it. "I'm not going anywhere with you. In fact, get the hell out." Furious tears slammed into the back of her eyes, prickling. "I don't ever want to see your miserable, lying face again."

He clenched his jaw. "You're pissed. I understand. I deserve it. Let's hash this out somewhere else. But you're not staying here alone and waiting for your unexpected houseguest to wake up."

Mark grabbed for her once more. Nicki jumped out of his reach.

"I don't need you. I can call the police all by myself. My sister should be back from her outing with Ashley soon. I'm not risking her running into this guy. And while he's not my best friend, Blade won't let anything happen to me, either."

"According to the unconscious criminal in your room, it seems your pal Bocelli hired him to kill you. Normally, I wouldn't put a lot of stock in what a speed freak says, but since he had no reason to lie and I was holding a gun to his head . . ."

The words hit her like a slow-motion punch to the gut. They sank deep, stunned, leaving her gasping for air. "But . . . why? I don't . . . Blade hired him?"

"Yes, and we're wasting too much time standing here and talking about it. If Bocelli realizes his latest plan has gone awry, there's nothing to keep him from marching over here with that shiny forty-five he wears under his leather jacket and dusting us both."

Mark stalked toward her. Nicki had no time to think, to react, before he cornered her and bent, slinging her over his shoulder in a fireman's carry.

"Put me down, damn it! I'll walk."

She beat her fists against his back. Her blows may as well have been water for the way they rolled off. Great, his Conan alter-ego was back.

"Where are your car keys?" he asked, marching out the apartment door.

"In my hand. I'd planned to use my house key to open the door." She paused, a thought occurring to her. "Which was standing wide open when I arrived. You broke into my apartment?"

Mark started down the club's stairs, holding her firmly in place with a large palm nearly across her ass. Nicki tried not to notice that his fingers brushed the sensitive skin of her inner thighs with virtually every step he took. She gritted her teeth. The lying ape might arouse her—but she wasn't going to give in to him ever again.

This time, she'd forget the scent of him still clinging to her own skin and remember Anne Boleyn.

"Well, if you found my business cards, I'm guessing you were on your own fishing expedition at my place."

"I was looking for a piece of paper, and a briefcase seemed like a logical start. What the hell were you looking for?"

Beneath her belly, she felt Mark's shoulder tense. The grip of his fingers tightened on her thighs and climbed higher. Oh, great. Just perfect. She was furious and betrayed and itched to give him a verbal kick in the ass . . . while his finger now bumped and rubbed her right . . . there with every step. She wouldn't be surprised if the bastard was doing it on purpose.

He didn't answer as he strode through the club with sure steps and wound his way to the back door. Kicking the door open, he erupted into the night, still carting her over his shoulder, still prodding the dampening flesh between her legs with each step. The fact arousal began to simmer low in her belly only pissed her off more.

Finally, he set her down next to the passenger door of her car. "Get in."

He unlocked it with a button, opened her door and tried to shove her inside.

Panting against her will, Nicki pushed back. "I'm not leaving my sister here with a killer."

"We'll call the police to take the ice head away. And Bocelli . . . he's not trying to kill your sister. In fact, I think there are lots of things he'd like to do to her, but killing her isn't one of them."

Nicki blinked. "What? You think Blade wants to . . . sleep with my sister?"

He snorted. "Doubt there'd be much sleeping going on, but yeah. That's the general gist."

Blade and . . . no. It didn't add up. Did it? "With Lucia?"

"Do you have any other sisters?"

The way Nicholas DiStefano liked beautiful women everywhere, no telling. He'd spread his genes more than once, both before and after he'd married.

Frowning, Nicki felt like she was playing for the slow team today. "You're saying that Blade has it in his thick Italian skull that he's going to have me killed, then pursue Lucia. Isn't that male logic for you?"

Mark lifted her and shoved her in the car. "We're burning time here. I'm getting you to safety with or without your cooperation."

Nicki started when Mark slammed the door. An instant later, he appeared on the driver's side, where he opened the door, inserted the key in the ignition and pressed the button to put the convertible top down.

Seeing her opportunity to escape the single-minded bastard who'd both lied to her and broken her heart, Nicki reached for the handle on her door.

Mark grabbed her wrist. "Don't even think it. I will bind you up like a calf at the county fair if I have to. But one way or another, I'm getting you away from Bocelli."

"Let go of me, you lying, domineering, slime-sucking bastard. I'm so pissed right now, I could—"

"Rant all you want," he broke in, his stare implacable. "At least you'll be in one piece."

"When you go out of your way to be a jerk, you're really a blue-ribbon winner, you know that?"

"Never do anything halfway." He shot her a bitter grin.

Finally, the top whirred down into place. Mark adjusted the seat all the way back and climbed in. His knees were still somewhere in the vicinity of his arm pits—served the jackass right—but he managed to start the car and place a call to 911.

A few turns later, he managed to zip onto the Strip, still crowded at midnight, while indicating to the dispatcher that the suspect was unconscious in Nicki's bedroom. As he turned off the busy tourist path, heading toward the older downtown section of Las Vegas, Mark ended the phone call with a sigh.

"Where are we going?" she demanded at a stoplight.

"I'm thinking."

"This is crazy. You drag me out in the middle of the night with no explanation, you lying slime. Nothing makes sense. Why would Blade try to kill me?"

The people in the next car over had their windows down and turned to stare. Tourists clearly. Still, she winced.

"Want a megaphone to go with that?" he ground out. "Maybe the folks out at the Hoover Dam didn't hear you clearly."

"Sorry," she grumbled. "I'm frustrated. You're pissing me off. I don't understand and—"

"Fifteen minutes, okay? Just give me that long to work out a plan."

She glanced at the clock on the dash and crossed her arms over her chest. "I'm watching the clock."

With another sigh, he dragged out the cell phone at his waist, hit a few buttons and lifted the little device to his ear. "Sorry for the nasty habit of waking you up, Rafe." He glanced over at her, with an expression he couldn't quite read. "Things have changed. Someone tried to kill Nicki tonight. I'll fill you in later. For now, I need someplace Nicki and I can hide."

Mark paused, listening. Nicki studied him. Tense, jaw clenched, one hand gripping the steering wheel so tightly she was amazed it didn't bend. Grim, like he hadn't smiled in forever. Golden hair whipping behind him in a wild tangle as he buzzed down the nearly empty side streets, he looked like a pirate, a loner. He didn't look merely lost, but desolate—and resigned to that fact.

In that moment, Nicki wanted to raise her hand to comfort him. Damn it, no! He'd lied to her about his name, wanting a job, where he'd come from—hell, everything. Nicki dug her nails into her palms to prevent herself from even thinking of offering him comfort. Mark had pretended to be involved with her, so he could investigate what? Her? Her club? No clue.

"Yeah," Mark said to Rafe over the phone. "And when I hang up, call in the Feds. This case is about over."

He'd deceived her, pretended to be conflicted about the fact he cared. He hadn't cared one iota. She'd let him touch her in ways no man ever had sexually, emotionally. She'd give her body again and again. Worse, she'd surrendered her heart. He knew it, too, and still kept deceiving her. And now he was calling the Feds? As in the FBI?

Nicki's chest contracted, pain gripping her. This was, in some surreal way, reality. She'd been a case to him, a mere investigation.

Lord knew why. Whatever she thought they'd shared had likely been nothing more than a way to earn her trust.

Biting her lip, Nicki struggled to hold in furious tears and four-letter expletives. She curled her hands into even tighter fists to keep from pummeling his barn-broad chest. Damn him!

"What?" Mark protested suddenly into the phone. "No, man. Be serious."

After another pause, he sighed and shook his head as he rolled to another stop before a red light. "Fine. I'll call you once we're safe and I've had a chance to talk to Nicki."

"Don't do anything I wouldn't," she heard Rafe taunt on the phone now that they'd stopped.

Mark snorted. "Since you'd do most anything, that doesn't leave me a lot to avoid."

"All kinds of possibilities while you keep her safe."

"Fuck off."

Mark snapped his flip-phone closed on the sound of Rafe's laughter, then sped off as the light turned green again.

He avoided looking at her.

Finally, they pulled up in front of a mission-style hotel. It was older and out of the way, but known everywhere for its Elvis-themed wedding chapel.

"Why are we here?" Nicki stared at him, wondering if he knew he was about to be all shook up by the very "Viva Las Vegas" place he was walking into.

"Let's go." He put the car in park, pried himself out of the little car, then pressed the button to put the convertible's top up again.

Nicki grabbed her key out of the ignition as he lunged for them. "I'll keep these. They *are* mine."

With hardly a ripple of those mile-wide shoulders, he reached out and snatched the keys from her hand. "You're not going anywhere until it's safe. If that means my hanging on to your keys until you start listening to me . . . oh well."

Ire bubbled up in her like a boiling vat of fury. "You make me

so mad, I could just spit! Your attitude only proves that you definitely belong in the prick category."

"I'm sure wanting to see you live another day makes me a pecker
of the first order. Let's go."

After pocketing the keys, Mark lunged at her and seized her
wrist. There wasn't enough room in the small space of the car for
Nicki to dodge him.

As Mark yanked her through the parking lot, she did her best
to keep up, but the hot tar and little pebbles littering the surface
both conspired to bruise the bottom of her bare feet.

She gritted her teeth against the discomfort. She'd let her lily
white ass get a sunburn from the fires of Hell before telling Mark.
Still, walking gingerly while Conan dragged her behind him was
impossible.

"What's wrong?" he turned and asked.

The sudden concern on his face made her pause. Damn it, she
was angry. She wanted to stay that way. He deserved every hurled
accusation she could dream up for his lies and deceit. But while she
couldn't deny that the bastard didn't love her, his concern was evident in the tilt of his golden brows above watchful hazel eyes. He
was trying to save her life . . . in his own overbearing way.

"I'll be fine if you give me a—"

With an exasperated shake of his head, Mark bent and lifted
her against his chest. "Stubborn woman. If your feet hurt, just say
so. Put your arm around my neck."

With an exasperated sigh, Nicki slid her arm behind his neck,
trying to ignore his woodsy-musk smell that never failed to ignite a
flicker of awareness. His breadth, his solid heat—damn, together
they nearly curdled her anger.

Then she made the biggest mistake of all; she raised her gaze
to his.

His stare, so intense. The green in his hazel jumped out to touch
her. Like a caress, it smoothed over her cheek, brushed her mouth.
The awareness she'd been fighting fanned its way to arousal.

She knew she should close her eyes against the sensation. It was all a lie. He didn't want her. He'd only been investigating her.

None of her self-talk worked. Nicki felt herself mutely drowning in his stare. Damn it, she'd never had the spine of a jellyfish. Why start now?

Because the thought that he'd betrayed her and would soon be gone left her feeling torn, unable to breathe. The thought of being without him made her feel like some part of her was missing, like she'd only be half the person she should be without him. It made no sense . . . but there it was.

When they reached the lobby of the hotel, an elderly bellhop opened the door for them, grinning as if gladdened by the sight of young love. Mark nodded at him, but otherwise ignored the man. Instead, he simply strode through the lobby, still cradling her in his arms—the most wonderful, dangerous place to be.

"You can put me down," she whispered once they were inside.

He ignored her as well, until they reached the front desk. Slowly, he set her on her feet, dragging her body down the length of his. Her breasts brushed against the steel of his chest. Her nipples hardened, deciding now would be a good time to come out and play. Nicki stifled a groan and looked away.

Mark stepped back pulled out some money from his pocket. The instant he let go, his strength and his heat disappeared. She felt oddly cold, despite the fact is was June in Las Vegas.

"There's a gift shop over there. Go see about getting us some toothbrushes and anything else you need."

With a nod, she took the money and turned away. Without a purse or any money of her own, she had no choice.

The gift shop sported shelf after shelf of items that shouted early Las Vegas tacky. She grabbed two toothbrushes and a travel-sized tube of toothpaste. The slogan on the box promised to make her mouth kissably fresh. Glancing around the corner at a grim-faced Mark talking to the desk clerk, she reminded herself that she shouldn't need to worry about her breath too much. She wasn't kissing him.

Once was enough to make her will evaporate. More that that, she might as well lie on her back, tear her clothes off, and start panting.

Grimacing at that humiliating thought, Nicki snatched up a comb, a mini-tube of mascara, and a nonfiction paperback about war atrocities that would surely curdle all sexual thoughts. She hoped.

On her way to the register, she encountered a fluorescent display of condoms in various flavors. Margarita caught her attention, and she added it to her pile. Let Mark buy a condom for his eventual replacement in her bed. That would be poetic justice.

As long as he didn't persuade her to spend it on him.

Shoving the thought away, Nicki paid for her purchases. The clerk didn't raise a brow as she packed it all away in a discreet little sack. Nicki supposed nothing raised brows in Vegas. After all, what happened here, stayed here, right?

Rolling her eyes at that, she clutched the bag and made her way back to the lobby.

"Let's go," he said, eyeing the little brown bag in her hand.

Nicki eyed the room key attached to the enormous palm tree keychain clutched in his fist. She was curious about that, really. But she'd be damned if she was asking.

They made a long, silent trek down a musty hall, to an elevator that might have been new when T-Rex ruled the planet, and reluctantly climbed in when the doors opened.

The tight quarters weren't helping, not with Mark half a breath away, taking up most of the space, all of the air. He slanted a look at her, one that questioned if she was still pissed. With a resolute toss of her head, Nicki looked away.

The ancient elevator dinged as it passed every floor. Damn, she could have crawled faster than this!

Mark coughed, inched closer. Their arms brushed. Awareness clashed with anger. Something volatile churned inside her. Nicki knew if she didn't get out of the elevator in about two seconds she'd scream. Or tear his clothes off and have her way with him here and now.

She backed away, leaning against the wall instead.

A few moments later, the elevator gave its final ding as it arrived on the fourth floor. Only two suites occupied this floor, one to the left and one to the right. Mark guided her left. They reached the tall door, freshly coated with white paint that nearly concealed the peeling layers beneath it. A brass plaque on the front simply stated BLUE HAWAII.

Mark inserted the key in the lock, the palm tree key chain dangling a good four inches, and turned. The lock popped open, and he pushed the door forward.

A blast of humid air greeted her first. But the decor was a close second.

"Oh my gosh. Elvis threw up in here."

Scowling, Mark pushed her inside with a hand at the small of her back and walked into the room. "I'm about to join him."

A canopied bed with white gauze curtains dominated the middle of the room. Behind it, a mural of the beach and the ocean beyond. Swaying palm trees bracketed the bed. To add a touch of reality, a hunk of wood carved to look like a palm's trunk had been nailed to the wall on either side of the bed and artificial greenery affixed to the ceiling above.

On the wall to the right of the bed, a tiki had been painted. A door that led to the bathroom gave the illusion of being the tiki's door. Clever . . . in a high-cheese sort of way. The wall on the left was a mural of the beach and ocean, with a lone island in the distance and dancing orange crabs and off-white shells.

Wandering into the room, Nicki set the bag of goodies down on a nearby dresser made of bamboo. Mark shut the door, and she turned to face him. On the wall behind him, Elvis crouched in the sand, wearing a loud Hawaiian shirt and a lei. He strummed a guitar and crooned to bikini-clad babes swooning on his left and right, while the endless blue ocean faded into a bright sunset in the distance. Even the ceiling had been painted an impossible blue with fluffy white clouds.

Nicki was sure she'd seen it all now.

Seeing her attention fixed on the wall behind him, Mark turned for a glimpse. His shoulders stiffened.

"I'm going to kill Rafe," he muttered.

"Is this your brother-in-law's idea of a joke?"

"Or romance. I'm not sure which."

Nicki scoffed. "If so, it's a miracle he's married."

"That's probably true."

Silence fell. Nicki glanced around for a place to sit—and found none. Behind a half-wall in the corner she found a jetted tub sunken into the floor and presided over by dancing starfish. But no sofa. No chairs. Just a big bed with a bucket of iced champagne beside it. Rafe had to have arranged that in advance.

Wasn't that just peachy?

Nicki sat on the edge of the bed, watching Mark with wary eyes. "Okay, I'm here. Blade can't possibly find me here. Even if he did, he'd have a laughing fit. Tell me what the hell is going on!"

Nodding, he threw the dead bolt into place and crossed the room. "Long story short, the FBI requested that Rafe and I investigate suspicious financial activity going on at your club. Bocelli was the primary suspect from the start. During the investigation . . . things happened that made me believe you and Blade were working together to launder money for some higher connection in the Mafia. It wasn't until—"

"*What?* Launder money for someone in the Mafia?"

Mark might as well have been speaking Greek. Nicki tried to pick her jaw up from the floor. But shock reverberated through her, making movement difficult.

"Yes."

"Are you serious?" she asked "You thought I'd use my own club to do something that stupid and illegal? And work with Blade to do it?"

"I had no hard evidence of your innocence or guilt, so I had to consider you a suspect."

"Why would you imagine such an asinine thing?" she demanded.

Tall, taut, Mark just stared with a battered stare. "Best I could figure, you were using your cut of the money to buy out your uncle's interest in the club. I know you're eager to get him out of your business. He's such an ass, I don't blame you for that."

"Blade works for my uncle." Her tone told him to try logic—and quickly.

"Nothing new in the underling screwing the boss, especially in the Mafia."

"Now you think my family is in the Mafia? Why?"

"I don't think. The FBI does."

A cold chill fell over her. Nicki settled back on the bed. "Pietro likes gangster movies and pretending he's Don Corleone. He's a typical Italian man with his hands in a lot of businesses so that everyone else does his work for him. I hardly think that makes him a gangster."

"That's between him and the Feds. But it doesn't change the fact Blade appeared to be using your club to launder money. He had access to your books and bank statements for months. He kept false records on Marcy's computer. On your computer, I found a set of genuine accounting records. Did you give him your passwords?"

Nicki struggled to keep up. The information whizzed by so quickly. The way he stated everything as fact before she had a chance to soak it in and examine it was dizzying. "I let him use it when Marcy's wasn't working. But what do you mean by passwords? I only have one. More than one would have confused me. Hell, the whole computer confused me."

"Well, he's been tampering with your machine, and he didn't want you to know anything about it. There was a password to your system, a different one to your accounting software, and a third to the actual accounting records."

His assertion took her totally aback. "I just established the one, after my favorite shoes."

"I guess he likes Ty Pennington and knows a guy named Frank, who's twenty-nine."

"Well, Marcy liked Ty, so maybe it was her. Frank . . . I don't remember her dating anyone by that name."

Suddenly, Mark frowned. "It's possible Marcy created some passwords. But she couldn't be the one laundering money. She's dead, and it's still going on. Anyone else ever use your computer?"

"Everyone. Lucia is writing her research paper on it. Zack keeps schedules. Blade . . . does whatever. Ricky wrote a term paper. My bartender, Leon, answers his e-mails sometimes. Marcy's computer quit for a while after she was shot. I finally got it fixed just before you arrived."

"That was probably by design, just like I think Marcy's death was."

Nicki's heart stuttered. "You don't think the drive-by was random? The police thought it might be some sort of gang initiation that—"

"No, I think Blade wanted her gone, the way he wants you gone. And that he hired someone to do his dirty work."

Pressing her forehead into her hand, Nicki tried to wrap her mind around his words. "Her death *was* suspicious, I suppose. I can believe that someone wanted her gone and made it look random. But Blade . . . he's had a thousand opportunities to kill me. He's never made a move in my direction."

"He's being watched, and I'll bet he knows it. He wanted to make your death look as much like an accident as possible. Falling lights, gas leak, intruder . . ."

"Oh my . . . You think Blade did that?"

Mark sighed and edged closer. "Before I came to Vegas, Rafe hired a private investigator—"

"Jacob T. Lane?" A razor had nothing on her sharp voice.

"That sounds familiar enough. Anyway, he pointed a finger at Bocelli as the most likely suspect. The coworker who framed me for embezzlement used to launder money through the bank that employed us for someone matching Bocelli's description. I even saw a picture of them together, leather stretched across his back as he was buried balls deep in this woman. In public. Who else would that be?"

Nicki sagged back against the pillow for a moment. Lord, her head was spinning. "You know for sure he's laundering money through the club?"

"I've got months' worth of false accounting records, bank statements, and analysis to prove someone at the club is laundering money."

Holy shit. Nicki sighed. "And why did you think I was involved?"

Mark tensed, backed away. "I got the idea you were helping Blade when you invited me to your apartment for sex for the first time and someone approved bank transfers while we were . . . busy."

"You weren't doing my accounting yet. I hadn't give you access to my records."

"That's right." His tone set her teeth on edge.

"*What?* You just—just barged into my records?"

"I—I was there to investigate, Nicki. Wherever that led, whomever looked guilty, I was there to check it out. I did my job."

Blinking once, twice, Nicki stared at him, stunned yet again. "So you took me to bed, pried into my financial records before the sheets were cold, and decided I was an accomplice, rather than imagining it might have been a coincidence." Her thoughts drifted back over that night and as the recollections came, a fresh stab of betrayal and pain accompanied it. "Oh, then when you decided I was guilty, you came back, fucked me, then left me like a cheap whore."

"Nicki . . ." He tossed up his hands. "The evidence wasn't in your favor. I was angry with you for looking guilty. I was angry with myself for wanting a suspect."

"Yes, everybody knows all women are guilty of using sex to distract men and get what they want. No woman has any amount of self-respect that would make her puke at the prospect of whoring herself to get her way!" she shouted. "You son of a bitch!"

He winced. "I didn't handle it well. I'm sorry."

She crossed her arms over her chest. "What made you suddenly decide I'm innocent?"

"It's tangled."

"Untangle it fast, pal. I want answers."

Nodding, he started, "When you asked me to be your accountant and threw Blade out of the chair, but the accounting anomalies continued, I wondered if you were the mastermind of the operation and simply trying to cut him out. It seemed even more likely after the gas leak, which I believed was an accident at the time. No money transfers occurred while you were in the hospital or down in the bed. At that point, I couldn't see how anyone else could be responsible."

Shocked didn't begin to describe how Nicki felt. She couldn't breathe. Thoughts raced, yet she could hardly grasp anything beyond the pain, the renewing sense of betrayal. She'd loved him. Heaven help her, she still did. And he didn't know her at all. She'd been nothing to him but a case.

"You think I have enough of a criminal mind to launder money for some big don in the Mafia all on my own? You think I'm that devious and immoral?"

"Nicki, I didn't know what to think."

"That didn't stop you from taking me to bed every chance you had."

Mark gritted this teeth. "You're right. I wanted you, and I wasn't good at resisting. That's my fault. But Nicki, my thinking you were guilty changed tonight. When the intruder tonight told me he'd been hired to kill you, things snapped into place. About a year ago, Blade told the person who framed me for embezzlement that he'd have control of this money pipeline by this summer. If you're not involved, baby, he'd have to get you out of his way to do that. All your "accidents" started to look more suspicious. Why would Blade kill you if he was innocent?"

"Maybe I cut him out and he wanted revenge?" she challenged.

"Maybe." He shrugged. "But the meth freak said that Blade told him he'd been trying to kill you for a while. I realized that a guy with Blade's reputation would have just finished you off if he was pissed. He didn't get a name like Blade because his mama had a knife fetish. All those accidents didn't seem like the work of someone angry. It seemed like the work of someone calculating. Someone with a master plan. A criminal trying to get a roadblock out of the way."

Mark's answer made sense as much as it flayed her feelings into raw strips of sensation.

"But it never occurred to you that I might be innocent because I wasn't the criminal kind of woman?"

He frowned, his face a seeming snarl of confusion and regret. "I . . . I didn't want to believe it. At times it seemed unreal, not like something you would do. But the facts were against you." He sighed. "To be honest, this was more about me. I've picked some awful women in the past. The worst. The baddest, raciest, and most audacious."

"And you thought I fit right in with that crowd. You know what? You've done nothing but deceive and use me since the day you walked in my door—"

"That's not true. I was as honest as I could be. My name really is Mark, although my last name is Sullivan, not Gabriel. I did work at a bank in Florida. I really was framed for embezzlement. I do have a sister named Kerry, a brother-in-law named Rafe—"

"Tiffany?"

He nodded. "An ex-wife named Tiffany. All true."

"And every time you touched me, it meant absolutely nothing. I was the means to an investigation."

Mark leaned close—disconcertingly close. He placed his palms on the mattress on either side of her thighs. Nicki was forced to lean back onto her elbows or endure his dangerous touch.

"Do you really believe that?" He grabbed her wrist and placed it over an erection like steel. "Do you?"

Nicki swallowed. A few feet away, with tension swirling between them, Mark had been a major distraction. With his cock under her palm, those mesmerizing eyes looking so green and challenging and staring right at her, while his lips hovered mere inches above hers . . . she wouldn't have a prayer in hell if she didn't do something quick.

"I need to use the bathroom," she lied.

Immediately, he backed away.

Nicki stood and walked past him, heading toward the room's lone toilet.

Before she could make a clean escape, Mark grabbed her arm and drew her close. His spice and body heat assailed her. Nicki had to fight the urge to sway against him.

"I swear," he murmured, "despite everything, I couldn't treat you like just a suspect. There's something about you that . . . it just won't let me go."

She swallowed. Nodded. Breathed in his earthy pine scent, went weak at the knees, and prayed for the strength to resist the sensual promise lurked in his eyes. "Thank you for that. Excuse me."

Mark hesitated, then lifted his hand, curling it around her neck. She saw him looming above her, coming closer, closer. *Turn your head! Push him away!* For the life of her, she couldn't do either.

Nicki knew she'd never have another opportunity to kiss him good-bye.

So she lifted her face to him in offering. Her eyes slid shut as he filtered his fingers through her hair. Mark surrounded her then, chest to breast, the gentle slant of his mouth settling over hers. He tested her response, caressing, silently imploring. Nicki sighed against his lips and opened to him.

Mark eased his way inside, groaning. He didn't force or barge; he had no need to. Instead, he slid in with a soft touch, stroking the inside of her mouth in lingering sweeps that made her dizzy. Made her ache—with desire, yes. But even more with pain. His potent kiss evoked poignant longing, like she was saying good-bye to summer before a long, frigid winter.

Like she was bidding farewell to the only man she'd ever love.

At that thought, tears stung the back of her eyes. Nicki broke off the kiss and covered her swollen mouth with her hand. She lifted her gaze to his. It was a mistake. Regret, care, need, frustration all churned in the brown-flecked depths of his greenish eyes. And he looked half a heartbeat away from grabbing her and taking her mouth again.

Maybe he did care for her . . . in his way. But there was too much water under too many bridges. He'd betrayed her for a job, taken her to his bed to further an investigation—and wouldn't let his scarred heart care too much ever again.

It was over. Nicki had known it earlier, but the kiss only brought it home inexorably. They were done.

Better to end it now, go make sure the police had taken the intruder from her house, find Lucia, and tell her about Blade's evil plans, then get them both to safety while she tried to think of a way to extricate her uncle's henchman from her business.

Nicki edged away from Mark and picked up the sack from the gift shop. She all but ran to the bathroom. She had a little of Mark's leftover money in that bag. If lady luck was smiling on her, the bathroom would have a window and the building would have a way down to the street.

Clutching the little paper sack, she entered and flipped on the light, shutting and locking the door behind her. Then she gazed out the little square window and smiled at the fire escape.

Jackpot!

Chapter Seventeen

SHIMMYING out the window and climbing down the fire escape proved as easy as finding a half dozen pairs of darling shoes at Sak's. Finding a taxi in the drive-through chapel part of town after midnight . . . downright frightening.

Swiping angry tears from her face, Nicki managed to look tough in a white dress with bare feet while marching toward a busy street to track down a taxi. At least she guessed she did since she didn't get mugged.

When she'd finally accomplished the first part of her mission, Mark's leftover money from the gift shop extravaganza convinced the cabdriver to take her to the club. It took every dime in her possession to satisfy what she owed. He scowled at the lousy tip, and Nicki regretted that she didn't have any more to give him, but her purse was in her car back at the motel.

After watching the taxi's taillights fade in the distance, Nicki turned and stared at the dark club. She wanted to just go in and see if her sister had returned from painting the town red. But was that the best plan? The police, if they had come at all, were gone now. Any chance the intruder was still there? If Blade really was out to kill her, was he just waiting for her to come back? She'd never particularly liked him, but murder?

A speeding car roared through the parking lot behind her.

Not just any car—Blade's black Lexus convertible.

Oh, shit! She started to run, but a totally unexpected voice stopped her.

"Nicki, there you are!" Zack shouted. "We've been worried! Where did you go?"

Frowning, she took in his mussed hair and pale face. "With Mark. What's going on?"

"No time to talk. Get in! I'll explain on the way."

"The way to where? And why are you in Blade's car."

"It's faster. Watch out!" Zack pointed to something behind her.

Blade exited the building and began stalking his way through the parking lot, his heavy stare locked on her. "Nicki, stay where you are!"

She blinked, watching in horror as Blade's furious face thundered closer, closer. Her heart thudded, threatening to break free of the blood and bone that trapped it inside. She'd always known she was going to die someday, but she didn't picture it happening before she turned thirty, damn it.

"Get in!" Zack yelled.

When Blade reached into his jacket, pulled out his shiny gun and pointed it in their direction, Nicki gasped and ran. She didn't have time to scream, and she wasn't going to argue. Instead, she scrambled around to the side of the car and hopped in the passenger's seat.

"No!" Blade roared in the otherwise empty lot. "Come back here!"

Then he fired his gun. If Zack hadn't peeled out and turned the car toward the road at that moment, the bullet would likely have planted itself in his temple.

Breath rasping in and out of her chest, Nicki trembled as Zack approached the edge of the lot. "Holy cow! I can't believe he nearly shot you. What is going on?"

Barreling from the other direction, her Crossfire suddenly charged into the parking lot. Damn, Mark must have realized she'd fled and chased after her in her car. Of all the times to take an after-sex interest in her, why did he choose now? Mark had barely stopped the little car when he scrambled out.

"Nicki, come back!" His golden hair flew around his face in the desert wind. Panic transformed his face as he ran toward the Lexus.

Her heart nearly broke at the sight of him.

Zack floored the accelerator and, with a screech of tires, the car darted out into the nearly empty night. She turned and watched as he sprinted after the car, shouting her name. But he only grew smaller and smaller as Zack put distance between them.

"Wait!" she ordered Zack, terror slicing through Nicki's belly. "You've got to stop. I can't leave Mark there. Blade will shoot him!"

He ignored her. Out on the street, streetlights whizzed by as the car picked up speed. Fifty, sixty, seventy, through the empty streets of Vegas. Nicki couldn't possibly bail out of the car without needing a full body cast when it was all said and done. Beating Zack was tempting . . . but not when he could introduce the car, along with both their heads, to a brick wall. Was he that afraid of Blade?

"Zack! What are you doing?" she demanded. "Turn around. We've got to rescue Mark!"

He turned to her with a dark stare that made the hair on the back of her neck stand up. A movement near his waist drew her attention. She looked down to see him point a small gun in her direction.

"Honey, if I were you, I'd start worrying about myself right now."

* * *

MARK watched Zack speed away with Nicki. He thanked God she'd gotten away before Blade could point the gun he held at her head and fire.

Staring at his nemesis across the parking lot, Mark suspected he wasn't going to be so lucky.

To his shock, Blade holstered his gun and drew out a cell phone. Cursing, he punched a few buttons and made a low-voiced request Mark couldn't quite hear. Was he sending someone after Nicki and Zack to finish them off?

"The game is up, Bocelli. I know about the money laundering. So does Nicki. I know you've been trying to kill her—"

Blade stomped in his direction. "We've got to find Zack and Nicki before they get too far away. You're going to help me. Now!"

Knowing it was likely going to get his brains splattered across the blacktop, Mark leaned into Blade's face. "You're going to have to kill me before I let you go anywhere near her."

Gritting his teeth, Blade grabbed Mark's shirt. "There have been moments when the idea would have thrilled the hell out of me. But we don't have time for this now." Blade released him. "You've got everything wrong. Damn it! Zack is your bad guy."

"Don't try to pull that shit on me, you motherfu—"

"Why did Norton send you here?" he growled and reached into his jacket. This time he pulled out a small leather case and flipped it open to reveal an official-looking badge. "Jon Bocelli. FBI."

* * *

NICKI stared at the cold, black metal of the gun's barrel hovering at Zack's waist—and pointing directly at her. Nervous laughter escaped her throat.

"Zack? If this is your idea of a joke—"

"Do I look like I'm kidding?"

She searched his face, gaze tracing the tense lines, the sweat running down his temple, and the grim shape of his mouth. No, he didn't look like he was kidding in the least. "Oh, no . . ."

"I hate to do this. I really do." He sighed. "I like you. It's nothing personal."

A cold terror rained through her blood. Zack was seriously threatening . . . to kill her?

"Whatever it is, you don't have to do this."

"I do," he huffed. "You're in my way. I tried to make the light fall on you. It would have looked like an accident since we'd had the lights serviced the previous day. You wouldn't have felt a thing . . . But no, that Viking buffoon had to knock you out of the way at the last minute."

"Oh my God . . ." Nicki muttered, shaking her head.

Zack slowed as he approached a red light. Nicki waited for him to stop, praying that in the precious moments he did, Mark might come after her or figure it out and send the police. Maybe she could jump out of the car. Something. Anything!

Bad went to worse when Zack didn't stop at the red light. He checked left, right, made sure no cars were coming, no police cars were evident. Then he sped on.

"When I cracked the gas pipe at the back of your stove," Zack went on, "I never imagined the blond hulk would come back from New York so suddenly and carry you out of there. Another hour, tops, and it would have looked like an unfortunate accident. Again, you wouldn't have felt a thing. Perfect."

"You hired the intruder," she blurted.

"I had to do something. I was getting desperate. You just wouldn't die! I love you, sweetie, but you've always been too stubborn for your own good."

Zack had tried to kill her—more than once. Not Blade. All this time, her stage manager and friend, trusted business associate— hell, he had signing authority on the club's accounts in the event something happened to her . . . Oh God, was that how he'd planned to control the money pipeline all along, by killing her? Nicki's gaze fell to the gun pointed right at her side. Scratch that. Was that why he planned to kill her tonight?

"Why?"

He sighed, seemingly exasperated. "Why does anybody do anything? Money, of course. Money laundering is dangerous busi-ness."

Shock cracked Nicki's numb shell. "You'd kill me for money? You were a friend. I trusted you . . ."

"I have to care for family first. You can't imagine that my grandfather's treatment is cheap. Old Frank's medication for his Parkinson's alone is a fourth of what I make. I have no health insurance, so I can't add him to my policy. Medicare isn't paying for much. I can't keep him at my place with a nurse at night anymore. He's declined too much. He needs assisted living, but I can't afford it. So, when I was contacted by someone who represented Cosa Nostra kinds of interests who offered me a way to make money, of course I accepted. It's either that, or watch my grandfather die a fast, humiliating death."

"I know you're distraught, but think it through. He's going to die, anyway."

"Bitch!"

Fury exploded in Zack's dark eyes. He raised a fist from the steering wheel and punched her in the cheek. Pain exploded inside her head, detonating every nerve with agony. The searing clawed through the muscles of her face, into her head. She cradled her cheek in her hand and looked at him as if he were a completely dangerous stranger.

He was.

"That man raised me, gave me everything when my own worthless parents were too drunk to care. When he was diagnosed, I vowed I'd spend my last dime to take care of him. And I have. It's not enough." Zack's voice broke.

"I'll help you. I have money—"

"It's too late." He shook his head. "Mark and Blade now know I was the one washing money through your accounts. I managed to hide the truth for over a year, but they were both suspiciously nosy. Blade is your uncle's lackey, so his prying didn't surprise me. I did wonder why he hasn't told Pietro about his suspicions. But Mark . . . I wondered if he's a cop or something. But then I realized neither trusted the other. I made sure it stayed that way."

He'd been very effective, Nicki knew. The two men could hardly be in the same room without coming to blows. All along she'd thought it was too much testosterone. Instead, it had been too much suspicion without enough facts.

"Even more delicious, I suspected Mark thought you were guilty of helping Blade. So I helped him believe it, planted clues, timed things just right, like not moving money while you were in the hospital. Worked like a charm . . ."

It *had* worked—all too well. Fury shook her. The man she'd thought of as a friend had done his best to ruin her life. Now he wanted to end it. "Who are you laundering money for?"

He shot her an incredulous frown. "Look, when you're presented with a great business opportunity, sometimes it's smart not to ask too many questions."

"You have no idea? That's crazy! This plan doesn't make any sense, Zack—"

"It makes perfect sense! I've been stashing my cut of the money and distributing the rest as I was instructed. The next group of real estate transactions was going to be to be my last. You were supposed to be dead so that nothing could stop me from withdrawing the last of the transaction's profits from your bank—along with your cash on hand. I could skip town before anyone figured out that I'd cleaned out the club's accounts. Frank and I would be settled and comfortable in the Caribbean. Now . . ." he raked a hand through his dark, spiked hair, "This is just a disaster."

Nicki couldn't decide what to do. Play on their past and their friendship and pray she could talk him out of it? Treat him like any other kidnapper or killer and fight to the last drop of blood?

"Zack, your grandfather wouldn't want you to kill for him."

"He's a frail old man. You think I'm going to tell him?" Zack made a quick left down a side street, wheels skidding.

Now they sped through an older section of town. Cracked sidewalks, aging desert landscaping with the occasional mature tree dotted the old neighborhood. She sensed they were nearly at their destination. Once they got there . . . Nicki shuddered, refusing to think about it now. She had to keep talking, keep him talking. Stalling until she found a better solution might be her only hope.

"There are witnesses now. Blade and Mark both saw—"

"I know," he roared. "They—they can be dealt with, too! The testosterone twins have been nothing but in my way."

Zack jerked on the steering wheel, sending the car zooming down a narrow alley. He parked between a Dumpster and his aging blue van, hiding Blade's flashy vehicle from the street.

"Get out." He poked her in the ribs with the gun.

Nicki scrambled to get out of the car. He moved to do the same on the other side. Screw this; she wasn't waiting for him like a good little girl to lead him somewhere so he could politely shoot her. Not a chance in hell!

She glanced at Zack unfolding his six-foot frame from the little car. While his knees were somewhere near his waist, Nicki started sprinting toward the street as fast as her bare feet would take her.

When the retort of his gun exploded in her ears and a bullet kicked up the cement inches from her feet, she began to wonder if she'd make it.

* * *

MARK wasn't sure how long it took him to collect his jaw from the hot tar of the parking lot.

He stared at Bocelli, utterly stunned. "*You're* the undercover agent?"

"Yeah. I'm investigating Pietro DiStefano's Mafia ties."

Mind racing, Mark tried to wrap his mind around the fact Blade was one of the guys in white hats, not the man trying to steal the money. Not the guy trying to snuff Nicki. But more importantly, Nicki was out there now with the real bad guy, who'd likely do his best to kill her—and quickly.

"We gotta get the hell out of here and get to Nicki," Mark insisted.

Blade nodded. "Let's go."

Mark hopped in the driver's seat of Nicki's little car. Blade all but hurdled the passenger door.

"Where to?" He took off, driving in the direction Zack and Nicki had disappeared.

"I've already placed a call. GPS Tracking is one of the features on my car. I'll get a call when—"

Blade's phone rang, interrupting him.

"Yeah?" he answered. "Is that south? Okay." He fished around in the glove box and found a pen and a scrap of paper. He jotted down a few numbers and a scribble. "Got it. Send backup."

While Blade ended the call, Mark gripped the steering wheel. "Where is she?"

"Older part of town. I have an address. Just keep going in this direction. We're ten minutes away."

Ten long minutes. Damn it! In ten minutes, a man with a gun could easily kill an unarmed woman. In a white dress, she couldn't hide well. With no shoes she wouldn't be able to run well. How on earth was she going to live another ten minutes?

Mark gunned the accelerator, willing the car to travel faster, to reach Nicki before the worst—the unthinkable—happened.

This was his fault. Totally his fucking fault. If he had, for an instant, suspected Zack . . . More, if he hadn't given her a reason to want to crawl out the window to escape him . . . If he'd been more capable of giving her what she needed . . . If he'd been capable of loving her like she deserved . . .

If he'd believed in her goodness . . . none of this would be happening.

Thanks to Tiffany, he just didn't have it in him anymore. His suspicions of Nicki only proved that his thinking was permanently warped, his heart eternally scarred. His inability to trust, coupled with choosing women who would likely star in a *Girls Gone Wild* video, simply doomed him from happily ever after.

But damn it if he was going to let Nicki die.

"So you're undercover?"

"Yep. My job is to get the goods proving that Pietro is big-time

Mafia. But Zack and his scheme aren't helping me. Pietro knew nothing about the money laundering, so in this case he's not guilty. The only consolation I have is that finding out is going to royally piss him off."

"You played the part of a Mafia thug really well," Mark commented. "Pietro has no idea you're a Fed."

Blade shrugged. "Been doing it for three years."

Mark scowled as a memory assaulted him. "Hey, you pointed a gun in my face."

"Just trying to calm you down, hoping to make you take a breath before you decided to try to pound me into the wall. I didn't know until this morning that you'd been sent in here to look at Nicki's books and help with the money laundering angle. Sorry if I offended you about the accounting crap. I didn't know you really are a CPA."

It didn't matter. Nothing did. Not until they found Nicki in one piece.

"You never touched Nicki," Mark challenged, "despite the line of crap you fed me."

"I never touched her. I only said otherwise so you wouldn't get too cozy at the club or with Nicki. I didn't need a Romeo in the middle of my investigation. Sorry."

Mark nodded. The explanation made sense, even though it had screwed with his head in a major way.

"Head southeast," Blade barked, switching gears. "My car went that direction. I've got the tracking downloaded to my phone now. I'll tell you where to go."

Mark nodded, tense, silent, mind racing as neon lights gave way to streetlights. He barely paused at traffic signals. Stop signs blew past his shoulder at forty miles an hour before he floored the accelerator again.

"I think Zack has been trying to kill Nicki for a while."

As if he needed to fucking hear that now? She was alone with a thieving lunatic who has a gun and a fast car. Fear twisted his gut into more knots than macramé.

Mark peeled his eyes from the road for a moment to stare at Blade's somber face. "I know about the stage light, the gas leak, and tonight's intruder."

"There's more. You have to understand exactly what we're up against. Zack tried to kill Nicki back in March."

"*What?*" The suspicious accidents had been going on that long. Why hadn't Nicki said something? Why hadn't anyone noticed anything sooner?

"Let me show you something."

Blade punched a few buttons on his phone, then thrust it in front of Mark's face. The little screen showed a picture of Nicki standing outside wearing a huge smile and a black trench coat on a rainy evening, with the club's lights illuminating the gloss of her long, dark hair.

"Yeah?"

"Hang on." Blade punched a few more buttons, then put the phone back in front of him.

This photo was of a woman lying facedown in a pool of blood, long, dark hair strewn all across narrow shoulders encased in a black trench coat.

The photo made him shiver. If he didn't know better, he'd think he had just seen a picture of Nicki again, this time in death.

"Holy . . . Is that the murdered accountant? From the back, she and Nicki could be twins."

Nodding, Blade took the phone back. "Exactly. Marcy had borrowed Nicki's coat that night for her drive home, since the heater in her car wasn't working."

"And you think Zack mistook her for Nicki and . . ." *Killed her*; Mark couldn't make himself say the words.

"Exactly."

It was one thing to believe that Nicki had fallen prey to a dangerous criminal. It was another to see a grainy color photo of a murder victim's pale cheek bracketed by Nicki's black coat and her own red blood.

"I never thought the drive-by was random." He sighed, tensely pushing his hair from his eyes. "I assumed that you"—he paused, shook his head, but it still seemed surreal—"Zack killed Marcy to get her out of the way."

But no, Zack had meant all along to eliminate Nicki. And he was serious—deadly serious. At the realization, Mark started sweating even more.

Dear God, what if . . . what if he couldn't reach her in time?

Chapter Eighteen

BLADE instructed Mark to stop Nicki's car a good hundred yards shy of the location the GPS tracking indicated his car sat.

Putting the vehicle in park, he yanked out the little key and shoved the driver's door open. Blade's hand on his arm prevented him from jumping out and running after Nicki like the possessed man he felt sure he was.

"I doubt Zack is onto the fact the car was being tracked, but be careful. Just in case."

Gnashing his teeth, he nodded. Bocelli was right. Getting his ass shot wouldn't do Nicki a damn bit of good.

Slowly, quietly, they exited the car. The night stood silent, its curtains drawn, displaying nothing, speaking of nothing. It was as if the air hovered unmoving, still.

It felt unnatural.

An old apartment building stood in yellowing testament to the number of years it had graced this Las Vegas street. Entrances to the building's parking lot sat on either side. A row of overgrown bushes in front of the building led to a railing dotted with peeling paint, illuminated by a faint yellow ray of light from its shadowed alcove. A rundown park across the street looked so empty, it felt haunted.

Had they gone in the building? Mark cast a sharp glance at Blade.

"I'll check around inside," he responded to Mark's unasked question. "He's probably in there."

In there with Nicki, doing God knows what. Anxiety clawed through him. He started to sweat.

Damn it, he had to stay focused.

"I'm going in with you."

Blade checked the chamber of his gun, saw it filled with ammo, then shut it again with a click. "We're more effective if we spilt up. I'm armed, so I'm going in. You stay out here in case the bastard hasn't worked his way inside yet. Hide, just in case. Look for anything suspicious. When backup comes, send them my way."

That made sense, even if he didn't much like it.

"Yeah." His voice broke, sounding scratchier than a twenty-year-old record. But he couldn't stop it anymore than he could stop his next words. "Listen, bring Nicki back safe. Whatever you do . . ."

Bocelli cocked his head. "This is more than a case to you."

It wasn't a question, and Mark didn't pretend to misunderstand. "Way more."

Nodding, Blade and his black leather seemed to blend into the night as he crept past the perimeter of the aging light and up the stairs, gun in hand.

Mark glanced around for a place to hide, finding next to nothing. The bushes in front of the building were overgrown but not large enough to conceal someone his size. He turned and assessed the park for possible hiding spots. Short of climbing trees or lying down in the grass and hoping to blend in, he didn't have many appealing options.

And all the while, he felt the clock ticking, heard the echoes of Nicki's pleas for help in his head. Damn it, he hated feeling this fucking helpless. No gun, hiding bad guy . . .

Then he heard a click and felt cold metal jammed against his neck.

"Hands up, Viking. Slowly."

Zack. He snarled the words, stuffing them with contempt as he backed away a few steps.

Damn it to hell and back! How had the little bastard crept up on him?

Raising his hands slowly, Mark swallowed. "Where's Nicki?"

"Somewhere around here. You're going to help me find her. Turn around."

Despite the gun pointed at his head, Mark breathed a sigh of relief as he turned to face Zack. At least Nicki had managed to get away and hide. And he was determined that she stay hidden until help arrived. Somehow, he had to keep Zack talking.

"I'd jump in boiling acid before I'd help you find her."

"Still determined to play the hero, huh?" Zack aimed the weapon at him.

"No, just determined to keep Nicki safe." *Determined to stop you.* But he couldn't get a clean jump at Zack. About three feet away, Zack would likely fire the gun, sending a bullet right through Mark's heart before he could ever put a stop to the money-laundering bastard.

"She is *not* going to ruin two years of planning and work!" Zack snarled.

Two years? Yes, he'd been laundering money all along, not Blade. Mark froze. Puzzle pieces clicked into place. Just as Zack had been creating suspicion between him and Agent Bocelli, Zack had also been doing his best to impersonate Blade when engaged in all things illegal and immoral.

The picture of a leather-clad, dark-haired criminal fucking Tiffany came to mind.

"You! You were the asshole who shoved my ex-wife ass deep into a life of crime!"

"Ex-wife?"

"Tiffany. The tall redhead in Tampa."

"Oh, her. Beautiful girl. Calculating. Loved the way her mind worked. She gave a great blow job, too." Zack shot him a ruthless smile. "So that makes you Mark Sullivan, the patsy who wouldn't go down. Not Mark Gabriel. Clever. I was fooled." His eyes narrowed with wicked glee. "You know, it was her idea to target you, rather than your boss. If she hadn't gotten greedy and sloppy, it would have worked perfectly and you'd be sitting in prison now, rotting away."

"You ruined her life, my life, our marriage . . . for some piss-ass piece of change?"

"Piss-ass piece of change? I have *millions* now. In cash. That's the money I've been stashing for a while, and it's just waiting upstairs for me. Once I collect it, cash out on the last transaction, and get rid of Nicki, my grandfather and I can go anywhere in the world." Zack growled. "Besides, Tiffany was a big girl who went into the scheme with her eyes wide open."

"And you fucked her. So your being gay was just another big lie."

"I test everyone's loyalty." Mark stared at the bastard who'd pretended to be Nicki's friend, watching as he shrugged. "I don't care what gender they are."

Mark shuddered. "You betrayed Nicki, lied, crushed the trust between you. Do you get off on destroying people?"

"I get off on money to help the last bit of family I have," he growled. "And I'm not about to give up the last big score I have planned because some slut of a nightclub owner wants to play hide-and-seek. Tomorrow, the last of the real estate transactions close, Nicki will be six feet under, and I'll be on the other side of the world soon after that."

None of that was going to happen, not as long as Mark had a breath left to take.

Despite the fact it would likely get him shot, he prepared to lunge at Zack and squash his big mouth and big ideas.

Zack retreated just out of reach and raised the gun again and pointed it right between Mark's eyes.

"Stay where you are," he growled in warning.

Mark held in a curse, backing off. Damn! He couldn't help Nicki if he was dead.

"Your girlfriend is hiding from me. Let's see if we can change that. Nicki!" Zack shouted. "You have one minute to appear, or I'm going to blow your lover's brains all over the sidewalk. I'm counting now. Fifty-nine, fifty-eight . . ."

Behind Zack, Nicki rose silently from the bushes in front of the rundown apartment building, amidst the overgrown bushes. She'd been right there all this time? He tried to keep his face impassive, but Mark's heart dropped to his knees at the sight of her. With her white dress smudged with dirt and hair a wild black tangle around her shoulders, she pushed the strands from her face and glanced at Zack's back.

Mark didn't look directly at her. Giving herself away would only get both of them killed. Instead, he tried to give her a discreet shake of his head, hoping she'd run down the dark street to safety, preferably to get help.

A moment later, her gaze drifted back to Mark again. She swallowed, shaking. Her tortured gaze connected with his for a long moment, rife with pain, remorse, the beginnings of tears—and sheer determination.

What was she planning?

"Fifty-two, fifty one . . ." Zack continued.

Pain tore through his chest. Beyond catching Zack and trussing him up like a Thanksgiving turkey for the coming Feds, Mark ached more than anything to hold Nicki, touch her.

Sorry, she mouthed.

Zack counted on. "Forty-eight, forty-seven . . ."

For what?

Then with a grimace of regret, Nicki tore her gaze away. She crept from the bushes, but instead of rushing away to safety, she ran up the stairs of the apartment building. What the . . . ? Mark would understand if she ran away; what else could a lone, unarmed woman do? But why would she leave him alone with an agitated homicidal criminal who had a gun pointed at his head and was counting down to the end of his life, only to run into his lair?

Mark mentally replayed his conversation with Zack . . . and a horrible thought blindsided him: Now that Zack had stated that the money was upstairs, was Nicki throwing him under the bus to go get the money for herself?

No, she wouldn't sell him out like that. She'd already chewed his ass out once for thinking that. But . . . she did want her uncle out of her business. The question was, how bad? Damn it, he trusted her. Didn't he? Tonight, he'd started to. It was fragile, though. And he couldn't help but wonder . . .

Should he trust her? Would it be a fatal mistake?

Was the determination on her face a drive to claim the money? Millions, Zack had said. Would she really forfeit him so she could get rich? He did not want to believe it.

But if that was true . . . dear God, Nicki would be Tiffany all over again—only worse. Nicki wasn't just going to dent his pride, she was going to shatter his heart.

Damn it, he always fell for the bad ones. He wanted so badly to believe Nicki was the exception. She had to be. But . . . if she was, why had she just abandoned him to a determined criminal with a loaded gun, to run toward a pile of quick, dirty money?

He closed his eyes as pain cratered his chest. The anguish was like an implosion, detonating everything inside him, torching hope, blasting his tattered heart wide open. He'd loved Nicki, despite trying his damndest not to, he'd gathered the pieces of his broken heart and laid them at her feet.

Had she really chosen money over his life?

"Thirty-four, thirty-three . . ." Zack laughed. "After you saved her life more than once, it doesn't look like she's going to return the favor, sucker. Thirty-two . . ."

Zack's stare told Mark he'd been duped. Mark felt that distinct possibility in his roiling stomach, in the stunned daze of his brain, now frozen by stock. The last thirty seconds of his life were ticking away, and he hurt too fucking bad to care.

In these last seconds, he realized he'd cared about Tiffany during their marriage, yes, and had wanted her to lean on him. He'd sought to protect her, coddled her seemingly fragile spirit. But he'd always held some part of himself back. Anything too aggressive, too male, too earthy, frightened her off.

He'd held nothing back from Nicki. In fact, the more he'd tried to hide from her, the more she'd drawn him out, seduced him, not just into her body, but into her light. She'd been his equal in temper, intelligence, grit. At the end of it all, nothing he dished out made her shy away. Being with her both challenged him and provided much-needed peace. That's why he'd fallen for Nicki; she'd been everything he needed—right up until the moment she'd left him behind with a killer holding a gun.

Which just seemed to prove that she could do without him utterly.

Whoever said that the truth hurt knew exactly what they were talking about . . . even if they'd been the master of understatements. It didn't just hurt. It raked and clawed, excruciating, unrelenting. God, he couldn't breathe.

"Twenty-five, twenty-four . . . Oh, how the mighty have fallen. How does it feel to have your balls kicked in by a woman?"

Mark blocked Zack's mocking voice out of his head.

He had a million regrets. That he hadn't seen Tiffany for who and what she was until it cost him nearly everything. That he'd been asleep while his mother bled to death in a convenience store. That Kerry had been forced to survive three hellish years in foster care before he'd been able to rescue her. That he would never see his niece's face. That he couldn't tell his sister good-bye.

Oddly, he didn't regret Nicki. Her duplicity, hell yes. That perfidy gouged him deep, all the way down to his soul. But actually being with her, touching her, knowing the woman who'd made him feel truly complete for the first time . . . Having that for a brief, sweet time he couldn't regret.

"Fourteen, thirteen . . ." Zack quirked a black brow in his direction. "Would you like to count down the last ten, or should I continue on?"

Mark would have liked to tackle Zack and kick his ass for that remark alone . . . but jumping on him would only get him a bullet in the brain at point-blank range.

"Fuck you. Nicki isn't coming. Are you playing a game, or are you really going to pull the damn trigger?"

"Eight, seven, six . . . You really have a nasty temper."

"You have no idea. If I get out of this, I'm making it a priority to show you."

Oh, hell, he was going to die either way. May as well go down fighting.

Taking a breath, Mark centered himself in preparation.

"Three, two, one." Zack shot him a cocky smile. "Say good-bye."

Mark sprang into action, bracing with one foot, kicking out with the other. He caught Zack in the gut. He grunted, his hold on the gun loosening. Mark took advantage of his weakness.

"Why don't you say good-bye, asshole?" Mark quipped.

Stalking closer, he smiled as Zack backed up a step and attempted to aim the gun with one hand while clutching his stomach with the other.

"Son of a bitch," he rasped out. "I'll definitely kill you for that."

"You can try. If I don't kill you first."

Before Zack even knew what was coming, Mark struck out with his right fist, catching the other man's chin. Zack's head snapped back. He never saw the next kick coming.

Anger surged through Mark as his foot connected with Zack's torso. Anger at Zack for having escorted Tiffany down the road to ruin, even if he hadn't loved her. Anger at Nicki for being as dangerous as Tiffany in the end. Anger at himself for having fallen totally and completely for a woman who had apparently abandoned him to his death.

He heard a cracking sound. Zack fell to his knees, clutching his ribs. He gasped for a breath, mouth open, face turning red in the center, white around the edges.

Mark grabbed the gun from Zack's hand and thrust it into the waistband at the small of his back. "I'd love to shoot you, but you weren't worth dying for, and you're not worth going to prison for, either."

"That's too bad. You could have saved the taxpayers some serious cash," joked Blade, who emerged from the alcove around the stairs to stand behind Zack. "A trial and prison digs are going to cost a pretty penny, damn it."

Speaking of pretty pennies . . . he had to address the issue of Zack's stashed millions. Duty before pain.

"You got him?" Mark motioned to Zack, who still clutched his ribs.

The criminal scumbag gave him the death glare, despite his obvious pain. "You arrogant shithead."

Mark held up three fingers to Zack. "Read between the lines."

Laughing, Blade answered, "Yeah, I got him covered. In my spare time, I think I'll cuff him and read him his rights."

Zack's head craned around so fast, Mark wondered if he'd learned the maneuver from Linda Blair. "You're a cop?"

"FBI, asshole. You're busted."

A long string of grunted curses littered the air.

"Did you see Nicki upstairs?"

"Yeah, she nearly mowed me down and told me to get my ass downstairs to save you. But by the time I got here, you looked to be doing pretty well on your own."

Surprise flared inside Mark. And hope. So she hadn't intended to just throw him to the wolves, to just leave him here to die while she found the money and used it to purge Pietro from her business. He hadn't believed in her before, in them. Maybe this time, like last, he'd jumped to conclusions.

But she hadn't come down with Blade. Why not?

"What was Nicki doing?" Mark asked.

"She said she had to find something."

Find something? What did Zack have upstairs? Maybe clues. Maybe something that incriminated Zack. Maybe . . . There were a thousand maybes. Fact was, he had no idea.

But he *knew* one thing was upstairs: the money. She'd never denied wanting more of it to pay back her asshole uncle.

Had she sent Blade to both save Mark and distract the FBI agent so she could make a clean getaway?

He didn't want to believe it. Everything inside him revolted. She'd said she loved him. But . . . Tiffany had proven someone could claim love and still totally screw their lover. They lived in the world of terrorism, child abductions, and marketing scams. Theft happened every day.

The rationalization couldn't keep a fresh rush of agony from burying him like an avalanche. God, he hurt everywhere, most of all between his pectorals, where he swore just over a year ago that he'd never let another woman hurt him again. But this hurt every bit as much. No more. Way more. He'd let Nicki in . . . and no matter what she did, Mark feared she'd be there forever, always nagging him, keeping him from peace like an untreated toothache.

"But now that you mention it," Blade continued, "I wonder where the hell Nicki went."

"Probably to find Zack's money and put it to good use. At least she sent you to help me." He shook his head, pain like acid in his chest. "She isn't a killer, just a thief."

A feminine gasp to his right brought Mark's head around.

Nicki.

She stopped in midstride as she approached from the side of the building, her blue eyes too wide in a face oh-so-pale as she clutched the arm of an old man at her side. Behind her, she parked a rolling suitcase. Hurt radiated off of her, bouncing all around them. She clutched at her chest as if trying to push back the pain inside.

"You son of a bitch!" she growled at Mark.

Her angry tears started.

Shock jerked his stomach clear through to his spine.

"Damn, why am I crying for you?" she went on, swiping away

at the wetness already on her cheek. Then she picked up the rolling suitcase and threw it at him. "Here! Have your fucking money."

Stunned, Mark didn't know what to say. He just stared, assailed with the terrible encroaching knowledge that he'd jumped to believe the worst and he'd screwed up big.

"You actually thought for even a second that I'd leave you here to die, so I could steal Zack's stash?" She frowned, the expression rife with hurt. "After everything we shared . . ." She shook her head. "Unbelievable. I must be the world's stupidest woman for not figuring out the truth. You weren't framed for embezzlement by just any bank employee, but by your ex-wife, weren't you? I overheard you talking to Zack. And it all makes sense now. If you had to have proof from Blade that I didn't intend to let Zack kill you, if you actually thought I intended to steal Zack's ill-gotten gains and use it to pay off my uncle, it should be obvious you're never going to let yourself forget Tiffany or heal."

"Zack tried to kill someone?" asked the old man in a shaking, bobbing voice.

He cast rheumy dark eyes to his grandson that looked ghostly with his silvery hair.

"Granddad, I . . ." Zack's gaze implored as he tried to explain the unexplainable. "I-I just wanted your last years to be good ones."

The old man drew back. "I don't want a life purchased in blood and treachery."

Mark barely spared a glance for the unfolding family drama. He focused on Nicki.

He had fucked up—bad. Worse than ever before. Dear God . . . When would he learn? Why hadn't he already learned? Maybe he simply couldn't.

Mark approached her, lay a gentle hand on her shoulder. "Nicki, I—"

"Don't say it, whatever excuse you've got! And take your hand off me." She shrugged off his touch. "I went upstairs to get Zack's grandfather, Frank, just so you know. He knew me. I'd been here before." She shuddered, fighting fresh tears. Instead of shedding them, she sniffed, swallowed, then went on. "I thought he could talk sense into Zack because none of us could. I brought the money as a bargaining chip. And after I gave you my heart, my body, tried to heal you . . . you thought I'd sold you out?" She shook her head. "You're never going to trust me, or yourself, no matter what. Damn you!"

Before he could open his mouth to respond, a hoard of unmarked cars pulled to quick stops lining the street, and lots of men in suits emerged, looking very bureaucratic.

The cavalry had arrived.

In an instant, he was swarmed. He answered questions, explained his investigation, placed a few calls to Rafe, who put the Feds on the scene in touch with Norton, who'd paid him to come in the first place.

But when he looked up again, Nicki was gone.

* * *

BY noon the next day, Nicki heard the knock she'd been dreading . . . but had known was coming.

Mark.

She licked suddenly dry lips and fought against too-wet eyes. After a nearly sleepless night, her eyes felt as if they'd sunk into the back of her head. Every muscle in her body protested the previous night's bout of drama and danger.

But it was her heart that ached—probably beyond repair.

Knowing the man she loved still thought there was a chance in hell that she would sell him out and steal . . . Damn, that hurt like a chain saw to the stomach. Yes, he'd absolved her of laundering money, but then assumed that she would take the fast cash in Zack's apartment, suspected, for even a moment, that she'd leave him there to die.

Did he think so little of her? Or just have zero trust in himself and his own feelings? Did it matter anymore? He was going to let that bitch of an ex-wife ruin his life—the life Nicki yearned to spend with him. And there wasn't a damn thing she could do about it.

Nicki's shoulders drooped in defeat. No matter how much she loved him, regardless of what she said or did to prove herself, it wasn't going to be enough. Mark hadn't let himself heal. And in truth, finding out that his ex-wife had framed him for her crime had been a shock to her. She could only imagine how much the event had stunned him.

Mark was closed, suspicious, unable to share his emotions. It made perfect sense after someone he'd trusted, maybe even loved, had deceived him so badly. Despite knowing why Mark behaved as he did, Nicki knew herself; she couldn't go on this way.

Yet she didn't see how she could go on without him.

The knock sounded again, reminding her that she was stalling.

Straightening her black yoga top and licking her lips again, she grabbed the knob in her shaking grasp and pulled the door open.

Whoosh! The sight of him stole her breath. God, he looked good standing there, golden hair glossy on his shoulders, contrasting with a tight gray T-shirt. His presence, coupled with the suitcases at his feet, hit her with all the subtlety of a crowbar to the chest.

The look in his hazel eyes impacted her like a death blow to her heart.

She couldn't breathe, felt her heart tearing to pieces. But the truth was there in his eyes. There was no pretending or denying that everything they'd shared was over.

"Can I come in for a minute?"

Silently nodding, she stepped back. She didn't trust her voice.

He shut the door behind him with a quiet *click*. And he looked at her intently. Unwaveringly. Deeply. She stared back, unable to look anywhere else.

Nicki had no doubt this was the last time she'd ever see Mark Sullivan.

Oh, it hurt. He wasn't even gone, and already she could feel her insides bunching into a knot of pain. Did the son of a bitch even know how much she loved him? How much letting him go was killing her?

"I came to say I'm sorry . . . and good-bye."

That deep voice that had once driven her fantasies was now making her nightmare a reality. God, she didn't know she could hurt this bad.

Nicki pressed her lips together, feeling the sting of unshed tears in her eyes. "I figured you were leaving."

"My flight is at three." He sighed, raised his hand to touch her . . . then lowered it with a sigh of regret. "I'd better not. If I start touching you now, I don't know how I'll stop."

Touch him, reach out to him! a little voice in her head urged. *You can persuade him to stay awhile longer.* She ignored the self-destructive advice.

"Last night only proved to me that I'm ruined for relationships, Nicki. I suck at trust. I don't think it's possible for me to change that, and it's not fair of me to make you believe otherwise."

That was crap. A cop-out to avoid dealing with the past . . . and the future. Nicki knew that if he didn't love her enough, if he didn't believe in himself, in them, she wasn't going to be able to make him learn to trust again. She couldn't go through life with Mark suspecting her of stabbing him in the back at the slightest little misunderstanding or infraction. He wouldn't be able to endure it, either.

Better to say good-bye—even if gouging her eyeballs out with an ice pick sounded like more fun.

"After last night, I know I don't deserve you," he murmured.

A part of Nicki wanted to rail and scream, wanted to kick his ass for hiding behind his pain. But fighting for him, for them, would do no good until he healed. If he ever let himself. At the thought, Nicki wanted to run crying, ask someone— anyone—why in the hell she hurt so damn bad.

Instead, she stared.

He looked down, as if he couldn't bear the look on her face. Finally, when he met her gaze again, Nicki saw a slip in his facade. Pain seeped in at the edges, tightening his face, dimming his red-rimmed eyes. And still, Nicki knew he'd take any agony to avoid hurting either of them even more. Heroic to the core, damn him.

"I'll never forget you," he whispered. "I'm not built for love or happily ever after. But if it's any consolation, if I was ever going to fall for someone and I could make it work, I'd be with you."

At those words, the tears she'd been holding back flooded her eyes, spilling onto her cold cheeks. She wanted to wail that he had tried—with the wrong woman. But it wouldn't do a bit of good. He was scarred and he was determined to go before he scarred her as well.

Too late.

Mark took her into his arms. Wrapping them tight around her, he pressed her face against the solid warmth of his chest. She inhaled that musky pine scent of his and wrapped her fingers around his shoulders, clung to the body that had provided both pleasure and comfort. She held him close for the last time in between wracking sobs.

As quickly as he enveloped her in his embrace, he pulled back and dried her tears with his thumbs. "Don't, baby. I'm not worth this."

But she couldn't stop. Nicki didn't see how anything could ever make it stop.

Especially when he brushed a kiss on her forehead, then stepped away.

"I'm sorry," he murmured, then exited her apartment and her life forever.

Chapter Nineteen

Nicki wondered if the person who'd said *That which doesn't kill you makes you stronger* had ever had a broken heart. She seriously doubted it. Nearly two weeks after Mark's departure, she still woke up every day feeling like she'd played a game of Chicken with a Mack truck and lost. Even the thought of food, much less the ingestion of it, made her want to hurl. And sleep . . . nonexistent.

Sighing, she sank down onto her sofa and glanced through résumés and pictures of potential dancers. Good looking, for sure. Many experienced and talented. Men who could replace Mark in her business.

Would anyone ever replace him in her heart?

Yes, she told herself. Someday she would move on. She'd meet Mr. Fabulous, give up the city for the 'burbs, have 2.2 kids and gush about her new minivan. It was only her crazy subconscious that plastered Mark's face and body over Mr. Fabulous every time she tried to picture it.

Tossing the résumés aside, she drew her knees to her chest and stared out the window at the vivid desert sunset over the Vegas city lights. But she saw nothing.

Everyone from Lucia to Dear Abby was telling her she'd get over Mark someday. Maybe that was true. She just didn't see it happening before she was eligible to join AARP. At the moment, Mark felt no less potent to her than an addictive drug. Some nights, she awoke in the wee hours, loneliness crushing her chest until she could hardly take a breath. Would she ever again feel like she could breathe without him next to her, inside of her?

At night, when she couldn't sleep, she replayed his comment to Blade. *She isn't a killer, just a thief.* It hurt again, just as much as the first time. It still made her want to pound some sense into that thick skull of his and hurt him bad while she did it.

Deep in her heart, Nicki knew Mark's comment wasn't about how he saw her. He didn't really think she was a thief, any more than she thought he was an asshole. This was about his inability to trust. Hell, in the same situation, he probably would have accused Mother Theresa.

Knowing that didn't change a thing. He was still gone.

The one silver lining: The experience had prompted her to call her mother. They'd talked for two hours and made peace. Having a broken heart really helped her to put her mother's life into perspective. Mom had never gotten over Nicholas DiStefano, despite the fact he'd left her. Well, history was repeating itself. Like mother, like daughter.

At least her mother had a child with the man she loved. Mark had always been too careful, too responsible, to leave behind a pregnant woman, so Nicki had nothing but bittersweet memories.

The phone at her waist chimed, jolting her out of her melancholy reverie. Nicki groaned. Who wanted what? Damn it, couldn't she have one evening to herself?

"Yes?" she barked after hitting the TALK button.

"What the hell is going on?"

Uncle Pietro. Of all the people she didn't have the energy to talk to . . .

"I have no idea," she said. "You called me, so why don't you fill me in."

"Where is your dancer slash accountant boyfriend? I want to talk to him."

Mark? Holy hell, what now . . . ? "I don't know. I think he went back to New York. What happened?"

"He sent me a note. And a check."

Mark had sent her uncle money? "What for?"

"So you had no idea that he was paying the balance of your loan to me?"

Nicki nearly dropped the phone. Surely she hadn't heard that right. "Mark paid the balance of my loan? That's impossible! I owed you three hundred thousand dollars."

"Hey, you callin' me a liar?"

Struggling to understand, to process, Nicki stuttered, "N-no, I just . . . It just doesn't seem possible."

"Well, I got a cashier's check today with a note that said I should consider your balance paid in full."

From Mark? Seriously?

Pietro went on. "You sure that Viking wasn't the one laundering money through your club, rather than your stage manager?"

Nicki gritted her teeth. "I'm sure. You talked to the FBI, same as I did."

"Yeah. Okay, I'm considering it paid. I'll send the paperwork over by Friday." He paused, and Nicki was too shocked to fill the silence. "And you didn't know a damn thing about this check?"

Mind racing faster than the land speed record, Nicki barely managed to get out, "Nothing."

Why would Mark pay her balance?

Guilt. He felt remorse for what he'd done to her—enough to send a small fortune to her uncle on her behalf . . . but not enough to grow and mend and come back to her whole.

The realization made her sad. Sad, hell. A ghost town couldn't feel any more desolate than her heart.

Where did he get that kind of money? How could she ever repay him? Certainly, she didn't want to *take* that amount of money, especially if it had been given in guilt. Paying back someone she couldn't locate, however, would be a big ol' challenge. She'd already tried to call his cell phone once in a moment of despair. It was disconnected.

"Typical broad. Don't know when an employee is running an operation that cleans a huge chunk of bling under your nose." Pietro's laugh brayed in her ear. "Don't know a damn thing."

Her bullshit threshold was never high even on a good day. This wasn't a good day. Nicki had no idea why Mark had sent Pietro that money, and at the moment, the only thing she felt was gratitude. Mark's guilt or whatever meant that she'd never have to put up with her bullying bastard of an uncle in her business life again.

"Bite me, you asshole," she bit out. "You didn't know what Zack was doing in the club's bank accounts, either."

"I wasn't there."

"It wouldn't matter if you had been. I still would have had to buy you a dog and named it Clue so that you'd have one. You've done nothing but belittle me since the moment I cashed your check to start this business. You criticize, terrorize, patronize, but you never *do* anything."

"Watch your mouth, girl."

"I won't. You're a great armchair quarterback, but who do you think runs this business day after day after day? I'll give you a hint: It isn't Blade."

"And who hired the queer who tried to rob and kill you?"

Nicki paused. Okay, she'd give him that one. But she wasn't giving him another inch. "Well, you sent me a thug who scared off half my employees and pointed a gun in my face, so your record ain't much better."

"Blade is loyal, which is more than I can say for you, judging from that tone."

"You're family, Pietro. Nothing is going to change that. But we're not partners anymore. And for your information, my assets are not all in my bra."

"You heard that one, huh?" He actually seemed to be laughing.

"I couldn't miss it. Stop hounding and disparaging me, and we'll get along."

Then she hung up.

God, it felt good to say that. If she ever managed to track Mark down to pay him back, she'd thank him for this moment. Either before or after she kicked him in the balls for breaking her heart. It was a toss-up which would come first.

But that was big talk, and Nicki knew it. The thought of seeing him again, of not seeing him again . . . She hugged her knees to her chest, put her head down, and began to sob.

Nicki had never been particularly fragile. Lonely as a child, with a father whose real family only included her on certain weekends. Dramatic as a teenager, with a flighty, jet-setting mother always on the prowl for Mr. Right and never finding him. She'd always taken care of herself. Suddenly, that didn't feel true anymore.

Mark had stripped her soul bare and taken away his strength, his support. And now that he was gone for good, she realized why she felt as if half of her was missing. It was.

Just as she knew she'd never be whole again without him.

* * *

"PUSH!" the doctor yelled, perspiration dampening the neckline and underarms of her blue scrubs.

Rafe got behind his wife and propped her back up while she bore down, sweat trickling from her hairline and down her temples. Kerry squeezed Mark's hand so tight he thought for sure she'd break half the bones.

"The baby's head is crowning. We're getting close," said the slight, middle-aged doctor. "Rest until your next contraction."

"Oh yeah, I'll just catch a quick two-minute snooze," Kerry quipped. "Heck, while I'm at it, let me flip out the lounge chair and grab a daiquiri."

Mark laughed. Rafe shot him a quelling glare.

"Babe," Rafe soothed, wiping away the sweat from her face. "I know it hurts—"

"You know nothing. You got the fun part. Let me tell you now; this is *not* fun!"

"It'll be over soon," the doctor promised.

"Ice?" Rafe offered Kerry some ice chips.

She glared at her husband. "You know where you can stick that ice?"

Mark laughed again, this time ignoring Rafe's nonverbal pleas to shut the hell up.

The next contraction hit moments later, faster and fiercer than the once before it.

"Push now!" the doctor barked. Rafe got into position again. Mark took Kerry's hand once more and encouraged her take out some of her pain on his crushed fingers.

"Breathe, babe," Rafe reminded.

"Why don't you?" she croaked. "I'm busy having a baby."

Then she screamed, long and loud, the sound so shrill, Mark swore it should have broken glass. Certainly, his hand had gone from throbbing to bloodless and numb.

The contraction subsided suddenly.

"Good, Kerry," the doctor coached. "The baby's head is out. One more good push and you should be a mommy."

Weakly, she nodded, then sent Rafe a wicked stare. "Then we won't be doing anything for the next ten years that could remotely cause pregnancy."

Mark laughed, knowing she'd likely eat those words as soon as the doctor gave them the green light. One thing he knew, Kerry and Rafe were solid. They loved each other . . . and weren't afraid to show it. He'd learned the hard way not to drop by unannounced on a Saturday night. Or a Tuesday morning. Or a Friday afternoon.

Suddenly, Kerry whimpered and grabbed Mark's hand again. Rafe tightened his grip around his wife's middle and murmured in her ear, "I'm here, babe."

"It hurts," she moaned.

"One good push and it will be over," Rafe whispered.

"Hold my hand," Mark encouraged.

She latched on with a vengeance. "Thanks for being here, big brother."

"Wouldn't have missed it for the—"

Kerry's earsplitting wail cut him off. She panted, then cursed, then screamed again. Mark began to wonder if both his ears and his fingers would be impaired for life.

Then a lusty baby's cry split the air. Everyone in the room stopped.

"It's a girl!" the doctor said. "Ten fingers, ten toes. Congratulations."

"We did it!" Kerry said on a happy sob. Tears brightened her eyes and slid down her flushed cheeks. He'd never seen her look happier.

Rafe shifted to her side and placed a gentle kiss on her mouth. "We did, babe."

Together they watched as the doctors and nurses cleaned the baby, examined her, took her Apgar scores.

A few minutes later, the doctor brought the squalling bundle to them and set her in Kerry's arms.

"Isn't she beautiful?" Kerry breathed.

"Like her mommy," Rafe murmured.

Mark stared at the baby's reddened cheeks, half-closed eyes and little bow mouth. A dusting of dark hair swept the top of her little head. "She's gorgeous."

Both Kerry and Rafe had a hand on their new daughter when they turned to him with identical smiles of wonder and joy. He'd seen the two of them get married and look ecstatic. He'd seen them settle into wedded life and make it look so effortless and breezy. But watching the two of them become three . . . clearly they'd taken their bond to a whole new level.

The doctor indicated they needed to remove the afterbirth and do a little stitching on Kerry. Rafe retrieved his minutes-old daughter and carried her to the nursery.

Mark walked out to the waiting room and sank into a lumpy brown chair to wait. Exhilaration bounced through his system, even as he felt humbled, stunned by the miracle of birth.

And completely empty.

He'd never have what Rafe and Kerry had. The security they knew in being happily married would never be his. The joy of holding a son or daughter of his own was something he'd never experience.

He'd been in New York for nearly three weeks and still, he couldn't smile, couldn't sleep. He worked twenty hours a day and stewed the other four. He ached. And wondered what Nicki was doing, and if she was all right, and if she missed him.

For her sake, he hoped not. For his sanity, a selfish part of him would be pissed if she forgot him so quickly or easily. He loved her . . . in his own dysfunctional, unable-to-show-it way.

Rising again, he paced. He couldn't stay here like this. Stuck between the past and the future. He couldn't sponge off Kerry and Rafe's love as if he had any part of it. As if it would somehow fill the empty parts of him that Nicki once had.

Sighing, he sat again. But what he had with Nicki was over. Accusing her of being a thief . . . She'd find it unforgivable. And she should. From his viewpoint, he couldn't do much worse to bring a proud, savvy woman down than to accuse her of being a criminal, then leave her.

Damn, he was fucked up. If he'd never met Tiffany, never given in to his urge to protect her seemingly fragile spirit and married her . . . He'd always wanted a family of his own, probably to replace the broken one he'd had as a kid. The day he'd married Tiffany, he'd been nervous, puking nervous. He'd tried to picture having kids with her, but had been unable to see past the next ten minutes.

Mark suspected if not for Tiffany, he would have married Nicki in a heartbeat and had no trouble picturing their kids, their future.

But it was never going to be, thanks to his ex-wife and the way she'd shattered and twisted his insides and made distrust his M.O.

"Hey, buddy." Rafe slapped him on the shoulder and handed him a chocolate cigar.

"Am I supposed to eat this?"

"You can't smoke in the hospital, and Kerry would have my hide for lighting up anything, anyway. Have to be responsible now that I'm a dad."

"Congratulations, man. She's a beauty."

"Yeah, I'm going to have to invest in a good baseball bat and practice fighting off the boys."

"I think you've got a few years," Mark said wryly.

"Never hurts to be in shape." Rafe shrugged, then cast Mark a concerned stare. "Hey, I didn't get a chance to congratulate you on Tiffany's conviction before your sister went into labor. You gave great testimony. How did it feel when the bailiff read Tiffany's guilty verdict?"

Mark shrugged. "Good. It was closure. Justice was served. I just hope Zack gets the same and worse. Discovering and nailing the right suspect added to the accomplishment, but I'm damn sorry to learn there's a whole Mafia structure behind the money laundering. I suspected it but . . . I sure hope to hell Zack gives up some names someday so we can put a stop to all this shit."

"As long as Zack doesn't talk, Blade's cover wasn't compromised. I hear he'll stay with Pietro DiStefano and try to see what illegal crap the Gamalini family is up to, so it's all good. Which makes me wonder why you look pissed."

"Not pissed, jealous. I'll never have what you and Kerry do."

"Never say never. The right woman comes along and changes everything."

Unfortunately for him, she'd already come . . . and he'd trampled her like a stupid ass. And there was no getting her back. "Nah, Tiffany ruined it for me."

"You sure about that?"

"Oh, yeah." Mark sent his brother-in-law a bitter smile. "She taught me a thousand and one ways to be the worst-possible husband material. And I was a quick study."

"Tiffany wasn't the right woman for you. Was Nicki?"

His smile evaporated. With his thumb and forefinger, he rubbed at the dull headache above his eyes. "Yes."

"And you fucked up." It wasn't a question.

"Yes."

Rafe paused. "I have to get back to your sister, but let me remind you that I screwed up and left Kerry. She forgave me and took me back."

"You didn't accuse her of being a criminal. In a crowd. With her listening."

He let loose a long, slow whistle. "I hope your groveling skills are really excellent."

Just his luck. Mark sighed. "They're rusty. But it doesn't matter. Tiffany put the nail in my coffin over a year ago. She made sure I didn't have a chance in hell of having another decent relationship."

"Now I'm guessing Nicki ruined the likelihood of you getting laid. At least before you went to Vegas, you got out regularly and serial dated. You haven't left your office in weeks, man."

He hadn't. And he didn't want to. Someday, he'd have to. Hell, he'd waited three months to see anyone after Tiffany's perfidy, and the hole Nicki had left in his chest was more like a gaping crater. What he felt for her was far more profound. Mark cursed under his breath and wondered if he'd be ready to look at another woman in three years, much less three months.

"Fuck off," Mark volleyed back.

"Ten-four." Rafe laughed. "Look, you can mope all you want, but your sister is worried about you. Maybe you should talk to Tiffany."

"Why start now?" Mark frowned, puzzled.

Incredulity transformed Rafe's face. "You *never* asked your ex-wife why she duped you?"

"The police reports and attorneys gave me all the motivation I needed to hear. What else was there to say? She used me, never loved me. I wasn't . . . joyously happy in the marriage, but I gave her everything I could. It wasn't enough."

"You have to come to terms with what happened . . . and how you want to use what it taught you. I'd tell you the past is going to catch up with you, but I think it already has, brother."

"I know what happened. I never denied it. As if I could!"

"But you never resolved it in your head." Rafe tapped a finger to his temple. "Trust me, I did the same thing with my old man, blamed him for everything. He was the reason I couldn't be with your sister in my twisted mind. And it was bullshit. *I* was the reason. Because I was afraid. Because I was still hung up on all the crap he fed me. I swallowed it and let it sour in my stomach, just like you've done. It isn't going to go away until you let it go."

Mark glared at his brother-in-law. Did Rafe think he liked being angry and bitter? He didn't particularly enjoy having such destructive forces ruling him. He couldn't find any calm or center these days.

"I've got to get back to your sister and that baby girl. Think about what I said."

Mark nodded, but his head spun with too many thoughts, all loud and insistent. Images of Nicki kept flashing in his brain: her smile, her face bathed in pleasure, her fury at his accusation.

She was permanently etched in his heart, and that wasn't going to change.

"What are you going to name my pretty little niece?" he asked into the heavy silence.

"Hope." Rafe smiled. "She and her mommy gave me all that and more."

* * *

THE next day, Mark sat in the visitor's area of the Hillsborough County Jail, tapping his fingers on the scarred Formica counter and wondering why in the hell he'd flown all the way to Florida. His stomach was one giant knot, he hadn't slept more than two hours last night, and he had no desire to actually see Tiffany. But here he sat, waiting for the guard to bring her to the visitation room before she was transferred to the federal penitentiary on Monday.

Rafe was right; he had to let this shit with Tiffany go. He had to dig up the past he'd buried and work through it. Somehow.

The hard plastic chair under him wouldn't let him relax. The ancient concrete floors with the don't-ask-don't-tell mystery stains brought back memories of the two hellish months he'd spent here awaiting his own trial—for the crime that had been Tiffany's. He shuddered. The minute hand on the black-and-white wall clock crept forward. Yet somehow, time felt as if it stood still.

Mark closed his eyes. Over and over, he played his final night in Vegas in his head. Every time he did, he cringed when he remembered how he'd measured Nicki using the yardstick Tiffany had created. He'd jumped to some bad conclusions about Nicki's doings and screwed up big—because he'd been too afraid to try again, to believe. He'd listened to the twisted logic Tiffany had taught him, not his gut.

Not his heart.

At that thought, his eyes snapped open. Lightning sizzled through his brain. He half-expected the heavens to part and rain down golden light.

That last thought made the whole solution to his problem snap into place.

He'd *listened* to Tiffany's twisted logic; she hadn't force-fed it to him. She hadn't even been there. *He* had. He'd allowed his fears to run riot in his head. He'd made the choice to believe the worst without getting all the facts.

He'd been the idiot that night, not Tiffany.

Mark rose. His ex-wife wasn't hanging up his future. Rafe was right; the pain Mark had ingested was. The fear of being hurt again. The mistrust he'd been drunk on since the divorce. Not Tiffany.

He had allowed his own destruction to occur, trampled on the best thing that had ever happened to him. Why? How had he let the ghost of their busted marriage lead him down such a bad path with Nicki?

He blew out a bracing breath. Rafe had been right again; he'd never dealt with the aftermath of his marriage. It had been easier to run. He'd never spoken to Tiffany again—except through attorneys. He changed his surroundings, sold his house, left the bank they'd both worked at. He moved to New York—totally different from Florida. Essentially wiped away all reminders of the past. He'd started dating a different girl every week, never did more than a round trip in her bed. Once she started talking third dates, he found new pastures. If he'd been lonely, well . . . he'd distracted himself with the TV or worked to exhaustion. He'd immersed himself in Rafe and Kerry's life.

He had not dealt with his own.

And it had bit him in the ass.

Nicki gave him light and sass and heat. She engaged him. Completed him. She loved him.

And he loved her so fucking much, he didn't want to breathe—to be—without her.

But when he'd come to a crisis with Nicki, he'd done the same thing he had after Tiffany. Left. Disappeared. Thrown himself back into work. Sponged off of Kerry and Rafe.

As he exhaled, the air left his lungs in hard rush. Holy shit! He felt like the ultimate doofus of the universe. Why hadn't he seen any of this before?

Because he hadn't let himself. No, that wasn't true. He hadn't wanted to. It was easier just to hide in a revolving door of women and stinking pile of bitterness.

Until now. Until Nicki.

Whatever happened going forward, the path of his present and future, was entirely up to him. He could either let his fears control him and dodge the pain so he'd be alone for the rest of his miserable life, or resolve to move on and have a future filled with the woman he wanted so much he couldn't see straight.

No choice.

He didn't need to talk to Tiffany to know what was wrong with him, or what he had to do.

He just needed to see Nicki.

And since Rafe had so ruthlessly pointed out that his groveling skills had better be in top form, Mark figured he'd better come up with a plan—fast.

Chapter Twenty

"WELL?" Lucia asked as yet another buffed up, G-string clad man found his way offstage—the latest in a long string of auditions.

After making sure he was out of earshot, Nicki sighed. "Nope. He's not going to work out, either. I've got to find a new dancer! Ricky is doing brilliantly as stage manager, but he needs a full cast."

"What was wrong with . . ." Lucia peered over Nicki's shoulder to see the last dancer's résumé. "Scott?"

"He could move . . . but I wasn't moved."

"You haven't been moved since Mark left."

Nicki closed her eyes. Wasn't that just like Lucia? Soft voice, soft smile, while she went for the jugular. She didn't need her sister to remind her of the man she'd loved . . . and lost. She thought of him, oh, every three seconds all on her own.

"You should be happy he's gone," Nicki pointed out. "You didn't seem that fond of him."

"I don't like the idea that he hurt you, but anyone who saved your life three times and paid off a huge loan to get Uncle Pain-in-the-Ass out of your hair deserves a medal in my book."

"He didn't just hurt me; he broke my heart," Nicki pointed out, voice sharp. "Whose side are you on, anyway?"

"Always yours, Sis." Lucia hugged Nicki and winked.

What the hell was up with that?

"So, do you have time to see one more today?" Lucia asked, then glanced toward the stage door.

"One more audition?" Nicki frowned, shuffling through all the papers in front of her. "I don't have any more applicants. I'm going to have to pick one and try to be happy with the choice."

"This one showed up last minute. I thought you might be interested."

And Lucia smiled once more. She was looking entirely too pleased with herself. Maybe Mr. Last Minute was a huge hottie.

Would you notice if he was?

Without Mark, she was feeling decidedly numb from the waist down. It wasn't fair! He was probably in New York, burying his past by living the party life with a different gorgeous woman every night. He'd probably already repressed the memory of her face and patted himself on the back for getting out of Vegas, out of her life, so quickly and easily. While she . . . well, since Mark had gone, she'd returned to having the personal life of a nun.

"I don't know. They're all starting to run together at this point."

"Poor you, having to look at half-naked guys all day. Life's tough."

Nicki shrugged. "I didn't notice you exactly cheering after any of the earlier auditions."

"True, but you said yourself when you started this morning that you never know when you're going to find the right one. This guy may be it."

Geez, she was relentless today. "All right, all right. Bring him in. If he's got you looking at a man besides Blade Bocelli, I'll kiss him on the spot."

Lucia blinked, suddenly all innocence. "I haven't looked at Blade like . . . that."

Nicki shot her a dubious stare. "This afternoon when he passed through here all decked out in his bad-boy best, I thought I was going to have to pick your tongue up off the floor."

Come to think of it, the way Blade had looked at Lucia was even more hungry. For as long as Bocelli was here, she'd better keep an eye on those two . . . And it better not be long. He was her uncle's lackey, and she wanted him gone. She'd told him as much, too.

"Do you want to see this audition or not?" Lucia snapped.

"I said I would."

"Good. And it doesn't matter if he moves me. If he moves you, definitely kiss him."

Before Nicki could question that odd comment, Lucia disappeared up the stage.

The door opened, then closed, a squeak that reminded her she still hadn't bought any WD-40.

The lights dimmed until the room turned damn near dark. Nicki frowned. Did this guy need major drama for an audition?

Slow footsteps crossed the stage. The shadow of a figure, tall, broad, rippling with power took his place in the center. Golden hair backlit by a dim overhead light, face concealed by intriguing shadows, white shirt with a turned-up collar, black pants—amazingly sleek. But the way he moved . . . it brought memories careening back.

Nicki's heart didn't just stop; it left major skid marks.

No. It couldn't be. Not Mark. This man had short hair. She could see the ends brushing the top of his stiff collar, hugging his scalp, flirting with the shadows about his face. But everything else . . .

No, it just couldn't be. Mark had gone. He wasn't coming back. No matter how tempting it was to hope that he would repair his scarred heart for her, it wasn't realistic. She had to stop wishing otherwise.

"Can someone get the lights so I can see him?" she called impatiently. "I can't audition someone I can't see."

Nothing but dark. Quiet. Damn it, where had her sister gone?

"What's your name?" she asked the dark shadow on the stage.

"Guess," he murmured.

The voice—that oh-so-familiar voice—sent a surge of lightning down her spine.

Oh my . . .

Before she could even complete the thought, a boom of music filled the air. A hypnotic beat followed, pulsing, seducing. The lights flashed on in a bright, blinding show, stunning her.

Mark!

Nicki gasped as he began to move, swinging his hips, shoulders rippling. Heat and shock flooded her insides, shutting down her brain. He was here? Here! A million questions formed . . . then faded as his intent gaze lured then captured hers in its relentless grip. He looked at her as if she was dessert and he was a man with a serious sweet tooth.

Her heartbeat took on the rhythm of a native drum. Breathing became secondary to looking at him, especially when he grabbed the front of his shirt and pulled it wide open, exposing miles of that glorious golden chest that made her mouth water and her fingers itch . . . and her heart ache with what could have been.

Desire hit her hard next. It was fair to say that she wanted the man—if want had suddenly taken on the same context as a life-altering craving.

Then yearning jabbed her gut in a one-two punch, nearly flattening her. She wanted more than his body. She wanted *him.* She wanted his time, his laughter. She wanted his love. Mark had to know that. So why was he here, teasing her?

He prowled closer, then unfastened the button of his leather pants. He winked at her before he reached for the zipper and pulled it down with all the speed of a teeth-grinding crawl. Beneath, she only saw more of those intriguing shadows. Was he naked under there?

Even the possibility made what few breaths she was taking nearly impossible.

Heat flashed over Nicki's skin as he stalked yet closer, closer, until only a narrow table separated them. So close she could see every inhalation make his abs ripple. So close she couldn't miss the pulse beating wildly at his neck. So close she couldn't escape that musky pine scent of his that sent her into hormone overdrive. So close she now read the determination in his hazel eyes.

He had come here for some reason. The possibilities made hope way too sharp, because it jabbed her in the chest, right in the heart. It would be much safer to believe he was here to collect his money.

Was it possible he'd come back for her?

Then he touched her, reached out with those long brown fingers and caressed her face.

His hand might have well been a live wire for the shock wave it sent through her. The man still affected her like no one ever would.

The music stopped. Nicki closed her eyes and took a deep breath. Did she assume he was here for her? No, the money. Three hundred thousand dollars was a lot. Certainly, he'd want to collect.

But why tantalize her with his half-finished striptease if he only wanted cash?

"Open your eyes, Nicki. Look at me."

Slowly, she complied. He wasn't a mirage. She could still see him standing there, all tall and solid and real. Still smell the heady woodsy scent of him enveloping her, both comforting and dangerous at once. Those eyes of his, wholly magnetic, seized her gaze again. But something was different. Very different. When she looked at him, his expression was wide open. She could suddenly read his every thought.

He was nervous. As he drew his fingers away from her face, his hand shook. He wanted her—in a big, bad way. That's what the fire in his green-brown eyes shouted. And his stare also told her he believed that being here was more important than his next breath.

Oh my . . .

"You're not here to collect the money you gave my uncle, are you?" she whispered.

He smiled, a hint of dimples flirting on his face. "No. I got a nice fat reward for bringing Zack in and turning the money over.

Apparently he was wanted for several things and had swindled more than one person lately. So when I got the money, I sent it to your uncle on your behalf. Your business is all yours now."

"Why?" She frowned, puzzled. If he said guilt . . . Damn, that would kill her.

"You found that cash. You deserved it, baby."

Her heart stuttered. "But you said—"

"A lot of really stupid things. Fucked-up things. I wish I could take them back." He walked around the table, removing the barrier between them. "I wish that more than anything."

Just like that, the ice inside her began to crack.

Mark knelt beside her chair and looked right into her eyes. His anxiety hit her first. But under that, she found more. Lots more. He took her breath away, not just with the whiplash of desire heating his eyes. But the warmth, like a thousand suns. It wrapped around her, suffusing her, like a comforting quilt.

Hope burst in a spiked rush all through her. Her gut clenched. Tears slashed at her eyes. "Mark?"

Her trembling voice betrayed her jumble of wishes and nerves and fear.

He reached up and laced his fingers through her hair before settling his palm against her nape. God, he usually did that before he kissed her . . . Her body knew that, too. She felt her breasts tighten, a rush of moisture down low. Her heart began to thud.

Well, at least she was no longer numb from the waist down.

"I'm sorry. I'm so damn sorry."

Sincerity made his hazel eyes shine so green. His expression held no shutters, nothing closed off from her. Nicki had no doubt he absolutely meant every word.

Slowly, almost reluctantly, he released her and peeled off his shirt completely. Then he turned his back to her and bowed his head.

His scars. He'd cut his hair, and he was intentionally showing these scars that he'd hidden for years, to her. She held in a gasp of surprise.

Now pink and fading with time against the warm gold of his

skin, they were ill-shaped blotches, five of them that spanned his neck. They bespoke his pain, uncertainty. His tense shoulders told her without words how awkward and afraid he was.

"I had three surgeries to have all this removed. I had radiation, chemo, more drugs than you can imagine. I got sick, lost my hair, lost my job, and puked my guts up until my toes turned blue. But I survived. And other than Kerry and my doctors, no one has seen these."

Nicki ran gentle fingertips across the unusually soft pinkish skin. Mark didn't flinch, didn't move. He just let her touch. The amount of personal trust he'd placed in her lap wasn't lost on her. The question was, why?

"Thank you for sharing that with me." She dropped her hand to his arm, squeezed. It felt so good to touch him . . . but he wasn't hers to touch. Reluctantly, she withdrew her hands to her sides. "I know that was a very difficult time in your life."

Mark faced her again. "Yeah. It was three terrible years. The cancer kept coming back, but I didn't give up until I beat it."

"You're not a quitter."

She smiled at him and wanted to believe his sharing meant something. But he had more to say—that was all over his face. She held her breath, hoping . . . even though hope could be so painful. What if the only thing he had left to say was good-bye?

"I'm not quitting now." His solemn face matched his vow-filled voice.

Nicki blinked, surprise curling through her. Did he mean he wasn't giving up on them?

"I want to explain what happened the night Zack was arrested. Will you let me?" he asked.

He wanted to let her into his thoughts even more? Nothing in the world would have made her say anything but yes. She nodded.

"I met Tiffany when we both worked at the bank. She seemed quiet and lost. She was new in town, knew nothing about working in a bank. I was assigned to train her to handle customers and be the branch manager's assistant." He swallowed. "We were both orphans from dirt-poor families. She leaned on me, made me feel . . . important. My sister was grown and had just moved out on her own. I was alone, and I wanted a family. Tiffany made me believe she loved me and wanted to be with me for the rest of our lives. Getting married seemed like a logical conclusion."

Hearing about his marriage . . . It hurt. Granted, he'd said it was logical, rather than emotional, but somewhere he must have thought himself in love with her.

"Mark, you don't have to tell me all the gory details—"

"Yes, I do. I want you to understand. Five more minutes, please. After that, if you want me to go, I'll leave for good. But I have to explain."

Nicki nodded, feeling the ice around her heart go beyond cracking to melting.

"We'd been married four months," he said, voice solemn, "when I was arrested one day. It happened in the bank, in front of my wife, my peers, and my boss, who lusted after Tiffany. All the evidence pointed to me. I had opportunity to embezzle from the bank, and I had motive, since I owed eighty thousand dollars in medical bills."

She gasped. "Didn't they investigate?"

"Enough to see that I looked guilty. The Feds locked me up, set a trial date, gave me a public defender who didn't know his elbow from his ass, and left me to rot. If Kerry and Rafe hadn't come to my rescue, I would have been convicted and carted off to prison for about twenty years."

Terror clenched her stomach. "Dear God! Mark . . ."

"But Kerry and Rafe did intervene. And they discovered that my own wife had framed me. Not only did she frame me, she only married me to frame me. And she tried to kill my sister. I found out later she was originally from Arkansas, her name was Ruthie Jo, her father was a traveling preacher, and she'd run away at fifteen and earned a living on her back for several years before deciding to find a more lucrative crime to commit. Despite being her first husband, I was just another victim in a long line of suckers."

"I'm so sorry." Nicki's heart melted completely and broke for him. No wonder he was damaged. Trusting anyone not to lie and deceive after that had to be damn near impossible.

"I picked up my life and moved to New York, close to Rafe and Kerry. I went to work for my brother-in-law. He's a fabulous hacker. He can crack just about any computer system in the world. As an accountant, he sucks, and lots of his cases require one. So I finished my CPA and added my brain to his.

"When this case came, the opportunity to nail the bastard who introduced Tiffany to money laundering was something I couldn't pass up. I was supposed to come in here, gain your trust, get inside your books, and figure out who was guilty and how to prove it. I just didn't expect you."

"Me?"

He smiled, something gentle that made her lose her breath. "I had a . . . um, very physical reaction to even a picture of you. You, in person, put me in meltdown. Getting to know you made all my barriers crumble. That night, on the kitchen table when I blurted that I loved you, I did. But I couldn't face it. Loving makes a man vulnerable, and I had a bad track record. You looked guilty as sin, and I couldn't ask you what was happening without blowing my cover. Even if I could have, I don't know that I would have trusted the answers. And through it all, I couldn't manage to stay away from you. I had to have you, touch you, be inside you every chance I could.

"What I felt for you, it got deeper and deeper. And I grew more confused. I didn't want to believe you were guilty, but I'd been so horribly wrong before. I didn't know how to trust you. I couldn't trust myself."

He sighed. Nicki wanted to interrupt, tell him that he didn't need to go on. She understood. Really. But she also saw that he needed to say this to her. This had to be the determination she saw on his face—the resolve to explain.

Was he looking for forgiveness?

She also hadn't missed the fact he thought he'd loved her once. Did he still?

"Go on," she prompted softly.

His hand tightened at the back of her neck. "This is the hard part."

There was more?

"When you and I talked in the Blue Hawaii suite, I'd finally let myself believe you were innocent. I wanted to take that leap of faith in you and in me. Tiffany had told me during our marriage that she loved me, but I realize now it never incited a need or an answer in me. The night you told me you loved me, I think my whole body exploded in happiness and pleasure. I knew I was in deep then. And it scared the hell out of me.

"But after I let myself believe you were innocent, I *needed* that to be true. Then you left me alone with Zack and his gun, and went after the money . . . All I could picture was Tiffany all over again. And your betrayal hurt worse. A lot worse. I enjoyed helping Tiffany and having her look up to me. But I loved you, and the thought of your betrayal ripped my heart out."

Nicki bit her lip as tears stung her eyes. "Oh, Mark, I—"

"When I realized how bad I'd screwed up, I didn't know how to put it back together. Or if I should. I knew I didn't have my head on straight. What good was I to you when you deserved so much more? But I didn't want you to hate me forever."

"I couldn't," she whispered. "I knew the problem. I just wish I knew how to help you."

"You can start by forgiving me."

How could she not? He'd been to hell and back, then come here to reveal his scars, both inside and out. He may not want her forever, but she admired his courage. And she still loved him.

"You're forgiven," she promised. "I won't lie and say it didn't hurt, you accusing me, not believing in me. But I hated that you didn't believe in you, either."

His brows drew into a frown. He was fighting emotion—and losing.

"You're an amazing woman. I've had a few weeks to think, put my past into perspective. I have choices. I refuse to assume the worst again. My gut led me to you. My heart latched on to you. I fell in love with you, Nicki. That hasn't changed."

He loved her? Really?

Tears and smiles hit at once. Lord, her face was probably contorting and her nose turning bunny pink, but she couldn't stop herself. "I tried to forget you these last three weeks. But you're unforgettable."

"Thank God." A relieved glance later, he grabbed her hands and squeezed and looked deep into her eyes, all the way to her soul. "Then if . . . would you—I was hoping . . . Damn, I suck at this." He sighed and squeezed her hands again and stared right into her eyes. "I want you to marry me, Nicki."

Her mouth dropped open. "Marry . . . You're sure?"

He nodded, an anxious half smile hovering over that tempting mouth of his. "Yes."

"Really sure? We can take it slow."

"Slow is for sissies. I love you, and I want to marry you, if you want me."

"There's no taking this back."

His smile widened. "I did give it some thought, you know. Lots of thought. Lots of planning, in fact. I even found this."

He reached for his shirt, unbuttoned the front pocket, and took something into his grip.

Looking straight at her, his eyes brimming with hope and affection, he placed the object in her palm.

A lone marquis diamond set in platinum. A big diamond. She gasped.

"I have the matching band already bought. You can't say no."

Nicki couldn't stop the smile from stretching the width of her face. "You didn't actually ask."

"On purpose. That way, I don't give you an opportunity to say no. Do you still love me?"

"I love you." She laughed through her tears. "You're changing the subject."

"I'm good at that, especially when I'm nervous."

Mark slipped the ring on her finger. Beautiful. Shimmering. Everything she ever wanted—just like him.

"Is that a yes?" he asked anxiously, gaze caressing her face. "You'll marry me?"

She smiled. "Well, to coordinate with my wedding dress, I would get to add a new pair of shoes to my collection."

"Hell, add two if that persuades you to be my wife."

"Well," she teased, "you didn't finish your audition yet. You're still wearing your pants, and I need to see the whole . . . package."

He shot her a seductive smile, complete with those heavenly dimples. "Say yes, baby, and my package is all yours."

Nicki took his face in her hands and placed a soft kiss against his mouth . . . then dropped one to glide down his back and cup his ass. She squeezed, and he shot her an amused glance.

"What's your answer?" he prompted.

She sent him a saucy grin. "Start stripping."

Shelley Bradley/Shayla Black

The author of twenty-plus sizzling contemporary, erotic, paranormal, and historical romances, national bestselling author Shelley Bradley/Shayla Black lives with her husband, her munchkin, and one very spoiled cat. In her "free" time, she enjoys reality TV, reading, and listening to an eclectic blend of music.

She has won or placed in more than a dozen writing contests, including Passionate Ink's Passionate Plume, the Colorado Romance Writers Award of Excellence, and the National Readers' Choice Awards. Romantic Times has awarded her Top Picks, a Historical K.I.S.S. Hero award, and a nomination for Best Erotic Romance of the Year.

A writing risk-taker, she enjoys tackling writing challenges with every book.